WAKING EDEN

RHENNA MORGAN

Ebbok ISBN: 978-1-945361-00-5

Print ISBN: 978-1-945361-01-2

ACKNOWLEDGMENTS

When it comes to writing, it doesn't take a village. It takes a horde. A fierce one that props you up when life tries to knock you over and runs interference while you're trying to get one past the goalie. Honest to God, I couldn't live without these peeps—Jennifer Matthews, Juliette Cross, Kyra Jacobs, Jaci Burton, Audrey Carlan, Dena Garson, Lauren Smith, Kami Adkison, Christina Gwin, and Lucy Beshara. Really, I couldn't do this thing without each and every one of you.

As always, I'm sending super big cyber hugs for my wonderful readers. If I didn't have you, writing these stories wouldn't be nearly as fun or rewarding.

To my daughters and my partner, Joe Crivelli, go the biggest thanks of all. Writing would be empty without your patience, your encouragement, and your love.

For my mom and dad. Your support, encouragement, and fathom-less love are the foundations of every story I write. Thank you for teaching me how to chase my dreams and making me the woman I am today.

CHAPTER 1

*T*rinity Blair's sweaty palm slipped on the steering wheel as she pulled into the parking lot of Plush and nearly took out a businessman fresh from the boardroom. God, what a nightmare. Fancy cars, bright lights, and shoulder-to-shoulder people decked out for prime time. Clearly, she'd lost her mind agreeing to her girlfriends' latest scheme. Girls' night out might be a good idea for other twenty-three-year-old women ready to usher in the weekend, but for Trinity it was bad, bad, bad.

Naomi waggled a twenty-dollar bill over Trinity's shoulder from the backseat, her blood-red nail polish a perfect match for her body-hugging dress. "Just do the valet, Trin. The parking lot's packed and I wanna save these heels for the dance floor."

Like that was going to be a problem. With Naomi's dark hair and mocha skin, she'd snag ample opportunities for dancing with or without her shoes.

Trinity ignored the cash and aimed her cost-conscious Accord toward the curb with a white-knuckled grip. "Twenty bucks for parking is insane."

Right up there with her agreeing to set foot in this place. Nothing but wall-to-wall opportunities for physical contact and the none-too-subtle blasts of everyone's dark and dirty secrets that came with it. "Y'all hop out and I'll find a spot."

"No way." From her shotgun seat, Tessa snatched the twenty out of Naomi's hand and motioned Trinity toward the waiting runners. Her sleek blond bob accented her modelesque jawline and bright hazel eyes. "Just park and let's get inside. We'll never get a table if we don't hurry."

"It's cool, Trin." Margo. Calm, cool, understanding Margo. Her average brown hair and modest looks matched her personality, completely unassuming. Trinity wouldn't trade her friendship or her willingness to run interference for anything. Some people just didn't get her phobia. "Drop us off and text me before you come in. I'll meet you up front."

Trinity shifted into park and the locks disengaged. The girls shimmied out curbside as the crowd's rumble and laughter filled the car's dark interior. Margo dipped for a quick wink through the front passenger's side. "Take all the time you need, girlfriend, but get your ass in here eventually. You've got your own place now and no nasty mom to deal with or answer to when you get home. You need this. You need people."

Both doors slammed before she could argue, dampening the social sounds behind the steady drone of her air conditioner.

Phobia indeed. More like an unfortunate result of her highly unusual parentage, though the haphephobia diagnosis all the baffled doctors had given her adopted parents did a good job of covering the truth.

Trinity navigated around a cluster of laughing women. Their long, spray-tanned legs were accented by short skirts and shoes that probably cost more than her car payment. She aimed toward the far end of the parking lot and checked her

2

hair in the rearview one more time. The cut was killer—super short in the back and flirty long in the front for a wild pixie look—but compared to everyone else, she'd probably come off like a hick in her simple Levis and white button-down.

Then again, it wasn't like she'd be going home with anybody. A simple kiss from a guy in freshman English comp had squashed any hopes for real intimacy. Instead of the raging heartbeat and delicious tingles promised in all her *Cosmo* issues, she'd earned a front row seat for every painful detail of his senior year. Talk about your mood killers.

A blinding white light flared from the passenger's side of the car and Trinity flinched, smacking her knuckles on the steering wheel. She missed sideswiping the front end of a sleek silver sports car by all of inches. "Damn it, Dad!"

"She's right, you know." Her father's low, almost deadpan voice barely registered above her hammering heart.

She rubbed the heel of her hand over her sternum and glared at the now occupied front passenger seat. "You gotta quit popping in like that. You're going to kill me."

"You're not that easy to kill, and it sure won't be your dad popping in on you that does it."

Not exactly a statement that made her feel better. Being part human gave her a vulnerability most people failed to appreciate. Being part Spiritu? That was a whole different enchilada. A big one with huge responsibility and access to way too much information. The guidance aspect to the Spiritu's purpose was beautiful, to walk beside their charge throughout their life, unseen and unknown, yet whispering words of inspiration and encouragement throughout their mortal lives. No sentient being went without a Spiritu, though not all of The Great One's creations chose to listen.

No, that part didn't bother her. It was the twenty-four, seven access to past, present, and future events that scared the ever-lovin' heck right out of her. Every Spiritu was hooked into it. A hive mind connection to The Great One for both the Light and Dark passions. A job necessity if they wanted to steer their charges in the right direction. Other people might appreciate a glimpse into the big events headed their way, but she'd opt for human ignorance and bliss any day. "I take it you know what actually will kill me?"

Her father, Kazan, stared out over the long rows of shiny metal, his simple black T-shirt and jeans a far cry from the customary and erotic attire most of the Dark contingent wore. He wouldn't answer. He never did. Spilling yet-to-be-unfolded information was a no-no, and Pops wasn't exactly on good terms with the higher ups. Not after the stunt he'd pulled with her birth mother, Anaya.

Trinity whipped into a tolerable slot in the next to last row. "You know, a benefit of having an all-knowing dad would be to get a heads-up on when I'm gonna kick it. At least let me get my affairs in order."

"Almost all-knowing. And everything can change. Free will has a way of rearranging the outcomes on a second-by-second basis. You know that."

Ah, yes. Free will. The trump card for all beings. Spiritus included, which explained her existence. A Spiritu revealing themselves without royal mandate was punishable enough, but tangling in a physical relationship and falling in love? It was a wonder her father hadn't forfeit his existence. Which was way more than she needed to contemplate with a bar full of too many contact opportunities in her immediate future.

Digging to the bottom of her knock off Michael Kors handbag, she found her lip-gloss, flipped down the sun visor, and smoothed on a quick touchup.

Kazan's stare weighed so heavy the tremor in her hand jumped a notch. "You could be tuned in yourself if you'd accept your powers."

And see what he saw day in and day out? No thank you. "I can't leave Mom. I'm all she's got." Well, not her real mom. Anaya had died shortly after Trinity was born. Her adopted mom, Carol Blair, wasn't the end-all-be-all in the realm of mothers, but she'd stuck by Trinity with her "phobia" when many others would've run like hell.

Never mind Carol also wielded her good deeds with a healthy dose of guilt when it suited her.

"You're stalling."

Trinity capped the tube of Raspberry Sorbet and glared at her father. "Wouldn't you? Dealing with humanity is hard enough at the library. There's so much skin in that club, I'm bound to come home with a truckload of TMI."

"Maybe you should stop fighting it. Take it in."

"It's not right. It's…I don't know…"

"Part of you." Kazan tucked a strand of hair behind her ear and his all-encompassing love wrapped around her solid as a bear hug. "Tonight's a big step for you."

The warm and fuzzy feeling wavered.

Trinity twisted in her seat. Her dad always came across a little pensive. Cold and reserved like a part of him was dead —particularly when it came to her avoiding her Spiritu gifts. But the groove between his eyebrows furrowed a little deeper tonight. Tension pinched the outer corners of his eyes, and his thumb skated back and forth on the door panel. The only other time he got this thoughtful and mysterious was when he talked about his brief interlude with Anaya. "Something in your all-knowing hive mind I need to know about?"

He shook his head and faced forward. "You know I can't tell you. You have to live your life. Make your own choices."

"Not helpful."

Kazan looked back, sadness and regret etched on his face. "I've already burned my one warning by loving your mother.

I'm not about to forgo the rest of my existence and get ripped away from you by breaking the rules a second time. You're alone enough as it is."

The tightness in her stomach doubled, and a weird unease settled in her chest. Whatever was eating him was more than just his customary moodiness, and it amped her need to run for the hills into overdrive. She rummaged for her phone and flipped on the overhead light. "Why don't we head back to the house? We can talk—"

Kazan clasped her hand, stilling her fingers over her smart phone. "You're on the right path, Trinity. You've got the kindest heart I know. Just like your mother. But don't forget, you've got my nature flowing through your veins too."

A Dark Spiritu. Unlike their Light brethren who spoke to conscience and goodwill, the Dark were advocates and inspiration for headier, more decadent passions. From the rush of a daring leap into something new and unknown, to the toe-curling thrill of a lover's first kiss, no being went without a Dark Spiritu's decadent encouragement. A mantra she'd heard over and over since the day Kazan first visited her on her eighteenth birthday.

"When passion hits you, don't run from it," he said. "Embrace it. Revel in it. Then you'll know what it means to truly live."

Okay, something was definitely wrong. Way too much mumbo jumbo and side-speak. "Dad, seriously. I'll text the girls. Heck, they're probably expecting it with my track record. We'll go have dinner and talk."

He released her hand and straightened in his seat. Formal. Distant. "It's better you go. Something you need to do." He fisted his hand on his thigh. "And this will be my last visit for a while."

"Why?"

His Adam's apple bobbed, and his gaze stayed rooted on the sea of shiny cars.

Oh, hell. Her crossroads. It'd been five years since he'd first been granted permission to visit her and explain who and what she really was. In that time, he'd crammed every bit of love and guidance he could into their stolen time together, trying to make up for the crap environment her adoption had landed her in. But he'd also hinted of a time she'd face an all-important destiny. "I won't push you for details, Dad. I'd rather have you here and *not* talk about whatever is bothering you than for you to disappear."

"It's not you I'm worried about. It's me who's bound to break the rules and share something you shouldn't know, even if I do it subconsciously." He closed his eyes, head dipped slightly, and then faced her. "I love you, Trinity. A father couldn't be more proud."

Why did he sound so desperate? So final? He couldn't be going for good. He was all she had. The only true connection with another living being who not only knew what she was, but could touch her in a normal, healthy way.

As if he heard her thoughts, he held out his hand, palm up. "If you ever change your mind and decide you're ready to receive your abilities, call out and I'll hear it."

Trinity gripped his hand in both of hers, like the contact might somehow prevent his form from fading. So tangible. Warm. She couldn't lose him. Not now. She wasn't ready. "I can't leave Mom."

"You can't save Carol from her bitterness. Only she can do that."

"She stood by me. Found a way to care for me when other people would've taken me back. How many parents would stick by a cranky toddler who can't abide touch?"

"Several." Kazan pulled his hand free and went back to glaring out the windshield. "My people should have done better looking out for you while I paid my sentence. Found someone less inclined toward fanaticism."

"Free will, remember?" Trinity nudged his shoulder, eager to pull him out of whatever morose thoughts held him tight. "Besides, I'm not living with her anymore. I've finally cut the cord and got my own place. That's a good first step, right? Maybe someday, when I know she's adjusted—"

"You don't have to explain. I know what we are scares you." He relaxed with a sad smile, leaned across the distance, and laid a tender kiss to her cheek. "I'm here. Always." He pulled away and jerked his head toward the building. "Now go. Try to have a good time."

He began to fade, and his gaze locked onto hers with an intensity that pierced her soul. "And remember, destiny is what you make it."

RAMSAY ZIPPED THROUGH DOWNTOWN DALLAS, the top down on his Porsche Spyder and Hinder's *All American Nightmare* cranked loud enough to mingle with the engine's growl.

Jagger twisted in the passenger seat and rubbernecked a leggy blonde in a short, pale blue skirt. "Makin' it hard to take in the scenery."

"Not like we can fly in," Ramsay shouted over the music. "Might as well do the next best thing. Been too damned long since I got to drive it anyway." Ramsay whipped left into Plush's parking lot then dodged right into the valet line.

Jagger eased the door open and unfolded himself from the cramped interior, drawing a host of head-to-toe scans from the women waiting in line. Not surprising. The fucker was as big as Ramsay and all the rest of his warriors, but had a golden-surfer-boy vibe women couldn't resist. "Man, you drive as crazy as you fly."

"You got that right." Life was meant to be lived full on. Passion pushing all boundaries, be it on a battlefield or a bedroom.

Or at least it used to be. Before Maxis Steysis resurrected the Lomos Rebellion with their jacked ideas of enslaving humans, and before his brother's mating kicked a four-thousand-year-old prophecy into play. They'd finally gotten a handle on the first problem now that Maxis was dead. That damned prophecy, though, was trouble waiting to happen.

Enough.

He opened his door and stepped out. Tonight he wanted a little of his easy-going life back. Just a hint. A taste of the no-strings existence he used to have instead of chasing his tail to keep everything from falling to shit.

The valet eyeballed the Spyder and nearly danced with impatience to get behind the wheel.

Ramsay snatched the outstretched claim check with a chuckle. "Once around downtown, but if you wreck it I do *not* want to find you."

There. One step back toward his carefree self. Now all he needed was a few hours with good music loud enough to vibrate all the way to his bones and the rest of the night tangled up with a woman who could match his pent-up energy.

"You sure you're up for this?" Jagger's voice resonated through their telepathic link. Unlike family links that were automatically formed, each warrior bond was purposefully created. An offering of trust and fealty given to Ramsay as their strategos, or commander in chief, at their swearing in.

The place was packed. Though at eleven on a Thursday night, that wasn't surprising. Friday and Saturday would only be worse. *"Why the hell wouldn't I be?"*

Jagger scanned him over one shoulder then went back to

recon. *"Cause you look more like a man about to rip the head off a bull than a guy out for a good time."*

"Only hit the portal two hours ago." Putting some distance between him and the lovefest in Eden felt damned nice. *"Gonna take a little more than a shower and a drive in a fine car to take the edge off."*

Jagger smirked and stalked toward a casual seating area clearing out near the bar. *"Eryx say how things went at council today?"*

Oh, he'd shared all right. Though the first thirty minutes of the download included nasty kicks and jabs at Ramsay's head while they sparred to unleash tension. Damn good thing Eryx was the malran for their race and Ramsay was just the heir. He'd just as soon fight an army solo than sit through the political tedium and bullshit kingly duties Eryx endured. *"Came here to let go, not rehash the state of the nation."*

Jagger sprawled in a big black leather club chair. *"Just makin' conversation, boss."*

Ramsay settled on Jagger's left in a black leather love seat with a perfect angle on the dance floor. He flagged down a waitress, a pretty little thing with short dark hair and a saucy gait. Right about now his blood could use some thinning in the way of good Scotch. "Got Balvenie?"

Her smile jumped a notch higher. Probably calculating how big their tab would be by night's end. "Thirty year's the best we've got. Crazy expensive though."

Figures. He could use a few drams of his brother's Fifty. "Thirty'll work."

She laid a coaster on the table in front of him and pinned Jagger with an expectant look.

"A stout." Jag barely made eye contact, his gaze a steady shuttle across the crowd. "Whatever you've got, but make it a big one."

A second coaster skated to the table's edge and the waitress cocked her hip, brushing Ramsay's knee in the process. "You need anything else?"

Sass and confidence. A killer combination in a woman. Not to mention she knew her Scotch and made it her business to shoot for the high end. A perfect first foray for the night.

And yet, he still wasn't into her. He smiled and looked away, a subtle no thank you without a single word spoken. Fucking chaos messing with his mojo. He wanted his world back.

The waitress sauntered off and Jagger ogled her ass.

Kind of weird running with Jagger. They were close, sure. All of the elite warriors were, but not like Ramsay was with Eryx and Ludan. Guys' night out with Eryx was out of the question. Too much sucking face with his new baineann back at the castle.

Ludan was an even worse option, lately. As somo, or bodyguard, to Eryx, his usual gruff demeanor was kind of expected. But in the last month, the burly warrior had gone from brusque to flat out dickhead.

Maybe that's why his game was off tonight. Too big of a change in wingmen.

"For a guy who's out to get laid, you look like your head's still back in your brother's library." Jagger blasted a devious smile at a passing gaggle of girls who looked too young to be in the place. "Find anything else on the prophecy yet?"

An even worse topic. Ever since that Spiritu showed and promised more prophecy developments, he'd been antsy as hell. Didn't help that the prediction was as vague as a politician on the campaign trail.

When a Shantos male takes a mate bearing the mark of a sword wound with ivy, so shall dawn a new era in Eden.

And damned if his brother hadn't taken a mate who'd

given him that exact mark. "Thought we weren't talking shop."

"Just thinkin' if you wouldn't chase it so hard, you wouldn't end up in a foul mood and need to get away in the first place."

"Better than sitting around waiting for something else to yank the rug out from underneath us. Lexi planting that mark on Eryx was one thing. Finding out there's more than Myrens and humans..." Ramsay shook his head and sipped his Scotch.

Spiritu. The alleged inspiration in everyone's thoughts. The whole concept of someone influencing anything between his ears cranked his pissed off level a little too high. "Kind of makes you wonder how much of our lives are our own and how much is our meddling fairy Godparent. If they're all about inspiration, where the hell are they now? I don't see any roadmaps lining out the prophecy."

"You never see what you need to see when you're looking for it. Same thing as fighting. Watch for the strike and you'll miss it. Let things flow, and you'll catch it every time."

Ramsay barked a laugh. "You gonna tell me to use the force, too?"

"Fuck you, Shantos," Jagger said, but there was zero bite behind his words. He smiled and stood, gaze locked on a quartet of scrumptious-looking ladies. A veritable smorgasbord of beauty with a little something for every appetite. "You ladies need a place to park yourself for a bit?"

Damn. Jagger might make a good wingman after all. He'd have to talk Eryx into more time away for Lexi's new somo.

A tall blonde with exotic eyes and a catwalk body held out her hand to Jagger. "I'm Tessa. You sure you don't mind if we share your space?"

"Sweetheart, I'll share more than my space," Jagger said.

Yep. Definite wingman material if the giggles from the girls were any indication.

"I'm Naomi." Where Tessa was elegant, the woman settling next to Ramsay was sex on legs, all curves wrapped in delicious mocha skin. She motioned toward the mousy brown-haired woman perched on the arm of the love seat. "This is Margo."

Margo smiled and nodded an unspoken hello. Kind of a knowing, Mother Theresa calm in a sea full of sinners. She leaned out and peered around him. "Trinity? You coming?"

Ramsay followed her gaze and his eyes locked onto pure sunshine in human form. Shorter hair, nearly platinum, and in one of those stylish cuts that crossed somewhere between windblown and freshly fucked. Her eyes were dark brown, almost black. And her curves, praise The Great One, whoever ran the Levi's marketing division needed to get a camera aimed in her direction. They'd make a serious mint in one campaign.

She wiped her palm on her hip and dipped her chin, hiding those amazing eyes. "Hi."

"I'm Ramsay." His hand was outstretched to take hers and he was standing. When the hell had that happened? And why wasn't she responding to what he offered? Histus, he was more off his game than he'd thought.

Margo stepped between them. "Take my spot, Trin."

Trinity stepped hesitantly forward and fiddled with the collar of her white button-down.

Funny. She showed about a tenth of the skin as every other woman in the club, and it only made him want to see the perfect form beneath even more. Or better yet, touch her. Undo the buttons, peel the sides apart, and kiss his way down her creamy skin. Maybe she'd taste like sunshine, too.

"She's a little shy." Margo's voice carried only enough to

reach Ramsay. Probably trying to cushion her friend's awkwardness.

Laughter and an abrupt shout pierced the steady rumble of the crowd, and a pair of giggling girls dodged some commotion.

One of the girls tripped, her trajectory dead-on for Trinity.

Ramsay shot forward, grabbed Trinity by the elbow, and righted her.

Trinity jerked away, overcorrected, and tumbled to the floor in the opposite direction.

"Trin!" Margo moved to help her up.

Ramsay beat her to it. "You okay?"

A bright red flush stole across her cheeks as she propped herself up on one elbow and rubbed her butt. "Fine. Nothing broken but my pride."

He offered his hand to help her up, but she refused it with a shake of her head. The neckline of her blouse gapped open, putting a whole lot of perfect flesh on display, punctuated by an ancient-looking pendent.

Ramsay froze.

Not just any pendant. An exact replica of Lexi's prophetic mark. A sword wrapped in ivy. Hanging from the neck of a human.

Oh, hell no. No way was he passing up information when The Fates dangled it under his nose. He gripped her hand, pulled her to her feet, and dove into her memories.

His whole body lit up, a painful fire shooting up his arm and blasting across his body while a battering ram took to his brain.

He vaguely registered letting go. And then nothing but black.

CHAPTER 2

*T*rinity dropped to her knees beside Ramsay and checked the pulse at his neck. Smooth and strong, unlike the frantic flutter of her own heart.

She smoothed a wayward strand of dark hair off his handsome face. Not just any man could pull off long hair without coming off girly, but this guy did it easily. Kind of a sexy barbarian who'd traded his leather armor for a skin-hugging T-shirt and jeans.

Ramsay's giant friend crouched opposite her and gripped his shoulder. What was his name? John? No. Jagger. That was it. Golden hair and eyes to match. Heck, the guy looked like he'd been created by Midas. "What happened?"

"I don't know." She checked the back of Ramsay's head. No blood, but she'd bet he'd sport a nasty goose egg come morning. God, his hair felt sinful. Thick and smooth. "He grabbed my hand and pulled me up. The next thing I knew, his eyes rolled back and he fell."

Jagger lifted Ramsay's head, clasped it at the back, and gripped his chin with the other. He scowled down at his friend. Or was he concentrating?

"I tried to break his fall, but he's, well…" She motioned toward Jagger's torso. "Huge, like you."

Ramsay's eyes popped open and he shook his head.

Jagger eased back on his heels and smiled. "You realize you passing out when you're coming onto a woman is gonna make for killer blackmail."

Ramsay studied his friend, then her, then her hand on his chest.

Her hand. On his chest. Not just touching him, but stroking. Small, comforting motions against hard, hot muscle.

She jerked her hand away and stood so fast, she nearly clattered onto the coffee table behind her.

Not one vision. Not before or after his fall. That alone should be enough to crow and dance around for days, but mixed with a good solid feel of those muscles, all she could think about was adding both hands to the mix. Minus his T-shirt.

Ramsay stood and narrowed his eyes.

Prey. Beneath his stare, she felt like a gazelle entranced by a black panther.

Jagger stepped closer to him, as though he meant to intercept. "You want to tell me what's going on?"

The question snapped Ramsay's focus. "Must've been the trip here. My head went fuzzy and that's all I remember."

Odd. His words made sense, but the tone and the way he eyeballed his friend made it sound like code for something else.

Jagger's gaze raked her head to toe before he nodded and ambled back to his seat.

Ramsay prowled closer, not quite as frightening as seconds before, but still on edge. Predatory. He offered his hand. "Let's try that again. I'm Ramsay."

Eye candy. The guy was pure unadulterated, grade-A eye

candy. She sucked with height estimations, but her lips were on a direct line with the rock hard pecs she'd shamelessly fondled and there were scattered light streaks in his dark hair. Not much. Only enough to imply her panther spent time lazing in the sun.

His voice rumbled, even more tempting than the rest of him. "I can wait all night." He held his outstretched hand steady, tanned skin tempting her as strongly as his words. Definitely a sun-prone panther.

She'd touched him twice already. Surely another wouldn't hurt. "Trinity Blair."

Their palms met, his hand encompassing hers in a delicious heat that radiated out in all directions and made her want to snuggle up so tight no space was left between them. The world stopped. The bar ceased to exist. No images. No fearsome emotions. Just perfect, addictive touch.

Tessa's voice cut through the cocoon of her thoughts. "Oh, my God. Did you just touch him?"

Trinity snatched her hand away and stepped back.

"Well, well, well," Naomi's sultry voice sounded from the loveseat as she reclined and draped one arm along the cushions. "This is turning into an interesting night."

Margo stood, jerked her head at Naomi to move, and motioned at Ramsay to sit. "Why don't you two take a load off? Me and Naomi are headed to the bar. Anyone want refills?"

Oh, boy. She'd seen that matchmaking gleam in Margo's eyes before, but never aimed at her. Definitely not good if she wanted to keep any semblance of control for the rest of the night.

"Sit with him," Margo whispered in her ear before turning and tugging Naomi along with her.

Ramsay grinned, clearly hearing her friend's traitorous instruction.

Mortified, Trinity dropped onto the loveseat as close to the edge as possible.

Ramsay settled close. His gaze rested on her throat before it jumped to her eyes. "So, no touching. Sounds like an interesting story."

More like the only thing interesting about her, and yet the one thing she couldn't talk about. Even if she could share something about her Spiritu self, her brain seemed to have gone on strike in favor of ogling the strapping god planted two inches away. "It bugs me, is all. Most people make me antsy. I guess…" She rubbed her thigh. "I guess you slipped in under the radar, and then after, I didn't have time to think."

Again his gaze dropped to her neck, and his smile faltered.

She checked her collar and made sure the sides were pulled together, hiding the pendant her adopted father, David, had given her before he died.

"You sure?" Ramsay tilted his head, considering. "I think we should try again. Test the theory."

Well, if that wasn't a perfect opportunity offered up on a silver platter. All her life, the only person who'd been able to touch her without impact was Kazan. She'd give anything to try something beyond a simple handshake.

Ramsay leaned in, his arm stretching along the seat back. His facial structure radiated the same power as his body. Proud nose, strong jaw covered in sexy stubble, and thick eyebrows, one arched a little more than the other. His warm, earthy scent surrounded her, clean with a hint of something exotic. Sandalwood maybe. "Touch me."

Hard to call it a command the way he said it. More of a dark, sensual dare. One that worked nerve endings she hadn't even know existed. "Where?"

As soon as the question left her mouth his eyelids

lowered slightly over stormy silver eyes. "Carte blanche. Lady's choice."

Her gaze locked on his lips. Full and firm. She'd bet her first paycheck he could kiss a blue streak. Not that she had much to compare to.

She opted for his sharp cheekbones instead. So warm. The rasp of his stubble diffused all the way up her arm.

"Seems to be okay." Ramsay trailed a touch along her shoulder, light, but still there. "Touching over fabric doesn't bother you?"

Trinity dropped her hand and stared out at the dance floor. What the heck was she doing? She didn't know this man from Adam. Whatever made it so she could touch him was either a fluke, or something dangerous. Given the conversion with her dad, she'd be willing to bet it was the latter. "It diffuses it a little. Most people don't get that. How'd you figure it out?"

Ramsay scanned her attire. "Nightclubs usually generate fewer clothes, not more."

Trinity plucked her clutch from between her leg and the arm of the loveseat and squeezed the tiny handbag tight. She should head to the car. Margo could always text her when the rest of the girls were ready for a pickup.

"Let's try it the other way." Ramsay leaned in, his heat registering at her side like an electric blanket.

"I'm sorry?"

"Let me touch you again and see how you do."

Her heart leapt. She shouldn't. Different probably meant dangerous. If she were smart, she'd head home and curl up with one of her fantasy books.

She nodded.

He lifted his hand.

Trinity held her breath.

He traced her lower lip with his thumb then skated his

knuckles over her chin and down her neck to the hollow at the base of her throat.

Her pendant shifted between her breasts, pinging a wakeup call to her touch-starved senses. She jerked back.

Ramsay's eyes were rooted to her neck, his focus so intense it was a wonder her shirt didn't fizzle to nothing. "Did it bother you?"

Heck yes, it bothered her. But not in the way it usually did.

He tilted his head and his panther-like scrutiny sharpened. "Where are you from, Trinity?"

Tingles broke out along the back of her neck, and a loud buzzing roared in her ears. A warning. The same one she'd experienced the day her adopted father died and countless times after. "I need to go."

She darted through the crowds, zigzagging to avoid contact. She failed one too many times and her head spun with erotic, vivid images, most centered on sweaty, wild sex. The kind she'd never be able to have.

From somewhere behind her, Ramsay shouted her name.

Trinity kept going, digging in her purse for her cell phone. No way in hell was she sticking around him any longer. His touch felt good. Great, actually. Insidious, check-your-brain-at-the-door-and-touch-me-all-night great.

But he was asking questions too. With her father's mysterious rumblings and promises of destiny still stomping around in her mind, no way was she taking chances. Better to stay touch-starved and safe than say more than she should.

CHAPTER 3

*S*erena smoothed the pale blue chiffon of her long-sleeved gown, making sure the grayed-out mark of her now-dead mate didn't show. Thyrus' voiced droned behind her. Do this. Don't do that. Typical lawyer-speak. The same blasted instructions she'd heard for the last four weeks.

She pushed from the table and paced to the tall arched window. Gold winked from Cush's taupe and ivory brick-laid streets, and the morning sun reflected off a row of weathered white domed roofs. The crowds had been thick when she'd arrived in Eden's capital two hours before, some having camped out overnight. Now they were even worse. "You'd think I was a Salem witch."

Thyrus paused mid whatever monotonous topic he'd been on. "Pardon?"

"A witch hunt from human history. Fanatics desperate for a hanging."

Thyrus waddled over, his maroon solicitor's robe stretched a little too tightly over his belly. He guided her away from the window. "Hardly that. More like curiosity. It's not every day a woman stabs her mate in the heart, let alone the leader of the Lomos Rebellion."

He pulled out her chair, the same one she'd been planted in since her arrival at daybreak. "Now, remember. Keep to your innocence. They can see your memories, but not the emotion that goes with it. It's the intent behind your actions that will sway the ellan one way or the other. If you keep to your claim that killing Maxis was all done out of love for the malran and a desire to protect him, the council will be hard pressed to convict."

"And my involvement in Lexi's kidnapping?" A stupid miscalculation on her part. She'd be smarter in the future. More distanced from the action. More effective in the outcome.

"Correct me if I'm wrong, but the truth of the matter is that Maxis did the actual kidnapping. You merely delivered the lure to the malress. Is that accurate?"

Serena nodded. Thyrus might be one of the most slovenly creatures she'd ever met, but he was damned handy in legal matters. Not to mention a staunch, yet quiet supporter of the rebellion.

"Then keep to that angle," Thyrus said. "Expound on your feelings of remorse as you carried out the act, but explain that it felt necessary to go along with Maxis' schemes to protect the malran. Trust me. They haven't a scrap to hold you to. Not with you taking Maxis out when no one else could." Thyrus shook his head. "A loss for the Rebellion, but a genius move on your part given how it makes you appear as though you'd meant to fight on behalf of the malran all along. Remind me never to piss you off."

A knock sounded on the door and a young man barely past his awakening stuck his head through the opening. "The council is gathering and the royal couple have arrived. You'll need to make your way to the main hall."

Royal couple indeed.

It should have been her beside Eryx. Not that human-raised commoner, Lexi Merrill.

Yes. She definitely needed to be more effective with her endeavors in the future. Particularly if it freed up the malress' throne in the process.

The steady rumble of voices from the main hall filtered down the long, shadowed corridor, and Thyrus' heavy foot-steps clopped beside her. They entered near the back, step-ping into the cavernous room with its domed three-story ceiling. Sunlight streamed through the glass-topped circle in the center to spotlight Eryx and Lexi seated on their thrones at the front of the hall.

That bitch. Fitted out in a platinum-colored gown, wearing a crown. The crown that should have been hers.

Serena looked away and clashed gazes with Angus Rallion, a lifelong politician who'd pissed Eryx off one too many times and now swam in the lowest layers of the polit-ical feeding pool.

He grinned at Serena. A smug, superior expression that made her fingers twitch for another dagger. If the idiot hadn't screwed their schemes up so badly, she might be in a different position right now. Preferably in Eryx's bed.

She smiled at Angus instead, lifted her head, and glided beside Thyrus to the defendant's table. Better not to burn any bridges. One never knew when inside influence would be needed. Low standing or not, Angus had connections. Powerful connections.

Three short raps of wood against marble clattered through the hall.

"All rise." It was the young man who'd called them into trial, his voice rich with formality despite his youth.

The ellan kneeling on long ivory cushions lined up in rows along the main floor, stood. Elders with higher standing peered over their second and third-story box seats on either side. Eryx and Lexi remained seated.

"By the authority of the malran and malress, Serena Doroz Steysis, baineann of the deceased, Maxis Steysis, is hereby brought to stand trial before the Myren council under the charges of attempted murder of our malress, treason against the throne, and violation of The Great One's tenets." The page looked up from the mammoth book perched on his lectern, and focused on Thyrus. "How does the defendant plead?"

Thyrus lifted his chin, the motion haughty despite his wiggling jowls. "The defendant is innocent."

Rumbles and poorly contained whispers rippled behind her.

The page scribbled something on thick parchment, the sandpaper rasp loud enough to carry as far as Serena's table. He motioned to the prosecutor's table and set his pen aside. "Simmons, you may begin."

A handsome man with a lithe build and sandy blond hair stood and tidied his papers. Vibrant jewels accented his stark white council robe, marking his rank as one of the highest among the ellan. Apparently, Eryx was pulling out all the stops in seeing she burned for her crimes.

Simmons set about his case, regurgitating news everyone already knew. Her former association with Eryx, a tame way of saying they'd fucked like animals and been quite an item a decade ago. Her involvement in Lexi's kidnapping and failed demise. How she'd mated Maxis and subsequently stabbed him in the heart in a public location with loads of humans looking on in Evad. "The prosecution asserts that Serena Doroz Steysis was not only an active participant in the actions of the Lomos Rebellion, but that she plotted to capture and enslave humans, and murder the malran and the malress."

"Hardly a valid assertion considering her fireann is dead by her own hand and the malran and malress are very much alive and well," Thyrus said.

Simmons lifted an arrogant brow. "The ellan represent the will of the people. It's their opinion I'm concerned with, counsel. Not yours." He paced to his table and slid a document closer to him. "The prosecution calls Neil Vernace."

Serena stifled an indignant huff, but barely. Really? A rookie Rebellion warrior was the best they could do?

The witness strode to the chair at Eryx's right, waited for a nod from Eryx, then sat at the edge.

Simmons looked up from his document. "You served the Rebellion, did you not?"

"For a short time." He glanced at Eryx. His rigid back and shoulders made it seem he was prepared for flight at the barest hint of irritation from the malran.

Poor boy. Hard not to keep from swallowing one's own tongue under Eryx's blatant stare. The malran was intimidating enough in normal council attire. Dressed for battle in his drast and leather pants ratcheted the intimidation factor higher.

"I didn't fully realize the extent of their goals," Neil said, still looking at Eryx. "If I'd realized they meant to hurt our fellow race, I would have never participated."

Traitorous bastard. She'd bet half her inheritance he'd have sung a different tune if she and Maxis had been successful. Especially if he had a few slaves of his own.

"Your beliefs and involvement will be addressed later." Eryx's warm, baritone voice reverberated through the hall. Powerful here for sure, but she preferred it up close and personal.

Simmons drifted away from his notes. "Neil, can you confirm the accused was sighted with Maxis at the Rebellion training grounds and played an active part in strategy sessions?"

"She did." Neil glanced at Serena then redirected to the prosecutor. "Only toward the end, but she participated."

"Participated?" Thyrus stood as he spoke. "Tell me, can you recount her contribution to said strategy sessions?"

Neil's gaze bounced from Simmons, to Thyrus, then to Eryx.

Eryx stared back, unmoving. A lazy predator unaffected by everything happening under his watch.

Serena knew better. The Shantos men missed nothing.

Thyrus settled into his chair. "The malran doesn't have any answers for you. Just answer as you remember."

"Watch your attitude, counsel." Eryx's warning snapped whip-sharp through the vast room. At the end of the day, he could overrule every outcome of her trial if he so chose. Probably would be tempted to do just that if it didn't mean losing political support.

With one last quelling glare at Thyrus, Eryx shifted his gaze to Neil. "Answer."

"Um, I don't recall."

"Nothing?" Thyrus pressed. "No suggestions from Serena of any kind?"

"No. Not that I recall."

Thyrus drummed the tabletop with his thumb. "Is it possible she was merely there? Watching and yet not contributing at all?"

Silence filled the hall and Serena's heartbeat kicked up a notch. If it weren't her own head on the line, she might actually enjoy the intensity.

"It's possible, yes."

Excellent. A small win, but a win nonetheless.

Thyrus shrugged as though Neil's admission were

nothing spectacular. Or, more to the point, expected. "Anything else from your witness, Simmons?"

Simmons shook his head and Eryx motioned for Neil to step down.

"If the malran would be so gracious, the prosecution would like to call the malress as its next witness."

Murmurs rolled along the crowd behind her, and she could have sworn the sound carried out into the streets beyond.

Thyrus stood. "My malran, if it pleases you, the defense readily concedes that my client did, in fact, deliver the message used to lure your baineann into danger. Further Serena admits to being in attendance while your mate was held hostage. I see no point in causing our malress further discomfort by rehashing the details."

"Then perhaps we'll discuss our malress' unique read on the situation when Serena delivered the message to her highness," Simmons said in an equally patronizing tone.

Lexi remained as stoic as her mate, the barest smile tugging at her lips. No telling what kind of telepathic commentary fired between the happy couple.

Eryx sucked in a deep breath and nodded.

Simmons gave a slight bow of thanks and directed his attention to Lexi. "Could you describe to the ellan your unique gifts, my malress?"

"I'm an emotional empath."

Serena's stomach clenched. She checked the impulse to throw the tablet poised near Thyrus' elbow across the room, but not by much. So much for her emotions being undetectable.

Thyrus toyed with his pen, mouth pursed and eyes thoughtful. For all she knew he was plotting his next meal instead of navigating the new land mine between her and freedom.

"For those unfamiliar with the gift, that means you can read the emotions of those in proximity to you?" Simmons asked.

"More like experience them. Just as a healing empath takes on the wound of another before healing it within their own body, I take on their emotions."

Simmons made eye contact with Serena. "Could you describe the emotions you registered the day Serena came to deliver the message that lured you to Maxis?"

For the first time since Serena had entered the hall, Lexi's gaze locked onto hers. "Hatred. Cold, calculated disgust."

"The type you'd associate with one out to do you harm?"

Thyrus pushed to his feet, his exasperated sigh carrying loud enough even Simmons seemed to take note. "Your pardon, malress. But is it possible the anger you registered by your most impressive gifts might be in relation to the situation Serena found herself in and not anything to do with you?"

"I highly doubt that." Lexi crossed her legs, displaying a long span of tanned skin as she reclined against the cushioned backrest.

Thyrus tilted his head and smiled the smile of a placating father. "Yes, but it is possible, correct? It's even possible she truly was angry with you, but was still willing to put herself, and you, in a tenuous situation in order to protect her former lover. Correct?"

More than one gasp rang through the hall at the none-to-sensitive reference.

Lexi glared at Thyrus from her throne, her body so still she could've been a cardboard cutout. "I suppose."

Impressive. Serena couldn't decide what pleased her more. Thyrus' clever maneuvering, or witnessing Lexi's discomfort.

Simmons moved on, calling more witnesses. Thyrus countered. Patches of sun inched across the stone floor.

Serena's back ached from her uncomfortable wooden chair and her ass had gone numb at least an hour ago.

The legs of Thyrus' chair grated against the rough floor as he stood. "The defense calls Reese Theron."

Reese made his way to the chair at Eryx's right.

His butt had barely touched the seat before Thyrus dove in. "Did my client come to you in order to share Maxis Steysis' plans and to beg for mercy from the malran?"

"She did." Reese met her gaze. His wild mane of long blond hair mixed with his warrior build to make him look like a lion straight off the Sahara. "Though the genuineness of her visit was questionable."

"You're making presumptions and offering opinions," Thyrus said. "Did she or did she not come to you and share Maxis' plans?"

"She did."

"Did she tell you she was sharing this information despite the danger it might bring her way?"

"She did."

"And did she ask for you to request mercy from the malran on her behalf?"

"Yes."

Thyrus ran his finger along the edge of his notepad. "Did her actions provide the malran with the information necessary to bring down the Rebellion leader?"

"I'd say that's a moot point considering she ended up being the one who did the killing."

Thyrus' head snapped up. "Exactly." He lumbered around the table and stood closer to Reese. "Despite her request for assistance and putting her own life in danger, she put the malran first and protected him from a man who'd forced her into a mating."

Whispers fluttered from all directions.

Lexi scowled from her throne.

Thoughtful, Eryx traced the smooth armrest of his own chair with his thumb. "Anything else, counsel?"

Thyrus pivoted toward his seat and shook his head. "No, my malran. The defense rests."

CHAPTER 4

*R*amsay dropped his head back against the plush couch cushions in Eryx's private council chambers and glared at the ornate ceiling. Four fucking hours he'd wasted in that damned trial. Five if you counted porting back from Evad and flying to Cush.

Trinity would be at the library by now, a detail he'd finally wrangled from her friend Margo after an hour and a half of assurances he'd do nothing to endanger Trinity. He'd sworn over and over he only wanted to get to know her. See how things went.

And find out how in histus she got that necklace. He wouldn't mind knowing how she'd flattened him when he tried to scan her memories either.

He'd been so close to another look at the pendant, her soft skin nearly burning his knuckles before she'd run off like a jackrabbit.

"Shit you not, man." Jagger directed his booming voice to Wes, Troy, and Ian, all fellow elite warriors gathered to support their malran and huddled near the conference table at the other end of the room. "One minute he was Don Juan on the move, and the next he was flat on his ass."

Sharp laughter filled the room, every eye on Ramsay.

All but Ludan. Physically, Eryx's best friend and somo was present, sprawled in a fancy wingback way too delicate for his massive frame, but he seemed about as far away as Ramsay felt.

"You couldn't let it go," Ramsay said to Jagger privately.

"Hell, no." Jagger lifted his glass of strasse, the bold and powerful amber liquor favored by most Myren warriors glinting in the sun as he waggled his eyebrows. *"At least I kept it in close company. You'd have outted me at drills if it'd been me who went down."*

Ian ambled toward the overstuffed chair at Ramsay's left, the chocolate color keeping with the overall dark decor of the room. Masculine sophistication, his mother had called it when she'd redecorated during his father's reign. "I don't doubt that for a minute."

Ramsay snapped his head up. Had Ian just said that out loud?

"What the fuck?" Jagger plunked down his drink and stalked closer. "That conversation was not for you."

Ludan's eyes came into focus, taking in the scene with a scary shrewdness.

Ian slumped against the seat back with a tired sigh and ran a hand through his salt and pepper hair. "Sorry." He locked gazes with Ramsay. "I try to keep it separate, but when there's a lot of talk going on, sometimes it's hard to keep it straight."

It was the impact of Eryx healing Lexi's human friend. Or at least that's what everyone who knew of Ian's growing ability to eavesdrop on telepathic conversations thought. Those in the know were a pretty tightly controlled group for good reason. The council might have conceded Eryx was right to heal the lethal wounds Maxis had inflicted on the man, but they'd have an altogether different reaction if they learned Ian was morphing into something closer to the Myren race as a result.

Ramsay motioned Jagger to back off and leaned forward, resting his elbows on his knees. "Any other gifts showing up?"

"Nope." Ian propped one foot on the coffee table. "Lexi spent an hour yesterday trying to teach me to fly or call a few elements. Not so much as a spark."

"And Brenna?" Ludan's unexpected, but restrained voice kept to their side of the room.

"Jillian says no." Ian fingered the fabric armrest and cocked his head at a considering angle, eyes distant. "I'm not so sure though. She's been...different lately."

"She's been Maxis' slave since she was eight," Ramsay said. "Considering how jumpy she was when we found her, I hope to histus she's a lot different."

Ian shook his head and drilled them each with a serious look. "No, it's not that. She's not just calmer now, she's... curious." He tapped his thumb in an absent, steady rhythm. "Kind of like a toddler who's figured out how powerful their fingers and thumbs are and sets out to use 'em everywhere... even where they shouldn't."

Ramsay relaxed back into the couch. "I'll talk to Eryx. See if we should—"

"Leave her alone." Ludan steepled his fingers. A contemplative pose for those who didn't know better, but the whites of his eyes burned neon vivid around his already bright blue eyes. That signaled one thing and one thing only for men of Shantos and Forte lineage: time to defuse the situation before earth, fire, water, and air all clashed in a cataclysmic event.

The study door opened.

33

"I cannot fucking believe it." Lexi stormed in, her cheeks a mottled red. A testy breeze that shouldn't exist in an enclosed space swept in behind her.

Eryx ambled in afterward and flicked his hand toward the door, shutting it with a thought. He gripped her shoulder. "Rein it in, hellcat."

Calm words delivered casually, but the tension in Eryx's shoulders made it obvious he wasn't too far behind his baineann in the pissed off department.

"They give the verdict?" Ramsay asked.

"Oh, they gave it all right." Lexi paced to the tall window at the back of the room and scowled at the packed streets. "Idiots."

"Reluctant accomplice." Eryx stalked to the sidebar and uncorked the strasse. "The council totally fell for her shit, but even more than that, they're relieved she took out Maxis. They confiscated the assets that passed to her on Maxis' death, and ordered probation for the next five years, her first year under house arrest with supervised excursions. If she violates probation, she'll be stripped of her powers and banned to Evad."

Jagger perched on the edge of the conference table, hands curled around the edge. "Histus, if that's the case we need to celebrate. Five years of probation? For Serena? She'll never make it."

Wes and Troy, both in at-ease stances behind Jagger and trying to look inconspicuous in the middle of the drama, chuckled.

"When's the verdict coming out?" Ian asked.

Lexi gave up her view of the crowds and rested one hip on the sofa. "Five more minutes. The ellan are on their way back now. They want this over with so they can get straight to this afternoon's session."

Ian whipped his head to face her. "Another one?"

"Status update on how our sideshow in Evad is playing out." Eryx strolled toward his mate.

Sideshow meaning the public display of Myren powers in Evad when Maxis tried to swipe a bunch of humans to fill his slave farm. Also conveniently the night Serena drove a dagger through his heart.

"We've covered that with them already," Ramsay said. "The only video that made it through you frying the electronics is too blurred to show anything meaningful. We give it time and the humans will move on to something else. Hell, the new Kardashians series starts in another week. It'll be fine."

"We can't ignore this, Ramsay. The tenets were broken, and the prophecy has people primed for panic." Eryx pulled Lexi in and kissed the top of her head. "If a regular report makes 'em feel better, then I've got no problem with keeping up surveillance and giving them a rundown every now and then."

"Who's the unlucky bastard doing surveillance?" Jagger asked.

"That would be me." Ian crossed his arms over his chest and leaned back in the chair with a shrug. "I don't mind. Jilly's curious about Evad, and it lets me get an Internet fix. I never thought I was much of an electronics junkie, but even an old man like me can get used to cell phones and Google."

Easy laughter moved through the room, diffusing what remained of the tension. Ian seemed to have that effect on people. Probably a gift honed through his years as a cop dealing with unsavory assholes.

"We've got to get back." Eryx stepped away and guided Lexi toward the door. "Ludan, do your mojo on Serena's memories as soon as she's released. Ramsay, I want detailed recon on Maxis' properties. The sooner we uncover his secrets and disassemble his infrastructure the better."

Fuck. Probably the right course of action where the Rebellion was concerned, but a kink in his plans for digging deep about Little Miss Sunshine. If Trinity worked a straight Monday through Friday shift, then he only had about five more hours to catch her before she left for the weekend, and patience was a pain in his ass.

Eryx glowered at Wes and Troy. "Get the word out. Any person suspected of participation in Rebellion activities will be brought in and tried. Those willing to come forward of their own volition to share what they know will be considered for special dispensation. Otherwise, they'll be marked a threat to the race."

Eryx opened the door, and Ludan and Jagger filed out in front of him and Lexi.

"Eryx." Ramsay shoved from the couch and followed his brother into the hall. "There's something else we need to talk about."

From the main hall, voices filtered down the dark corridor, their two somos already standing sentry at the exit.

Eryx watched the ellan file past and let out a weary exhale. For a split second, the composed mask he held in place for the world slipped, fatigue weighting his features. "Yeah?"

Lexi laid her palm on his chest and nestled in the crook of his arm, as though she sought to bolster his strength through touch.

News of Trinity and her mysterious pendant shriveled on his tongue. Adding more to his brother's plate would only make it worse, not to mention yank his new shalla around with the possibility she might have relatives. "Just thinking you two should probably take a little time away from the limelight for a few days. I can cover here, and you can get a change of scenery. Maybe head to Evad."

Eryx squeezed Ramsay's shoulder and started down the hallway, Lexi at his side. "Another week or two and I'm gonna take you up on that. Assuming no more flaming piles of shit get tossed in our direction." He waved over one shoulder without looking back. "In the meantime, handle Maxis' estate."

Ramsay nodded, but it went unnoticed. The newlyweds were too close to register anyone else in their last few moments of privacy. They looked right together. Comfortable. And The Great One knew Eryx had worked his ass off to earn it. Tracking a woman you weren't one hundred percent sure existed took huge amounts of patience, not to mention a little insanity.

Not his kind of gig. Relationships were messy. Cumbersome. Dangerous.

He shook his thoughts off and took two steps into Eryx's private chambers where Wes and Troy waited. "You two with me." He spun and headed down the corridor, his warriors' heavy footfalls behind him. "We've got three hours to get squads put together and assigned out. Wes, you're on point to lead everything at Maxis' estate. Troy, you're on the warrior camp."

Wes piped up at his left. "Thought you were going to head this up?"

"I am heading it up. I'm just delegating the grunt work." And freeing himself up for reconnaissance in a whole different arena.

They stepped out of the gray stone council foyer and into the bright Myren afternoon. Curious citizens spread out in a peaceful swath at least two blocks deep in all directions. Vendors made the most of the situation with their bright, covered carts.

"If we're the grunts, what are you doing?" Troy asked at his right.

A heady, almost urgent impulse pounded his feet. "I'm going hunting."

◠

TRINITY SQUEEZED THE STEERING WHEEL, focused on the pretty gold flowers fronting her mother's tidy white house in lower Greenville, and replayed her new life mantra for the fifteenth time.

Show up. Listen. Speak your truth. Let go of the results.

It was time to maintain her boundaries with her mother. Being kind didn't mean she had to let her mom walk all over her or pummel her with negative crap about her life. She was a single woman out on her own now. No strings. No rules but her own.

Yeah, how's all the positive jive workin' for you?

Trinity puffed out an exasperated scoff at her mind's negative jab and snatched her purse from the passenger seat. A healthy mental attitude took too much damned work.

After a click of her car alarm and a quick check left and right, she trudged across the street toward the homiest version of hell on earth. Her necklace lay heavy on her chest beneath her crewneck sweater set, but she checked the neckline to be sure it was hidden. God forbid her mother find out she was still wearing it.

Her fingers drifted higher, circling at the hollow of her neck as her heels clicked against the sidewalk. The memory of Ramsay's touch last night was as sharp under the noonday sun as it had been when she'd finally drifted off to sleep last night. She still couldn't decide if running had been the smartest or stupidest thing she'd ever done.

Probably smart. Questions, shrewd eyes, and her telltale warning tingle? The whole thing had *danger danger* written all over it.

Still, he'd been able to touch her.

She groaned and rang the doorbell. All this mental back and forth was exhausting.

The white painted door opened and rattled the old screen door.

A familiar woman with short dark hair and a kind smile pushed the screen door open, Trinity's mom hovering behind her. "Trinity!"

Trinity scrambled to place the woman and, without thinking better of it, shook her outstretched hand to cover the awkward moment.

The world dropped away.

A tidy but sparse and aged study, the decor at least two decades old.

The woman in her mother's doorway stood beside a man whose dark-haired head was bowed over a large desk.

"Please, don't make me go there," she said. "God forgive me, but she's the most judgmental, sanctimonious person I think I've ever met."

The dark-haired man looked up. "I need you, Lisa. You can reach her. Someone needs to. She's making the rest of our parishioners nervous."

Trinity dropped the woman's hand and reality rushed to greet her.

"I'm Lisa O'Dell. My husband's the minister at your mother's church."

That's why she seemed familiar. Trinity had only been to her mother's church-of-the-month a few times, much to Mom's dismay. "That's right. I remember now. It's good to see you again."

Lisa stepped out onto the stoop, making room for Trinity to pass through. "Such a nice daughter to come and spend a quiet lunch with your mother."

Behind her, Trinity's mother scoffed.

Lisa didn't seem to notice. "Now remember what I said, Carol. I know you mean well, but the church is about tolerance and love. Take a few days to think it through, and if you feel you need someone to talk to, I'll swing by for another chat." Her words were sweet and her smile was locked in place, but she bee-lined it to the car before her mother could answer.

Trinity pulled the screen door closed and shut the main door behind it, blocking out the cheery noonday sun. The dreary room matched everything about her mother—thinning, dull blond hair with ample gray, and clothes in every shade of drab. "What was all that about?"

Silly to ask. After all these years with her mother, the routine seldom changed.

"I simply shared with the minister my concerns about the youth at church and their wanton behavior." Her mother crossed her arms and frowned, the wrinkles around her mouth etched deep from years of scowling. "Evil must be stomped out before it can take root. The smallest amount of tolerance can lead to ruin for their souls."

Trinity sat her purse aside and glided to the small kitchen. The scent of spice and bubbling cheese filled the room. Mexican chicken casserole if she had to guess. The thought of eating while sitting through one of her mother's vile spiels made her queasy.

She pulled her old emotional armor tight. If those innocent children were sporting evil in her mother's eyes, then Trinity was the devil himself. "Lisa's right, Mom. Let their parents handle it and know that The Gr—God—will see to their needs."

Carol opened her mouth to argue.

"So, anything else interesting going on at church?" Trinity grabbed plates from the old white cabinets and set the table. Her mother's social life consisted of worship service, charity functions, meddling in the lives of churchgoers, and praying for her adopted daughter's soul.

Her mother shuffled to the kitchen sink with the dated, cornflower blue Formica surrounding it, and washed her hands. "They're holding a pot luck and a silent auction tomorrow night. I told them you'd be there after the library closes down."

Show up. Listen. Speak your truth. Let go of the results.

"I'm sorry, I can't. I'm working extra to get the hang of my new job." Damn. Not the truth. Speak the truth. "And after a long day of good work, I want to go home and get my new place settled."

"Well, that's a little selfish, don't you think?" She dried her hands on a faded green towel nearly as old as Trinity and leaned one hip on the counter. "You can unpack your things after church on Sunday. I'll come help."

Shit. At this rate, she'd have to speak her truth with a baseball bat to make an impact. "Mom, I appreciate the offer, but this is something I want to do, and I want to do it tomorrow after work. On my own."

Carol dropped the casserole she'd pulled from the oven to the maple table with a clunk. "You're awfully quick to distance yourself from me and the church. Ungrateful, if you ask me."

Well, I didn't ask you.

The television on the side table in the corner soundlessly streamed the midday news and the clock on the wall showed twelve-twenty. Twenty more minutes and she'd have an excuse to leave. "How's your back feeling?"

"Hard to get around. I spent most of yesterday resting in bed, but doing a little better today." She spooned enough casserole onto Trinity's plate to feed a lumberjack. "Of course, if you'd been here, I never would have injured it in the first place."

Twelve twenty-one. Note to self: seriously re-think visits to Mom and limit to no more than thirty minutes.

"A mother shouldn't have to bribe her daughter with lunch to see her."

"I offered to come, Mom. I wanted to check on you, find out how your back's doing, and see if you needed anything done while I'm here." More like ease her guilty, mother-fueled conscience for moving out in the first place. Boy, was that plan a bust.

"I don't need anything from you, Trinity. I'm fully capable of taking care of myself."

Ah, backhanded guilt. Awesome. Well played.

Carol's gaze locked on the television. A frozen video clip stretched to cover the whole screen, a black Pegasus with its wings outstretched and ready for flight on a silver background. At least she thought it was a Pegasus. The detail was horrid. Beneath it the caption read, *Clues Emerge in North Texas High School Phenomenon.*

Without so much as a blink, her mom snatched the remote control and upped the sound.

"For nearly a month now, forensic video analysts have been combing through blurred images captured at what dozens of Friday night football spectators claimed was a preternatural combat in the North Texas High School parking lot. Government and military officials engaged in researching the footage when witnesses claimed that the fighters, all large in stature and comporting themselves in a way consistent with military training, cast either flame or electrical strikes from their palms.

"Today reports surfaced indicating that the image you see on your screen has been identified as a type of insignia on more than one of the men in question. Facial recognition is still unavailable, but authorities assure they will continue to identify and locate the men in question."

The remote clattered from Carol's hand to the kitchen table. "Devil's work." Face tight with fear, her gaze slid to Trinity.

Tingles started at the base of Trinity's neck, cupping the back of her head like a specter's hand. A roar filled her ears.

Bad news. Very, very bad news. That fanatic gleam in her mother's eyes never boded well. Combined with Trinity's built-in warning radar, she could only expect something close to emotional Armageddon.

Her mother's lips firmed, her frail body nearly shaking with whatever fury was gaining speed beneath the surface. "You're one of them, aren't you?"

Damn it. She should have expected this. "Mom, I'm just a girl. Nothing more, nothing less."

"Normal girls don't see the future."

"I don't see the future." Well, not yet anyway. Only if she caved to Kazan's urgings and accepted her gifts.

"Then tell me how a seven-year-old girl can warn her father not to leave the house on the same day he gets killed."

"It was a fluke, Mom." Not that her warning had helped save David's life. It was also the last time she'd ever opened her mouth to share such a feeling in front of her mother. "I just didn't want him to go."

"Devil's work. I knew it then. I thought I could do my part to save your soul, but I was wrong."

God, she was so tired of this. Maybe Kazan was right. Maybe she should accept her mother's tenuous grip on reality and let her go. Carol had always been a little intense, even before David died in a car wreck. After that, it turned into something more. Something sick and scary. But she'd still cared for Trinity, despite her inability to touch.

The weatherman droned in the background, promising fall's first cold front. Twelve thirty-two. Close enough to call lunch finished. She could fathom her next steps with her mother in the sane, controlled safety of work. "It's time to get back to work. Do you need me to do anything before I leave?"

Carol shook her head, gaze aimed through the big window overlooking the small, plain backyard. "Go." Her hands opened and closed over and over into tiny, nervous fists. "Get out and let me get on with what I need to do."

The urge to placate and soothe her mother's anxiety with blithe assurances that everything was fine bubbled to her lips.

No. This wasn't her problem. Not anymore. She was free. On her own and no longer beholden to this woman in anything beyond loyalty and love. "All right then. I'll check in with you in a few days."

She pushed from the table and snatched her purse. She could do this. Just walk out the door and keep her mouth shut.

She opened the front door and the sun lit up the dark entryway like a breath of fresh air.

"Trinity."

Mid-stride across the threshold, Trinity glanced back and the buzz-tingle combo flashed back to life.

Her mother's flat, brown eyes glared from the kitchen entry. "I know what you are."

Trinity pulled the door shut behind her and jogged down the sidewalk. Her mother couldn't know. Not really. But God help her if she ever found out.

CHAPTER 5

*R*amsay hustled across the plaza in front of the downtown Dallas library and dug his iPhone out of his back pocket.

Four-forty-five. Way too damned close. Maybe he'd catch a break and learn she worked a later shift, but odds were on her being an eight-to-five girl.

The library's sand colored exterior with dark tinted windows and clean, once-thought-futuristic lines screamed eighties architecture. He opened one of the many glass doors and strode across the neutral, yet dated marble floors to the main desk.

An older woman straight out of a textbook librarian image peered up at him with a friendly smile. A white security badge dangled around her neck, the name *Martha* in big black letters. "Can I help you?"

Rows of teak-colored tables stretched behind her, all walks of life taking up random seats while others roamed in and out of the tall shelves on either side.

"I'm here to see Trinity Blair." His words came out more winded than he cared for, a fact he'd like to blame on the rush to get there. Truth was, his body hadn't stopped pulsing since he'd stepped foot out of the council building.

Martha scanned the row of offices along the far wall, all with doors closed except the one on the end. "I'm sorry, but she appears to be gone for the day. Is there something I can help you with?"

Not unless she knew a convenient way to rewind this whole damned day so he could show up thirty minutes earlier. "Any chance she'll be back in this weekend? There's something I wanted to run past her and was hoping I wouldn't have to wait until Monday."

She grabbed a pink pad with *While You Were Out* blazoned in blue text at the top. "It's against our policy to give out employee schedules, but if you want to leave a message, I'd be glad to pass it on."

"Oh, this isn't business." He flashed his most charming smile, the one he used on Orla when he was tired of bachelor food and wanted a particular meal. "Trinity's a friend of mine. I needed to ask her a quick question."

Her mouth pursed in an attempt to hide a knowing grin. She failed miserably. "If you're friends, then I'm sure you've got her contact information. You can call her and ask when she'll be here again or meet her outside of work."

Damn. Schooled by a little old lady he could snap like a twig. His pride rebounded. "You're right. I'll shoot her a text and see what her schedule looks like. Thanks for the help."

The lady smirked, but went back to her work.

Great. Now what?

He meandered toward the offices, winding through the aisles until he was sure Trinity's guard dog, Martha, had forgotten he existed. He pulled a book from a nearby shelf and pretended to check the contents. With a mental push, he tried the doorknob on the first office.

Locked.

He tried the other closed doors.

All locked.

He snapped the book shut and shoved it back on the shelf, no doubt plugging it in the wrong spot.

All wasn't lost. He could hit Ian up to do a search. Maybe see what his PI skills turned up. Still, approaching Trinity at her house wouldn't go over well. Not with a girl like her.

A pair of women with the same library identification tags ambled into the main lobby from a side hall, one of them gesturing wildly to match whatever story tumbled from her lips.

He might not be able to charm info out of Martha, but women under the age of fifty were a whole different ballgame.

"Excuse me." He strode toward the girls, checking to make sure Martha kept to her business. "Trinity's office is locked up, and I was supposed to meet her here before she went home. Any chance you guys know where she's parked so I can catch her before she leaves?"

Manufacturing an innocent, good-natured boyfriend expression wasn't one he had any experience with, but he gave it his best shot.

The dark-haired woman who'd been telling the animated story brightened and pointed toward a door at the end of the hall, a green Exit sign overhead. "Oh, no problem. We just left her. Out that door and over to the parking garage. If you hurry you can catch her before she gets there."

"Thanks!" He winked and jogged down the hallway, giggles from the two girls trailing behind him.

The security door *kachunked* open.

He blinked against the blinding afternoon sun. A mom hurried across the street with two toddlers in tow. Businessmen and women exited the buildings on all sides, some on phones, some chattering with those next to them. Cars raced between the stoplights and the drone and honks of traffic from the nearby freeway buzzed behind him.

Fuck. Where was the parking garage?

The light across the street turned green and a cluster of people stepped off the curb. A flash of blonde caught his eye, the owner's petite form moving more leisurely than the rest of the crowd.

"Trinity!"

His shout garnered more than one turned head, but the blonde head in question turned more sharply than the others.

He jogged to catch up with her, earning a honk from an impatient driver before he cleared the curb.

Trinity took a cautious step back. "What are you doing here?"

Ramsay kept his distance, her death grip on her briefcase's shoulder strap and the fear in her eyes slapping his conscience. "Sorry. I was trying to find you to apologize."

"And you knew to find me here how?" She might be nervous, but the bite in her tone said she didn't lack backbone.

"I, ah…" Ramsay ducked his head. Shit. Coming clean on this one was going to be tricky. He looked up and cocked what he hoped was a sheepish grin. "Your friends mentioned where you worked."

Her cheeks flushed a bright red and she turned for the garage. Yep. Definitely a backbone.

Ramsay darted forward and gripped her arm. "Wait."

She spun around so hard her briefcase nearly took out a woman passing on the sidewalk.

Ramsay held up his hands. "They only told me where you worked. I promise. And believe me, that took some doing."

Trinity scanned the street. Was she planning to run or looking for a cop?

"Listen, I'm afraid I came off like a class-A dick yesterday," he said. "I was kind of hoping I could make it up to you. Maybe get some coffee. Something public. Simple."

What the hell was he doing? Coffee? The extent of his conversations with women usually centered on music, social life, and sex. With Trinity and a coffee shop he'd be in a whole different realm of shoptalk, unless he got lucky and her librarian side had an affinity for military history. That he could talk about.

She took a deep breath and stared past the parking gate to the dark shadows beyond.

"Come on," he urged. "Just coffee. Or dinner, if you're hungry. Someplace quiet where we can talk." He motioned toward the cars parallel-parked in front of the library. "I've got my car parked around front. We can stay close. You pick."

Trinity shook her head, straightened to the peak of her whopping five-foot height, and headed for the garage. "I don't think that's a good idea."

He followed, but kept a decent distance. "I promise. I just want to get to know you. Make up for the way I acted. What can I do to make you feel safe?"

She stopped and ran a hand through her hair. A chunk of her nearly platinum locks fell across her brow in a sexy tousle.

Damn but that was a good look on her. One he'd give a lot to see under entirely different circumstances.

She shoved the strand out of her face and held out her hand. "Give me your license."

Well, she wasn't storming off anymore, so that was something. He dug in his back pocket, tugged his license from his wallet, and handed it over.

Trinity plucked it from his fingers. "Oklahoma?"

"My twin and his bain—wife live there."

"So you're here on business or pleasure?"

Don't fuckin' blow it, lover boy. Stick close to the truth. "A little of both. They're newlyweds and driving me nuts. Plus I needed to research some things for our family business. The trip here covered both."

She tapped the corner of his license for a minute then dug in her purse. She whipped out her phone, snapped a picture of his license, and handed it back. "I'm texting a copy to three of my friends. I'll call them before we go in and after we leave."

She pursed her mouth in the cutest way. Her lips were a pretty pink. Pale to match the rest of her coloring, not at all like the darker skin tones prevalent with his race. And they were full. Kissable.

Wait a minute. He was here to find out about the necklace, who the hell she was, and how she knocked him on his ass. Not lock lips and see if that perky personality of hers transferred to the bedroom. "So, where are we headed?"

Trinity readjusted her shoulder strap, dropped her phone in her purse, and squared her shoulders with a determined air. "How do you feel about pizza?"

SERENA GLIDED through the stark council hallways toward her first taste of freedom in weeks, Thryus waddling beside her. She opened and closed her right hand, willing the tingles left behind from Ludan's perusal of her memories to fade.

The bastard. Signing over all she'd inherited from Maxis, including his palatial estate, had been bad enough. Being forced to submit to Eryx's somo was the worst kind of torture.

Thank The Great One for Thryus' intervening gift. Most solicitors had the ability to act as a gateway for memory scans, keeping the browser to the parts of life that were under evaluation and leaving the more intimate details in the shadows.

"I know you're disappointed not to be fully exonerated," Thyrus said between choppy huffs. "But considering how things might have gone, you're really very blessed. Try to look on the bright side."

"The bright side?" Serena froze. "I'm one misstep away from being cast out of Eden with no powers. No one in my family has so much as raised a hand to acknowledge me, and I have no idea where I'm going to sleep tonight."

Thyrus patted her shoulder and urged her to keep moving, completely unaffected by her outburst. "Not to worry. I've got a few apartments you can choose from for the time being. Give yourself a day or two to settle and see what develops."

An apartment? Was he out of his mind? Her room at her family's estate was bigger than most warrior homes.

They turned the corner, the council foyer abandoned but for a few straggling ellan and warriors guarding each door. A slow steady burn started behind her chest. This wasn't how things were supposed to turn out. She was meant for more. Greatness. Power. Not driveling behind her solicitor and accepting his handouts.

The doors opened and the late afternoon sun washed over her, warm and soothing. A step up from the dark confines of the warrior training grounds where she'd been held.

A respectable crowd waited, not a crush, but at least fifty people up close and several others in scattered huddles further away. Maybe another hundred.

She moved to the first of the council steps and two people moved in on her right.

She halted, and her hand jerked to her throat. Not just random watchers, but her mother and father. Their heads were held high, proud smiles on their faces, the picture of support and concern.

"What are you doing here?" she asked her father, smoothing her expression to mask her surprise.

Reginald wrapped one arm around her shoulders and guided her down the steps. "Why, supporting my beloved daughter, of course."

The four of them navigated the crowds, Thyrus leading the way.

"Odd, I didn't notice any support while I was locked up, or through the trial." Outwardly, she might be the epitome of grace under pressure, but she made sure her disgust was evident in her tone.

"That was before you built a following." He handed her a news flier folded to accent the header of the top story.

I Did It For Love.

Reginald tightened his grip on her shoulder, more of a warning than anything born of affection. "Chin up, dear. You're a bit of a blooming celebrity. Have a mind to how you use it."

CHAPTER 6

*R*amsay zipped into a parking spot outside what looked like a dive bar. White stucco walls stretched to form a simple square building with a flat roof and blue trim. Above the matching blue door hung a cheesy blue and pink neon sign in the form of a martini glass with *Louie's* in cursive beneath it. "This is a pizza joint?"

Trinity fidgeted with the leather tassel on her purse. If she was impressed with the Spyder's swank interior or the price tag that went with it, she sure wasn't showing it. Not at all the kind of reaction he normally got from women. "Martini bar, actually, but they're known more for their pizza."

She opened her door as soon as he got it in park.

He hurried around to her side, barely making it before she shut the door. "Makin' it hard for me to show good manners."

"Oh." Trinity's gaze back-and-forthed between him and the car. "Sorry. I guess I don't…"

"Don't what?"

She tucked a strand of hair behind her ear and put a lot of work into studying her sexy as hell black pumps. Her matching skirt hit just above her knees and her prim blue sweater set rounded off the whole hot librarian vibe. "Dates usually mean touching, so I don't do it much."

Not many dates. Which meant not much in the way of kissing. Or anything else.

Untouched.

The idea detonated inside him. He *could* touch her. Give her what no one else could. Explore and teach her all kinds of wicked things.

Fuck. He had zero business entertaining anything along those lines. Not with this woman. He needed answers. Not sweaty sex with a probable virgin.

"Well, then, you're due for some much needed practice." With a light touch on her arm, he steered her toward the entrance, avoiding skin-to-skin contact.

Inside, the bar was packed. Not at all the kind of place he'd expected his buttoned-up librarian to pick. One side was older, dark with remnants of heavy smoke from days before the ban on indoor smoking, and small, black-top tables that had probably been around since the fifties. Not a single chair matched. The other side was newer, an add-on with exposed brick walls, party-sized booths, and a whole lot more light.

Ramsay gave the hostess his name while Trinity plastered herself to a wall in the shadowed entry, arms crossed and tucked in tight. Damn, but that must make her life miserable. Forget about sex. How'd she get through growing up without so much as a hug? Surely she didn't have this issue with her parents.

The hostess motioned for them to follow and trotted toward the newer side.

Trinity hesitated, gaze darting between the loitering bodies as though plotting out a safe path.

"Come on, Sunshine." He pulled her against him and navigated the crowd. "If you're big enough to let a guy grovel over dinner, the least I can do is run interference."

The hostess showed them to a booth and offered Trinity a menu.

Trinity accepted it at the furthest corners.

"How long have you fought the whole touch thing?" Not exactly a subtle conversation starter, but dancing around the topic seemed silly at this point. Besides, her condition might somehow feed into the rest of the information he wanted.

Trinity made a big show of perusing the menu, tapping the corner with her index finger. Unfortunately, her eyes never lingered on any item long enough to make the act convincing. "Since I was six. It took about a year, but the doctors finally diagnosed me with haphephobia."

"Fear of touch."

Trinity's head popped up, her mouth slightly ajar. The non-stop tapping stopped.

"What?" He winked at her and set his menu aside. "You think a guy like me doesn't know big words?" A guy like him had all kinds of time to learn multi-syllable words. One of the benefits of being one hundred and fifty-two years young.

She coughed and fisted her hands in her lap. "Sorry. That was rude of me."

"Hardly. More rude for me to tease you about it. Though it's kinda cute the way your ears turn pink when you're embarrassed."

One hand shot up to the side of her head. "They do not."

"Do too. It's cute."

She traced the shell of her ear, lingering for a second or two.

"It must have been hard on your parents," he said.

Her shoulders dropped and her sweet smile vanished. She shut the menu and set it away. "Harder after my dad died. He meant everything to Mom, and when she lost him..." She frowned at the table. "She stuck by me, but she was never the same again."

A waitress with deep maroon hair and cobalt blue streaks sauntered up and broke the tension. She was a tiny thing, four-foot-ten at best, but her demeanor screamed of good-natured rebellion. Kind of a renegade faery minus the wings. "You two know what you want?"

Ramsay motioned to the menu and grinned at Trinity. "You pick. I'll eat ten of whatever you're having."

The waitress laughed, a full belly rumble that made the two tables beside them turn to take notice. "Damn, girl." She sidestepped to get a better angle on Ramsay and winked at Trinity. Her eyebrow piercing glimmered in the overhead fluorescents. "Lookin' like that and giving you carte blanche? Sounds like you're in for a fun night."

Trinity's cheeks pinkened to match her ears, but she kept eye contact. "A merlot for me, and we'll have a large, thin crust with chicken, jalapenos, onions, and feta."

Wild child scribbled on her note pad. "Large thin crust, chicken, jalapenos, *no* onions, feta. Got it."

"No, we want onions."

The waitress dipped her chin and peered down her nose at Trinity. "You're missing me here. You've got a good-looking guy offering whatever you want on a date. You do *not* want onions. Get me?"

Ramsay couldn't help the chuckle that slipped out. Under different circumstances, Wild Child would be a hell of a lot of fun to hang with for a few hours. Come to think of it, she seemed a little familiar.

No. He'd have remembered the hair. "She's right, you know. I'll give you whatever you want…with or without onions."

"Daaamn…." Wild Child fanned herself.

Trinity's whole face turned beet red a split second before she ducked her chin and rubbed her palms on her thighs.

"Make that two larges," Ramsay said. "And a beer for me."

"On it!" The waitress spun away and hurried to the kitchen.

Praise The Great One, Trinity was sweet. The kind of innocent sexy a man wanted to horde all for himself. "Trinity."

No response, not so much as a twitch in his direction.

"Give me your eyes, Trinity. I want to see the way they look when I say something that makes you blush."

Her head snapped up, nothing short of raw and inexperienced hunger on her face. God, everything about her was pure goodness. Expressive and honest.

He laid his hand on the table palm up. "Take my hand."

She stared at it and worried her lower lip.

"It's just a touch. Two people holding hands while they get to know each other. You're safe with me." His conscience flinched. He'd never willfully hurt a woman, but he had a funny feeling he could seriously injure Trinity if he didn't tone things down.

She slid her hand in his.

The hesitant contact sizzled through him, more erotic than a practiced courtesan playing nice with far more intimate body parts.

He tightened his grip and the muscles in his biceps flexed with the impulse to pull her across the table and onto his lap. He had work to do, damn it. Information to get and puzzles to solve. What he needed was a safer line of conversation. "Why a librarian?"

Her answering smile nearly flattened him, so bright and happy it warmed him from the inside out. "Because I love books. The things I learn, the places they take me..." She giggled and rested her chin on her free hand. "I swear I even love the smell. That makes me kind of weird, huh?"

Weird? Unlike most of the women he talked to, she was genuine. Candid and unpretentious. "Men like the smell of gasoline and motor oil. I'm not gonna give you a hard time over books."

She laughed, tugged her hand free, and reclined into the back of the booth as the waitress delivered their drinks.

The conversation flowed easily. Likes and dislikes. Wine versus beer. Sports and Trinity's appalling lack of knowledge thereof. As promised, the pizza surpassed Trinity's claims, not one onion located on either one. Languid with food and drinks, they strolled toward his car.

Ramsay recaptured her hand in his and stroked the inside of her wrist with his thumb. So soft. A tiny flutter at her pulse point.

Her breathy voice floated around him. "So, what do you do?"

Tricky. Too much information and she could search for him. Not enough and he'd look evasive. "My brother has a geological research company in Tulsa. I work for him."

Not a lie as far as actual corporations went. In truth, he wasn't sure he could find the office without a little assistance from Google. "Have you always lived in Dallas?"

Her shoulders sagged, as though some of the happiness she'd built up through their light conversation eked out before she could catch it. "Ever since my parents adopted me."

Ramsay stopped. The rumble of the bar crowd inside barely registered above the random street traffic, and a dirty streetlight buzzed three cars over.

Adopted.

Like Lexi.

"So, it's just you and your mom?" he asked. "No other relatives?"

She shook her head. "But you have a brother, right?"

"A twin, actually. And a sister." The Great One help him if Galena ever learned how he was going about getting info out of Trinity. She'd string him up by his nuts for sure. Maybe a touch of directness wouldn't hurt. "Why do you think I can touch you?"

Trinity huffed out a laugh and traced the lower ledge of the passenger door window. "I have no idea."

"But you said others could, right?"

She nodded, still distracted.

"Who?"

She shook off whatever thoughts held her and moved so he could open the door. "I don't want to talk about it."

"Bad memories?"

"No, just private." She motioned for him to open the door. "I've gotta get home. I moved last week, I've got boxes to unpack, and I was up early this morning."

Ramsay leaned a hip into the door and crossed his arms. "You know, strong men are especially handy to have around when it comes to moving."

She mirrored his move, though it looked a whole lot sexier on her. Especially the way her crossed arms lifted her killer rack up for exaltation. Even more impressive, she didn't have a clue what the pose did for her. "I've already moved."

"Yes, but are all the boxes emptied? Or are there more to move around and unpack?"

She hung her head so her hair obscured her face. The moonlight shone bright against the platinum color and her shoulders shook on a silent laugh.

Damn but he hated it when she hid her eyes, and she did it a lot. A nervous habit he wanted to help break.

He lifted her chin.

Her chuckles ceased as she met his gaze, and a tiny smile lingered on her lips. One and a half centuries on this earth and he'd never met anyone like her. Standing next to her was like having his soul plugged into a power outlet, a high voltage one at that. "Call your friends if you want. Have them come over. I understand you need to be safe. I just want a little more time with you."

Her gaze roamed his face.

The space between them sparked with untamed energy. Heady. More punch than any top shelf booze and twice as addictive.

She rubbed a spot beneath the neckline of her sweater. The exact place her pendant would be. "I'll call my friends and ask them to check on me in a few hours."

CHAPTER 7

*T*rinity opened her front door and fumbled for the light switch, the jingle of her car keys practically broadcasting her jitters to Ramsay close behind her.

The kitchen light overhead flickered to life on their left. Packing boxes were stacked in haphazard patterns along the ivory quartz countertops, and cleaning supplies littered what little space was left. Her ancient hardwoods could use a Swiffer, but she hadn't exactly planned on company when she'd left this morning.

"There's not much in the fridge." She motioned Ramsay toward the tiny knockoff stainless steel refrigerator and strode toward the living room. *Please, please, please, don't let me have left anything embarrassing out.* "Margo might have left a six-pack from moving day. I know there's milk and bread. I think I put glasses in the cabinet to the left of the stove."

A squeak sounded behind her followed by the *schleep* of the refrigerator door.

She snatched yesterday's shoes off the floor and tucked last month's well-worn *Cosmo* in the end table drawer.

The bedroom. What if they ended up in the bedroom?

She hurried to the larger of her two bedrooms. Talk about rash moves. She never brought home strangers. Bed made, closet closed up tight, bathroom...yep, toilet flushed. All good.

"You've got a half-empty bottle of merlot and two beers," Ramsay called from the kitchen. "You want something?"

The guy sounded way too comfortable in this situation. Waaaay more comfortable than her. Of course, he also appeared to have a social life. More than a social life, actually. He lived. His whole demeanor practically screamed *bonsai*!

"You drink the beers," she called and checked her makeup in the mirror. Not too bad. Hair a little flat and eyeliner on its last leg, but otherwise okay. "I'll stick with the merlot."

She paused at the bedroom door, hand bolstered on the jam. Surely this wasn't a mistake. Her body buzzed, the mere idea of a man touching her, even if it turned out to be nothing more than a kiss, whipped her insides into a three-ring circus.

He sure liked to ask questions though. But that was a good thing, right? Last week Naomi had ranted about a date where the guy only talked about himself. Ramsay had been the opposite.

"Sorry, I rushed out this morning without a mind to company coming." She rounded the corner and jerked to a stop.

Ramsay sat on her gray chenille sofa, elbows planted on wide knees while he flipped through a photo album splayed across her coffee table. An album from her much younger days.

"Where did you find that?"

He motioned to a box on the floor. "It was open. I'm a sucker for embarrassing teenage pictures." He grinned and turned the page, but the way he held himself didn't match his joking tone. Or maybe it wasn't his posture so much as his focus.

He closed the album and stood, scanning the few boxes that remained in the living room. "Where do you want to start?"

Her mind plastered an insta-picture of the two of them naked and sweaty on her bed, a much less tidy bed than the real life version she'd left behind.

He picked up a full wine glass off the table and offered it. God, he had sexy hands. Long, strong fingers. Manly. What would they feel like between her legs, stroking her to a slow, yet powerful orgasm?

Her heart tripped and a ripple filtered from her belly button to the top of her thighs.

"Trinity?"

She lurched forward and took the wine. "Are you any good with electronics? I can strain a broadband signal with the best of them, but I'm pretty clumsy setting up a network."

"And here I thought you wanted me for my brawn." The playful glint in his eyes sparked a pleasant heat beneath her skin. "Show me where you want everything hooked up and I'll do my best to impress you with my limited knowledge of routers. A warning though. This means I'll have access to your Internet browser and I'm not above scanning your browser history."

He leaned in and all the oxygen in her lungs scattered to make room for his dark, delicious scent.

"Kinda curious what naughty sites a girl like you visits when no one's watching." He backed away and waggled his eyebrows, seemingly oblivious to the fact he'd taken what was left of her rational thoughts hostage. "So where am I headed?"

"Down the hall, second door on the left, dirty boy." Impressive. More than two words put together in a complete sentence, and she'd actually managed some spunk. No small feat considering her mind was busy backtracking through her Internet sessions. How long was that kind of stuff stored in history anyway?

She trailed behind him. His loose, long hair was the sexiest snub to conformity she'd ever seen, and his overall size was, well, big. Especially compared to her. Tight, defined muscles, wide shoulders, narrow waist, and a backside that made his easy swagger downright lethal.

He turned. His white T-shirt was tucked neatly into his low-slung jeans. Yep. The total hot guy package. Hard not to imagine the impressive parcel underneath.

"Trinity?"

She blinked and tried to force her mind back online. Oh, God. Totally busted staring at his crotch.

He grinned. Not just any grin, but a genuine shit-eating, caught-you-with-your-hand-in-the-cookie-jar grin. "Your router and cables?"

She staggered to the opened packing box on her desk and rummaged inside. At least she could hide her embarrassment behind the box flap at this angle. "I'm pretty sure they're in here, but can you check the one by the bookcase?"

Deep breaths. She couldn't be the first woman to ogle the guy. Not that his ego needed any extra boosts.

"Got 'em."

She peeked over the flap and found him untangling two gray cords.

"I'll put the router on top of the bookshelf so you don't clutter up your desk. That work for you?" Every move was smooth and efficient. Confident, like he did this every day.

She nodded and situated her computer, snapping to hand him whatever he asked for and otherwise aiming to stay out of the way.

He glanced up from behind her computer and lifted his

chin toward the picture frame on her desk. "Those your parents?"

A pang knifed her heart. "Yeah. That was taken about a year before David died." Carol looked so much different then. Happy and hopeful, even if she was still a little high-strung.

Trinity had come along and ruined life for both of them.

The clunk and rattle of hardware and cables stilled. Ramsay rested one arm on the top of her monitor. "If it makes you sad, why put it there?"

"They don't make me sad. I just wonder if they would've ended up happier without me."

Whoa. Where the heck had that come from? She never talked about her family with anyone but Kazan.

Ramsay twirled a cord between his thumb and fingers. "How could anyone be happier without you in their life?"

Trinity laughed, the sound bubbling up with a hint of resentment. "Well, you've only known me a total of twenty-four hours, so I'm not sure you're a suitable judge."

"Then educate me." His intensity crept across the room and held her by the back of the neck, his silver eyes glinting.

No. Going there would only drudge up the sludge she'd fought to escape. Mental health meant accepting all your old junk, letting it go, and moving on. "It's a long story best left behind." She motioned at the cord in his hand. "Where's that one go?"

He studied her for a few seconds and moved to the book-case. "All right, if you're not willing to talk, then you have to learn." He held out the cord. "Get over here, and I'll teach you how to do it for next time."

The way he was situated against the wall with the book-case in front of him, she'd be sandwiched mighty close to his big body. Too close.

Her abdominals fluttered and the muscles between her

legs tightened. That's why she'd agreed to bring him here. To see if anything else would happen. Maybe find out what real touch felt like.

She inched forward.

Ramsay straightened, the predator she'd glimpsed in him the night before rushing to the surface.

Her pulse pounded in her head, drowning all ambient sound, and her deepening breaths echoed in her ears.

With a hand at her shoulder, he guided her into the space between him and the bookshelf. "Take this." His voice was deeper. Distracted. "Plug it into the one that says WAN."

Trinity slid the blue box closer, fingers locked on the cable with a death pinch. It was either that or drop the damned thing and lose the incredible heat radiating off his body.

The connector snapped into place.

"Now this end." He handed her the other end of the cord, simultaneously closing what remained of the distance between their bodies so every amazing inch of his front pressed against her back. His other hand curled around her hip and his lips hovered beside her ear. "Plug it into the cable modem."

The what?

She dropped her hand. The cord dangled between her fingers, her muscles unresponsive to anything but the man behind her. "I..."

His hand at her hip slid in and splayed low across her belly, nearly hip to hip. Powerful and confident.

He pressed his hips into her back, the package she'd ogled needing absolutely no imagination now.

A low, frustrated growl rumbled from his chest. "Turn around."

She turned on autopilot.

He braced one hand on the bookshelf and cupped her

face with the other. His fingertips pressed against her scalp, the urgency of his touch prickling all the way down her spine. His breath fanned warm against her face. "Have you ever kissed a man, Trinity?"

The proximity of his lips brought a tingle to her own. Her voice sounded different. A little broken and a lot breathless. "A small one. Quick."

He leaned closer. The side of his nose grazed hers as he splayed the hand he'd braced against the bookcase to the small of her back. "Tell me you want more."

Huh? Why was he talking? Her entire world centered on his mouth, the plush, wet contact she'd always fantasized about the only thing worth entertaining.

"I won't take what you don't offer." The arm around her back tightened. "Tell me."

"Yes." A million times yes, if he'd shut up and get with the program.

His mouth tilted in a wicked grin and he cupped the back of her head, hair tangled in his fingers. "I promise." His lips skated over hers in a teasing whisper and his husky voice rattled her senses. "This won't be small. Or quick."

The claim crashed over her a second before his mouth captured hers.

Perfect. So full and warm, their breath mingling as he licked the seam of her lips.

She parted them, eager for more of his taste, the faint trace of beer, but something more powerful behind it. *Him.* Rich and frighteningly addictive.

He groaned into her mouth, his tongue encouraging her for more. He shifted his stance and muttered against her lips. "I was right. You taste like sunshine, too."

Her shoulders and back met wood. The bookcase.

He tilted her head and deepened the kiss, hands at either side of her neck.

She didn't have a clue what he was talking about. Couldn't care less. Not so long as he kept kissing. Stroking those perfect lips of his back and forth, licking into her mouth to tangle his tongue with hers.

Cool air assailed her stomach and his rough, erotic stroke teased above the waistline of her skirt.

Her cardigan was gone, only the tank from her sweater set still in place. When had that happened?

Her heart tumbled and her fingers tightened in his hair. Intimacy. This was what it felt like. Explosive and languid all at once, nerve endings on high alert and laid bare for contact.

She moaned and arched into his touch, needing more. Higher. Preferably without the confines of her bra, which felt two sizes too small.

Ramsay kissed along her jaw, down her neck. "A kiss isn't enough." He nipped her earlobe, his thumbs teasing the undersides of her breasts through the silk covering them. "I want more."

So did she. Hours of it. Starting right now. She fisted the hem of his T-shirt and tugged, slipping her hands underneath. Hot skin and hard muscle rippled beneath her palms. Amazing. So alive and powerful.

A hiss sounded at her ear. "I'll take that as a yes." In one smooth move, he peeled her sweater up and over her head, tossed it to the floor, and froze.

RAMSAY STARED at the ancient black filigree pendant dangling between the swells of Trinity's breasts, the shock of Lexi's mark ripping his lust from underneath him.

Somewhere in the night he'd forgotten his mission. Gotten lost in Trinity's bright, crisp scent and her warm, sweet taste, eager to see what lay beneath her prim and proper sweaters, only to crash head-on into what had brought him here in the first place.

"Did I do something wrong?" Her innocent, breathless voice lashed his conscience even as her heavy lidded eyes and flushed cheeks drew him back in. Praise The Great One, her breasts were full and lifted by lavender silk and lace like a damned offering. He'd bet everything he owned her nipples matched the pale pink of her lips. They wouldn't stay that way long, though. They'd be a nice, rosy color after he'd licked and sucked them like a ripe fucking peach.

"You've never done this." It wasn't a question. More like his common sense talking out loud.

She flinched and tried to cover herself.

Idiot. He snatched her wrists and pulled her close, her tight nipples rasping through the thin silk against his chest.

A subtle tremor racked her body. "I'm sorry, I don't know—"

"Shhh." Ramsay stroked her hair and shifted against her, his cock an uncomfortable ache behind his jeans. "You didn't do anything wrong." Hell, if he was honest, she'd done everything right. Enough to make him forget his purpose.

Praise The Great One, he was a leech. She was adopted. Probably didn't have a clue about the necklace. He should have done this all different. Researched her through records or talked to people she worked with.

But you didn't because you want her, pendant or not.

The thought lashed him. Hard. He leaned back, not enough to let her escape, but enough for eye contact.

Chocolate eyes stared back at him. So honest and vulnerable, like a direct line to her soul. Guileless. Hungry.

"I've never been anyone's first kiss." The realization rushed past his lips before it fully registered in his thoughts. Something foreign, almost primitive, flickered to life.

You could have all her other firsts too.

Oh, hell that was dangerous territory. Dangerous and barbarously pleasing. "Do you want more?"

She bit her lip, fear creeping into her eyes for the first time since he'd walked through her front door. "I'd like that."

He nudged her head higher and stroked her jawline with his thumb. "Then I'll give you more. Whatever you need. But we go slow."

"Why? I was fine and then you—"

He stopped her with a finger at her lips. So soft and swollen from his kiss. The picture of them stretched around his cock flashed with excruciating detail. "Details, Sunshine. A woman like you deserves them."

Another shudder moved through her, but this time her breath caught with it.

A bed. His mind stamped the demand and calculated the steps it would take to get from her office to the queen-size bed he'd marked on his way down the hall. Ten seconds max with her body pressed against him.

He swept her into his arms and strode out and around the corner to her lamp-lit room in under five. Lowering her to her feet, he kissed the spot above the pendant. Her waist was tiny beneath his hands. Delicate. And yet a substantial power radiated from her core. One that drew him in with a velvet, iron fist.

Slowly he turned them, teasing the swell of one breast with flicks of his tongue at the edge of her bra. He sat and centered her between his legs. With a lingering kiss against her sternum, he looked up and slid one hand to the closure at the back of her skirt.

Her eyes were shut and her fingertips bit into his shoulders.

"Give me your eyes, Sunshine." He unfastened the button and pulled the zipper down. "Watch me while I look at you."

Her grip tightened, but she opened her eyes on a shaky exhale. "I'm scared."

Fuck. Responsibility and something else he couldn't quite define settled on his shoulders.

Her skirt hung loose on her hips, tiny scraps of lavender lace peeking out to tempt his fingers. One push and she'd be nearly bare, only curves, silk, and sexy heels left to shred his patience. "No pressure. Only what you want. However much you want."

He circled her belly button with his thumb and the muscles beneath quivered.

"I want." She slid one hand to the back of his head and urged his mouth toward her stomach.

Her crisp scent surrounded him. Filled his lungs so there was nothing else save the faint musk of her arousal. The Great One be praised, he wanted the taste of that on his tongue. Needed it.

Pushing away from her urgent grip, he eased back. It was either that or break his promise and devour her. "Show me."

Shock and an uncertain quaver moved across her features. She glanced over one shoulder at the door.

Oh, hell no. The woman was a walking sun goddess in petite form. No way was he letting her get in some bullshit headspace. "Stop."

Her gaze snapped back to his.

Ramsay scooted to the top of the bed and rested his shoulders on the padded headboard. He motioned to the side closest to him. "Come here."

Her hands fluttered awkwardly at her waist and she wobbled unsteady on her heels beside him. Her black skirt teetered at the widest stretch of her hips.

"Give me your hand," he said.

Her eyebrows pinched inward.

"Your hand, Sunshine. Give it to me."

She held it out, cautious, as though ready to snatch it back.

Ramsay stroked the inside of her wrist and tugged her closer. "You wanted to run. Why?"

Her gaze zeroed in on his touch at her pulse. "I've never…" She swallowed and met his gaze. "No man has ever seen me."

His cock jerked and lengthened farther. A barely contained growl vibrated at the hollow of his neck. He pressed her hand to the insistent bulge behind his jeans. "You did this." He guided her palm up and down his shaft and flexed his hips into her touch. "Your smile, your words, your kiss." With a pointed look, he scanned her semi-dressed body. "And that was before I saw a damned thing underneath."

He relinquished her hand and tucked both of his behind his head. "Now show me. Own it."

The challenge brightened her dark eyes. She straightened and her shoulders pushed back at a tentative, but proud angle as she sucked in a deep breath. She rested her hands at her hips and licked her lower lip.

He fisted his hands, biceps straining to stay situated.

The skirt swished to the floor and pooled around those prim but oh-so-naughty black pumps.

Damn. He gave up keeping his hands contained and palmed his cock through his jeans, eyeballing the most amazing curves and creamy flesh on the planet. "Oh, no, Sunshine. You do not doubt your beauty. Ever."

He stroked the curve of her hip, her skin as soft as the silk panties barely covering the sweet stretch between her legs. He was *so* getting his tongue there. Licking and sucking until she screamed the damn building down.

Trailing his gaze up to her face, he squeezed her hip. "Still with me?"

A pretty flush stretched across her collarbone and cheeks, and her breath moved in and out raggedly. "Very."

Best. Answer. Ever.

Unleashing more of his power than he should, he dragged her across him and onto the bed and took her mouth. Her flavor consumed him. Hell, everything about her did. Scent. Touch. The whole package.

He tugged her bra straps over her shoulders, teasing her skin along the way with the gentle scrape of his nails and licking between her breasts. A quick pinch of his fingers behind her back and the hooks slipped free. He pulled the offensive silk away and tossed it to the floor.

His breath seized and a maddened hammering started up in his chest. Perfect. Soft ivory globes tipped in pale pink. Not too full, not too small. Just enough to fill his hands and tempt his mouth.

He rose to his knees and savored her innocent yet sultry pose, one knee cocked to cover the last scrap of fabric. His eyes locked on the heels she still wore. God, this woman had abso-fucking-lutely no damned clue how much power she held.

He circled one ankle, teased the arch of her foot with the barest stroke, and pulled the shoe free. It clattered to the floor with a muted thunk.

Her hand splayed wide across his thigh, as if the contact might somehow better ground her. "What are you thinking?"

Ramsay shifted, kneeled between her ankles, and slipped the other shoe off. "I'm thinking I'm one scrap of fabric away from being the luckiest bastard on the planet." He kissed the inside of one knee and nuzzled her soft thighs. "I'm thinking it's a damned shame you've never enjoyed this before, but am thrilled I'm the one giving it to you." He slid his hands under her perky ass, curled his fingers into the waistband of her panties, and tugged them over her hips. "And I'm thinking there is absolutely nothing I want more right now than my mouth on your pussy."

Her startled gasp rasped through the room.

He pulled the silk free and tossed it aside, splaying her knees wide before she could recover from his crude but dead-on accurate statement.

Sweet, delicate pink folds, swollen and begging to be touched. He stroked the back of her thighs and kissed the tightly trimmed thatch of curls. "You're wet, Sunshine."

Slowly, he worked his hands toward her core, ready to lift her hips up to his watering mouth. "I can see it." He closed his eyes and inhaled deep, the light musk as bright and addictive on his senses as the rest of her. "Smell it."

"But you…" She tried to scoot away.

Ramsay slid his hands beneath her ass and held her fast. So close. Inches from sucking the tiny clit peeking out from its hood. "What, Sunshine?" He blew on the sensitive spot and reveled in the flex of her hips. "Tell me what's wrong."

"Your clothes." She gripped his forearms, a satisfying storm of desperation in her eyes. "I'm naked and you're—"

"Trinity." He lifted his head just enough to hold her gaze. "You do not worry about me. You do not think. As of right now, the only thing you do is watch, let go, and feel."

He gave into his hunger and swiped his tongue through her folds.

Her legs jerked and a surprised squeak shot through the room.

A slow, steady rumble built in his chest. His lips and teeth sucked and nipped her sweetness with even more intensity than their kiss. Damn but this was powerful. Her hands in his hair, breathy moans in his ears, and hips lifting to meet his devouring mouth.

The Great One help him, he was out of control. Her taste

and the need to feel her release on his tongue nothing short of compulsion. An unrelenting demand from the universe.

He teased her entrance, sucked her clit deep, and slid a finger home.

She cried out and arched off the bed, her pretty nipples hard and begging for attention.

Ramsay pressed another finger to join the first and kissed his way up her body. Tasting her was one thing. Watching her expression the first time she came for him? No way was he missing that.

He latched onto one nipple and suckled, flicking the tiny nub with his tongue as his thumb worked her clit. He pulled away and blew on the tip. His cock pulsed, angry and aching for the tight slick surface surrounding his fingers.

He swirled his tongue around the other peak. "That's it, Sunshine. Ride my fingers." Another lick. "Take what you need and show me how hard you come."

Her eyes flashed open, pupils so dilated they burned pitch black. Her nails bit into his scalp and biceps, and her breaths came in ragged, needy mewls.

Pressing deep, he crooked his fingers and stroked the sweet spot along her front wall.

Her thighs tightened and shook.

He ground the heel of his hand on her clit.

"Ramsay!"

Her walls clamped around his fingers, and the hottest groan he'd ever heard in his life rang long and loud.

His name. She'd cried *his* name.

Mine.

The thought slammed into him, an unmerciful demand to take and claim. To make her come again. To feel her pussy clench and release on his cock the way it sucked his fingers. To feel her slick release as he rode toward his own.

His cock jerked in agreement, the ache shifting to a demanding throb.

Her soft sigh drew his gaze from the lazy push and pull of his fingers at her core to her closed eyes and parted lips. Her head was angled to one side, languid and easy. Peaceful.

Innocent.

Untouched by anyone but him.

His stomach clenched. Reason stomped past the raging length between his legs and scowled at his conscience. Getting her off was one thing, but taking her innocence would shoot them to a whole different level of intense. He might be mercenary in getting information for his brother, but he'd be damned if he fucked Trinity over with something as important as this.

He shifted and pulled the comforter over her.

Her head lulled to one side and she yawned. Actually yawned. It was cute. Like a kitten settling into a cozy spot.

He tucked her close, her back to his front. "Relax, Sunshine. Give into it. I'm not going anywhere."

Not until morning, anyway. He'd hold her. Revel in being her first, in this at least, and then take a shot at researching her tomorrow. The right way.

His dick would just have to live with it.

CHAPTER 8

*T*rinity snuggled deeper beneath her blankets, her quiet cocoon cooling just enough to tug her from sleep. Gentle sunshine danced behind her eyelids and a dark, sensual scent clung to her pillowcase.

Saturday. Perfect for lazing a few extra hours—

Dark scent?

Ramsay.

She shot upright and blinked to clear her vision. She didn't have a stitch on, and her clothes were scattered over the floor. The sheets and blankets were twisted in a chaotic mess. Not at all the tidy, barely-ruffled pattern from a normal night of sleep.

She hadn't imagined it. She'd actually gotten naked with Ramsay and had her first mind-blowing orgasm with a man.

So where the heck was he?

She scrambled out of bed and snatched her robe off the back of her bedroom door. Light pushed between the blind slats, and the shouts and laughter of kids somewhere down the block flittered through the windows, but her apartment was silent.

The bathroom door sat open, no lights on. Her office was empty too. She rushed down the hall to the living room and kitchen.

Nothing.

She fisted the sides of her robes between her breasts and glanced back at her bedroom.

The picture of Ramsay poised between her thighs, his dark hair tickling her skin, flashed in excruciating detail, and the muscles in her belly rippled. Oh, no. Her imagination was excellent. Freakishly creative, for that matter, but she did not make that up. No one could make something like that up.

She padded to the kitchen. Maybe he'd needed to run an errand. Or had work to do. Whatever it was, she could figure it out over coffee. Everything puzzled together better with coffee.

She rounded the bar separating the kitchen from the living room and marched toward the pantry. Next to the coffeemaker was a paper towel with black writing in sharp angles, the Sharpie from her office perched on top.

> Need a few days to wrap up an issue at work.
>> Dinner when it's done?
>
> R
>
> P.S. You're cute when you sleep.

He'd left his number, which was a good sign. Wasn't it?

God, the things he'd done. The way he'd touched her and the way she'd responded. Maybe her dad was right. Maybe she really did have some of the legendary passion of the Black contingent flowing in her veins.

She leaned into the counter and studied Ramsay's broad scribbles, fingering the rough edge of the paper towel.

You're cute when you sleep.

Sleep. Holy crap! She'd actually slept without her ear buds. She never slept without them. Too much noise from her Spiritu self trying to break through her unconscious. At least that's what Dad claimed.

It must have been the orgasm.

An unpleasant and weighty sensation spread from head to toe.

Ramsay hadn't had one. She'd come harder than she ever had in her life and promptly fallen off to Snoozeville. He hadn't even gotten his clothes off. Was she out of her freakin' mind?

Trinity gripped the countertop and squeezed her eyes shut. No wonder he'd left. Hell, he probably ditched her in the middle of the night. What kind of woman had a monster orgasm and left the man who'd given it to her high and dry?

She opened her eyes and picked up the paper towel. His number was scratched toward the bottom. Maybe she was jumping into full-fledged freak-out mode too quick.

Ugh. The back and forth was giving her a headache.

She snatched the coffee from the pantry and counted off scoops. Coffee first. Then she'd call Margo and figure out what to do next.

CHAPTER 9

*R*amsay re-read Ian's info on Trinity a second time and tossed the folder across his new friend's desk. "That's it? Three days and the only things you can tell are where she went to college and that she's an upstanding citizen?"

"Hey, you didn't exactly give me much to go on." Ian eased back in his desk chair and propped one booted foot on the corner. "No birthdate, no social, and no birth city. Plus your brother kind of trumps you on my list of priorities, and he's got me busy tracking videos from the North Texas thing on gossip sites."

Ramsay bit back a curse and stalked to the window over-looking Ian's aging neighborhood. Tulsa might not be the hub of sophistication Dallas was, but with Ian's PI setup already in place here it made keeping a pulse on humanity kind of handy. "Not your fault."

The postman's oversized white box truck with its blue and red stripes trundled along the far side of the street, the diesel engine surging from one mailbox to another. Now what was he going to do?

The sweet, hesitant voice from Trinity's message replayed in his head for the five-hundredth time in seventy-two hours.

"Hey, it's me. Um...Trinity."

Like he wouldn't register her voice the second it hit air.

"I got your note." A whisper in the background. *"It was nice...being with you last night. I think dinner once you get your work stuff taken care of would be great."* A raspy, indrawn breath. *"So, you should have my number on caller ID. Just let me know when you're available. Good luck with work."*

He smiled. Christ, that woman did wonky things to him. It was a voicemail for crying out loud, and just remembering it lightened his mood.

Except he'd never called her back.

Foolish. No, scratch that. If he was honest with himself, she scared the ever-lovin' shit out of him.

"There is one thing I didn't put down," Ian said. "Her adoption." he nodded at the report perched sideways on the desk.

"Same place as Lexi. Though that's all I've got to go on." Ian dropped his foot and planted his elbows on the desk, one of those don't-jack-with-me-I've-seen-it-all expressions on his face. "You wanna tell me what's going on?"

Damn. Both of them from the same place, and Trinity with that pendant? There wasn't a whole lot he could say without dragging everyone into the mix. No way was he ready for that. "It's just a hunch. Anything else turn up on the videos?"

Ian sipped his coffee, those wise eyes of his glaring a "not buyin' it" over the rim. He thunked the mug down on the desk. "Almost dead. We got a little worried when your family emblem popped up, but they've gained zero traction since. Most outlets have either dropped the story or knocked it to the bottom of their feeds. A few more days and it'll be all but forgotten."

Well, thank The Great One for that.

"Thinkin' that means I'll be able to research your girl a little more now," Ian said.

Bait. Pure and simple. But Ramsay wasn't biting.

"Been kicking around suspicious shit my whole life, Shantos. Not stupid enough to ignore a man tracking a pretty girl who happens to have been adopted from the same place as Lexi. If there's a chance she and Lexi are related, then trust me when I tell you, holding that back from Lexi is going to piss her off when she does find out, no matter what your intentions are."

"What if they're not related?" Ramsay said. "How's it going to make Lexi feel if she gets her hopes up and we find out it's all a bust?"

"That's not your problem. A smart man would let her and Eryx be a part of the decision. Group conscience is better than one anyway, and you avoid the backlash." Ian stood and stared down the hallway to where Jillian perched in front of the TV in the living room. "Trust me when I tell you, finding someone after a crazy long search is worth the risk."

Eighteen years Ian had tried to find his missing wife and daughter, only to have The Fates deliver him to his surviving daughter through his association to Lexi. A long time to be without people he loved. What if Ramsay was keeping something from Lexi he shouldn't?

Ramsay opened the folder back up. A Bachelors in Library Science. Uninterrupted residence in Dallas, Texas. "Lexi never mentioned she suspected she had family."

"Not directly, no. But she's always wanted one. She's inherited yours through Eryx, but there's nothing like blood."

He was right on that score. And what adopted child, especially one who'd grown up in some seriously nasty foster homes like Lexi, wouldn't hope to find someone they could call their own? If he was smart, he'd spill what he knew while he had the chance.

But you won't because it's Trinity and you don't want to share.

Certainty blasted through him. The minute he came clean with his suspicions everything would change. Not just for him, but for Trinity too.

"Dad!" Jillian shouted from the front room.

The clipped, professional voice of a male news anchor ratcheted high enough Ramsay and Ian caught it as they strode down the hallway to join her.

"So far, six reports have been confirmed across North America. Individuals insist an unseen being transported them to a fantastical, parallel realm their guide referred to as Eden. One of the interviews was conducted by reporters from our sister station in Austin."

Jillian whipped around and her dark blond hair spun out at her shoulders. Her hazel gaze locked onto Ian. "They were covering the latest on the videos and this came on."

A big, burly guy with long, mostly gray hair flashed on the screen, wrenches and screwdrivers lined up in organized chaos on a pegboard behind him. "Damnedest thing I've ever seen. Kind of like here, but more like things were in the old days. No wires. No towers. Lots of colors though. Crazy colors. You should've seen the sky. Cool rainbows everywhere."

Long blond hair and the reporter's profile flashed at the corner of the screen. "Can you tell us how you got there?"

Eyes distant with a cock-eyed grin on his face, the man scratched his head. "Sounds nuts, but we walked through a big 'ole swirling gray tunnel. Had fancy sparkles in it. Kinda like those glitzy dresses women like to wear. I'm telling you, Gene Roddenberry would've been all over that —" *Bleep.*

The reporter floundered for a minute at the crass commentary. "Any idea who your guide was?"

"Claimed they were one of the folks from that hubbub up in North Texas. Kinda weird though. Those sure looked like men to me. Big men. And I'll be damned if it wasn't a woman."

"A woman?" the reporter said.

"Had to be. I might not remember a face, but whoever it was had the best damned perfume I've ever smelled. Something you'd find in one of those high-end specialty stores."

"Serena," Ramsay blurted to no one in particular.

Ian jerked his gaze from the TV. "What?"

"He's right." Jillian thumbed the volume down enough to talk over the reporter's wrap up. "I could always tell when Serena had been at the castle. It's not bad, just unique and stands out because it's so rich."

Ian cocked his head. "Kind of a ballsy move given the sentence they gave her, don't you think? I mean, why take a chance? What's she got to gain?"

A damned good point. But Serena would do just about anything to cause Eryx trouble. Or, better yet, cause Lexi trouble.

"I don't know," Ramsay said. "She's nuts enough to think she could get away with it."

Jillian punched to another station.

Lost World of Eden Rediscovered stretched across the bottom of the screen. An older woman of Asian descent spoke to a reporter off screen.

"What if it's something else?" Jillian spun from the newest story. "What if it's not Serena?"

Ramsay crossed his arms. "Who else would do something this stupid and leave a perfume calling card?"

Ian held up a hand to cut Ramsay off. "What do you mean, Jilly?"

She shrugged and went back to flipping channels. "You heard the Spiritu. We still have the prophecy to deal with. What if this is part of it?"

Every muscle in Ramsay's chest contracted. The image of Trinity's pendant flashed in his head, and a cold, sharp dread blasted from the inside out. It couldn't be her. He'd been with her all night long. And she sure didn't reek of anything close to what the man had described.

But that didn't mean she or something about her didn't factor into the prophecy.

Shit.

He tugged his iPhone from his back pocket. Eleven-thirty. If Eryx had council business, he'd be back at the castle soon. "How long will it take you to research the other reports?"

Ian stuffed his hands in his jeans pockets and frowned at the TV. "I don't know. An hour. Maybe two. Depends on how much has made it online."

Ramsay stalked toward the kitchen. So much for keeping things quiet until he ran all the possibilities. He jerked open the ancient fridge. "Good. I need a beer before I tell my brother."

CHATTER. Lots and lots of high-pitched, non-stop chatter. Serena's vision glazed over as the mouthy little chit perched on the plum brocade wingback across from her went on and on about some drivel from her home region.

What day was it now anyway? Wednesday? Thursday? She counted out the days since being welcomed back into her family home, keeping her expression attentively neutral.

Damn. Only Monday. Three whopping days since the trial, but it felt like a century. She'd die before she made it a year, let alone five. Especially if all she had to occupy her time were endless visits from vapid socialites.

"Don't you agree, Serena?"

Serena beamed her most dazzling smile and added a fluttery laugh for good measure. What in histus were they talking about?

The receiving room doors opened, and heavy footfalls sounded on the marble beyond.

"Your highness, if you'll but give me a moment to introduce—" Their family butler, Otter, hopped to the far side of the threshold, barely escaping a head on with Ludan Forte.

Eryx strode in behind his somo, his brother beside him, all three decked out in standard issue drast and black leather.

The seven chatty women situated through the room surged upright in an almost perfectly orchestrated move, and their gasps and murmurs rippled in all directions.

"My malran." Serena rose and joined the rest of her guests. Her pulse quivered at her throat, and her mind sparked for the first time in days. Every one of her gossip-hungry visitors zigzagged expectant gazes between her and Eryx.

Well. Wouldn't want to disappoint a captive audience. She clasped her hands between her breasts and floated forward. "I've missed you, Eryx. I'm so glad you came."

Right on queue, the girls sighed behind her. She could practically hear the stories buzzing through the capital already. *The malran visited her personally. Without the malress in attendance.*

A muscle ticked at the back of Eryx's jaw.

Ramsay crossed his arms and lifted a bored eyebrow, and Ludan growled.

Oh, yes. Eryx's appearance couldn't possibly have been better timed. Father would be thrilled.

Eryx pinned her with a bland expression. "I can interrogate you on more Rebellion activities in front of your guests, or we can go it alone. Your choice."

"My malran, the ellan found me—"

"Don't push me, Serena." His gaze drifted over the women, far too much calculation burning in his silver eyes.

Better to take her small win and get her audience out while she had the chance. "Ladies, I apologize for the inconvenience. Perhaps you could visit again tomorrow? Your company is such a comfort as I face my time alone."

Ludan scoffed loud enough to make one of the women jump as she hustled past him.

The rest of the women squeaked farewells and promised future visits between none-too-subtle glances over their shoulders.

No doubt they'd be back. Those in her circle loved gossip even more than they loved her unrequited love story.

Serena settled into her chair and crossed her legs. Unrequited love indeed. Matings were about power and, if you were lucky, exceptional sex. "So, what brings our benevolent ruler for a house visit? And without your half-breed mate, no less?"

Eryx prowled across the room.

Ramsay held his spot near the door, and Ludan crossed his arms and scowled.

"Where have you been the last few nights?" Eryx said.

Was he joking? "Where in histus do you think I've been?"

He stopped little more than a foot away. At six-foot-four inches, he towered over most people, but from her seated angle, he seemed double that. "I asked you a question. You get one more shot before I unload the last scrap of civilized I've got left."

The whites around his steel gray eyes began to glow. Not enough to batten down the hatches and duck for cover yet, but enough to know he was one flippant comment away from making it enough. "I was here. Right where I'm supposed to be. If your guards can't confirm it, then I've got a string of visitors who can."

His eyes dimmed.

Serena crooked her head and smirked. "I'm not sure you've heard, but it seems the public has a fondness for unrequited love."

"I've heard. Your father may as well have hired street criers." He strolled to the far side of the room and peeked beyond the window curtains, staring out at the front lawn. "How's it feel to be your father's most recent marketing ploy?"

Bastard. One of these days she was going to find a way to take his smug attitude and shove it up his tight and very fine ass. "Better than how you must feel knowing I've got sympathizers."

He snapped around and lasered her with a killing look.

She lifted her chin.

"You're pretty cavalier about the whole situation." Eryx glanced at Ludan and jerked his head in her direction.

Ludan stalked closer.

Eryx remained by the window. "If you've got nothing to hide, then you won't mind Ludan checking to see exactly where you've been."

"That depends." Probably shouldn't have poked the tiger. The smart move would be to call Thyrus, but damn it, she'd been playing by the rules, as much as it bored her to tears. "Has there been a charge leveled against me?"

Ramsay huffed a harsh laugh. "Aiding and abetting the Rebellion isn't enough?"

"I'm paying for my poor judgment." She reclined into the wingback and shrugged. "Besides, I offered my memories already."

"You call this punishment?" Ludan's coarse voice raked

through the room, an auditory affront compared to Eryx and Ramsay's easy baritone. The freak. Scary and decidedly lethal, but a freak nonetheless. Just once she'd like to swipe that superior expression off his face.

She focused on Eryx. "I'll ask again, what exactly do you think I've done?"

Eryx paced to the artful floral arrangement centered on a marble-topped stand between the windows. He stroked the petal of one white bloom hanging low over the vase's edge, a deceptively gentle move. "Seems someone decided to bring half a dozen humans on a sightseeing trip to Eden. Every last one came back with wagging tongues and accurate descriptions. The only thing they can't remember is their tour guide's face."

Interesting. She feigned a bored expression. "Sounds terribly exciting. Or terrifying. Maybe it's fallout from your," she waved at the mark on his arm, "prophetic mating. Still not something I can help you with."

"So you were here and can corroborate it with your memories?" Eryx said.

Serena froze. Waiting for Thyrus would be safer. Not only for keeping Ludan out of places he shouldn't be, but from a pure witness perspective. Then again, nothing felt better than calling your ex's bluff.

She held out her hand to Ludan. "See for yourself."

Ludan grinned, though there wasn't anything happy about it. More like a demon looking forward to eating its own young. His big hand gripped hers.

Cold, stinging and brutal, stabbed up her arm and down her spine. Her vision dimmed and a loud roar barreled through her head.

She ripped her hand free and looked up at Ludan. Her chest heaved as though she'd sprinted four miles. "What the hell was that?"

"Time conservation," Eryx answered from beside her.

When had he moved? Ludan had only gripped her hand for a second or two.

"It's also a comprehensive record all rolled up into one," Eryx said. "Ludan's handy with memories."

"Feel good?" Ludan's eerie grin stayed locked in place, but frustration marked the corners of his eyes.

She fisted her hand in her lap and forced her jaw to unclench. To histus with him. With Eryx and his twin too. They had nothing on her. Her memories proved it. "If Ludan's so talented, then you know I was here."

Ludan ambled back to his place near the door. "Nothing but black space at the time the humans say they were here. Could be sleep, could be you blocking."

"Oh, please," she said. "I'm not that good."

Ramsay laughed. "Like to get that on record."

Serena stood, adrenaline making her movements jerky and awkward. She faced Eryx. "Why on Earth would I want to jeopardize myself to bring humans here?"

"Maybe you're out to stir up trouble and claim it's the prophecy," Ramsay volleyed from behind her.

She kept her focus on Eryx. "Maybe you're worried I'm getting more positive press than your new baineann."

"Maybe it won't matter." Eryx ambled around her and headed to the door. "Ramsay, check her room. Gather up everything she's got."

Ramsay grinned and opened the doors with a flick of his wrists.

Eryx kept moving toward the entry.

Serena trailed them, a shaky urgency rattling through her torso. "Everything I've got of what?"

Eryx stopped in the foyer and watched his brother dart up the grand staircase. He waited until Ramsay disappeared from sight and faced her, eyes triumphant. "When the humans were interviewed, they all said the person had a unique perfume. One they couldn't get out of their head." A deadly smile stretched across his handsome face. "One screw up, Serena. That's all I need and you can spend the rest of your life without power surrounded by people you detest."

His gaze drifted to Ludan still behind her, and he jerked his head toward the front lawn. The two strode to the main courtyard without another word, leaving the doors wide open to the bright Cush afternoon.

Ramsay's voice floated down from her rooms on the east wing, mingled with surprised squeaks and placating words from her maids.

The son of a bitch. Eryx was setting her up.

She should have called Thyrus. Should have put Eryx off and gained more details before she gave in.

Smoothing her silk gown, she returned to the empty sitting room and the window overlooking the front lawn.

With the rest of the guards gathered round them, the two men waited, arms crossed and silent.

It didn't matter. None of it. Eryx could try to spin this new twist however he wanted, but there was no way in histus she was going down without a fight.

CHAPTER 10

*R*amsay landed beside his brother outside the main castle entrance. Late afternoon sun dipped behind the high walls and cast the wide stone veranda in cool shade.

Ludan touched down a heartbeat behind them.

"Track 'em down, Ludan," Eryx said, not breaking stride. "Find the humans, scour their memories, and see if you can find anything that ties Serena to this mess. I want her ass gone."

Ludan stayed tight on his heels. "Send someone else. I'm with you."

Eryx spun so fast Ludan barely avoided a collision. "Do what I. Fucking. Asked!"

Ludan took two steps back. One and a half centuries they'd been in each other's shit, but Ramsay had never seen Ludan so dumbfounded.

Eryx planted his hands at his hips and hung his head. He sucked in a powerful breath. Gone was the anger, replaced with something far more raw. Vulnerable. He lifted his head and looked at Ludan. "I don't know what I'm up against. I need someone I can trust. With your gift, you can get in and out faster than anyone."

Ludan stared, his body locked in place. Histus, for a minute Ramsay wasn't even sure his brother's somo was breathing. "I don't like this. Serena. The Rebellion. The prophecy. The Dark rogues. None of it."

Eryx shook his head. "It's not the prophecy. Don't ask me how I know. I just know it's not. The prophecy is something else. Something bigger. Better."

"What if it's not?" The question leapt from Ramsay's mouth before he could sensor it, every one of the suspicions he'd had the last few days fueling its power.

Eryx snapped to attention. He edged closer and narrowed his eyes, a move that would have been threatening if Ramsay hadn't been on the receiving end of his brother's suspicious focus since they were toddlers. "Is there a reason I should think otherwise?"

Just what he needed. His damned brother was like a rabid hound dog when it came to scenting trouble. "Um, yeah. You got it firsthand from the Spiritu at Reese's swearing in. I think her exact words were, 'It's only a matter of time before the prophecy begins to unfold.' Can't get much closer to the horse's mouth than that."

"Uh-uh." He stepped closer, bringing them nose to nose. "You said, 'What if it's not?' As in I-know-something-you-don't-know-yet."

"Oh, give me a break, Eryx."

"He's right," Ludan said. "Spill it."

Son of a bitch, he needed to learn to watch his mouth.

Both men glared, feet firmly planted on the gray stone terrace like they'd stand there all day if necessary.

He wasn't ready for this. Not yet. "You need to get Lexi."

Eryx held his place. "You need to tell me what the fuck is going on."

"Not on this one I don't. Trust me when I say she's gonna be pissed enough to know I waited. More if she's not here when I share."

The whites around Eryx's eyes glowed and the muscles along his neck strained.

"Calm down, already." He'd call his brother a hotheaded asshole, but the truth of the matter was that was usually Ramsay's M.O. Eryx was always the cool one. Unless the topic involved Lexi. "It's not a bad thing. If it's what I think, it's good. I just don't know how it all ties with what's going on in Evad."

The tension in Eryx's eyes lessened, no doubt buffered by a telepathic contact with his mate. He waved a hand and the massive entry doors flew wide open, cracking against the stone at either side. "My study. Now."

Ludan ambled beside Ramsay as they followed Eryx into the cool shade of the castle foyer. "You holdin' back intel's not your style."

"Yeah?" Ramsay said. "Wait until you hear before you judge."

Or until he saw Trinity. No way would Eryx or Ludan blame his hesitation once they factored in the details.

He hoped.

Lexi hustled into the study she shared with Eryx, the jeans and form-fitting tank top she wore a pretty good indicator she'd had her fill of Myren attire at council. Seriously, she and Ludan were kindred spirits. "What's up?" She glanced at Eryx's murderous face and her steps slowed. "Whoa, big man. Who pissed you off?"

He jerked his head at Ramsay.

"Okay." She nestled close to her mate and stroked his chest like he was a cute kitten instead of a raging, unleashed beast. "You two not sharing your toys again? Or did you throw a bachelor party and forget to invite him?"

Ramsay laughed despite the situation. Damn, but he loved his new shalla. He hoped to histus she didn't hate him by the time he was done.

"Talk." Eryx pulled Lexi in front of him, hands at her shoulders.

Ludan perched at the edge of Lexi's desk.

Ramsay let it all out. The night out with Jagger and meeting Trinity. The pendant. Trinity's adoption and her tie to the same agency as Lexi. Her inability to touch most people, but that he seemed to be the exception. Even the fact she'd shocked him unconscious when he'd tried to scan her memories.

The details on what went down in Trinity's bed? That and the pull she had on him he kept to himself.

"You think she's Myren." Eryx's voice had evened out alongside his tension.

"I think she's not human," Ramsay said. "Or at least not like any human I've ever met."

"You think we're related," Lexi said, blunt and to-the-point as ever.

"That's just it," Ramsay said. "I don't know what to think. I've been trying to find out. First by taking her out, then with Ian. But then this thing with humans hit us out of left field and—"

"Hold up." Lexi held up a hand. "You went out with her?"

Ramsay glanced at Ludan.

His deadpan expression stayed locked on the drama unfolding in front of him, legs crossed at the ankles.

Yeah, no help from that quarter.

Ramsay shrugged. Better to play it off as innocent at this point. "I wanted to find out who she was, so I asked her out. Thought I'd see if I could get a better look at the pendent while I was at it."

"How?" Lexi straightened. The only thing preventing her from stepping forward were Eryx's hands at her shoulders.

Ramsay kept his feet locked in place. Barely. "How what?"

"How did you plan to get a better look?"

Something snapped. Frustration. Anger. Loss. It all coalesced at once and dropped like an axe on his conscience. "Any. Fucking. Way. I. Could."

Lexi lurched forward.

Eryx dragged her back, arms wrapped around her shoulders and his cheek pressed to her temple.

Her face was livid red, a fierce protector ready to charge the man who'd dare defile someone she didn't yet even know.

"She's innocent," Ramsay blurted.

Lexi stilled.

Ramsay took a shaky breath, the oxygen weighting his lungs ten times heavier than normal. "I don't know who she is. I don't know what she is. But I know she's as innocent as they come. A damned beacon for everything good in this world."

And you want her.

Lexi's eyes narrowed, a feminine version of Eryx's hound dog behavior only minutes before. "You like her."

Well, this was awkward. He really hated his shalla's emotion sniffing abilities. "Everyone likes her. The diabhal would like her. She's a perpetual ray of sunshine. So, yeah. I like her." Ramsay fought the need to fidget. The space between his shoulder blades itched from the weight of Ludan's stare behind him.

"I want to meet her." Lexi turned to eyeball Eryx. "Prophecy or not, she's got a connection to my past and I want to learn about it." She aimed a raised eyebrow at Ramsay. "Might want to learn about other things too."

Leave it to Lexi to whip out her handy emotional radar at

the worst time. Ramsay gave into his need to pace and angled toward the windows overlooking the gardens. "Turn those feelers of yours off. It's rude."

"Oh, so it's rude for me to sniff around at what you're broadcasting, but you diving into someone's head isn't?" Lexi crossed her arms and leaned into her fireann's chest. "Personally, I kind of dig knowing someone knocked your ass silly for trying."

True. Much as he hated to admit it. When Lexi found out how far he'd gone to learn more about Trinity's background, she'd be ready to dish out even more justice, even if he'd ended the night with an entirely different goal in mind.

"What does she look like?" Lexi asked. "Do we look like sisters?"

"On the surface? No. She's light to your dark. Blond hair, almost black eyes, and a lot lighter skin. You've got an easy four inches on her height-wise."

He paused and really studied Lexi, beyond her striking slate blue eyes and soft black hair. "If you look past that though, maybe. Same oval face and jawline. And your eyes are shaped the same too."

"Set it up." Eryx grumbled. "We'll do it on her turf."

He knew it. Ten minutes they'd known about Trinity and already they were pushing into territory he wanted all to himself.

Shit. Not the kind of thoughts he should be having. He did *not* want a relationship. Not now. Maybe not ever. "What about the tenets?"

"What about them?" Eryx said. "She's got a mark around her neck to match my mate's and has some kind of mojo to knock you on your ass. I've got more than enough cause to cover divulging who we are. It's not like I'm carting her over here. So, set it up."

Ramsay scratched his head and stared out the window. "Yeah, it may not be that easy."

The quiet thickened to a near hiss.

"What did you do?" Lexi asked, her voice indicating judgment was about ten seconds from being handed down.

Ramsay faced them. "I haven't exactly called her back since I saw her last."

Eryx's shoulders snapped back. "You slept with her?"

"No." This so wasn't going the way he wanted. "I mean, I was going to, or get things far enough along I could get a look at the pendant, but…"

Eryx and Lexi both glared at him.

"Look, I realized it was a dick move, okay? I made it right and got out. Nothing but straight and narrow since."

More quiet. More accusing glares.

Eryx lifted that imperial fucking eyebrow he used to intimidate damned near everyone. "You made it right how?"

"None of your damned business."

"Oh, yeah." Lexi grinned in a way that made Ramsay's insides cramp. "I wanna meet this girl."

CHAPTER 11

*T*rinity slid the gearshift into park with way too much force.

Men. Stupid, stupid men. All of them.

She jostled free of the car and slammed the door shut. Usually she enjoyed coming home to her new place. Once a large home in the popular M streets of lower Greenville, it was now sectioned off into four modest, but trendy apartments. Tonight she'd have enjoyed a visit with a punching bag a whole lot more.

God, she had great friends. Really. They'd poked and prodded her into a night out with the best of intentions, primarily to keep her mind off the uber player of all times, Ramsay Shantos.

Stupid. Stupid, stupid, stupid Trinity. Opening herself up and thinking he'd actually call her back. Worse, she'd gone and tried to prove Ramsay's ability to touch her was a fluke by shaking hands with a clean-cut guy at the bar tonight. She shuddered all over again, remembering the disgusting images the light contact had brought. Yeah, not so clean cut after all.

Her heels clicked against the concrete and the porch light cast a soft glow over the entry stoop.

Across the street, a car door opened.

She jogged up the three steps and glanced back. The streetlight reflected off the door of a black and chrome Hummer. A pretty decked out Hummer. The drug dealer variety.

With shaky fingers, she punched the code on the security pad and missed the last digit. The red light flashed an angry, "Nope, you're a bumbling idiot, try again."

Footsteps sounded behind her.

Her heart picked up steam.

Four-two-seven-nine. Enter. Green light.

Thank God.

She yanked the knob.

"Trinity."

At the sound of Ramsay's voice, she froze.

The door clattered shut and the lock re-engaged. Damned hydraulics.

She went for the numbers again.

"Trinity, wait."

A second later his hand closed around her shoulder. Way too fast for him to have covered that kind of distance.

She flinched and braced for a flash of his unwelcome thoughts.

Nothing.

Her muscles uncoiled and a fresh surge of anger bubbled up behind it. Not one flash. Not a doggone thing. Yep, definitely should have found a punching bag tonight instead of those glasses of wine.

She spun to face him. "I might not have a lot of experience with men, but I know a brush off on a pretty intrinsic basis."

Ramsay released her shoulder and held up both hands. "I

get you're mad I didn't call. You have every right to be, but if you let me come up I'll explain."

Oh, no. The last time she'd let him in she'd really *let him in*. No way was she crossing either of those thresholds again. "You can explain right here."

He glanced at the Hummer. "Actually, I'd rather show you."

As if on cue, the Hummer back door opened. A set of booted feet appeared beneath the door, followed by another in heels. A beat later they moved into the street.

Whoa. Ramsay hadn't lied when he'd said he had a twin, but something about the way the man carried himself screamed power. The woman was no slouch either. Together they strode toward her with movie star confidence.

"You didn't tell me you brought an audience." And here she was looking like Miss Marple.

"Actually, I brought a lot more than that, but I'd rather talk to you inside if you're up for it."

This was nuts. Letting Ramsay anywhere near her, let alone her apartment, was certifiably insane. What was the saying?

Insanity is defined by doing the same thing over and over and expecting different results.

Yeah, that one.

The couple stopped a respectful distance from the porch. Ramsay's twin was a weird mix of everyday Joe and Conan the Barbarian. Jeans, T-shirt, leather jacket, boots. And braids. Lots of them. All halfway down his back and tied off with what looked like metal beads. The woman had a lithe build, the kind you'd expect on a long distance runner, and something about her radiated exceptional force.

A buzz kicked in at the back of her head. Not as crippling as her warning signs and not altogether unpleasant.

The woman eased closer to Ramsay's twin and gripped his arm.

The twin covered her hand and squeezed. A peaceful, reassuring gesture.

"I've got work in the morning," Trinity said.

Ramsay dipped and met her eyes. "Understood. We'll share what we need to and you can decide where we go from there."

She punched the keypad, slower than before, but still shaky. Understandable considering the adrenaline firing out in all directions. She might have sensed a crossroads before, but now she felt as if she was standing in the middle of it with about fifty cars headed right toward her.

Ramsay and the couple followed her down the hallway with its scarred wood floors and up the narrow flight of steps. She keyed the bolt and fumbled for the light as Alicia Keys and a steady bass serenaded from behind her neighbor's door.

"You've been busy." Ramsay stood between the kitchen and the living room and scanned what boxes remained.

Trinity tossed her keys on the kitchen table and shrugged out of her jacket. "I've had time and incentive."

Ramsay winced.

The woman and the man beside her smirked.

"Yeah." Ramsay ruffled the hair at the top of his head. The hint of red in his cheeks was mildly gratifying. He dropped his hand and straightened. "Trinity, this is my brother Eryx and his baineann, Lexi."

Eryx. That was a nice name. Odd, but nice. And what had he called Lexi?

Eryx held out his hand. The sleeve of his leather jacket rode up, revealing the edge of a tattoo.

Trinity stared at his hand. Not shaking it would probably be a huge insult. And she'd been able to touch Ramsay. Then again, a guy like Eryx had to have some scary stuff in his head. "What's a baineann?"

"Wife." Lexi tugged Eryx's hand back and looked up at him. "Don't push her."

Trinity whipped her gaze to Ramsay. "You told them?"

"There's a reason," he said. "I promise."

Lexi urged her intimidating husband toward the living room and motioned for Ramsay to follow. "How about we sit instead of looming by the front door and scaring the hell out of her." She shrugged at Trinity. "Sorry, I'm a bit blunt sometimes."

"I don't mind blunt." Heck, considering the situation, blunt was freakin' great. She frowned at Ramsay. "Thoughtless kind of bugs me though."

Lexi laughed, one of those big uninhibited ones. She shoved Ramsay, who still hadn't moved, to join Eryx, leaned close to Trinity and whispered, "Pretty sure it's more like scared shitless."

The two settled into her tiny sitting area, Eryx at one end of the couch, Lexi nestled right beside him. Ramsay plunked in the lone club chair angled next to the sofa.

Trinity hesitated, too hung up on Lexi's comment to initiate momentum. Ramsay? Scared? Of what? She'd never met a more self-assured man. Her gaze slid to Eryx. Okay, maybe there was one other more confident man. The two of them had the market share in spades.

And they were staring at her.

Right. Explanations.

The only space left on the sofa was way too close to Ramsay, so she stood opposite the coffee table and crossed her arms for a little extra oomph. "I doubt bringing your brother and his wife for a visit has much to do with your lack of common decency, so why are you here?"

Ramsay glanced at Eryx.

Eryx dipped his head. More silent permission than any kind of agreement.

Ramsay cleared his throat and rubbed the back of his neck. "I didn't call you back because I was trying to learn more about you."

Okaaaay. Not where she'd thought he'd go. "You mean like a background check?"

He frowned at the floor. "Not exactly."

Lexi chuckled.

Ramsay's head snapped up, aimed at her. "You're not helping."

"Sorry, I never thought I'd see a little bitty thing like her make you fidget."

Eryx squeezed her arm and Lexi rolled her eyes.

Ramsay let out an impatient breath and refocused on Trinity. "That night I met you, when you fell and I helped you up, I saw something. Something I never expected to see away from home."

"Oklahoma?" Sure, Texas was a little more cosmopolitan than their northern neighbor, but it wasn't exactly edgy like New York or California.

"Eden," Ramsay said.

"As in New York?" she said. "I thought you said you lived in Tulsa with your family."

Lexi's laughter bubbled up again, though this time it was more along the lines of a sympathetic girlfriend. "Clearly, my geography sucks because that wasn't my first response."

The pleasant buzz in Trinity's head kicked back in. "Well, where else is there?"

Ramsay stood, eyes locked on her, and took her hand. "*The* Eden, Trinity. Though the history for the one you've probably heard about isn't entirely accurate."

She tried to jerk her hand away, but Ramsay tightened his grip. Not hard, but firm. "Take a breath and hear me out."

He trailed his fingers down her neck. They dipped beneath her crewneck sweater and under the chain of her necklace. A second later the pendant slipped free. "Your necklace, this symbol, it's kind of a big deal where I'm from. Everyone's talked about it for a long time, but no one had seen it until about a month ago."

Lexi leaned forward, her mouth slack and eyes riveted on Trinity's neckline. "Holy shit, it's identical."

"Identical to what?" Trinity fought the need to move. To hide. Run. Do something besides stand there while they all gaped at her. Even Eryx seemed a little shell-shocked, and she'd be willing to bet that took a lot to accomplish.

Her guests glanced from one to the other, their expressions shifting like they were holding a conversation without words.

Eryx stood and shrugged out of his jacket. He tossed the jacket to the sofa and faced her. Stretched up and down Eryx's arm was a replica of the necklace her adopted father had given her. An exact replica.

Trinity stumbled back, dimly registering Ramsay's steadying hand at her shoulder.

No. Freakin'. Way.

"Now you see why I was so surprised," Ramsay said quietly beside her. "Why I started asking all those questions. That mark means a lot where I come from, more now than ever."

Trinity shook her head and stepped away. She gripped the pendant. The black filigree bit into her fingertips and her heart pounded against her hand. "My father gave me his. Yours looks like a tattoo, so how did you come up with the design?"

"It's a mating mark," Eryx said. "When I took Lexi as my mate, I took her family symbol as well, just as she wears mine." He smiled down at his wife. "We found her here in

Evad, what we call the human realm. She was one of our lost, though at the time we didn't have a clue she was Myren, let alone what her family mark would be."

Trinity's gaze snapped to Lexi. "Family mark."

Lexi's lips tightened and she stood, gripping Eryx's hand. "Exactly. Every family has its own and they're not repeated. The fact that you have a necklace that matches it makes us wonder if we're not...well, related."

The buzzing she'd felt when she saw Lexi. Not unpleasant so much as familiar.

Obviously Kazan hadn't spilled all of his secrets.

But he wouldn't have been able to. Sharing her history was one thing. Sharing someone else's would've crossed the line.

This was it. Her crossroad.

Her heart lurched and tumbled, and her mouth ran so dry it almost hurt to speak. "What's so important about this mark?"

"It's the focal point of a prophecy. One that's been around since our earliest generations." Ramsay sidled closer. "They say that when a Shantos male takes a mate bearing that mark, a new era will dawn for our race."

Vague. No direction or consequence of any manner. Which, if the fantasy books she loved were any indication, was the norm for such predictions. "That tells you almost nothing. How are you supposed to know what it means?"

Eryx sat on the edge of the couch and pulled Lexi down with him. "We were kind of hoping you could tell us."

Trinity drifted to the club chair in a daze. Ramsay's hand rested on her shoulder, the other at the small of her back, so maybe he was guiding her. Her mind was too muddled to clarify, or even care.

A prophecy. A different realm. A different race, if she'd

caught that detail accurately. What had they called themselves? Myrens?

Oh, and she might have a relative, too.

Her breath kicked up and the space behind her chest
burned. Kazan definitely hadn't spilled everything from his
almost-all-knowing hive mind.

And Ramsay. What he'd been after was information. The
touching, he'd been after a visual, not really interested in her
at all.

"So this…" She looked up at him, standing tall beside her,
and waved between them. "It was all just to learn about me?
Find out what I know?"

Ramsay crouched in front of her and gripped her limp hand
from the armrest. His eyebrows drew in tight, sharpening the
impact of his silver eyes. "At first, yeah." His thumb stroked her
knuckles. "I realized it was a dick move and I backed off."

So the touching after he'd gotten an eyeful had been a
pity thing. Excellent. And she'd called him like an eager
puppy the next day.

Lexi stood abruptly and motioned her husband toward
the door. "Let's go."

Eryx gazed between her and Ramsay, and then slowly
joined her.

Lexi turned back with lips pinched tight, and jammed her
hands in her pockets. "I know you'd probably like to kick his
ass out the door, but if you can tolerate him a little longer,
you could at least prod him for more information." She shot
Ramsay a death glare. "He might even pull his head out of his
ass and own up to what he's too afraid to acknowledge."

Tugging her hands free, she took a tentative step toward
Trinity and held out her hand. "I'm guessing a hug is too
much right off the bat, but I don't want to leave without
telling you I'm thrilled to know I might have family."

Trinity stared at her outstretched hand.

Family. Not adopted parents. Not a mystical parent incapable of a normal relationship, but an honest to God, flesh and blood human.

Well, maybe not human.

Lexi lowered her hand and shrugged with a wry smile. "It's okay. You've had a big night." She raised an eyebrow at Ramsay. "Might be bigger, who knows."

She ambled toward the door, and Eryx splayed his big hand at the small of her back.

Trinity shot to her feet. "Wait."

All eyes whipped to her.

She rubbed her hands on her slacks to steady them and paced toward the door, Ramsay close beside her. It was a wonder she didn't choke on the violent pulse at her throat.

She could do this. For family, she could sure try. "If there's a chance we're relatives, maybe we could try a hug."

CHAPTER 12

*R*amsay held his breath and braced to intervene as Lexi hugged Trinity's petite shoulders. He'd yet to get Trinity to tell him how the whole touching thing impacted her, but the way she guarded herself from humanity made it obvious it wasn't pleasant.

Trinity tension unwound on a relieved exhale, and she wrapped Lexi up at the waist.

"All good?" Lexi cupped the back of Trinity's blond head.

Trinity jerked a tiny, awkward nod.

Part of Ramsay relaxed and offered up thanks to The Great One. Another, far more selfish part, bristled. So much for him being unique for Trinity.

Lexi stepped back, hands on Trinity's shoulders, and smiled. "Maybe us being able to touch means we're related. It would explain the necklace."

"Probably more race-specific than relationship." Eryx edged closer to them and offered his hand. "Either way, it's a good thing. No touch isn't healthy."

Trinity hesitated, then slid her hand into his. She smiled

up at his brother a heartbeat later, one of those killer sunshine ones that stopped a man in his tracks.

Yeah, not as thrilled with the growing population of people who could touch Trinity.

Lexi locked eyes with Ramsay. *"I dangled a hall pass for you. It's up to you to kiss ass and get back in her good graces, but so help me God, if you hurt her again, I'll cut your nuts off."*

Eryx agreed with a telepathic grunt, pulled Lexi against his side, and held out his hand palm up. "Keys."

Ramsay tugged the Hummer's fob from his jeans pocket. The second it was free, it shot from his hand and across the room to Eryx's.

Trinity jumped a good foot away from all three of them and fisted her hand at her throat. "Whoa."

Ramsay moved in to steady her and glared at his brother. "She just found out a whole new race exists. You think now's the best time to showboat?"

Eryx grinned, if you could call it that. More like taunted with evil glee. "Just giving your girl extra reason to keep you around. Someone's got to explain the details."

Meddlesome jackass. "I seem to recall you spoon feeding Lexi all kinds of information when she first came to Eden."

"I knew she was my mate and wanted to protect her," Eryx said. "What's your motive?"

Mine.

The claim rattled through him as clear as it had three nights ago when she'd come riding his fingers.

"Where are you two going?" Trinity asked. "I mean..." She glanced at him, wide eyed, fidgeted with her necklace, and zeroed in on Lexi. "I'm thinking more viewpoints and explanations might be better."

Safer, that was for damned sure. He didn't want a relationship. Didn't want the responsibility that came with an innocent like Trinity. He wanted light and fun like things used to be. Relationships only set people up for disappointment.

He moved to her anyway and pulled her back against his chest. Protective. Claiming.

"I've got this," he said to his brother, and *only* his brother. Lexi wouldn't understand the need to be alone with Trinity with this. Not like Eryx would.

Without hesitation, Eryx tossed the key fob into the air, caught it, and steered his mate toward the door. "Can't. I've got one night's reprieve from the chaos at home with my baineann. She deserves a little taste of home while we're here." With one last pointed look at Ramsay, Eryx winked at Trinity and wrapped his hand around the doorknob. "Ramsay will take care of you."

The door clicked shut behind them.

Trinity wiggled out of his arms and half stumbled, half marched to the kitchen. She turned on the tap, wetted a dishrag, rang it out and started wiping down counters already so clean they were fit for surgery.

"Anyone would be a little freaked out to learn the things you heard." Ramsay paced closer to the tiny bar separating the kitchen from the living area. "Lexi's about as open-minded as they come, and even she was disbelieving."

Trinity shook her head, moved her shiny stainless steel toaster out of the way, and kept cleaning. "I wouldn't say I'm freaking out." She shifted to the far side of the counter and repeated the whole process with the cobalt blue storage containers artfully arranged by height in the corner.

Slowly so as not to completely push her over the edge, he inched in behind her and covered her hand with his.

She froze.

He opened his senses to gauge her emotions through his own gifts, but hit the same mental wall as when he'd tried to scan her memories. He smoothed his thumb along the inside of her wrist instead.

Her pulse hammered back at him. Not frantic like someone ready to run, but powerful.

"Talk to me." He laced his fingers with hers and pulled their joined hands up to her chest. "Tell me what you're thinking."

Her gaze stayed locked on the counter, distant. "You didn't want to talk before."

Shit. Man, he had this ass-handing coming. And honestly, he deserved whatever she wanted to dish out. Probably best to get things on the table so they could move on. Whatever that looked like. Problem was, he didn't have a clue where to start.

"I screwed up." It was something at least, and nothing short of the truth. He wrapped his other hand around her waist and squeezed the one intertwined with hers. "This prophecy thing has me worried for my brother, and I didn't stop long enough to think it through."

His conscience punched hard and fast.

Liar.

Trinity nodded and tried to move from his arms.

"Wait." He tightened his grip and rested his cheek at her temple. "That's not entirely the truth." He dragged in a slow breath and closed his eyes. Her clean, sunshine scent surrounded him. Innocent and provocative all at once. "I wanted answers. I also wanted you."

Trinity tensed.

"Everything we did, I wanted," he said. "I lied to myself plenty to get us both to that point, but I wanted it." He turned her, trapping her with his body against the countertop.

Trinity stared up at him with wide, cautious eyes, and her lips parted.

God, he hoped that meant she'd give him a chance. At

least long enough to explain. He cupped her face and stroked her cheekbones with his thumbs. "Everything was genuine. The only reason things didn't go further is I realized the truth. I wanted to back off and do things the right way."

Trinity fisted her hands at his chest and pushed. "I need some space." She paced to the living room and rubbed her palms against her dress pants. "Your race..." With most of her apartment between them, Trinity turned and braced one hand on the back of the club chair. "You think it's because you're different that you can touch me?"

So much for making headway on the intimate scale. Not that he could blame her wanting to sidestep that issue. Histus, he wasn't even sure he wanted things to register on that scale. "Probably a good guess. But you said others have touched you, right?"

Her eyes shifted toward the floor. "My dad."

And he'd died when she was little. Possibly before her phobia had fully developed. So maybe it was race specific.

"So..." She steeled her spine and sat on the edge of the chair, rubbing her hands. "Tell me about you. Your race."

"You want to narrow that question down a bit?" He strolled closer, edging between the simple coffee table and the sofa to sit beside her. Close, but not too close.

She shifted another two inches away, one hip pressed hard to the far edge of her chair. "Pick a spot. The beginning, I guess."

Praise The Great One, this was not his forte. Battle, yes. Sex, oh yeah. History, no.

He rubbed his chin. "Well, for starters, we're not supposed to tell anyone anything. Not humans, anyway. There are two tenets we're bound to; no divulging our race to humans and no interfering in their destiny."

Trinity sat up straight, her eyebrows arching high. "I'd say you've blown number one tonight."

"If you and Lexi are related, then you're not human."

Her mouth slackened. Had she really not put the two together? Although, she'd also had a lot thrown at her. "You think I'm one of you?"

"Lexi was what we call a lost Myren. Someone who's grown up in Evad, unknowing of their race. We took her to Eden. A few days later, she underwent the awakening ritual and came out whole and hearty on the other side."

Trinity's face blanked a split second before she ducked her head. She traced the cuticle of her thumb. "I doubt that's the case with me."

Damn, but he hated seeing her this uncertain. Even dodging contact in a crowded restaurant, she'd seemed confident. Determined to find a way to make it from point A to point B. Now she acted like someone had played Yahtzee with her whole life.

Oh, wait. They had.

To heck with distance. Ramsay sat on the coffee table in front of her and grabbed her hands. "Trinity, look at me."

She frowned at the floor and shook her head.

"I think it's possible you're exactly like Lexi. There's something different about you."

She surged to her feet and moved a good five feet away, keeping her back to him. "There's not a thing different about me. I'm just an average girl." She spun to face him, arms flaring out with more drama than he'd ever seen from her. Or maybe it was frustration. "I'm a librarian, for crying out loud. I'm as plain and ordinary as they come."

"Not ordinary. Not by a long shot." He stood sharply to punctuate this statement and prowled toward her. "It was you who knocked me out."

"I what?"

"You shocked me." He stopped short of reaching distance. "Or I guess I should say something inside you shocked me."

"I did not."

Ramsay laughed. How could he not? The woman had flattened him as good as any steel I-beam, and now she wanted to debate it. "Yeah, you did."

She leaned in a fraction and frowned.

Damn it all to histus. This really wasn't his strong suit. He rubbed the back of his neck. "When I saw the necklace, I knee-jerked and tried to scan your memories."

Trinity snapped to full height. "You did what?"

"Tried to scan your memories."

"You got in my he—"

Ramsay threw up his hands. "It's not something we normally do. It's considered impolite and I'm usually not comfortable using it, but seeing your pendant made me worry about my family."

Trinity crossed her arms, breaths coming short and fast. "What did you see?"

"Nothing." The Great One knew he wished he'd gathered something. Anything. For all their sakes. "That head of yours has got a mighty strong security system. Definitely not like any human I've ever met."

She lifted her chin and strolled to the window overlooking the street below. She kept her arms crossed, fingers digging into her biceps so hard she'd have a mark the next day.

He let her have her thoughts for a minute, replaying through everything he'd shared. Maybe he needed to focus on the benefits of being a Myren instead of the drama and intrigue. "Does the idea of being Myren scare you?"

"Right now a lot of things scare me."

Couldn't blame her for that. He moved in behind her and cupped her shoulders, her fresh, light scent seeping into him and ratcheting down a hefty amount of his tension. "Being Myren's got its advantages."

She turned her head. Not enough to truly give him her attention, but enough she could see him from her periphery. "Like slinking into people's heads?"

"Like that." The little fox. "But we can levitate too, our bodies and objects. Just like Eryx did with the keys." He slid his hands around her waist and pulled her against his chest. "Family and mates can talk telepathically. Everyone has gifts tied to the elements, and most have one or two unique gifts they excel in."

Her hands covered his, the touch both tentative and that of a woman gripping a lifeline.

He nuzzled the spot behind her ear, her hair silky smooth against his cheek. "It's beautiful there. Similar to Evad, but special in its own way."

She let out a shaky breath. "Special like the way those people described on the news? The ones who said they went there?"

His arms tightened around her at the reminder. "Just like that."

"Who's taking them?"

"We don't know. It's one of the reasons Eryx agreed to take a chance and come clean with you on everything. We were hoping you might have clues to help us see if it's prophecy related."

Trinity sucked in a deep breath. "I'll tell you what I know, but I wouldn't get your hopes up about me being one of you."

A warning brushed his senses. Nothing dangerous. More of an alertness. He turned her in his arms and angled her face to his with a firm grip at her neck. "Why? Would it be so bad?"

She smiled up at him, a sad one lacking its usual sparkle. "I think it sounds amazing. But there's no way I'm Myren."

CHAPTER 13

*D*amn her stupid mouth. Trinity shook the wooly melancholy off her thoughts and stomped around Ramsay toward the kitchen. She needed Ramsay focused on another subject pronto. He and his family might be willing to risk breaking their tenets, but sharing her heritage came with a nasty price. She might not know the details of said penalty, but it was bad enough to keep Kazan in line since her mother died. That was enough warning for her.

She snatched a bottle of Ménage à Trois Red from her clearance sale Pier One wine rack. "I think I've earned a drink. You want one?"

Ramsay's eyebrows pinched inward hard enough to leave a permanent dent. "Why don't you think you're Myren?"

Screw a drink. She'd earned the whole bottle. "I've got a better question." She worked the bottle corkscrew into place. "Tell me what Lexi was talking about?"

Silence floated behind her.

"Lexi said you're afraid to acknowledge something." She pulled the cork free and served up way more than the standard restaurant pour. "What was she talking about?"

Ramsay dropped into her comfy club chair and rubbed his neck.

"You said you'd give me answers. I want this one." She stifled the *harrumph* that rushed up behind her question, but just barely.

"Lexi's an emotional empath."

Trinity stopped with the wine glass midway to her mouth. "A what?"

"Emotional empath." He met her gaze across the room. "Kind of like an emotional radar. When she opens her senses, she can feel what people feel. Usually as a physical sensation before the emotion registers. Fear, for instance. It's got a metallic taste that hits before you feel it."

Well, that could be handy. A heck of a lot better than the movie-grams she got from touching people.

Wait a minute. "You talk about it like you've felt it yourself."

Ramsay's gaze slid to the sofa. "A little bit."

"You must be really tired. I didn't come close to buying that one."

He leaned forward, elbows on his knees, hands clasped together. Those delicious lips of his screwed up to one side, like he couldn't decide if he wanted to choke her or share dirty fantasies. "I have all Myren powers. So does Eryx. All Shantos men do. Eryx is our malran."

Well, shoot. The guy was a walking Myren lotto winner. No wonder he'd been cagey. "Malran?"

"King, as you'd understand it."

Whoa. "So, Lexi's a queen?"

"Malress. And yes. A pretty feisty one, too. When Eryx found her in Oklahoma, she was tending bar and doing college part-time."

Okay, that was *so* cool. An honest to God queen. And they might be related. Definitely a story to pull out of Lexi someday when she wasn't busy tiptoeing through informational land mines.

Ramsay pushed to his feet and prowled toward her.

Not good. He might have been reticent and tired of her questions two minutes ago, but the saunter headed her way said he'd recouped and re-strategized.

She sat her drink on the concrete countertop with an unsteady clink. "So what does that make you? A prince or something?"

Ramsay grinned, the distance between them closing fast. "A spare for the throne, and strategos for our warriors. What you'd probably call a commander in chief."

He wrapped his arms around her, one hand sliding up to the back of her neck and tilting her face to meet his. "You scare me."

The man had perfect lips. So close. Full and sinfully skilled.

Wait. "Me?"

His gaze roamed her face. "You."

She swallowed, the lingering trace of wine sticky at the back of her throat.

"Everything about you tempts me into places I'm not sure I'm comfortable going."

She smoothed the fine cotton stretched across his chest. "You mean sex?"

He studied her a second, his thumb moving in a hypnotic glide up and down her neck. "I mean serious."

So, that's what Lexi had been referring to.

"You're...different," he said. "Special. The kind of woman a man knows instinctively she'll be worth walking through histus and back for."

He tucked a strand of hair behind her ear, and the contact flamed out in a wild current through every nerve ending. "The truth? Aside from my brother and sister, and maybe her fireann, Reese, I don't think I've even considered letting anyone else in. Too risky."

"Why is that?" The question barely registered, her throat still in shock from his touch and his honesty.

Ramsay fingered the pendent between her breasts. "Too much disappointment. You let people get close, and then find out they're not there when you need them." He lifted his gaze and gave a wry smile. "Have I suitably owned up to everything now?"

And then some. She wasn't sure how she'd sleep tonight with all his commentary clattering around in her head. "I'd say you're covered."

"Good, because Lexi threatened to cut my nuts off if I didn't get it right." He pulled her in for a tight hug. Not at all a sexual move. More comforting than anything. And wasn't that disappointing.

"I didn't hear her say that," she muttered into his hard chest. She could wallow in his scent for days. A little spicy. Definitely exotic. Maybe she could get him to give her sheets a quick brush over before he bailed on her.

"Telepathy, remember?"

Huh? Oh, Lexi threatening to cut his nuts off. Right. An ironic laugh bubbled up from deep inside her belly. The two of them were the most bizarre paradox. Both of them afraid of intimacy, her physically and him emotionally.

"What's so funny?" His question stirred the fine hairs at her temple and fired a perfect ripple down her spine.

She wanted more. More touch. More experience. More memories. And who knew? Maybe they could help each other in the process and find some middle ground. "You want my help, right? To learn what you can about my background and see if it can untangle the prophecy?"

He pulled back, the eyebrow scowl working on that perma-wrinkle at the top of his nose again.

Trinity gripped his shoulders and held on tight. "Hear me out. That would help you and your family, right? To go through my past and see if there's anything you can use?"

He nodded, though definitely cautious.

"And you feel…" Damn, what was the right word? "Something…for me. Enjoyable. You just don't want the strings."

"You make it sound selfish."

"Not selfish. Honest." She urged him closer, a part of her needing his inherent strength to feed her courage. "We could help each other. I can show you what I know." Well, everything short of her Spiritu background. "And you can give me…"

Oh, brother. She was out of her damned mind.

Something lit behind his silver eyes. Something devious and oh-my-God naughty. "What?"

Just spit it out. "Touch." She licked her lip. "No strings, just physical enjoyment. Everything you know. Anything you can dream up while we research my background."

A wicked grin split his face, the kind that worked her body like a pair of super-charged jumper cables. "Trinity Blair. I do believe you've just propositioned me to be your fuck buddy."

Trinity would've staggered and crashed into the tiny breakfast bar if it weren't for his steady hands at her waist. Her shoulders shook, a none-too-ladylike laughter bubbling up from her belly while her cheeks tightened on a huge smile. It felt good. Like someone had offloaded about fifty tons off her big toe. "I do believe I did."

She hiccupped on a particularly loud guffaw and clamped a hand over her mouth. Did she just say that? Out loud?

But wait a minute. Ramsay wasn't laughing.

She looked up and sucked in a harsh breath.

Heat. I'm-gonna-twist-your-panties-inside-out heat. The

kind that made his silver eyes more like liquid steel with little flecks of white. And it was all centered on her.

She braced her unsteady hand on his chest, and the muscle flexed beneath her palm. "Does that bother you?"

For crying out loud, who was she, Jessica Rabbit? She sure as heck sounded like it.

"Bother's the wrong word." His crooked grin disappeared and he focused on her lips. He moved in closer, and one hand tangled in her hair at the back of her head. "Rock-fucking-hard and eager are much better choices."

She couldn't breathe. The space between them was too thick. Too clouded with something combustible and dangerous.

He ran his nose alongside hers, those yummy lips of his so close her mouth tingled. "You want me to teach you? Show you all those delicious sensations you've been missing?"

Oh, yes. Exactly that. Over and over again with a chance for extra credit. "Please."

His breath fluttered across her cheek, warm with a hint of something sweet. Cinnamon maybe.

"I like that word on your lips." He traced her collarbone. "I think I'll make you say it a lot. Make you beg. Maybe toss in a few naughty words for fun." He tilted her face up to meet his gaze. "Would you like that?"

Her belly flip-flopped and her thighs tightened against the steady throb setting up shop between her legs. "I'd agree to anything if you'd stop talking and kiss me."

He tangled his fingers in her hair and a raw and primitive expression moved across his face. "Deal."

He slanted his mouth over hers, harsh and unforgiving, while his arms caged her against his body. His tongue plunged deep, slicking across hers and dueling in a way that made her insides clench for an entirely different invasion.

Damn, but this was good. Slow, seductive Ramsay was one thing, but this... What the hell was it? Ravenous. Merciless.

And it was perfect.

She held on for dear life, one hand buried in his hair, the other nails-deep in his shoulder.

"Legs." He nipped her lower lip and cupped her ass, lifting her.

Her mind might not have comprehended what he meant, but her body sure did, her legs wrapping around his hips and locking him up tight.

He thrust against her core, the hands at her backside making damned sure she felt every inch of his hard length.

"Ohhh." She ground herself against him and centered on the bundle of nerves. Was he laughing? No wait. It was a groan. Or both. And they were moving.

Her back met the mattress a second before she took his weight square between her thighs.

"Praise The Great One." He worked her tailored blouse off with jerky movements. A snap sounded, followed by the *plip* of a button hitting hardwood floors. "Need to see you. Want my mouth on your pussy again."

She fisted the hem of his T-shirt with both hands and yanked upward, their arms colliding as shirts went flying. His lips crushed against hers, frantic. Almost bruising. His hands were at the clasp of her bra, even as her shoes and slacks were pulled free.

She jerked back as her pants slipped to the floor. "How'd you do that?"

He grinned and pinned her hands at either side of her head. "Telekinesis, remember?" He eased back and took his sweet time pursuing every inch of her nearly naked body. The nude lace thong sure wasn't doing much to cover what remained. "Convenient when a man's got his hands on more important matters."

He slid his hands down her arms, the heat from his palms almost scalding as he cupped her breasts and flicked the hard tips with his thumbs. His warm breath coasted along her sternum, and a hint of stubble at his chin teased her skin. "Much more important matters."

His mouth closed around one nipple.

She cried out and arched into the wet, delicious heat. God, she could get used to this. How had she lived without it? Worse, how would she live without it when he was gone?

No.

She shook the morbid thought away and reveled in the wicked path his lips and tongue trailed down her belly. He licked around her belly button and curled his fingers into the stretch lace at her hips. He pulled her panties free and nuzzled her cleft, inhaling deep while he pressed her thighs wide. "Yeah. Definitely, want this sweetness on my—"

"Ramsay." She scrambled out from underneath his diabolical mouth, rolled up, and faced him on shaky knees.

He straightened beside the bed, a predatory wariness marking his face. "You wanna tell me why you just took away my snack?" Playful words, but packed with edgy bite.

She dropped her gaze and nearly swallowed her tongue. So she hadn't imagined his size. Even with his jeans still on, it was obvious he was every bit as big and hard as he'd felt while she'd ground against him.

"I was thinking..." Her mouth went dry and her mind tripped and tumbled, completely at a loss for words. She swallowed and crawled off the bed, standing in front of him. She could do this. He'd given her everything and she'd given him nothing. Even gone so far as to fall asleep on him.

With a tentative touch, she traced his length through his jeans. "I was thinking this time I could take care of you first?"

A low rumble sounded. Somewhere between a growl and agony. "It's not about tit for tat. It's about making each other feel good."

She flattened her palm and stroked, keeping her gaze locked onto his chest where it was safe. "When you—" Shit. What should she call it? "—took care of me. Did you enjoy it?"

He flexed into her touch. "Watching you come? Knowing I was the first man to bring you there?" He palmed her nape. "Oh, yeah. Made my fucking century."

Tell him what you want. Just look up and say it. She scraped her nails against the denim on an upstroke.

This time she got a definite growl out of him.

She met his eyes. "If I told you I wanted to learn how to make a man feel good, would you show me?"

His grip at her neck tightened and the tension between them jumped from sparks to razor sharp need. He covered her hand at his crotch with his own, pressing her palm harder against his shaft. "Baby, right now you could ask me to run naked in Times Square and I'd give it serious thought." Another stroke, his gaze scorching hot and never leaving hers. "You sure?"

No. Not at all. But then she'd left the bulk of her reason near the bottle of Ménage à Trois Red. "Yes," she whispered.

He cupped her face and traced her lower lip with his thumb. "The word stop means something where I'm from." The words came out raspy. Broken and deep. "If it's too much, you use it."

She nodded, the movement as jerky and awkward as the rhythm of her heart.

"I want to hear it. Tell me you understand."

"I get it," she said quickly, trailing her fingertips up and over the defined ridges at his abdomen. "I'm not afraid." *Liar.* "Teach me."

He rested his forehead against hers. Their chests rose and fell in the same heavy rhythm for three or four breaths. And then he pulled away. A pillow levitated off her bed and plunked to the floor in front of her. "Get on your knees."

Oh, boy. She'd never seen a man look that way, let alone aim such a hungry gaze at her. A cold shiver worked its way from her head to her toes. Her breasts grew heavy and tight, and her nipples ached. The sweetest flutter centered between her legs.

"Now, Trinity." He stared her down, his muscled shoulders pushed back in a daunting pose, his erection a demanding presence behind his faded jeans.

She swallowed and kneeled.

"If you want to pleasure me, Sunshine, you'll have to touch me."

Right. Touch. That tiny detail she'd gone most of her life without. Damned if she wasn't making up for it now.

The top button popped free and Trinity jerked back with a gasp. Dear Lord in heaven, didn't the man own underwear?

Ramsay's chuckle wrapped around her even as he stroked the back of her head. "Got a few more to go, and my cock would feel a whole lot better if you'd give it a little wiggle room."

No blaming him on that count. She pulled the other buttons loose and his staff sprang free, hard and more than a little angry looking. She tugged the sides of his jeans, mindlessly shoving the fabric as he stepped out and kicked them away.

No hair. Wasn't he supposed to have hair? Was that a Myren grooming thing or did they come that way? And what must he think of her? She wasn't Rapunzel by any stretch, quite the opposite with what she called her landing strip, but he had nothing.

She looked up to find his silver gaze locked onto hers,

tension making his cheeks and jawline more pronounced. "What do I do?"

His lips crooked in a ragged smile. "You touch me. How ever you want."

Funny, it didn't look up close like she'd thought it would. Hard, yes, but soft too. Carefully, she traced the stark ridge below the head.

His cock jerked and Ramsay hissed.

Trinity tried to snatch her hand back, but Ramsay caught it at the wrist.

"Sorry," she said.

"Nothing to be sorry for. Best damn one-second touch of my life." He guided her hand back to the base of his cock. "Wrap your hand around me."

Wow. It really was soft. Sort of. In a pillow-topped concrete kind of way.

She squeezed and Ramsay flexed into her palm with a moan.

"I can feel your breath." His gaze was locked on her, his eyelids languid and sexy while every other muscle in his torso seemed ready to snap. "It's fucking hot as hell, and all I can think about is how much hotter it'll feel when my cock's inside your mouth."

A tremor rattled through her, and her muscles did the most amazing Kegel demonstration of her life. Damn, but the man had a filthy mouth, and there wasn't a single nerve in her body that didn't approve. The realization knocked something loose in her psyche. Like her reservations had lost a foothold and another part of her stepped out of a cold dank cell into the bright sunshine for the first time.

She leaned in, never breaking eye contact, and flicked her tongue against his length.

He fisted her hair. "Fuck, yes. Scorching." He nudged her closer, his free hand angling his cock toward her lips. "More."

She closed her eyes and gave in, sliding her mouth along his shaft and licking the raised veins from base to tip until her tongue swiped through a bead of moisture at the head. Salty, but not unpleasant. Her eyes snapped open.

Power.

She was the one on her knees, Ramsay towering over her, but Trinity was the one in control. The one making the muscle at his jaw tick in an unsteady pattern. The one causing his hand to fist her hair and his quads to clench harder than steel.

And she wanted more.

She took him in her mouth in one swift move, her lips stretched in a pleasant discomfort around his girth, yet nowhere near taking all of it. Over and over she worked him, stroking the base of his cock while her tongue played along the hard ridge beneath his head.

Ramsay moaned, his muttered curses and ragged encouragements floating around her. His hips flexed into each bob of her head.

"Trinity." He tugged her hair, his grip locked up tight at the roots. "Sunshine. You gotta stop. It's your first time."

She kept going, standing taller on her knees and angling to take more of him.

"Fuck." No muttering that curse.

Good. She wanted him half as crazy as she felt. Half as undone. Out of control.

A low, feral growl radiated from him and out along her skin. "You want my cum, Trinity? You want me to lose control and spill in your mouth?"

Oh. My. God. Yes. That was exactly what she wanted.

She moaned around his staff and hollowed her checks on an upstroke, sucking harder.

"You want that, then you're going to come for me while you do it." He gripped his cock at the base and pulled free of her mouth. "Sit back on your heels, knees wide. You want to use those pretty hands, then cup my balls."

His gravelly voice vibrated across her skin, and she'd swear a cool gust of air rushed down her back and around her butt. She did as he asked, cupping the tight sack in one hand and bracing with the other at his hip.

"Smart call, hanging on." He slicked his wet cockhead along her lower lip, coaxing her mouth open before sliding in. "If you thought undressing you with my mind was good, wait until you see what I can do with the elements."

Another rush of air met her skin, this one finer than what she'd sensed seconds before and swirling around her spread thighs in a deliciously unnatural way. Her gaze snapped to his.

"Oh, yeah." His wicked grin fired an urgent pulse between her legs, need knocked aside for something closer to primal demand. "Myren gifts have their benefits. Air isn't an element to be discounted, is it?"

A sharp stream slipped between her wet folds and her whole body shuddered. Her hands at his hips and sack tightened.

Ramsay hissed. "Maybe you need something else. Something more tangible."

Invisible fingers cupped her breasts, kneading the sensitive mounds and plucking her hard nipples. She moaned around his cock and took him deep, urging him on with a faster, frantic rhythm.

"My girl wants more."

More. Yes. She didn't dare stop, the need to take him as far as he'd catapulted her driving every hard pull against his flesh. She met his eyes instead, willing him to give her more. Begging without a word.

"Oh, Trinity." He caressed her cheek. "Been alive six times as long as you, and I've never seen anything sexier than you right now." A teasing touch brushed her mound. "Going to be even better when you come screaming around my dick."

Contact. Slick, decadent contact. Invisible fingers sliding through her wetness. Circling her entrance, and playing with her clit.

He tugged her head back. "Look at me."

Bright eyes bore down on her. Bold silver surrounded by an almost neon white. A wild animal sighting its prey. "You gonna get there with me?"

She tongued his shaft's sensitive ridge in lieu of a nod and stroked the velvety underside of his balls with her fingers.

"Sweet. Fucking. Sunshine." His hips surged forward and his cock jerked inside her mouth. Cum, warm and salty coated her tongue, and his nearly triumphant shout rang in her ears.

A sensation every bit as real as his fingers plunged inside her, hitting that perfect spot with a tantalizing scrape. Pressure pinched her swollen clit.

And she was gone.

Floating.

Riding each veiled thrust and bobbing her head to match the undulations of his hips. She was lost. Dazedly coasting down from the most erotic event of her life.

Ramsay's big hand cupped the side of her face, pulling himself free of her swollen lips. "The Great One help me." Strong arms wrapped around her, holding her nearly boneless body tight against warm hard muscle.

Safe. And so damned relaxed.

Her body jostled in his arms and the rustle of sheets and blankets screamed through the quiet. The dim light of her nightstand lamp disappeared from behind her closed eyes.

"I see my girl's got a thing for catnaps after she gets off."

Oh, shit. Her eyes snapped open, thirty pounds heavier than normal and damned hard to keep focused. "We didn't finish." She pushed against his chest and tried to sit up. "You were going to teach me—"

"I am teaching you." He tugged the sheets up to cover her and rolled her on her side, facing away from him. "It's not about a man getting his dick in you. It's about feeling good and not being sorry about how that happens." He curled in tight behind her. "Now let those pretty eyes of your close and go to sleep."

So warm. Powerful and yet gentle at the same time. A girl could get comfortable with a long-term arrangement like this in short order. "Will you be here in the morning?"

Quiet settled in the darkness. His exotic, manly scent covered every inch of her, the taste of his climax still vaguely on her tongue. Sleep pulled her down, reality fading to ether.

"Yeah, Sunshine," he said, his voice grated, yet strangely peaceful. "I'm not going anywhere."

CHAPTER 14

*S*erena crept down the servants' staircase at the back of her family estate, the narrow passage dark save for the pale shaft of moonlight from the kitchen at the landing below.

Of all the nights for her father's staff to be doggedly efficient. Normally they'd meander to their rooms or private homes within hours of cleaning up the evening meal. The one night she tried to sneak out, they up and decide to linger until nearly midnight. Another hour and she'd have had to delay her secret trip. She'd barely make it to Uther's home in the Underlands and back before sunrise as it was, and she damned sure wanted time to read Uther the riot act for leaving her high and dry after her arrest.

Moonlight glowed pearlescent off the black stone countertops and lingering coals smoldered a warm orange in the wide fire oven along the far wall. She cut around the massive island at the center, headed toward the back door.

Sharp pain fired from her pinkie toe and all the way up her spine. Damn it all! She held her breath and mashed her lips together to stifle a scream. Stupid shadows. This was why she needed warriors. Someone better equipped to handle stealth and dirty deeds. The right skills and specialized training. Planning she could more than tackle. Masking and creeping around in the middle of the night, no.

She hobbled to the tall window overlooking the back gardens. No guards near the doors and none by the garden edge. At least Eryx's henchmen hadn't lingered with the same fortitude as her father's servants.

The iron door latch snitched beneath her hand.

Her father's voice cut through the darkness. "I'd thought you were smarter than that."

Serena whirled and plastered her back against the door, her heart lodged squarely in her throat. "Father, you startled me." Just what she needed. Another complication. "Smarter than what?"

Reginald stalked from the shadows of the main hallway, the one closest to his study. "Don't play false with me, daughter. Your claims of innocent love might resonate with weaker minds prone to such folly, but I know you better than to buy it."

The son of a bitch. He was bluffing. In all her one hundred and thirty years, he'd not so much as given her the time of day, treating her as little more than an empty-headed sheep. No way would he suddenly believe she held enough wits to mastermind all she'd managed thus far.

"Play false?" She paired her innocent retort with puppy dog eyes and a fluttering hand at her chest. "I don't understand. I merely couldn't sleep and thought to walk through the gardens. All this talk of prophecy and changes for our race has me frightened. I worry for Eryx."

His lips twisted in a wry smirk. "Well presented. Still not buying it, but well presented, nonetheless." He pulled out a stool tucked beneath the island counter and nodded at the back door. "Don't be deceived by the lack of guards. They're there. More than double since the malran left this afternoon."

Damn it.

Reginald chuckled. "Yes, I know he was here. Your mother met your brother and me at the back door this evening, breathless with news of his visit. I've encouraged her to spread further tales of his arrival, perhaps adding a bit of fanciful elaboration on what may or may not have occurred during his stay."

She had to give it to her father. Tacking any kind of falsity to the malran's visit was a sizable risk if it ever tied back to their family, but it would be markedly good for business. Still probably not in her best interest to let on she was onto his schemes. "While my heart would be overjoyed with any romantic inclination on the malran's part, he showed me no such affection. Why would you represent him otherwise?"

Her father's eyes narrowed. "Because your newfound popularity benefits our family and our profits. I'd be a fool not to bolster your reputation further." He glanced at the door then back to her. "I'm even wise enough to ensure you don't ruin it with ill-planned actions."

"You misunderstood. I don't—"

"Leave off, Serena. I know you. I also know about the gifts you think you've kept so well hidden. Do you honestly think I could live under the same roof with you for all these years and not be keen to the fact you're a natural influencer?"

Everything inside Serena locked up tight. Her mind, her breath, even her heart stuttered. How could he know? She'd never once shared knowledge of her gift with anyone, not even Maxis. Histus, it had taken her years after her awakening to even realize what her gift truly was.

"I see I've struck a nerve." Her father traced a slow pattern against the black stone countertop. An absent-minded gesture, as though he were clueless to the way he'd upended the most cherished aspect to her life. "I know your gifts, Serena, because they're my own. It's why I'm a merchant. What better way to ensure our wares and vendors find their way home with people than to manipulate their feelings? I felt it in you only days after your awakening. Revealing my knowledge would have shown my hand. Better to let you gallivant unaware. Ignorant people show the hands they've been dealt too quickly."

All this time. All those years brushing her off. Ignoring her. A slow, sizzling burn fired in her belly, and a furious shout knotted in her throat to the point she could barely breathe.

Reginald sat taller on his stool and crossed his arms. "The malran's reported to the council someone is spiriting humans to Evad for a little sightseeing. No one can describe the one bringing them here, though they uniformly comment on a distinctive scent being present the entire time. One not unlike an expensive perfume." He tilted his head, more indirect accusation than curiosity. "I assume this was the true nature of the malran's visit?"

The muscles in her forearms ached from the constant pressure of her fisted hands, and her feet itched to pace. She nodded instead.

"And your near-disastrous stroll through the gardens tonight was what?" he said. "Another outing to Evad to stir further trouble for the malran?"

"It wasn't me."

He raised a pompous eyebrow.

"It wasn't. The malran's somo checked my memories. There was nothing."

"Nothing to prove you were there, but nothing to prove you weren't, either. The black of delta sleep gives you not a leg to stand on. In fact, the malran could argue you were blocking the time you were away."

"I wasn't." Despite the cool room, a bead of sweat slid from her nape and between her shoulder blades, and a fine sheen of moisture built along her brow. She should have waited for Thyrus.

Reginald stood and ambled to the window. "I know it wasn't you."

What? Surely he hadn't just defended her.

With a look over his shoulder, he raked her with a loathsome gaze then returned to his study of the gardens beyond. "Your stealth leaves something to be desired. Not surprising. You're a woman and not trained in such matters."

"My sex holds no bearing on my skills, and I'll be damned if I abide one more person relegating my capacity because of it." The sexist bastard. All men were. He'd bleed like anyone else, and she'd prove it once more if she had a dagger in her palm.

"This errand," he said. "I suppose it serves to find the individual laying suspicion on our doorstep?"

Our doorstep. Years of neglect and now he wanted to make it about *them*?

"I won't be framed for this," she said. "There is someone I can speak with who can determine the truth and protect me. Someone loyal."

Reginald crossed his arms, one hand raised as he rubbed his chin. A classic picture of thoughtful consideration hiding the shrewd cutthroat within. He faced her, eyes narrowed and lips pursed in a way that had boded all manner of childhood scolding. "You'd best hope they're loyal, Serena. You may not enjoy the life you lead with this family, but you'd find the life of a powerless human even worse. Particularly one of their homeless."

He studied her attire, the black leggings and tunic grossly outside her usual fare, but displaying her assets quite well. "Though I doubt you'd be without a protector long. You do have a way with men." A snide chuckle shook his chest and his lips twisted in a cruel smile. "All except for the malran, of course."

With a dismissive lift of his chin, he strode toward the hallway and his study beyond. "Tomorrow. Prepare to leave at seven a.m. Your mother has a daylong event volunteering at Sanctuary. Such a trip is protected under house arrest. Tell her you're consumed with worry over the latest developments and wish to pray to The Great One that the prophecy brought on us by the mating of your beloved doesn't spell the worst for our race."

He stopped before the shadowed hallway and looked back. "Make no mistake, daughter. Your usefulness to the family is the only reason for my assistance. I'm not without my own means of distancing us from you just as quickly." He turned away, his last words nearly swallowed by the darkness. "I suggest you make your venture count."

CHAPTER 15

*R*amsay rolled away from the sunlight slanting across his closed eyelids. His morning stubble scratched against the soft pillowcase, and Trinity's spring and linen scent filled his lungs.

His eyes snapped open. No Trinity, just a dent on the pillow beside his. He checked the sun's position with his senses. No more than six or six-thirty. Surely she hadn't—

The bite of strong coffee drifted from the kitchen. Oh, no. Not gone. Looked like Trinity was doing the domesticated sex kitten routine. And praise The Great One, was that bacon?

He threw back the covers and padded to his jeans across the room. God, this woman was amazing. Drop dead gorgeous, innocent heart, wild as fuck in the bedroom, and she cooked bacon. Perfect. Abso-freaking-lutely perfect.

He gave up finding his T-shirt and ambled through the living room half dressed. Only the kitchen lights were on, leaving the rest of the apartment in the soft glow of morning.

Trinity shifted from behind the stove and tossed a utensil in the sink.

Guess he'd found his T-shirt, and damned if she didn't look good in it, the hem reaching almost to her knees. A wallop of something he'd never felt before pushed his shoulders back and puffed up his chest.

He crept closer. Not just bacon on the menu. Toast, potatoes, and eggs too. "Not sure which I like better. You making food that won't leave me hungry in five minutes, or what you wear doing it."

Trinity spun around and smiled, a wide, killer one at full wattage. "I hope you don't mind. I've read a ton of stories where the woman wears a guy's shirt the next morning, and I've always wanted to do it." Her smile turned sheepish and her cheeks pinkened. "It smells like you."

So honest. Not a bone of pretense in her body. Was there a better word than perfect? "You like my scent being on you?"

The blush flared a hotter red and she twisted to the stove.

So, she did like it.

He liked it too. A lot.

The image of his family's mark on her arm splayed across his mind. Dangerous, but damned inciting too.

He settled on a barstool. Even if he wanted a baineann, she'd have to be Myren to take his mark, not that Trinity seemed too keen on the idea of being Myren. And why in histus was that, anyway? "You care if I get coffee?"

"Help yourself. Cups are over the coffee pot. There's creamer in the fridge and sugar in the small container." She motioned to the smallest of the blue containers nestled in the corner and flipped the potatoes. The steady sizzle from the pan flared to an angry hiss.

Maybe she needed a less sexual demonstration of the perks of being a Myren. He opened the cabinet with his mind and pulled out a handcrafted tan ceramic mug.

Trinity froze, a strip of bacon dangling off the end of her fork and eyes locked on his trick.

He slid the carafe free, poured a full cup, and slid it back on the burner.

Trinity pivoted and followed the levitating cup of goodness across the room with wide eyes.

"Black works fine for me. Though the stuff we brew at home kicks a bigger punch, so I'll usually go for cream there."

The mug clinked atop the concrete countertop.

"That is so cool." She might try to fit the unruffled librarian mold, but in that second her face lit up like a seven-year-old at Christmas.

"Ah, so you like my daylight parlor tricks better than my bedroom performance." He sipped his coffee and winked. "I'll have to keep that in mind."

Her levity melted away, replaced with a shudder and softening mouth. So adorable. Runway models paid damn good money to get mussed hair and kiss-swollen lips like hers. "I liked that too. Though I don't really get how you did it."

"As simple as a thought. An impression of touch guided by the mind. Not much different from how I moved the coffee pot." He took another drink. "That was only half of what I could've done. If you were Myren, I could have made it much better. As it was, I had to hold myself in check to keep you safe."

"Safe?"

Ramsay sat the mug aside. "If you are Myren and unawakened, too much energy could trigger your awakening. You're not even willing to consider you might be one of us, let alone be ready to take on your powers."

She smoothed his T-shirt at her stomach and cleared her throat. "I was thinking I'd stop by my mom's house and pick up some stuff the adoption service gave her."

Ah, the none-too-subtle change of topic approach. He'd go with it for now. "Is that where you found the necklace?"

Trinity ducked back to work and flipped off the burners.

"I think that's where it came from. Dad gave it to me when I was little." She pulled two plates from the cabinet overhead and plated the food. "I get off work at five. I can pick it up on the way home and meet you back here."

"Why not meet there? I can help."

Trinity hesitated mid-spoonful of fried potatoes. "Mom's a little difficult."

The plates were done and her coffee full, but she still wouldn't turn around. "Difficult how?"

She shook her head and pivoted with a plate in each hand, her face blanked with a kind of impassivity that seemed like a mortal crime on someone as bright as her. "It's a long story. Not worth telling."

"Not worth telling, or don't want to tell?"

"Don't want to." She dug into her food and waggled her fork at him between bites. "Don't you have...I don't know... more important prince stuff to do?"

She didn't want to talk about it, fine. He'd play along. But it was damned weird seeing her lock up. "Actually I could use today to catch up on how we're doing with the Rebellion."

"The what?"

Oh, that's right. He'd missed that detail the night before, somewhere between getting her to admit she might be Myren and her fuck-buddy proposition. "The Rebellion. They're a bunch of fanatics who think The Great One made us superior to humans so they could be our slaves."

Trinity semi-coughed/choked on a mouthful of eggs.

"Shit. Sorry." Ramsay stood and smacked her on the back.

She waved him off and covered her mouth, trying to suck in a steady breath. "Warn a girl before you scare the crap out of her, would you?" She poked her fork at his plate. "Eat. I'd like to make sure you've got enough energy to keep your local bad guys from ruining the rest of my life."

Ramsay shrugged and got to work on his food. "Yeah,

well," he said around a mouthful. "It doesn't help they've got rogue Spiritu helping them."

Trinity's fork clattered to the countertop. "Rogue Spiritu?"

Ramsay grinned. He couldn't have stopped it if he'd wanted to. The look on her face was priceless. Big eyes, loose jaw, kinda like he'd just told her he could sprout two more heads and a tail. "Guess I kinda fell short on explanations last night, huh?"

She picked up her fork, studied the plate and pushed around what was left of her food.

Weird. She'd taken everything else no BFD, but this seemed to suck the life right out of her.

"You don't sound like you like these Spiritu too much," she said.

"Dislike probably isn't the right word. Histus, I barely know them. It's what they do that bugs me. Inspiration is what they call it, but the idea of someone pushing ideas that aren't mine in my mind?" He shook his head and scooped up the last bit of potatoes. "It rubs me the wrong way. Too close to brainwashing, if you ask me."

Trinity scraped her plate clean over the trashcan and loaded it up in the dishwasher. Everything about her seemed empty. Void of the usual life that energized her movements. Unplugged.

To hell with that. He wanted his sunshine back. To see her smile and put some of that innocent swagger back into her hips. He left behind his own plate and slid behind her, hands at her waist. "Did I mention breakfast at Trinity's house is now my favorite pastime?"

Her knuckles went white gripping the sink ledge, but she tilted her neck to give his lips better access. "I'm not sure I have time for a lesson before work."

"This isn't a lesson. This is enjoyment."

"Doesn't this..." She eyed him over her shoulder. "I don't know, muddy the waters?"

He splayed his hand across her abdomen, so soft. And damned if a quick dip with his fingers didn't confirm she didn't have a stitch on underneath. "Not to me. Touch, sexuality, intimacy, it's the norm in Eden. Natural. Even PDAs are no big deal. I'd say they're practically expected between two people in a relation—"

His mouth locked up the second the word registered.

Trinity slumped and she frowned, though she clearly tried to couch it as a smile. "That's what I meant." She turned and urged him back. "I respect your boundaries, Ramsay, but you have to respect mine too. Don't pull me into something you're not ready for."

Son. Of. A. Bitch. How had he not seen that coming? And even more importantly, why did he want to tug her right back against him and tell her to hell with boundaries?

"I've got to get to work." Trinity snatched the dishtowel off the counter, wiped her hands, and headed to the living room. "Do you need me to drop you somewhere?"

Praise The Great One, where was his head? He'd forgotten he didn't have a car.

Still stuck on figuring out if the cost for the candy you're craving is worth it.

His conscience was a lippy pain in the ass. "No, I'll port over."

Trinity drew up short and looked back. "Port over?"

"To Eden." As far as parlor tricks went, portals were one of the best. Second only to flying. And The Great One knew she needed some serious pepping up after his flubs this morning. "You wanna watch?"

She glanced at the kitchen clock. "I still need to get dressed and get to work. Do we have time?"

"Plenty." He eyeballed her in his shirt and grinned. "But

one way or another I've got to get you out of my clothes first."

SERENA TOUCHED down a few feet outside Uther's front door, Underland's noonday sun blasting down on her bare shoulders. Knowing her luck, she'd end up with noticeable tan lines and blow her one big covert task on a wardrobe misfire.

Praise The Great One, she hated this place. As close to a human desert as you could get. Scorching in the daytime, and bitter cold at night, but without any hope for an oasis. How Uther's family had survived here so long, she'd never understand.

She knocked on the weathered front door, and the crumbling whitewashed finish scraped her knuckles.

The door opened.

Uther stood with one arm propped on the door's edge and the other on his hip, his chocolate linen pants and loose ivory shirt more indicative of a laborer than the Rebellion strategos he'd once been. He scowled and looked her up and down. "Took you long enough."

She pushed past him and headed for the kitchen. The tiny place barely held its own against her family's gardener shack, but compared to the brutal outside it was paradise. "What do you mean, 'Took you long enough'? I'm on house arrest. By the way, thanks for all the support."

She ran water over the shallow cuts the door's dried paint left behind.

Uther tossed a mostly clean hand towel in her direction. "I knew where you were."

"Then why didn't you come help me?"

"Couldn't be sure you wouldn't throw me out as bait to get yourself off the hook."

Well, he was right on that score. Any longer cooped up at the warrior's training facility and she'd have thrown her own mother out as bait. "You could've come after."

"Nope." He strolled to the navy blue couch across from the well-used but unlit fireplace, settled in, and kicked up his feet on the scarred walnut coffee table. "Needed to be sure I had something to keep you in line first. Any woman who'll knife her own fireann can't be trusted."

Serena tossed the towel aside and crept closer. Goose bumps raced up her arms and across her shoulders. "Keep me in line how?"

"Put a little more skin in the game for you." He stared at the empty hearth, unbothered to even meet her gaze. "Make sure you had enough incentive to help me out."

She lurched into his field of vision. "So you forced me to break my house arrest? Is that it? Do you have any clue how many guards are on me at any given time? Praise The Great One, they're even saying someone's bringing humans to Eden and claiming it was me."

At her last shrieked word, his gaze snapped to hers. "I know exactly what's going on because I'm the one bringing them here."

Serena's thoughts tumbled. "You set me up?"

"Keeps the malran busy while I take care of my own business," he said, not the least bit concerned with the fact her lungs wouldn't work right.

"They'll strip my powers if they prove it was me bringing humans here. Histus, I doubt Eryx will even be held to proof. Supposition will be more than enough."

"Oh, I don't know. Seems you've got quite the following lately." He smirked. "Unrequited love suits you."

"Stop it!" She stomped to within an arm's reach. Even standing on her feet she barely towered over his seated height. "This isn't a joke."

"I'll bet Maxis didn't think his plans were a joke either, but you took him out quick enough didn't you?"

Fuck this. She straightened and schooled her features to that of a fearful, innocent woman. "I was afraid." She nudged a wave of sympathy toward Uther, a barely detectable cloud of emotion to skew his natural response. "He was about to give us all away to Reese. I couldn't risk him sacrificing all we'd done. If anything, I protected you. And now you put my powers in jeopardy? They'll cast me out."

"Then you'd be wise to work with me. I can plant something more substantial next time." No concern or capitulation at all. Just a steady, cold glare. "I sure as hell won't use your perfume again, though. Took three showers to get it off me."

Blast it, why wasn't he responding? No one but Eryx— "Wait, the people you brought over, how do they not remember you?"

His grin grew to a full smirk.

The memory of Uther's blocking demonstration in this same cabin only a month before blazed vivid in her mind. "You blocked it. The same gift you use to block attacks, you blocked their memory of you."

He dipped his chin, more of a salute to her deduction than agreement.

"Any other handy tricks I should know about?"

"There's very little you need to know about me. What you do, I'll share when I'm ready." He stood and strolled toward the cluttered desk situated against the far wall.

Damn, but she was fed up with men giving her their backs. Dismissing her with less care than a muddy pair of shoes. "Then tell me what's so important you deemed it necessary to blackmail an innocent."

"An innocent?" He looked up from rummaging through

the papers on the desktop and flat out laughed. "You are many things, Serena. Innocent isn't one of them."

"What is it you need?"

He flipped through a beat-up tablet, a modernized legal type from Evad. Not altogether surprising considering how much less they cost compared to those made in Eden. He tossed the notepad aside and scowled across the room. "I want access to old records. You have it. I don't."

"Then by all means, visit Cush and bury yourself in books at the leabrash."

"Don't patronize me, Serena. If it was something that simple, I'd have gone there by now."

"By all that's sacred, get on with it and tell me exactly what you need!" Her pulse pounded at her temples and her throat scratched from the outburst. Even worse, her pride stung at the loss of control.

Uther eased back, rested against the desk, and crossed his arms and ankles. "I need a specialized text. One from ancient times like Maxis had in his library."

Her instincts prickled, all the frustration and anger she'd mustered since Eryx's visit sharpening on the man in front of her. "Why?"

"I told you. When I want you to know, I'll share."

"Bullshit. If you want me to risk my neck any further, then I want to know there's something in it for me."

"You won't lose your powers and you won't get tossed to Evad. I'd think that was enough."

"Enough for bare bones, maybe." She meandered closer and pushed an emotional urge to cooperate his direction. "Give me an incentive." She swayed her hips with each step. "Something to make me want the risk."

The closer she got, the more his eyes narrowed.

Give me what I want. Forget your caution and loosen that tongue of yours. She wove the thought around him, light so as not to raise suspicion with too great a stir of energy. She laid a hand on his chest. His heart thudded steady and strong beneath it. "Just a hint."

"I have leads on the prophecy." His biceps flexed and his eyebrows pinched in the center. "That should be sufficient impetus for you, particularly if it means upsetting the throne."

She smiled, the first lighthearted flush she'd felt in over a month, making the drab room feel positively radiant.

Aside from one tiny detail.

"I can't get to Maxis' possessions anymore." She paced toward the soot-covered hearth, excitement pushing her blood along at a heady pace. "They confiscated the lands. All of it."

"A minor problem considering your connections." He pushed away from his desk and headed to the front door. "Surely you have contacts with access to the sacred halls. You get me the texts I need, and we'll see where we go from there."

"What's that supposed to mean?"

He opened the door and the blast of sunshine nearly blinded her. Heat wafted behind it. "It means you've got four days to get your hands on the translation texts for our mother tongue."

Was the man daft? "Our language has been dead for thousands of years. No one has those kind of records."

"Maxis did."

She shouldn't be surprised. Maxis' grandmother, Evanora, spent the bulk of her life with the sole intent of dethroning the Shantos line. Being left pregnant at the altar in favor of a commoner would do that to a woman.

"The translations exist," he said. "Get them and we'll see if we can't use what I know of the prophecy to get you what you've always wanted."

"And if I don't?"

Even with the glaring sun blinding her, there was no missing the evil twist of his lips. "Then it's likely more tangible evidence will be left behind for Eryx and his men to track in Evad. One that leaves culpability on your doorstep with a big, shiny red bow."

CHAPTER 16

Too close to brainwashing if you ask me.

Trinity glared through the windshield at the aged, but warm exterior of her mother's house and replayed Ramsay's off-hand comment for the seven-hundredth time. She tapped out a frantic rhythm on the steering wheel. All this time she'd been scared to death of sharing the truth about her Spiritu heritage, when what she should have been worried about was the possibility her race might fall on the unsavory list.

Didn't that just figure.

She dropped her hands in her lap and let out a frustrated huff, the new leather seats creaking at her sudden move. Where did Ramsay get off judging the Spiritu anyway? Like one rogue sector should color an entire race? Whatever rogue Spiritu were. Her dad had never mentioned them before. Another topic he'd conveniently sidestepped.

A shadow fell across the driver's seat and a knock sounded on the window.

Ramsay grinned down at her, the picture-perfect playboy

—loose, shoulder-length dark hair with sun-kissed streaks, jeans, and turquoise T-shirt.

She popped the door open and snatched her purse from the passenger's side. "I didn't see you pull up." The door shut with a muted chunk. "Where's your car?"

"Cars are for fun more than necessity." He pointed to the sky and steered her around the car with a hand at her elbow. "The friendly skies are faster and easier. Less traffic, no rules."

She froze so fast her purse nearly whacked her off balance. "Come again?"

The man beamed a shit-eating grin to melt a nun's panties. "I know I got sidetracked with the explanations last night, but I'm pretty sure we covered telekinesis this morning."

She lifted both eyebrows and bobbed her head for him to continue.

He mocked the same smug expression back at her, only on a far more playful scale. "So, if I can move a coffee pot and tweak all the right spots on your body with my mind, then I can move me too." He tapped the tip of her nose and urged her into motion with a tug on her arm.

Trinity dug in and snatched her elbow from his grip. "You're telling me you fly."

"I'm telling you I fly."

"In the sky."

His lips twitched. "On the ground wouldn't be flying."

Smart ass. "Don't people see you?"

He guided her forward again, this time splaying his big hand at the small of her back. God, the things that man could do with his hands. Or more precisely his fingers. Just thinking about it made her want to bypass her mom's house and head back home for her next lesson.

"Remember the portal?" he said. "How I masked it? Same thing."

Oh, yeah. She remembered. Coolest thing she'd ever seen. Levitating a coffee pot times about a million. Gray and white swirls in the form of a mystical cave with pixie dust sparkles thrown into the mix. If she didn't think it would get Ramsay in hot water, she'd be all over a little adventure trip so she could see the inside next time.

They got to the front door and Trinity fished her keys from the bottom of her purse.

Ramsay held the screen door open. "So, what's in the box?"

"It's been a long time since I looked." The key slid home and she wiggled the bolt until it finally budged. "A brown book. Or a journal, maybe. Some news clippings and a few pictures of my mom, if I remember right."

"Kind of vague for something unique to your past."

Trinity led the way into the dark, depressing room. The house had been built in the early sixties, but the decor was stuck in the seventies. How anyone ever found wood paneling attractive she'd never know.

"The one time I tried to see inside didn't turn out so well." Her breaths shortened and her throat constricted. For a fall evening, the room sure felt more like August. She shut the door behind them and headed to the kitchen. "I was about thirteen. Mom had left me alone for the first time to go to a church meeting. She'd have never done it if I wasn't sick."

"And?"

Trinity checked the kitchen, then her mother's room. Her mother hadn't answered when she'd called on the way here, but a little extra caution couldn't hurt. Carol Blair plus Ramsay Shantos would only equal major pain in the butt for Trinity.

She shrugged as she passed Ramsay and headed to the

garage. "Mom forgot something and came back. Caught me looking."

"So? It's your stuff, right?"

She opened the back door and flipped on the light. No car. Fingers crossed Mom had a big thing keeping her busy at church.

Oh, who was she kidding? Mom always had a big thing at church. She shut the garage door and faced Ramsay head on. "My mom blames me for Dad dying."

To his credit, Ramsay didn't flinch. His eyebrows dipped into a stern V, but otherwise he held stock still.

"He was taking copies of something from the box to a language expert out of town when he was killed by a drunk driver." It was the first time she'd truly correlated the buzzing sensation with an impending significant event. She'd done everything to stop her adopted father, including telling him she thought something bad was about to happen.

Her mother had been convinced she was evil ever since.

"Your mother blames a seven-year-old kid for a guy getting hit by a drunk driver?"

Trinity strode back through the house and tossed her purse and keys on the sofa on the way to her mother's room. Funny how it sounded, a logical question next to her mother's illogical behavior. Her mom had latched onto religion, seeking comfort, and ended up twisting decent teachings into ideas even the most fanatical churches shied away from.

Thank God Kazan had taken his concerns toward Carol's behavior to the Black King. If he hadn't been granted dispensation to reveal himself and her heritage to Trinity, she'd have faced the next thirteen years alone with nothing but endless reminders of her evil nature.

"Grief does crazy things to people." She flipped on the bedroom light. The faded blue comforter and nondescript furniture matched her mother's worn out demeanor. "Anyway, I never tried to look again. She stuck by me, even with my inability to touch people, and always took care of me. It seemed the least I could do."

She opened the accordion-style closet doors. Years of conservative clothing hung bunched together, the colors bland as dirt. She shifted the shoeboxes on the top shelf.

Ramsay pulled a few out of her way. "So, the book's written in a foreign language?"

"I guess so. I never got far enough to see for myself. Dad was trying to honor my heritage. Said it was important I know where I came from." She dropped her arms and studied the crammed contents of her mother's closet. Where the heck was her box?

She stroked the pendant beneath her button-down. The memory of the day she'd chanced a peek inside the box flashed as clear as the day it had happened. "Mom tried to take my necklace. I told her I lost it and hid it ever since." She shook her head and focused on Ramsay. "It's the only real lie I've ever told."

Well, up until now. Did not sharing her heritage with Ramsay count?

She shoved the hanging clothes aside, checking along the back wall. It had to be here. It had always been here.

"Something wrong?" Ramsay asked.

"It's gone."

Ramsay stepped in closer and checked both sides. "What's it look like?"

"Dark brown wood. There was a horse carved in the top. Beautiful. With wings like Pegasus."

Ramsay spun, his eyes sharper even than the night they'd first met. He opened his mouth to speak.

"Trinity?" Her mother's high-pitched voice rang from the kitchen and the back door slapped shut.

Ramsay snapped to attention. "Your mother?"

She nodded and dove back into her search, shifting and tossing boxes off the shelf and onto the bed behind her. It had to be here. It was hers. All she had of wherever she'd come from.

"What are you doing?"

Trinity spun at her mother's shrill voice. A sensation she couldn't quite name rushed from the depths of her stomach to clog her throat. Fury. That was it. Hard, cold, choking fury.

Her mother scowled at Ramsay, seemingly not intimidated by his formidable size and build. "And who are you?"

Trinity lurched between her mother and Ramsay. "Where is it?"

"Where's what?" The words might have been right, even tinged with the necessary amount of innocent intonation, but her fanatical eyes burned with righteous indignation.

"My box," Trinity said.

"Notes and scribbles from the devil, you mean." Carol straightened to the peak of her five-foot frame and flicked a superior glance over Trinity's shoulder at Ramsay. "I turned them in."

Trinity inched closer. "Turned them in to who?"

"The authorities," her mother said. "You saw the mark they found on those videos. It matches the one on the box. I might have been willing to harbor a child in the name of saving a soul, but I won't protect someone who might cause God-fearing people harm."

"What the hell is she talking about?" Ramsay's low voice rumbled behind her, his anger a nearly palpable presence at her back.

"She thinks I'm evil," Trinity answered.

"What else could you be?" A mottled flush spread across her cheeks, and her skinny frame shook with an eerie kind of energy. "Only a child of Satan would be able to predict the things you do. To warn of her own father's death. What type of being can't touch another human soul?"

"That box was mine." All the long-stuffed loneliness and suffering lumbered its way from the pit of Trinity's stomach, punching and clawing until her insides roiled with nausea. "I lived with you. Supported you when your family and normal friends abandoned you. Never once disobeyed you. And you give away the only thing I had that was really mine? What is wrong with you?"

"I'm a virtuous Christian woman."

"You're so far past Christianity, most churches are terrified to see you sitting in their pews." Trinity whipped around to Ramsay. "We're going."

She stomped out the door, Ramsay's firm footsteps behind her.

"I know my calling." Carol's voice trailed them. "I'll do the Lord's work no matter the cost."

Trinity snatched her purse and keys off the sofa and strode toward the front door. She needed air and about fifty miles between her and her mother's toxic bullshit. "I'm glad you're so strong in your convictions, Mother, because they just cost you the only family you had left."

She swung the door open.

Ramsay pulled her to a stop. "We need that box," he said low enough only Trinity would hear.

She snapped her gaze to her mother, who hovered at the edge of the living room. "Where is it?"

Carol shook her head, the zealous gleam in her eyes enough to make Trinity's stomach heave. "With the authorities where it needs to be. They've got your contact information as well, though for your sake, I asked they handle matters with as much discretion as possible."

"For my sake?" What kind of mother not only threw away her child's history, but tossed her to the wolves of public scrutiny in the name of religion? And Trinity had given up how much of her life trying to stand by her? "You mean for your sake. Heaven forbid people find out you've been harboring evil spawn all these years, right?"

Trinity looked at Ramsay. "That memory thing you do. Does it hurt?"

Ramsay shook his head. She'd swear his entire being swelled to that of a giant prepared to attack. Protective and lethal all in one package.

Trinity shut the door, blocking out the early evening sun, and crossed her arms. "Then do it."

CHAPTER 17

*R*amsay squeezed the steering wheel so hard it was a wonder the reinforced plastic didn't snap. The world sped by around them, Trinity's Accord not at all prepared for the punishment of the man driving it.

Trinity stared out the passenger's side window, her profile troubled and strained, her thumb shuttling back and forth along her lower lip.

He'd never wanted to gut a woman before. Not until he'd blasted through Carol Blair's memories.

Praise The Great One. The things Trinity had endured. No touch. Her father's death. The vilest emotional abuse dressed up with the pretense of decency and love. Yet, Trinity was still Trinity. Good. Sweet and considerate.

The steering wheel groaned beneath his torturing grip. He turned onto Trinity's block and took another calming breath. "Tell me about the premonitions."

Her thumb stilled.

"Surely you can't think the concept would surprise me," he said. "Not with the things I've shown you in the last twenty-four hours."

She clasped her hands in her lap. "I wouldn't say I predict things. I just get a nasty buzz in the back of my head when something important is about to happen." She glanced up at him, the hurt in her eyes so fierce and sharp it pierced his heart. "Hardly something to mark me as a child of Satan."

He zipped her car into the driveway and killed the engine. The sudden silence held a tangible weight. "It could be a sign you're Myren."

Her lips tightened and she reached for the door handle.

Ramsay pried himself from the car and met her as she hurried up the sidewalk. "Lexi had something similar. Her intuition was strong her whole life. Turns out one of her gifts is emotional empathy." He stopped her at the apartment complex door. "There aren't many seers in Eden, but there are a few. Maybe that's your thing."

Trinity shrugged him off and swung the door open. "You need to let it go."

Like histus he would. Why wouldn't she even consider it? Lexi had fired right up to the idea. Or at least she had after they'd convinced her she wasn't in a drug-induced coma and imagining the whole thing. Then again, Trinity had spent her life with a mother accusing her of being evil. Maybe Trinity was afraid to accept anything that seemed supernatural as a birthright.

For the time being, he followed her up the outer-staircase. Two wall sconces cast a cool white glow against the foyer's stock gray paint. Inside her unit, a single light burned above the kitchen sink, the rest of the place sinking into night's shadows.

Trinity tossed her keys onto the counter, and the clatter of metal on concrete jolted the quiet. She snagged the unfinished bottle of red from the night before and yanked the cork free with unnecessary force.

Seeing her like this, raw and angry, seemed to cross every

synapse in his mind and body until all he could process were sharp, needling shocks. "I need to thank you," he said.

Trinity hesitated mid-reach for a wine glass. "For what?"

"For offering your mom's memories." He slipped behind her and gripped her shoulders. The contact calmed him. Not enough to wash the sensations away entirely, but enough his lungs found a solid rhythm. "Your journal may tell us what we need to know about the prophecy."

She poured two glasses and re-stoppered the bottle. "You don't have to thank me. I told you I'd help." Her voice was cold and flat. Distant.

He gave her time to take a good, healthy drink, turned her to face him, and pulled the glass from her hand. "We'll get your box, Trinity." He set the wine aside and wrapped her up tight, guiding her head to his chest while he stroked the length of her spine. "Jagger and Ludan are already on their way to the police station. They'll grab your stuff and meet us back here and no one will be the wiser."

She shoved his chest, not enough to actually make head-way, but enough to meet his eyes. "They can't do that. You've got enough problems with the press."

So sweet. Always thinking about everyone else. Even the ones who'd abused her soul. "The masking, remember? We're pretty good with locks too, if we know where they are." He tapped his temple. "Telekinesis has its benefits."

He tucked her head so it rested against his sternum. "Trust me, as long as the place isn't up to Fort Knox standards, it'll be no big deal. Until then, you and I will hole up here and take some time to recoup."

"I missed so much," she whispered against his chest. Her fingers dug into his back, almost desperate. "I did everything she asked. Walked and talked the way she said was right. Lived a life so far removed from the world it's a wonder anyone knows I exist. And for what?" She looked at him.

Pain radiated from her nearly black eyes. "I missed everything."

He cupped the back of her head, barely couching the need to fist the soft strands. He wanted to roar. Fight. Tear someone or something into tiny bits if it would rip that look off her face. "We'll make up for it," he said instead. "All of it."

Her expression shifted, one second lost and agonized, the next as resolute as a man braced for war. She licked her lips. "I still haven't had sex."

The Great One be praised. His cock took note and hardened so fast it was a wonder he kept his feet. "I gathered," he choked out, his voice apparently impacted by the rush of blood to his dick as well.

She tightened her arms around him, crushing those perfect tits of hers against his chest. "I want to fix that."

Fuck.

"I want to feel more. Do more." She gripped his neck and urged him toward her mouth. "Please."

Her plea fluttered against his lips a second before he caved and kissed her.

God, but he loved her taste, the rich wine on her tongue mixed with her own unique flavor. He pinned her against the countertop, greedy for more, angling her with hands at either side of her head for his assault.

Trinity gasped into his mouth and gripped his shoulders.

Slow, dumbass. She's had a shit day.

He rested his forehead against hers and fought to calm his breath. If his brother or Ludan saw him now, they'd never let him live it down. The best living strategist for their race, thrown off kilter by a barely-five-foot ray of sunshine.

He stroked her cheekbone. Her jawline. Peppering each stroke with easy kisses.

"You don't have to be soft with me."

Oh, histus, yes he did. She'd suffered enough today.

Suffered enough her whole life. She deserved to be cherished. Not thrown on the kitchen counter and taken wild. "It's your first time. You need soft."

"Is that how you'd be with other women? Soft?"

Ramsay gripped her chin. "I won't ever be with you the way I am with anyone else. Ever." The sooner she understood the distinction the better.

Her head jerked back as if he'd slapped her. She shoved his shoulders and wiggled free, then stomped toward her room. "God, I'm an idiot. Not good enough for my mother. Too Goody Two-Shoes for you. Figures."

He shot across the room so fast the lamp perched on her end table wobbled and the blinds rattled against the window jam. He spun her to face him, the hunger he'd kept in check fighting its way past all his barricades. "I think you misunderstood."

Trinity took a cautious step back.

Something inside him snarled at her response. He wrestled his instincts and kept his hands to himself. "If you want edgy and raw, I'll give it to you. I'll hold you down, fill your ears with every fucking dirty word I can come up with, and push your boundaries until you fly, but there will never be anything between us as empty as what I felt with other women."

The world around him stopped. The import of his words slammed into his soul as hard as one of Ludan's right hooks.

Shit.

She'd never be like anyone else. Couldn't be.

Mine.

His muscles unlocked, every fiber in his body unwinding in a liberating stretch. A wild animal freed from a cage it hadn't even known existed. Powerful. Fucking invincible.

"You shouldn't say things like that." Trinity's voice shook. "We set boundaries and you're crossing them. You're supposed to be teaching me, not toying with my head and my emotions."

"Boundaries." He stalked her, every one of his steps forward answered with a backward step of her own, herding her through the living room. "You're absolutely right. I think we need to clarify."

The hallway shadows closed around them.

He shifted, steering her into her room without so much as a touch. Another step. Then another, the bed looming behind her. He flicked the small bedside lamp alight with his mind.

"You're scaring me." Trinity's legs met the mattress.

"Do you think I'd hurt you?"

Her mouth opened on a tiny O. "N-no."

He palmed her nape, massaging her tense muscles. It was either that or wrench her head back and claim her perfect lips. "No, I won't." He sampled the column of her neck, licking and sucking a path up along her jawline, freeing the buttons down the front of her prim pink shirt.

"I'll tell you what I will do." He pushed the crisply starched shirt off her shoulders and unlatched her matching bra with just a thought. He pulled the sweet lace and silk number free and tossed it aside. The pendant that had drawn them together hung heavy between her breasts, dark filigree against creamy skin. "I'll devour every glorious inch of your body, and I'll keep at it until you don't know where you end and I begin."

"Ramsay." She gripped his shoulders and tried to pull him close, her nipples hard and practically begging for his touch.

He nudged her off balance so she fell back onto the bed and made quick work of her tailored brown slacks, sliding them and her panties down her trembling legs and thumbing her prim pumps off in the process. "Scoot back, Sunshine."

She hesitated, one hand fluttering to rest between her breasts.

"You said you wanted to feel." He pulled his T-shirt off and threw it to the floor, his muscles twitching with anticipation, craving the contact of her soft, giving body. "Stretch out for me. Show me you're ready."

She pushed toward the head of the bed, her arms shaking and her eyes wide with a mix of passion and uncertainty.

The minute her head hit the pillow, he stroked an invisible touch along the inside of her wrists, lifting her arms until they rested at either side of her head, and pinned them in place.

"Ramsay?" So much said with just his name. Apprehension. Innocence. Hunger.

"Shhh." His cock throbbed, hard and straining with the single-minded focus of sliding home. He mirrored the calming stroke at her wrists along her hips, warming the air and guiding it in a sensual slide against her skin as he shed the rest of his clothes.

Trinity arched into the warm gust. Her eyes slid closed and her legs parted a fraction. Welcoming, yet hesitant.

"Look at me." He crawled onto the bed and nudged her legs apart with his knees, soothing the inside of her thighs with his hands.

Her eyelids fluttered open and her breath caught. Her gaze locked on his raging erection before snapping to his eyes.

"You wanted to talk boundaries, so let's talk." He leaned over her, one hand anchored in the mattress beside her and the other splayed across her belly. "I don't want any."

She gasped. "What?"

He cupped her breast and teased the tight skin with his thumb. "I plan to knock down every last resistance and fill every decadent craving you've got. I'll be the one to teach you, the only one, but my fuck buddy days are over."

Beneath his palm, her heart hammered and her sweet breath fluttered across his face. Breathless. Vulnerable. "I don't understand."

His.

"I'm saying I don't want distance." He pressed his hips against hers, giving her his weight and rocking his shaft through her wet folds.

So close. Almost home. Exactly where he needed to be. "I want what's mine."

Trinity's breath hitched then froze in her chest. Every inch of her burned, straining for more of his wicked touch, craving the fullness he promised but stopped just short of giving.

He wanted her. Not just sex, but her. Trinity Blair. The bookworm who'd always kept to the corners. The woman who didn't have a clue how to touch or seduce a man outside of a *Cosmo* article.

"You're thinking too much." He nipped her earlobe, the delicious rumble of his voice vibrating in all the right places. He pinched her nipple and a ripple fired through her belly straight to her sex.

Her hips flexed into his and the muscles at her core contracted. God, she wanted him. Every hard inch, fast and deep. "Please, Ramsay."

"Please, what?" He shifted again, the wide head of his shaft slicking through her wetness, so close to the sweet contact she ached for, then gliding up and teasing her clit. "Please fill you up? Take your sweet pussy and claim you?"

A short squeak eked past her lips. The muscles in her

abdomen spasmed and her thighs squeezed his hips, trying to keep him in place, to urge him on...something. Anything to ease the pounding need.

"Say it, Sunshine," he muttered against her mouth, the sound of his voice as grated and broken as what was left of her thoughts. "Tell me who you belong to, and I'll give you want you want."

So dangerous. Her mind grappled and clawed, trying to find a little reason to cling to. To keep from tipping out of balance and exposing her heart to his blistering fire. Her body sang, every inch of her skin prickling with heightened intensity, her core desperate for the connection he withheld.

Destiny is what you make it.

Her father's last words rattled through every fiber of her being. Caution lost its grip and her spirit unfolded. Her eyes snapped open.

Silver eyes blazed wild and bright into hers, flecks of white sparking almost neon around the edges. "Say it," he demanded, his hand moving between them to guide his cock into place.

Live.

Feel.

Love.

"I'm yours." The words escaped, releasing with them a rush of emotion so powerful every vein pulsed as though charged with lightning.

He gripped her hip, pinning her in place, and smiled as only a triumphant predator could. "Damn right."

He surged forward in one bold thrust.

A ragged, nearly inhuman cry shook the room. Hers. And God, didn't that make sense. The sensation was perfect. Her sex full, stretched to the point of near-discomfort, and yet the most incomparable pleasure.

Slowly, he pulled back, then powered home. Then again.

And again. Slow. Hard. Slow. Hard. A wicked, sensual rhythm that marked her very soul.

Wet, exquisite heat surrounded her nipple, followed by an erotic tug. His cheeks hollowed as he sucked, and his dark hair spilled against her skin.

She moaned and fisted the smooth strands with both hands, anchoring him in place.

He shifted to her other breast. Plumping the mound he'd left behind, he flicked his tongue across the untouched peak. His narrow, deliciously defined hips undulated between her thighs.

He lifted his head and straightened the arm beside her, raking his gaze down her torso and locking where their bodies joined. "Look at us, Sunshine." He pistoned with long, steady strokes, his abdominals flexing and contracting in the most carnal display of physical perfection. His focus was singular, angling each stab to scrape the sweet spot inside her. "Do you have any idea how fucking tight your pussy is around my cock? How hot? Every time I hit the end of you, your walls ripple and tease me with how good it will be when you come."

His gaze met hers. His long hair fell around either side of his face and his eyes burned with an intensity she felt all the way to her toes. An avenging God staking his claim. He circled her clit with his thumb, up one side and down the other, and his mouth tilted in a wicked grin. "I want to feel it, Trinity." Another circle, each thrust more powerful than the last. "Call me a greedy bastard, but I want to feel it, and I want to feel it now."

Unseen fingers cupped and kneaded her breasts, squeezing her nipples. She arched into the hedonistic touch, chasing the zing that shot between her legs.

He speared deep and pinched her clit.

Every muscle locked up tight, the walls of her pussy

contracting in a rapturous pulse that matched the pounding rhythm of her heart.

His shout rang out, ragged and victorious. His hips slammed against hers, seating him flush against her sex.

She rode the sensations, flexing and fisting around him. Luxuriating in the frenetic jerks of his cock and the unsteady shake of his arms as he held himself above her.

This was life at its most primitive. Ideal and without parallel. And Ramsay had given it to her, drawing out pieces of herself she'd never known existed. Dark. Carnal. Spiritu.

The aftermath of her climax billowed up and embraced her, relaxation and sleep mixing with Ramsay's languid kisses along her shoulder and neck.

Slow and easy, he worked his cock inside her. Lazy, intimate strokes. His chuckle rumbled in her ear. "Love the way you get sleepy after you come. Like a kitten hopped up on warm milk."

That was nice. She did feel a bit like a kitten, only he scratched her itch in far more delicious places. All she needed now was a window ledge and she could snuggle in for a nap.

He brushed his lips against hers and answered the thought before it fully registered. "Let go, Sunshine. I'll be here when you wake up."

CHAPTER 18

So warm. Safe. Trinity nestled closer to Ramsay, reveling in her early morning haven and drifting between sleep and wakefulness. Hot skin. Cool sheets. Arms wrapped around her and a firm chest beneath her cheek. Perfect.

She inhaled deep, filling her lungs with his warm, elusive scent. He wanted her. Said he wanted to claim her. Whatever that meant. And she'd slept without her ear buds again, the same as every other time he'd held her. Strange the way he kept her Spiritu buzz at bay with nothing more than his presence.

Ramsay's breath fluttered against her hair. A girl could easily get addicted. Heck, if she was honest, she was already halfway gone. What if she was reading everything he'd said wrong? What if it was all a ruse to get her in bed?

But that didn't make sense. She'd asked him, more like begged him, to get between the sheets. So, maybe what he'd said was genuine.

And here you are lying to him.

The thought yanked her out of her post-sleep haze and dropkicked her heart into overdrive.

Ramsay flinched, shot upright, and tugged the sheet up to her shoulders, gaze locked on the hallway.

The front door opened.

He rolled out of bed and snatched his jeans off the floor. He was fastening the last few buttons when a huge man walked into her room. "Praise The Great One, Ludan, you ever think of knocking?"

Another man came up behind the stranger. This one she recognized from the club.

"Hi, Jagger." Well, that sounded a bit lame. Kind of pip-squeaky and not at all befitting of what was probably a wicked case of bed head and tousled sheets.

Jagger grinned.

The stranger studied her with a curious, but still lethal gaze. "No time to knock. Need to get your woman up and gone."

"Kinda rough to do that with you two ogling her in the doorway." Ramsay tugged his T-shirt down, grabbed his boots, and settled at the foot of the bed. "You fuckers wanna give her a minute and wait in the living room, or would you rather I pry your eyeballs out with my pinky?"

With a smile as big as Texas, Jagger tipped his chin, and headed for the front room.

Ludan barely managed a smirk, but followed suit.

The second the men were out of the doorway, the door swung closed on its own.

"The whole moving objects thing is going to take some getting used to." She scrambled and gathered up her clothes. "Who's the scary guy? And what's he talking about me leaving?"

"Ludan. Eryx's somo. Bodyguard in the human language.

Though most of the time he's just a grumpy pain in the ass. You already know Golden Boy."

Trinity shimmied into her favorite pair of jeans and tugged a T-shirt from her top dresser drawer. "You call Jagger Golden Boy?"

"Have you looked at him?"

Trinity paused midway into her shirt. Gold hair, gold eyes, and a tan so rich it might as well be gold. "Well, okay, I guess that makes sense, but what about the me getting gone part?"

"Think that means the press is on to what your mom shared with the cops." Ramsay stood and pointed to her closet. "Grab some shoes. Something comfortable."

Going by the men's attire, she nabbed the pair of cute black ankle boots she'd bought a few weeks ago but still hadn't had a good excuse to wear, and followed Ramsay into the living room.

"You couldn't head home and link me?" Ramsay said to Ludan.

Ludan stood with arms crossed near the door. He jerked his head toward the street. "Need to move. Got the box, but had to stir the pot to do it. Press was there and her name's been leaked. Pics too. Already got a good crowd outside."

Stationed at the window, Jagger eased the blinds back into place. "Two more crews just pulled up."

"I give it ten minutes, tops, before the cops are here," Ludan said. "Our commotion didn't last long. Cops had already figured out the box was missing when we left. No doubt they're gonna check here first."

Ramsay zigzagged a glare between Jagger and Ludan. "What the fuck did you do, Ludan?"

Ludan shrugged. "Got the box. Had to start a little fire in the stairwell to get their eyeballs off it."

"Damn it!" Ramsay paced to the window and peeked through the blinds.

Damn it, indeed. Cops and TV crews didn't sound positive, but they got the box. The least she could do was thank the guy and introduce herself. She stepped forward and held out her hand to Ludan. "Thanks for helping us. I'm Trinity."

He eyed her for a minute and the smirk he'd thrown her from the hallway inched up into something both sexy and terrifying. He took her hand, the size of it encompassing hers in a way that made her feel two instead of twenty-three. "Ludan."

She pulled her hand away and rubbed it on her hip. "So, um, where exactly am I supposed to go?"

"Could take her to Ian's place," Jagger said to Ramsay and Ludan. "Lay low and get a read for how far the press reaches."

Ramsay shook his head and faced the men. "Nope. All the affiliates are here already. Tulsa's slow to pick up on stories, but not that slow. Better to take her home where we know she can't be tracked."

"Home as in your home?" Trinity stomped to the window. "I can't go there. You said humans are a no-no."

Two vans, a mid-sized SUV, reporters, all strung out on her lawn.

Ramsay spun her around. "For all we know you're Myren. You show all the signs."

"I'm not Myren!"

Everything in her apartment wrenched to a standstill. She'd swear even the clock on the wall with its purely cosmetic pendulum hesitated a beat. She hurried to the kitchen. Coffee would be good. Surely they had time for coffee before they turned her whole world upside down.

Ramsay stalked in behind her. "What aren't you telling me?"

Trinity pushed a filter into place and shoved the plastic holder back into place. She needed a minute. Okay, more like five minutes. A little time to catch her breath.

"There's something else, isn't there?" Ramsay said from behind her. "More than just funny feelings when something big's about to happen."

Trinity ducked her head and tried to pull a decent amount of air into her suddenly very tight lungs. "I'm afraid to tell you, all right?" She fisted her hands on the counter, the pressure behind her heart so big it was a wonder the thing didn't quit altogether. "I want to. Believe me, after everything you've shared with me, I want to."

"Why can't you?" He steered her to face him. "I'm a pretty reasonable man. What could possibly be so bad you can't tell me?" He moved close and lowered his voice. "I can't help you if you don't give me the facts."

Voices from the crowd outside filtered through the window.

He hated the Spiritu. He'd never used those exact words but his tone pretty much screamed it. She'd been a fool to let go with him. To believe the things he'd said the night before. The minute she told him the truth, he'd hate her, like he did the rest of her race.

If it changes everything, was he worth your heart to begin with?

All the fight in her, all the tension, deflated. He'd been good with her. Honest. The least she could do was give him the same. "You told me yesterday about the Rebellion. How the Spiritu helped them. You made it pretty clear you don't trust them at all."

Ramsay laughed. Not a happy laugh, but a disgusted one. "No one trusts the Rebellion. They're a bunch of damned sociopaths who think humans were born to be slaves."

"I wasn't talking about the Rebellion." God this hurt. The minute she opened her mouth she'd be alone again. Even more so now with the loss of her mother. Who knew when Kazan would be back. "I was talking about the Spiritu."

Ramsay frowned.

Ludan and Jagger crept into her periphery.

Trinity swallowed, the process turning into more of a choked cough. "I was afraid to tell you because I'm human." She pulled in a deep breath and closed her eyes, praying for some kind of salvation. "But I'm also part Spiritu."

HUNDREDS OF BATTLES and countless sparring sessions, and never once had Ramsay taken a sucker punch like Trinity's. And she hadn't even lifted a finger to do it.

Behind him, Ludan and Jagger were as slack-jawed as he'd been. "You don't think telling me a little earlier you're Spiritu might have been a good idea?"

"I couldn't." Trinity took a quick step forward, registered the look on his face, and jerked back again. "I mean, I didn't think I could at first. I didn't know you knew about them and revealing their race would've made my dad's life forfeit."

"I thought your dad was dead."

For a second she looked confused, then she shook her head. "Not my adopted father. He died in a car accident like I told you. I mean my real father, Kazan. The Spiritu. It took a dispensation from the Black King before he could even reveal himself to me. The only reason the king allowed that much was because of how crazy Carol became after David died."

"And after you learned we already knew about them?"

"You made it pretty clear you don't like them." Trinity ducked her head. "At that point I was afraid you'd lump me in with everyone else."

"So your dad's a rogue?"

Her head snapped up, a defensive fire burning in her dark eyes. "I don't know about any rogues, but my dad's not one of them. He's a Black. Passionate. Indulgent, maybe, but not evil. And by the way, judging a whole race based on a few bad seeds is no different than lumping all Myrens in with the Rebellion."

The growing sound of voices and the steady purr of engines from the street rumbled through the windows.

Trinity met Ludan and Jagger's stares one by one then finally landed on his. "I'm sorry." She lifted her chin, but her lower lip trembled. "I was scared. I was trying to process it. To figure out what to do. Then we had our run-in with my mom and came back here..."

Oh, yeah. When they'd come back there and he'd gone hell bent for leather for someone giving him only half-truths. Even without her deceit he'd never really know how much of what he felt was genuine and how much she'd manufactured in his head. "The touching, that part of you being Spiritu?"

Trinity nodded. "When I touch someone, I get a blast of what they're thinking. What's immediately impacting their lives." She crossed her arms and trembled as though the temperature in the room had dropped twenty degrees. "Nine times out of ten it's not something anyone wants to see."

"But not with me," he said.

"No, not with you." Her gaze slid to his men behind him. "Not with any of you. I'm guessing it's because you're Myren."

Well, that was good at least. He felt violated enough. The last thing he needed was her knowing how far down she'd pulled him. "Can you influence people like the rest of them can?"

"You see? This is why I didn't say anything," she said. "You talk about us like we're contagious. And we don't influence.

Those who've accepted their powers offer thought. Ideas. Inspiration. Any being's will is completely uninhibited."

"But they can be bent." Ludan's deep voice shot through the her tirade, his eyes on Ramsay. "The rogue at the deal in North Texas took Serena's will and stabbed Maxis."

Trinity sighed and dropped her hands. "If they can, I don't know how. I didn't even know rogues existed until Ramsay told me. My dad rarely talks about his world other than to try to get me to accept my gifts, which I don't want. If I did, I'd be hooked into their hive mind, which freaks me out. Plus, I didn't want to leave my mom alone." She huffed out a bitter chuckle and fisted her hair at the top of her head. "Though in hindsight I'd say that wasn't wise."

A siren chirped outside the building.

Jagger strode to the window and checked between the blinds. "Cops are here. We gotta make a move and do it quick."

Ramsay flexed and clenched his fists over and over. All this time he'd been so convinced she was Myren. Didn't it figure he'd finally wrap himself around the idea he'd found someone, only to get smacked sideways in the process.

"It's okay." Trinity motioned to the box perched on the counter and headed to the hallway off the living room. "You guys take the box. I'll be fine." She all but growled the last bit. Her tone implied she referred to more than just answering questions from the cops and shoving through a bunch of frenzied reporters.

Ludan snatched up the box and paused by the front door. "We've got enough bad press without adding cops to the mix. Let's move."

Jagger watched by the window and waited.

Damn her. And damn her race with their meddlesome thoughts. Ramsay strode to the door and reached for the knob.

Kind of the pot calling the kettle black, aren't you?

He froze, the metal against his palm as cold as the idea of leaving her alone to deal with the mess he'd created. Hadn't he done pretty much the same thing to her? Going for information without being honest up front? Would she have come clean if the whole snafu with the cops hadn't bubbled up?

He stomped down the hall toward her room.

Empty, but a ragged exhale sounded from her office. He followed the sound and found her braced with both arms on her desk, eyes locked on the picture of her adopted parents.

He whirled her around and gripped her shoulders. "I'm going to go home, spar, and beat the fuck out of Ludan or Jagger until I can breathe without wanting to break something. Then you and I are going to have a very long talk." He pried his hands free and took a step back, leaving a path to the doorway. "You can walk, or I can throw you over my shoulder, but either way, you're going to Eden."

CHAPTER 19

*S*erena drummed her fingers on her father's desk and studied his collection of liquors across the room. Crystal decanters filled with the finest Myren and human spirits, all neatly arranged on a mahogany bar, with vintage red wines angled in the racks below. She'd more than earned a drink. Several, really. Between almost being discovered slipping back into Sanctuary and Uther's ultimatum, sleep would be a long time coming. A little boost before she went to bed wouldn't be a bad idea.

But not until she talked to Thyrus, wherever he was.

She checked the sun's position. Only thirty minutes since she'd sent for him. Barely enough to leave his house, let alone fly across the capital. This late at night, she'd be lucky if he answered at all.

Rows of leather-bound books in jeweled colors stretched beside the bar, most as crisp in their coloring as the day they'd been purchased, their spines barely even cracked, if at all. A show of sophistication more than academia. Unless, of course, it pertained to economics.

Well-worn, crimson journals lined a shorter row of

shelves behind her father's desk. The Great One only knew what secrets they held.

A knock sounded and Serena's heart leapt. "Enter."

The door clicked opened and their butler stepped into the library. His towering frame curled forward at the shoulders, his wiry, thinning hair more disheveled than normal. "The solicitor, Thyrus Monrolla, to see you."

Thyrus lumbered into the room and angled toward the desk. He might have been out of breath, but his voice sounded not at all disturbed. "Your messenger said you had an urgent issue?"

Perhaps being summoned at all hours of the night was the norm in his line of work. Then again, she was compensating him for his time, and probably at an inflated rate. She settled back into her father's chair. "I need access to the sacred archives."

With a mangled tablet halfway free from his bag, Thyrus looked up. "The sacred archives?" His eyebrows lifted so high it was a wonder they didn't smack his hairline. He stuffed his tablet back in the bag and harrumphed so forcefully a loose parchment fluttered to the floor. "If I'd known that's what you were after, I could have saved us both some time and trouble. Only ellan and the royal family have access to those records."

"I'm well aware of that. Unfortunately, my house arrest makes it such that you're the only person I can reach out to without raising suspicions, and I need in those archives to protect myself."

"To what end? The malran's solicitor mentioned Eryx's concerns and his visit. He also admitted your memories proved insubstantial. There's no need for you to go digging around in ancient texts." Thyrus peered down his nose at her. "As a side note, that was a terribly foolhardy move. I should be present for all such scans. My gifts and my status ensure the malran or those acting on his behalf keep to the time in question, and particularly far away from memories of our private conversations."

Shit. She'd forgotten about those.

"I wouldn't concern yourself." He buckled the worn leather briefcase and tugged the flap tight. "The malran might not favor our race leading those lesser than us, but he usually acts with honor. I doubt he'd take action he couldn't hold up to public scrutiny."

Ah, but Eryx hadn't been the one to look. Ludan had. And Ludan didn't give a damn about scruples or public sentiment. Particularly when it came to her. What had she and Thyrus spoken of in recent days? Surely Ludan hadn't been able to get the full breadth of their conversations with such brief contact.

Thyrus hefted his briefcase and turned to go.

"I still need the records. Translation tablets for our mother tongue. As far back as you can get them."

He bumbled to a stop and faced her. "I've already told you. We can't—"

"Contact Angus. If anyone can get in, he can. You've sold him on our ideas before. Maxis even went so far as to say he doubted anyone else could have lured Angus into our fold as eloquently as you did." Nothing wrong with slathering Thyrus' ego while she was at it.

"Those documents aren't supposed to leave the sacred halls. If Angus is caught taking them past the front doors, he'd either be ejected from the council entirely or worse. Particularly with the bad blood between him and the malran. Even Maxis couldn't have sold Angus on such a risk."

"Not even if those texts pushed Eryx off the throne?" Serena stood and paced the room. She trailed her hand along the books beside her. "I don't need everything. Only a few. The oldest he can find. If he's smart about it, no one would be the wiser. For all I care, he can smuggle the damned things back as soon as we're done."

"We?"

Damn. If she didn't get a grip on her emotions and thoughts, she'd end up hanging herself long before she reached her goals.

"Uther," she said. "He's got information we may be able to use against the malran, but it's in the old tongue." A vague enough statement to stir Thyrus and Angus' interest. Not enough to admit she hadn't actually laid eyes on said leverage. "Speaking of which, I need a few of our warriors. Two you're sure are loyal to the Rebellion."

Thyrus shook his head and crossed his arms. Barely. Hard to get a grip when you had to fight so much girth. "I'd have better luck convincing Angus to help us. The malran's proclaimed all Rebellion men who surrender and offer what information they know will gain leniency. All the ones with a shred of common sense have taken him up on it. I'm not sure there's a Rebellion man to be found at this point."

Fantastic. An opportunity to unseat Eryx and she had a whopping army of none. She tapped her fingernail against the bookcase. There had to be a way to figure out what Uther was up to. Even with her piss-poor masking skills, she'd give combing his home a try if she could make it past the front door.

She'd deal with that task after she got this one under control. Four days was all she had to get her hands on the texts before Uther came calling. "Fine. Work on Angus and see what he can do." She strolled back to her father's desk and made herself at home in his well-worn chair. "One way or another, I'll make sure it's worth his risk."

❧

HOLY COW. If Walt Disney could see Trinity now, he'd have put a whole different spin on Future World at Epcot. A cool gray fog surrounded her in a long and comfortably wide tunnel. Diamond-like sparkles glinted in vibrant shades of teal, cotton-candy-pink, and pearlescent white.

Ramsay's hand tightened on her arm as they walked, whether to stop her from gawking or making sure she stayed upright, she wasn't sure. God knew she had a right to swoon. She'd have happily skipped into the mystical portal on a normal day, but Ramsay swishing her out her apartment window and up into the skies like Superman kind of jumbled her insides.

Ludan's deep, almost angry voice behind them seemed blasphemous in the peaceful space. "Eryx know we're coming?"

Ramsay nodded. His jawline strained so hard it would probably snap in two if she so much as tapped it.

The surface beneath her feet shifted from something solid to mushy and inconsequential. She wobbled to the left.

Ramsay clenched her arm harder.

"I could have taken care of myself," she muttered, more embarrassed than angry. If she was bound for public enemy number one in Ramsay's world, she'd at least like to have a little grace in getting there.

A muscle flexed in Ramsay's cheek.

"You've got the box," she said. "You don't need me anymore, so you may as well save yourself the pissed off bit and let me go home."

He jerked to a stop, and Ludan and Jagger halted behind them. He glared at her for all of two seconds, then motioned Ludan and Jagger toward the sparkling darkness at the end of the tunnel.

Jagger rolled his eyes and shook his head, but the men marched on as directed.

Ramsay inched closer, his hand still brutally clamped around her arm. "You think I'm pissed about bringing you to Eden?"

"Oh, so now you want to talk. Well, fine. We'll talk." And then she'd make sure he knew exactly where he could stick it. "What I think is you're mad I didn't tell you about my secret sooner. But if you'd pull your head out of your butt, you'd see it's the same thing you did to me. Only I forgave you. If you're not willing to do the same, then let me go and quit punishing me. I did what I thought I had to do, same as you."

He snapped back and studied her face. "It's not the deception. It's something I'm not even sure you're in control of and not a topic I'm gonna dive into until I know you're safe and I have a chance to clear my head."

"Then do you think you can at least unwind the He-Man grip?" She rolled her shoulder to accent her point. "I can walk fine on my own and I'm not particularly partial to bruises."

Instantly, he loosened his grip and shoved the sleeve of her T-shirt out of the way with the other. "Fuck." His eyes met hers, and his silver gaze darkened to match the tunnel fog. "I'm sorry. I just…" He shook his head and refocused on the bruises already setting up shop. With a tender touch, he traced the patterns left behind on her skin.

A funny tingle filtered into her muscles, followed by a sharp sting and an odd knotting sensation. Like a flu shot, but in reverse.

He let her go and waved toward the end of the tunnel. "I'll follow. If you need me—"

"I'll be fine." She stomped toward the exit. Stupid men and their double standards. She understood she'd hurt him holding back, but what the heck else could she do beyond apologize?

Ugh. She'd think about that later. She had her own issues

to wrap her head around. Ramsay had said Eryx was expecting them, so maybe she'd get to see Lexi again. It'd be nice to have some time to get to know her, especially if they were related. Even better if they'd let her peek in the box and see if there were any mementos from her real family.

Not twenty feet from the tunnel's edge, the fine hairs along her arms and the back of her neck stirred. Almost as if she'd walked into an electrically-charged cloud. Funny, but the air felt cooler too. The kind of chill that invigorated your body and made for perfect campouts and bonfires.

The bruises on her arm pulsed and burned. Not so chilly there.

She inhaled deep, and the crisp bite of grass and something floral whisked through the entrance now a stone's throw away. Two more steps and—

Trinity stumbled onto a soft, yet far more substantial surface.

"Whoa!" Feminine hands reached out to catch her. "Easy."

Lexi. And Eryx stood behind her.

"That's a trickier exit than it looks," Trinity said.

Ramsay cupped her elbow to steady her and a perfunctory thank you queued up on her tongue.

A fat silver streak shot across the sky and wiped the polite comment away along with the rest of her thoughts. Velvet night skies stretched as far as she could see with more of the sparkling streams streaking in random patterns. Even the grass—at least she thought it was grass—sparkled with a kind of metallic sheen.

"You made her walk her first time out?" Lexi asked and aimed a nasty glare at Ramsay.

"I offered to carry her."

"You said I could walk or you'd sling me over your shoulder," Trinity said. "You'll forgive me if I opted for the upright option."

"Christ, Ramsay what the hell's wrong with you?" Lexi said.

Eryx tugged Lexi against his chest. "Let it be, hellcat." He nodded toward a building in the distance, but kept his gaze locked on Ramsay. "Ludan and Jag are securing the box at the castle. Lexi can get Trinity settled in and give her a tour. Why don't we head to the training grounds?"

Trinity spun in the direction he'd indicated. Her heart leapt a good two inches and she choked on a girlish squeal. A castle. A real, live castle made with soft gray stone and fanciful turrets glowing in the moonshine.

Ramsay barked, "I've got plans with Ludan."

"Not anymore, you don't." Eryx kissed Lexi's temple and nudged her toward Trinity. "I need a full rundown and you're going to give it to me. You want to throw a few swings in the process to pull your ass out of the funk you're in, then you're welcome to try to land them."

Trinity barely stifled a snort. Neanderthals. Every damned one of them. Dizziness rushed in behind the thought, and the spot on her arm throbbed angrily. She must have moved or swayed, because every head snapped in her direction.

Ramsay's eyes narrowed and he stepped toward her. "You okay?"

She waved him off, and opened and closed her fist to stave off the sensation. "I'm fine." More like a little buzzed, but who could blame her under the circumstances? "Go spew your anger somewhere else. Trust me, your prophecy pawn isn't going anywhere soon."

His gaze shot sideways, and his lips mashed together in a way that made her regret her words.

Eryx steered Ramsay away with a hand at his shoulder. The two men were identical in stature, the only difference between them Eryx's nearly barbaric-looking braids, and Ramsay's stiff, angry stride.

In the distance, a wide stone structure spanned about two football fields with flaming torches mounted in regular intervals along the walls.

Trinity rubbed her arm and rolled her shoulder to ease the building tension. She should've trusted her instincts and leveled with him from the start. Yes, he'd screwed up too, but what was the old adage? Two wrongs don't make a right?

"You wanna talk about it?" Lexi said.

Hardly. And even if she wanted to, what would she say? *"Hey, I kept a really big deal under wraps with your family and I shouldn't have? Oh, and I might have messed up something special with a kick ass guy in the process. Oopsie."*

"I'd rather have a bucket of Ben and Jerry's," she said. "But something tells me you don't have grocery stores here."

"Nope, but we have Orla, which is even better." Lexi guided her toward the castle, thankfully choosing the arm that wasn't burning a blue streak up her shoulder and neck. "Now, come on. You can tell me what my idiot briyo did and we'll plot some sort of nasty revenge."

CHAPTER 20

*R*amsay dodged left, barely missing Eryx's roundhouse kick to the head.

Before he could re-center, Eryx jabbed and clipped his jaw.

"Fuck!" Ramsay jumped back and shook his head to clear the lingering rattle. His muscles had bypassed any kind of healthy burn an hour ago and throbbed with a bone deep ache.

"You're distracted," Eryx said between heavy breaths. "Either focus or give it up."

He probably should give it up. They were both drenched in sweat, shirts tossed aside less than thirty minutes into their match, but his mind wouldn't shut the hell up. He staggered back into the game, chin down and hands up. "More."

"Bullshit." Eryx feigned another kick, levitated into a spinning barrel roll over Ramsay's head, and smacked him on the temple before landing in a crouch. "You're too damned stubborn to own what's going on."

The verbal barb pierced deep, stinging worse than the

bitch-slap his brother landed. He lashed out, one kick after another interspersed with ruthless punches. It wasn't Eryx in front of him anymore. It was everything else. A black blur of frustration. The prophecy. Trinity's heartless mother. The Spiritu.

His fist connected with bone, and his vision cleared in time to see his brother's head snap to one side. "Shit."

Eryx leaned over and braced himself with his hands on his knees, and a drop of blood splattered to the sand.

"Eryx—man, I didn't mean—"

Eryx waved him off and straightened, wiping his mouth with the back of his hand, but he was grinning. Lopsided, but grinning, his teeth streaked with more blood. "Thought you'd never get around to that."

Ramsay's thoughts, his breath, even his body shook with a dangerous mix of fatigue and adrenaline scrambling for stability. "I shouldn't have let that out."

"Actually, it's exactly what you should have done, but about an hour earlier." The words were garbled, hindered by what Ramsay suspected was a broken jaw, but there was no missing the message in his tone. "You keep that stuff locked up and it'll ruin you from the inside out." He pressed his palm to his cheek and concentrated on healing the injury Ramsay had caused.

Ramsay spun away, a whole new flavor to his already manic emotions jumping into play. He'd sparred with his brother in one way or another since before they'd been born, but he'd never attacked him like this. His outburst was a complete lack of control. The purest kind of rage, indiscriminate of anything in its path.

The tall stadium wall with its ivory stone spectator benches stretched out on either side of them, an impressive five hundred feet total. Only a handful of torches burned in the center where they'd fought, making the arena seem even older than it really was. How long had it been since they'd had warrior competition just for fun? Bright sunshine pinging off the gold flecks in the sand and stone while spectators cheered on their favorites? Certainly not in the last year. At this rate, he wasn't sure they ever would again.

"Let's go."

Ramsay turned at his brother's sharp and much clearer words.

Eryx shuttled his jaw back and forth, prodded the bone near his chin as though checking his work, and took off for the tunnel leading to the locker rooms. "We need a drink."

"I need to get back to Trinity."

Eryx kept going and snatched his drast from the dirt. "According to Lexi, Trinity went to her room nearly dead on her feet an hour ago, so she doesn't need you." At the entrance, he pegged Ramsay with a warning look. "What you need is to spill whatever crazy thoughts are spinning in your head."

"I'm fine."

"Really? Tell that to the jawbone I just mended. Which, by the way, Galena's gonna be pissed if I screwed up and she has to reset it."

Pissed was putting it mildly. The last time she'd had to do it had been when Ramsay broke his arm and mended it himself. She might not usually show the pain she took on when she healed a person, but experiencing the re-break process with him had been too much to hide.

Ramsay sighed and ambled behind Eryx to the private locker room they shared. His sweat-soaked jeans abraded his skin almost as badly as his jumbled emotions scraped his insides. He'd have hell peeling out of them later. Eryx was damned lucky he'd only have to wrestle off leathers.

189

Dropping into an oversized leather chair, Ramsay glared at the ceiling. A crystal tumbler floated into his line of sight filled nearly to the top with strasse. He grabbed the glass and knocked back a dangerous-sized slug.

"So?" Eryx kicked back behind his desk and propped one foot on the gleaming black surface.

Ramsay shook his head and tried to stifle the burning cough that bubbled up in the strasse's wake. A heck of a lot easier task than wrangling words to make sense of what was in his head. "What do you want me to say?"

"How about owning up to whatever it is that's got you scared shitless?"

"I'm not afraid of anything."

"Said the little boy whistling past the graveyard." Eryx took a much more reasonable-sized drink, his eyes narrowed daringly over the rim. He exhaled loud through his mouth, a kind of fire-breathing necessity brought on by the liquor. "Now be a fucking man and spill it."

Son of a bitch. The end-all taunt between men. Ramsay squeezed the tumbler tighter and the indentations of the crystal pressed into his fingers. Sweat broke out on his neck and forehead. The strasse in his belly lurched toward his throat. "I started to believe in her."

"Yeah, she seems like a pretty straightforward, honest girl."

Ramsay clunked his glass down on the marble table top beside him. "That's not what I meant and you know it."

Eryx grinned back in a way that said, *"I know that's not what you meant, but I'm not making this easier and sayin' it for you."*

Ramsay gripped the leather armrest hard enough the wood frame creaked. "I thought she might be someone permanent."

Silence.

He didn't dare face his brother. Histus, he could barely look at his own thoughts, let alone try to process anyone else's. "I thought she might be mine."

"What makes you think she's not?"

She couldn't be. It hadn't been anything more than a ruse. At least that's what part of him insisted. The rest of him clutched his brother's challenge as permission to move forward. He surged from his chair and paced the spacious room. The cool gray stone beneath his bare feet was a welcome relief against his heat-stifled skin. "She's a damned Spiritu, that's what. They push all kinds of thoughts that aren't your own in your head. How am I supposed to know which thoughts are mine and which are hers?"

"You're shittin' me, right?"

Ramsay halted in front of Eryx. "What? Don't tell me you haven't wondered the same thing since the Spiritu showed up."

"Actually, I haven't. If anything, I kind of liked knowing who to thank for leading me to Lexi." He sipped his drink. "Then again, I can see where you'd be hesitant of anyone who leads you toward an actual relationship with someone outside of me, Galena or Ludan."

"What in histus is that supposed to mean?"

"It means you've lumped everyone except the three of us in the too-dangerous-to-care bucket ever since we were kids. The closest you ever came to stepping beyond that zone was building a friendship with Reese, and you used his deception to refortify those walls."

Ramsay fought to keep his feet still. To keep from flinching or hightailing it somewhere he could lick the deeply covered wounds his brother had ripped open. What he felt didn't have a thing to do with relationships. It was the

Spiritu and the way they muddled with people's heads. Wasn't it?

At one end of the room, the circular stone map of Eden perched on a marble pillar. The thing was at least two thousand years old. His dad had spent hours reviewing the detailed topography with his sons, one of the few times Ramsay actually remembered their father finding time for them.

"Our parents were distant," Eryx said, low and free of judgment. "I felt it the same as you. But not every relationship has to be that way. Not everyone is going to meet you at the same level you want or expect, but that doesn't mean they'll all let you down."

The sentiment ricocheted in his chest, and the hooks and levers that held his carefully structured, carefree life in place snapped free, leaving him flailing without an anchor. He didn't want this. Didn't want to feel this exposed and vulnerable.

The scrape of wood on stone reverberated off the walls, followed by the clink of crystal on the sidebar. He felt more than heard his brother moving closer.

"The Spiritu aren't puppet masters. They're inspiration. Ideas. It's what you do with them that matters." Eryx gripped his shoulder. "If Trinity makes you feel a tenth of the way Lexi makes me feel, then I'd say you could do worse." He let go and left Ramsay alone with the silence and his thoughts.

So much introspection and not one damned scrap of tactic to go on. Between the fighting and the strasse, his body idled in neutral, and his mind did little more than pace in a non-ending loop. The aloneness of the empty training grounds pressurized his body until it hurt to even breathe.

He snuffed the candles with a thought and strode down the long corridor to the outside, desperate for air. For sound or touch.

The moon shone bright above him, the well-worn path to the castle easy to follow. Silver streaks of energy darted bold against velvet night skies. How many times had he walked this same path growing up? Running home, eager to tell or show his mom and dad something, only to find them unavailable? It was always Eryx who'd stepped in to fill the void and cover the loss, putting on a brave face for Ramsay.

A slow breeze buffeted his face and chest, the fresh, clean scent that went with it not unlike waking up next to Trinity. He quickened his pace and took the steps to the terrace two at a time. He could deny the connection he felt with her all he wanted, but it was there. A demanding pulse that thrilled and comforted. Possessive and needy.

And she accepts you just like you are.

The vacant rooms between the castle entrance and his suite blurred past him. Despite every caution and protective barrier he'd built, right now all he wanted was to see her. To know she was safe. Protected.

Still twenty feet away, he opened the door with his mind and a soft pool of candlelight spilled out into the hallway. As he entered, sheer black panels lining the open windows stirred and the twin flames at his bedside fluttered. Trinity's tousled blond hair barely peeked above the covers, the rest of her huddled deep beneath the blankets.

If Trinity makes you feel a tenth of the way Lexi makes me feel, then I'd say you could do worse.

Him. In a relationship like Eryx and Lexi. The idea knocked around in his head, clumsy, but determined. Had he been using the Spiritu as an excuse to hide behind his feelings?

Only silence answered. That and the need to feel Trinity next to him. He could hold her tonight and face his questions in the morning.

He peeled off his still damp jeans and doused the candles.

He owed her an apology too. A big one. Somewhere in the vicinity of groveling might be enough. He pulled back the covers and stopped, letting his eyes adjust to the shadows.

She was still in the clothes she'd worn to Eden and her body was curled into a tight, trembling ball.

He cupped her neck. It was drenched in sweat, as was her back and hair. He rolled her to her back and shook her shoulders. "Trinity, wake up." He re-ignited the candles and lifted each eyelid.

Unresponsive.

He straddled her shaking body and tossed the covers completely off the bed, sending out an urgent call to Eryx and Galena. Damned if he'd wait for them though. He speared his spirit into her body, checking her vitals and organs with an almost instinctive desperation. She'd been fine when they got here. She should be safe with him. Healthy. Able to hand him his ass on a platter.

The door slammed against the stone wall, Eryx's voice ramming home right behind it. "What's wrong with her?"

Galena shoved his shoulder. "Ramsay, move and let me check her."

Ramsay held his ground. Didn't dare move. His spirit too focused on the riotous energy swirling through her torso. The same pattern every other Myren suffered at some point in their life.

"Ramsay!" Galena shouted and slapped his cheek.

He sat back on his heels, hands fisted on his thighs. In the tunnel. The bruises. He'd healed her and not thought a damned thing about it.

"Ramsay, you need to move if you want me to help her."

He shifted to the side of the bed and sucked in a much needed lungful of air. "You need to anchor her."

Galena slid in and pressed her hand against Trinity's forehead. "What?"

"You need to anchor her." He looked back at his brother, comprehension settling into Eryx's face even as shame and terror stomped around in Ramsay's chest. She might not have thought she was Myren, but there was no denying what he'd seen. "I triggered her awakening."

CHAPTER 21

*M*uted, rumbling voices and sharp commands sounded around Trinity. Not at all a fit to the soft white light in he mind's eye and the weightless sensation in her limbs. Kind of like she was dreaming, but still registering the real world all around her. Last she remembered, she'd crawled into Ramsay's bed.

Her body seemed to be situated at a slight incline. Whatever held her upright wasn't a bed. It was too warm for that. Too…powerful.

A body. Strong arms wrapped around her.

Ramsay.

"You've really got him in a tizzy." Kazan's voice jolted loud and clear through her head, though no body accompanied it in her dreamscape.

"Dad?"

"I'm here."

She angled her dream self in all directions, the endless white nothingness almost the same as groping blindly in pitch black. "Where?"

"Doesn't matter." His voice reverberated all around her,

somewhat like a thought, but more concrete. "Just know I'm here and you'll be fine."

"Fine from what?" Where was she, anyway? "Did something happen?"

Kazan's ironic laugh echoed out in all directions. "You could say that."

Blasted men and their attitudes. She'd had enough male posturing in the last twenty-four hours to last her a decade. She tried to wriggle upright, ready to head-butt her dad, Ramsay, or any other man stupid enough to open his mouth.

The dreamscape spun the same way her room had the first time she'd gotten drunk, and a blowtorch heat wave blasted through her torso. "Whoa."

Had she moaned the word out loud? Or only thought it? She could've sworn she'd felt her chest vibrate as she'd said it, followed by the tightening of Ramsay's arms and a string of muffled shouts around her.

Okay, so moving wasn't the smartest idea. She focused on her father's unseen presence and narrowed her thoughts. "What's wrong with me? Tell me what's going on."

She felt more than saw Kazan's spirit shift, an invisible specter her eyes refused to register. "You're mid-awakening."

Mid-what? "I told you I wasn't ready to receive my gifts. I can't. Not right now. Ramsay needs me—"

"Not your Spiritu gifts, sweetheart. Your Myren ones."

Wow. She must have been more exhausted from the trip to Eden than she thought. Even with a direct mind-to-mind convo, her father's comments weren't registering right. "I don't understand."

"You don't understand because you never made it to the information in the box your grandfather left you," Kazan said.

The box. Lexi had offered to take her to it after Trinity finished unloading the details of Ramsay's asinine behavior on the walk back to the castle. She'd bypassed the chance in favor of a good night's sleep, exhaustion and the killer ache in her arm too much to deal with.

Her heart rat-a-tat-tatted about thirty times faster than normal and her strangely weighted torso clenched on a bated breath. "I think it might be a good idea for you to start with the most relevant information and work your way into the details, starting with the grandfather bit."

Kazan's sigh fluttered around her. "You were supposed to find out naturally. It was the agreement I made with the Black King."

"Find out what?"

"I was allowed to share your Spiritu heritage, but you were to learn of your Myren blood as The Great One intended."

Spiritu *and* Myren? God, was there anything human about her? "And?"

"Free will has a tendency to monkey with destiny." A comforting stroke drifted across her cheek, a phantom touch but still comforting. "Don't get me wrong. Destiny never gives up. It circles around until you're ready to own it, but a person's will can keep it at bay longer than necessary."

Even in her detached state, she itched with the need to move and pace, like the motion might somehow speed fitting all the pieces together. "But we got the box. We were going to study it."

"And Ramsay healed your arm. He thought you were only half human and half Spiritu. The action triggered your awakening."

The bruise from his grip in the tunnel. The burn she'd felt afterward. By the time she'd fallen into bed, it radiated through her torso, alongside a case of fatigue so deep she wasn't sure how late she'd sleep.

Her father's spirit shifted. "Honestly, if I couldn't see the fear in Ramsay's eyes right now and the way he's holding you cradled against him, I'd beat him black and blue."

Quiet stretched long and loud in her dreamscape. In the real world beyond the white, the voices steadied and a soft, calming stroke registered at her shoulders. "He's afraid?"

"Very." Kazan didn't even try to hide the pleasure in his voice. "They don't know what they're working with and Ramsay's too damned stubborn to let his Spiritu in to help."

Well, that wasn't surprising. Ramsay didn't appear to be interested in letting anyone in. Or when he was, he found the fastest escape hatch he could find. That wasn't her problem though. Right now she needed to get through whatever his insta-band-aid trick had started. "Am I going to be okay?"

"You'll be fine," he said. "Another two or three hours and you'll be able to play with your new powers. I'm holding the pain away while you transition. A whole lot better than even Ramsay's healer sister could have done for you by the way."

"If I'm awakening my Myren gifts, does that mean I can't ever accept my Spiritu gifts?"

"It's still possible, but to embrace both, to live in their world and see their futures as they unfold without guiding them unduly? I wouldn't wish that for you, sweetheart. Keeping guidance from you all these years has been the worst kind of torture. The only thing that held me back was knowing you'd have no one to truly be there for you." He paused.

The pregnant silence practically flashed a neon sign for her attention.

"You have someone now though, don't you?" he said.

Did she? Ramsay promised they'd talk once he got his head clear, but who knew if it would actually happen. For all she knew he was only saying that to get away from her. "I'm not so sure about that. Not anymore."

A comforting touch feathered her forehead, one that

filtered through every inch of her with the same warmth of a down blanket on a cold winter morning. "We'll see."

Her spirit self stilled and focused on the strength of the man holding her. He was here, right? Maybe she wouldn't be alone when she woke up. "So I'm not human?"

Kazan's chuckle billowed out, more distant now than a moment before. "Stop asking me questions I can't answer, Trinity. Relax, let the process work, and let your old man take care of you."

CHAPTER 22

*S*erena stifled a yawn and started over on the same paragraph for the third time. Praise The Great One, scholars made for dry delivery. The damned history book she'd pilfered from her father's library was over a thousand pages long. How many different ways could they drive home the fact that their mother tongue was dead, dead, dead?

A loud thud and the clash of something tinny on marble sounded from the foyer. Shouts of concern and heavy footsteps clipped toward the sound.

Great, another accident. The sixth or seventh she'd inadvertently caused today. Her father had stormed into her suite after the second and insisted she get a grip on whatever angst had her influential skills spinning out of control.

Thank The Great One he never set foot in their home midday. Otherwise he'd be forcing the sedative he'd threatened her with down her throat.

She tuned out the chaos from the hall beyond.

With the more accelerated growth of the human race and the inclination of Myrens to fluently interact with their sister inhabitants, the original language for our species began to rapidly wither around one thousand years after the earliest Myren recordings. More scholarly and language-conscious intellectuals assumed knowledge of other tongues, but the predominant language naturally adopted was English. Given the limited means for recording important records at such a primitive time, few original texts remain. Those available in a consumable format are translations of the originals and prone to incorrect interpretation or error.

Lovely. A fancy way of saying even if she found a translation, she may not end up with more than she knew right now.

She slammed the book closed. Where in histus was Angus, anyway? He should have been here an hour ago.

The door behind her swished open.

Serena stood and spun.

Their butler blocked the doorway, his scraggly salt and pepper hair slicked back in a tight queue.

With a flick of her hand, she opened the doors the rest of the way and cut the servant off before he could utter a word. Behind him, Angus stood in his stiff white, unadorned council robes. "I've got this, Otter. Have refreshments sent for my guest."

Angus shuffled into the room and smirked as Otter closed the door behind him. His hands were crossed at his stomach, and the way the sleeves covered them made him look like a well-dressed human monk. "Home confinement not agreeing with you, Serena?"

Don't react. Stay calm. Bury the emotion.

She'd already burned one of the four days Uther had given her. Finding another source would be next to impossible. "You never truly appreciate something until it's gone. I suppose you and I are somewhat alike on that score."

A suck-up and a reminder at the same time. Eryx might have lopped off her freedom, but he'd demolished Angus' lifelong political career in less than five minutes. All because Angus had dared to act in the malran's stead while Eryx searched for Lexi.

"Indeed." Angus frowned and tottered deeper into the room, studying the room's details. "A most ornate home. Reminds me of the humans' peacock, all show with little purpose."

Not a surprising reaction considering the man's upbringing. The room was ornate indeed—lush lavender and plum furnishings, fine crystal and china accents, and dove gray, handmade rugs. Unlike her, Angus had earned everything from the ground up, scraping for every ornamentation and honor. Now he was little more than a figurehead.

"Thyrus tells me you're in need of some of our most ancient texts." Angus eased into one of the more comfortable chairs facing the door. "Care to tell me why?"

"Don't play coy. I've no doubt Thyrus already told you." She picked up the book she'd been studying and settled beside him, laying the large tome so he could see it better. "I'm researching the prophecy. Looking for clues that might aid in unseating the malran. Between Eryx's new mate and the mysterious instances of humans being brought to Eden, I couldn't help but wonder if more knowledge might benefit our cause. Something we might be able to use to our advantage." Fiddling with the fine overlay of her ivory gown, she wrapped him in a subtle cloud of influence. *You want to unseat Eryx. You want your power and prestige back.*

Angus puckered his wrinkly mouth. "And this idea came to you out of nowhere? Out of the blue?"

"Where else would it come from?"

"I haven't a clue," he said. "But the timing is intriguing. Just this morning, the royal couple made an unexpected and unprecedented appearance at the sacred halls and carted off all books documented in the original Myren language."

Serena shot to her feet. "They what?"

A crash from above shook the room, followed by muffled sobs and shouts.

"I see I've struck a nerve." Angus eyeballed the ceiling for a second or two and chuckled. "Perhaps it's you who's being unnecessarily coy. I find it hard to believe your request is based on simple research."

Serena strode to the window, fists clenched so tight her wrists and forearms ached.

Two guards stood at attention near the gold-flecked brick streets, a matching set outside the front door.

Angus gripped the armrests hard enough to turn his already pale skin whiter and one of his legs bounced in a nervous tick, but other than that, he seemed unaffected by her emotional outburst. Probably because he'd only been exposed to her for five minutes instead of twenty-four hours.

"I need those books," Serena said.

"Well, I'm certainly not going to ask the malran for them, so I'm afraid I can't help you on that score." His voice trailed up at the end, as though he had more to say.

"But you might be able to help me on another?"

"Depends." Angus released his death grip on the chair and reclined against the cushions, arms folded on his belly. "What's in it for me?"

Serena smiled, a welcome wave of appreciation and downright respect dissipating the moroseness of her thoughts. Hard not to like the crotchety bastard when he copped such an attitude. "You want Eryx off the throne, correct?"

"I don't think I've made that a secret, not even from the malran."

Serena strolled toward him, grateful for the emotional equilibrium. "When he's gone, the new ruler would require an advisor. Someone with extensive experience and connections. Someone well decorated and powerful in their own right."

"I don't see any contenders for the throne."

"Just because you don't see them, doesn't mean they don't exist."

Angus studied her, his nondescript hazel eyes sharp despite his nearly six hundred years. "The strategos. The one who brought me to Evanora's place."

Yes, definitely shrewd. Angus had met Uther only once and yet quickly discerned his abilities. Granted, the one meeting comprised of Uther finding, capturing, and bringing Angus to Maxis' hidden warrior camp, so it was bound to make an impression. "Do you care so long as you get what you want?"

Angus' lips twitched. He stood, the motion surprisingly spry considering how long it had taken him to sit. "It'll take a few days."

"I don't have a few days. I need them now."

Angus shuffled toward the door. "Tomorrow by sunset at the earliest." He opened the door with an insolent flick of his wrist and turned at the threshold. His stooped shoulders gave his frail form an almost sinister look. "You'll owe me for this, Serena. I might be old, but I'm not the one with banishment and the loss of powers hanging over my head." He turned to exit. "I have no compunction ensuring evidence comes to light to make that eventuality happen."

CHAPTER 23

*R*amsay leaned forward in the chair beside Trinity and propped his elbows on his knees, hands clasped between them. She looked so tiny in his big bed. A damned sunshine faery minus any sign of consciousness. It freaked him out seeing her void of expression, like someone had offloaded every scrap of her vibrant personality and left only a living shell behind.

The scratch of paper on paper startled him.

Reese slouched deeper in the wingback across the room, all attention riveted on the book he'd pretended to read for the last hour. He'd never known Reese to be a reader, and given his warrior's attire, it sure wasn't how he'd planned to spend his morning. Galena had probably guilted him into babysitting and brought the book to avoid meaningful chitchat. Still, good of the guy to keep Ramsay company. Especially when he factored in what a dick he'd been to Reese for the last seventy years.

Prying his fingers from their death clench, he stroked the area he'd healed on Trinity's arm. Smooth, creamy skin. Not one mark left behind.

Well, no mark except the drastic change in her physical capabilities.

Idiot. He'd known better than to use that kind of energy on her. Healing humans was one thing, but healing a Myren with such an uncontrolled blast? Nothing short of a transition hot-wire.

"It was an accident." Reese sat the open book in his lap and right-angled one leg over the other. "You didn't know she was Myren."

Well, technically he'd considered it. Hell, he'd hoped for it. But then he'd gotten so damned zeroed in on her being Spiritu, he'd forgotten the possible ties to his own race. "I was angry. I wasn't thinking."

"People do stupid shit. But the smart ones figure out where they went wrong and recalibrate." Empathic words from a man who'd had his own lessons to learn. Seventy years he'd hid his ugly secret and lost everything he'd ever wanted in the process. Now he was a changed man, free of secrets and mated to the woman he'd always wanted.

"I guess that makes you pretty smart then," Ramsay said.

"Took me long enough. Worth it though, to be with Galena."

Ramsay flopped back in his chair, knees wide. "Still can't believe we hung for four years and not once did you let on you had a thing for my sister."

Four years of warrior training. Four years of having a friend of his own outside Ludan and Eryx. Until he'd used Reese's perceived deceit to split ties and destroy the man he'd once called a friend.

Reese shrugged and shut the book. "You going to tell me you wouldn't have punched me back then?"

"Not past punching you now." Damn, but he hated when Eryx was right. He really had kept everyone at bay. He smoothed the back of his fingers against Trinity's forearm. If he hadn't been so stubborn, so guarded, things with Trinity could have gone a whole lot differently. "I owe you an apology."

Reese cocked an eyebrow. "Thought we already covered that."

He could let it slide. Not say another word and mosey on down the road. No vulnerability. Safe, but a total chicken-shit approach. "I apologized for judging you. Can't say I'd have coped with Maxis being my brother any better than you did." His lungs hitched and his tongue froze up, his mind glitching off line. "Truth is, I had no intention of letting you back in. Too risky."

"Takes a while for trust to rebuild. Don't blame you for that."

Ramsay shook his head and refocused on Trinity. "You're giving me too much credit."

"Or you're not giving yourself enough. Hate to point it out to you, but for a guy not interested in letting an old friend back in, it kinda sounds like you just took the first brick off that wall."

Fucking Reese. Always able to see to the heart of everyone. Except himself. Probably the reason they'd gotten along in the first place. He shifted in his chair and fought to keep his feet still. He'd give anything to pace, maybe take about thirty minutes on a heavy bag to let out some tension.

"Why don't you go check in with Eryx," Reese said. "Grab some food. Bathe and change at least. If she does wake up, you're going to scare the hell out of her."

Ramsay held her hand. Warm, with a steady beat at her wrist, thank The Great One. "She doesn't know you. I don't want her to wake up without someone here she knows."

If she wakes up.

The stupid thought had slammed around in his head so many times, his brain tissue was bruised. No one slept this long after an awakening. Even Lexi, who'd had the ritual from histus, woke up hours before this.

"Galena's going to be here in another five minutes," Reese said. "Go. Change. Stretch a little bit. I swear I'll let you know if she wakes up."

"She doesn't know Galena either."

"Really, man? We're talking about your sister here. The one person in this family who could charm the horns off a demon."

True. Whether it was her healer skills or her warm personality, Galena could put pretty much anyone at ease.

"Seriously," Reese said. "What's going to happen while you're gone?"

Well, for one, she might wake up and demand someone take her back to Evad without letting him grovel and beg to let him make it right. Or worse, she could get the wrong impression right off the bat. Nothing said *I don't give a shit* like waking up and learning the guy who pushed you into Myren culture couldn't be bothered to stick around and see if you lived through it all.

"I can't leave her like this. I owe it to her to stay." Ramsay needed to make it right almost as bad as he needed to breathe. To earn back what he was scared shitless he'd lost.

Not that he'd share that last bit with Reese. Chipping away at emotional walls was one thing. Full-blown demolition wasn't on the agenda. Not with Reese, anyway.

Trinity though…

"Have you looked in a mirror?" Reese said. "The only thing you're gonna do if she sees your haggard mug is scream or feel guilty. Now, go. I've got this."

His back cracked in none-too-subtle agreement. Twenty-four hours of nothing but sitting in this chair had left his muscles in wicked knots. If he looked half as bad as his body felt, Reese might be right. He stood and the joints in his knees snapped. His heart overcompensated and thumped out enough blood to fuel a race. "You'll call me if—"

"Get out, Shantos. Galena's headed up the back staircase now, and I can smell your bedside cologne from here."

Fine. He'd catch a quick shower. Or maybe he'd scout out Lexi first and see if she'd be willing to sit with her. Trinity would want to see her could-be relation when she woke up. If he was lucky and threw on a decent load of groveling, he might even talk his shalla into a little girl-to-girl PR on his behalf.

CHAPTER 24

A tickle lodged in Trinity's throat, ripping her out of the weirdest dream. She hacked in a not-at-all glamorous fashion and squeezed her eyes harder to block out the light behind her eyelids.

"Well, good morning, sunshine!"

Ugh. The feminine greeting rattled the gruesome hum in her head up a notch. Whoever it was clearly hadn't gone on the same bender as Trinity. What time was it, anyway?

The steady swish of fabric and soft footsteps moved around her. "Oh, come on, Trinity. It can't be that bad. Compared to my awakening you looked snug as a bug in a rug."

That voice. She'd heard it before. If she didn't think the harsh light would obliterate her eyeballs, she'd check the face that went with it.

"Awakening?" Trinity's eyes snapped open and the sunshine speared to the base of her skull. She rolled away from the window and covered her head. The conversation with her dad powered through her memories. Ramsay's healing, her awakening, and all the mysterious comments her dad had tossed in for good measure.

The mattress dipped beside her and a gentle hand brushed her hair off her forehead. "Hey." The same voice only quieter. Concerned. "Galena, what's wrong with her?"

Another hand cupped her shoulder and warmth radiated up her neck and down her spine. "Nothing's wrong. Just a bit of an awakening hangover. Nothing I can't take care of." A different woman, this one with a soothing voice. Like warm honey and tea on a cold winter day.

The warmth on her nape intensified and seeped into her muscles and bones. The sharp pain in the back of her head lessened, a slow fade mixed with uncoiled tension.

Trinity opened her eyes.

Lexi. She knew she'd recognized that voice.

"Hey." Whoa. Hangover was a bit of an understatement. Her voice sounded like she'd sanded a brick wall with the inside of her throat.

"Well, hello to you, too." Lexi beamed beside her, her dark hair sparking glints of blue in the sunlight. Unlike the casual jeans and tank she'd worn the last few times Trinity had seen her, she had on a cool-looking blood-red outfit. Kind of a modernized toga-type top that hung to mid-thigh with a high-end set of matching leggings. "Galena's mojo make the nasty stuff go away?"

Galena?

Lexi motioned to the other side of the bed. "Trinity, meet our family doc, Galena. Galena, meet my possible new relation and the one woman who's single-handedly brought my new briyo low."

Talk about elegance, Galena set the standard. Beautiful auburn hair plaited in a wildly complex, but enviable arrangement, curves men lusted over, and a simple, but elegant emerald green gown. She laughed and poured what Trinity hoped was water from a cobalt blue pitcher into a matching glass.

"What's a briyo?" Trinity focused on the clear liquid.

Galena handed it over and eased onto the bedside chair. "Brother-in-law, or in this instance, Ramsay."

Trinity coughed mid-swallow, her throat hitching in time with her stumbling thoughts. She wiped her free hand across her mouth and tried to pull in a steady breath. Surely Lexi didn't think Ramsay and she were an item. Maybe they'd had a chance before the whole Spiritu reveal, but now?

"Hey, how come she's not all itchy and skitzy like I was when I woke up?" Lexi didn't seem the least bit phased with the fact Trinity had damned near swallowed her tongue.

Galena shrugged. "Not everyone comes out as overloaded as you were. And we've already figured out you carry more power than the average Myren woman. Could also have something to do with Trinity's Spiritu heritage." She focused on Trinity. "Frankly, I'm surprised yours went as well as it did. I kept trying to slip into your mind to anchor you, but I couldn't get past whatever natural defense mechanism you've got. I'm sorry I couldn't do more."

Trinity pushed herself upright and rested against the backboard. Whoever had taken care of her through the whole ordeal had shucked her jeans and T-shirt and replaced them with the softest white cotton nightgown she'd ever felt. "It's okay. My dad helped me."

Galena and Lexi eyeballed each other.

"The Spiritu? He was here?" Lexi scanned the room as if she expected him to pop out of thin air.

It was a huge room. Gray stone walls, thick black carpet with matching drapes lining an eight or ten-foot wide arched window. Heck, the bed could probably sleep six adults comfortably. Not the kind of thing you could pick up at the local Mattress King. "Sort of. More like he was in my head." She caught Lexi's gaze. "I'm sorry. I didn't know I was Myren or I would have said something."

"Why would you be sorry?" Lexi said. "I love the fact you're Myren. A little jealous you skipped the skitzo phase and got to sleep for a solid twenty-four hours after it was all done, but happy as punch I'm not the low man on the totem pole anymore."

Well, that was something at least. Good to know she had one person on this side of the...wherever she was. She stroked the soft black blanket covering her lap. "Does Ramsay know?"

Lexi grinned, a gleeful evil smile that almost made Trinity feel bad for the guy.

"Oh, he knows," Galena said. "I couldn't pry you out of his grip until you settled into a sound sleep. The only reason he's not here now is Reese told him he'd scare you off if you got a good look at his face."

"Why? What's wrong with him?"

"Nothing seeing you up and about won't fix," Lexi said. "Assuming you want me to tell him you're awake? I can sneak you out of here, put you in a room near mine, and keep him out if you'd rather."

Come to think of it, she'd felt Ramsay while she'd been out of it. And her dad had teased her about it, in a back-handed, hound dog sad kind of way. "So he was here? He's not mad?"

Lexi scowled. A momma bear ready to read her cub the riot act. "Trinity, he triggered your awakening without your permission, even if it was an accident. Why on Earth would he be mad at you?"

"Ashamed is more like it," Galena said.

"And worried," Lexi added.

"But he was upset about me not telling him I was part Spiritu. I assumed he'd be mad about this too."

Galena reclined in her chair, her emerald gown making the casual movement look elegant. "My brothers can be Class-A jerks, but they've got more honor than that. Ramsay's a little slower getting around to the emotional side of things."

"Speaking of," Lexi said. "Ramsay just pinged me on the family tele-plan. He wants to know if we need anything else from the kitchen. I figure you've got about a minute and half to decide if you want me and Galena running interference or skedaddling."

Oh, shoot. It was way too soon for her brain to function, let alone deal with any heavy topics. "What should I say to him?"

"What do you want to say?" Lexi said.

Show up. Listen. Speak your truth. Let go of the results. "I'd like to kick him in the shins for being an ass, and then curl up with him for about thirty minutes. Though that's probably not the clearest message."

Galena laughed and stood, patting Trinity's shoulder. "Honey, no woman should be expected to send a clear message when their man's been an ass. Let alone right after they've suffered almost thirty-six hours of alterations to one's molecular structure."

The door opened with a muted thunk of metal on metal.

Ramsay strode in, carrying a tray loaded with oversized black mugs and an old-fashioned porcelain pitcher. The scent of fresh brewed coffee hit her a second before he looked up. His eyes locked on her for all of two seconds, and then shuttled to Lexi. "You said you'd tell me when she woke up."

Lexi shrugged one shoulder. "I got distracted." Gaze on Trinity, she lifted both eyebrows in silent question.

"I think I'm good." A total lie. She couldn't remember the last time her emotions were this tangled up and twisted, but dodging issues wasn't her style.

That evil grin of Lexi's slid back into place as she stood. She leaned in to give Trinity a hug and whispered in her ear. "If he doesn't grovel, you can always kick something higher up than his shin."

RAMSAY HAD STARED down some serious battles in his one and a half centuries, but three women with an axe to grind against one solo, self-proclaimed playboy had to be the most dangerous. Galena, Trinity, and Lexi weren't exactly aiming death glares his way, but he pretty much tasted feminine schemes in the air. "Everything okay?"

Galena tugged the empty blue glass from Trinity's hand and refilled it. "She's fine. Had a little hangover when she first woke up, but she's settled now. As long as she was out, a little movement will do her system good, not to mention keep her energy balanced. Get her up and outside for some fresh air."

She refocused on Trinity and handed her the water. "Reese and I are staying here tonight and maybe tomorrow to be sure you're stabilized. If you feel anything that worries you, let Ramsay know and I'll be there."

Ramsay zeroed in on Lexi standing beside the bed with her arms crossed. *"I thought you were going to help me."*

She wiggled a girly finger wave at Trinity, sashayed his direction, and snagged a coffee mug from the tray. *"How do you know I didn't?"*

"Oh, I don't know. Maybe because there was enough estrogen swirling in here to castrate a giant."

Lexi's laughter echoed in his head as she turned for the door, Galena in her wake. "You're safe on that score. For the kind of sucking up you've got in front of you, you'll need balls the size of Texas. Don't want to send you in unarmed." She paused at the threshold and waggled her eyebrows at Ramsay. "Y'all have fun."

The door clicked shut.

Yeah, definitely bad odds. A weird sensation rattled down his arms and shook the coffee pot lid. Fear, maybe, but a whole different variety than he was used to. He tightened his grip on the tray. "Hey."

"Hey." Trinity sipped her water, her face tilted down so he couldn't gauge her eyes. She tugged the black blanket closer to her neck and smoothed the fabric until it laid flat against her chest.

Damn, but she was pretty. Twenty-four hours out like a corpse and seven more before sweating through a life-changing upgrade, and she still managed a sexy-sweet look. Rumpled hair and sleepy eyes, reclined against his headboard and nestled in his sheets. Kind of made him want to swagger out a victory lap. Though considering he wasn't in there with her that might be a bit of a premature celebration.

He tucked the satisfying image away for later and sent the tray floating toward the bedside table.

Trinity flinched and her water sloshed over the rim. "Shoot!"

Ramsay plucked the glass from her wet hand and grabbed a towel off the table. "Thought you'd be used to my tricks by now."

Trinity took the towel and mopped up the mess, paying more attention to the barely touched blanket than her own skin. "Considering everything that's happened, I kind of forgot."

Ramsay perched on the edge of the chair beside her. "So, Galena explained things?"

She nodded, half petting, half plucking the bedcover, gaze locked on her lap. "My dad, too."

Her real dad. As in Spiritu. "Forgot they could drop in wherever they wanted. He came here?"

Her lips twisted in a wry smile and she tapped her temple. "More of a mental visit. He anchored me."

"Huh." Guess that explained the force Galena hadn't been able to breach. "Seems like he did a bang up job. You were a whole lot quieter than Lexi was with hers." And thank The Great One for that. Trinity's whimpers had damn near killed him. If she'd have screamed the same as Lexi, he'd have torn down at least one wing of the castle with his bare hands.

Silence settled thick between them, a kind of awkward barricade he didn't have a clue how to scale. He motioned toward the tray. "You can do those things now if you want. Telekinesis. Telepathy. The elements."

Trinity's fingers stilled.

"I'd like to teach you," he said. "If you'd let me."

She looked up, her beautiful dark eyes penetrating in a way that not only staked him in place, but hushed all the garbled emotions he didn't have a clue how to process. "You would?"

"Seems only fair, considering what you've taught me."

She tilted her head and frowned. "I haven't taught you anything. You were the sexual guru, remember?"

Sex. Praise The Great One, he'd be able to pleasure her a whole different way now. Share his energy as well as his touch. And damned if his body didn't get on board with the idea quick.

Not a topic to contemplate at the moment. Right now

was about earning back her trust. Rebuilding the damage from his wrecking ball reactions, not exploring all the different ways to make her body sing. The only way he was going to kick the weird distance he'd created was if he put his shit out there where it was good and vulnerable. Let her know she could take him seriously.

He sat beside her on the bed.

Trinity fiddled with the blanket's edge near her throat, kind of an absentminded check to ensure her armor was in place.

He tugged her hand free and clasped it between both of his. Amazing how different they were. Small to large. Cream against tan. Soft versus rough. He liked all of it. "I've been alive a hundred and fifty-two years. In all that time, I've never had a serious relationship with a woman."

Trinity's gaze locked on the rock wall opposite him.

He gently squeezed her hand. "Look at me, Trinity."

Her lips tightened and he'd swear for a second she held her breath before meeting his eyes, the fear and doubt that radiated out of them slicing cold as a blade.

"I let you in," he said. "I let you in and it scared the shit out of me. You being Spiritu was the perfect excuse for me to run. A way to keep you out." His throat seemed to close in on itself, like it knew instinctively the danger behind the words bubbling up. "Laying there during your awakening, holding you and wondering if your Myren lineage was enough to get you through the transition, I realized running was the last thing I needed to do."

"I—I'm not sure I follow."

He cupped her face. Funny how touching her, being close to her, soothed and comforted his anxiousness. "I'm saying I've never contemplated what love might feel like, much less felt it. What I feel for you, I'm not sure there's a word for it. Powerful, maybe. Whatever it is, it's huge, and you're the one who gave it to me. Dared me to face it just by being you. For a man who's held himself apart from everyone his whole life, I'd say that's a pretty impressive lesson."

Trinity blinked over and over. Her hand twitched between his, and her shaky exhalation fluttered across his face. "What are you saying?"

This was it. The biggest battle of his life, fought with nothing more than words. Words he never thought he'd say. He palmed the back of her neck. A calm, almost fated certainty settled over him, bits and pieces of his purposefully disconnected life snapping together. "I love you, Trinity. I've got a short fuse sometimes and don't know the first thing about how good relationships work, but I'm smart. Smart enough to know The Great One made you for me. I'm not about to let you go."

"You love me," she muttered, quiet and broken.

"I knew it that last night at your apartment. Had it driven home when I held you through your awakening."

Her gaze roamed his face. "You barely know me."

"I knew you were special in the first five seconds I saw you. In the time it took me to blink, everything about my world changed. I just didn't realize what it was at the time. And for the record, I come from a long line of quick study men—my father, Eryx, my grandfather. Every one of them fell fast for their mates. I don't see why my Shantos genes would be any different."

Trinity pulled her hand free, her mouth slightly ajar and rounded. Like her body was ready to protest but her mind was too upended to cough up the right words. Not at all the response he'd hoped for. Reasonable, but still a long way from taking that victory lap.

Ramsay stood and stuffed his hands in his front pockets. "So, I guess you might need a little time to process all that." He checked the tray, the bedside table, even glanced out the window. Give him a battle over intimate conversation any day. It was a hell of a lot easier. "There's coffee if you want. Might want to add some creamer. Ours is a little stronger."

Trinity stared at him. Was that shock on her face, or good old-fashioned disbelief?

He motioned to the double doors in the corner of his suite that led to the bathroom. "There's a shower and a tub through there. I laid out everything you'd need while you were sleeping. One of Galena's outfits too. I figured Lexi's a little too tall for you. Actually everyone's a little too tall for you, but Orla's rounding up your own wardrobe."

Geez, Shantos, shut the fuck up already.

He scratched the back of his head and stared at his boots, gathering up what was left of his pride. "I'll give you a little time to yourself. Maybe after you're dressed we could head to the beach, try out some simple skills. Unless you'd rather work with Lexi. I'm sure she'd—"

"I didn't know I was Myren."

Her statement scrambled his jagged exit strategy. "What?"

"When I told you I was Spiritu and human, I really meant it. My dad never told me anything else." She shrugged. "I didn't want you to think I was holding anything else back."

He sat on the bed, most of the awkwardness shattered by the simple sound of her voice. "I don't care what you are, Trinity. Yeah, the Spiritu thing surprised me, but I just want you. You being Myren's icing on the cake."

"Why?"

"Why what?"

"Why is it icing on the cake?"

The answer to her question rushed in, loud and clear, staking the most profound claim of his life. He leaned in and kissed her forehead. Her crisp, clean scent filled his lungs and fueled him to the point he felt invincible. He met her eyes. If he told her the truth, he'd likely ratchet the whole crazy awkward vibe back into the stratosphere.

Fuck it. He'd already laid one big boom. Might as well throw in full bore. "It's icing because if you're Myren, it means you can be my baineann and take my mark. And I'm prepared to do whatever it takes to make that happen."

CHAPTER 25

*S*erena jolted from a deep sleep. A large, calloused hand clamped on her mouth, and she strained to focus in the darkness. Only a sliver of moonlight filtered through a crack in the drawn curtains, outlining a towering masculine body.

"Not a sound, Serena."

Uther. The bastard was early.

The sun's position registered well below the horizon. Past midnight, close to one in the morning. She nodded beneath his firm hold, her frantic exhalations rebounding off his hand and onto her face.

He eased back, his broad shoulders blocking what was left of the light.

She lit a single candle on her dresser, one far enough from the windows not to rouse the warriors watching the house, but enough to level the visual playing field. "Are you out of you mind coming this late?"

"Would you rather I come in broad daylight?" He eased onto the rose silk chaise nestled in the corner of her room, arms stretched out along the sides. "Nice security you've got these days, by the way."

She snapped her covers aside and swung her legs free. "Thanks to you and your stupid tricks in Evad."

"You get the books?" He crossed one leg over the other, completely at ease. Like he'd been in her room countless times and hadn't just masked his way through The Great One only knew how many guards.

Her silk robe lay neatly situated near the foot of her bed, an elegant dusty pink that matched her fitted nightgown. She ran her fingers along the smooth fabric, eyes to Uther. Four days she'd debated how to handle this moment. Four days of powerlessness and not enough options. Only two choices, actually. Meet Uther head on and gain his trust over time, or grasp the upper hand quick with good old-fashioned seduction.

He held her stare, an interesting stir of power flowing between them.

Forgoing the robe, she gave Uther her back and locked eyes with him once more in the dresser mirror. "I'm not comfortable getting you anything or jumping into your schemes without more information." Her silk nightgown shimmered in the candle's glow, the fabric whispering with each step. She pulled her hair over one shoulder, exposing the low dipped back and the snug lace trim barely covering her ass. She picked up her brush.

"Are you saying you're not willing to comply?"

"I'm saying I need to understand what I'm supporting." Brushing the inconsequential knots from her hair, she imagined the two of them naked and tangled in her bed, his powerful torso flush against her breasts, the rhythm of his hips against hers. She pushed the image and emotion his way.

Uther uncrossed his legs and splayed one along the chaise. "I think it's safer you don't know."

She sat the brush aside and prowled toward him, hips swaying with invitation. He'd be a powerful lover. Demanding without all of Maxis' psychological whips and chains. A means to an end, yes. A sacrifice? Not in the least. Especially if it gave her the knowledge she wanted. "So you're looking out for me then?"

"You don't need looking out for."

She halted just outside his spread legs. Her breasts tightened, nipples straining against her nightgown. "I'll take that as a compliment."

With a slow, deep breath, she kneeled between them and imagined taking his cock with her mouth. The stretch of her lips around him. His taste. She pushed the thickening sexual tension that came with the thought around him and leaned in, enough to make her nipples strain at the lace trim of her neckline. "You're right. I can look out for myself. But only if you tell me what I need to know. Make me a partner in this, Uther. Maxis trusted me. You can trust me too."

A slow growl rumbled from his chest and he gripped her nape, pulling her to him. His lips were close. Warm and full. Heaviness weighted his eyelids, his sage irises more evergreen in the shadows.

No, not a sacrifice at all. She could easily envision him above her, thrusting fast and deep. She reveled in the sensation, let it mushroom around them both, her pussy clenching at the thought.

His nostrils flared and his fingers tightened on her neck. "Get back."

Her heart thrashed inside her chest, torso seizing as surely as if she'd been doused in ice water. "You don't mean that. You want me as much as I want you."

Praise The Great One, it was the truth. Right now she

wanted him with or without information. The heat coming off him alone was delicious. She could only imagine what he'd feel like naked and commanding her body.

He gripped her shoulders and forced her backward.

Serena stumbled to a stand, nearly ripping her gown's hem in the process.

The room crackled with his energy, angry and sparking against her skin. "If I wanted pussy, I'd get it from someone without political aspirations and a love for daggers."

"You bastard." No one treated her this way. Let alone some scrapper from the Underlands. She pointed at her bedroom door. "Get out."

"Not until you give me what I came here for."

"And you're not getting anything until you give me information."

"Why should I?"

A lifetime worth of emotion surged to the surface, flaring as dangerously as a challenged cobra. "Because I don't want to live the next year cooped up in this house. Because I don't want to watch my every step for the next five. Because I want the throne that should have been mine, even if it means getting Eryx off his to get it."

"Not a damned bit of which means a shit to me. So again, why should I?"

Reason pinged a subtle note in her mind, penetrating the anger and mortification of Uther's rejection. She settled with it a moment. Breathed through the emotion. Maybe he just needed to see the true value she brought to the equation. "Why don't you tell me what you're after, and I'll tell you how I might help you get it."

Uther studied her room, his gaze traversing the fine rose and gold accents, lingering last on her sumptuous bed. "You ever think about what it would be like living without rank? Without a place in society? Limited gifts and resources?"

"Only so far as to be glad I'm not in that situation."

He scowled at her, though there was an element of appreciation to it. "At least you're honest." He glanced to his left where open doors led to a bathroom bigger than his shack's kitchen. "That's all I've ever had. A family that lived on the fringes of society with nothing to our name. Of all of us, my powers are the strongest. A fluke compared to the rest of my line. Everything I have I've sweated for and made my own name." He pegged her with a stare that resonated through every pore. "I want more."

"You want the throne?"

"I want power. Enough of it I make my own rank, whatever the fuck that means. What I'm working on will give it to me."

Interesting. Something to work with. She paced toward her bed, head down, mind racing ahead. "What kind of power are we talking about?"

"What kind of power do you think is capable of creating its own rank in our society?"

Serena stopped and faced him.

Big power.

The kind of power that had allowed the Shantos line to rule since the beginning of their race. The sum of all known gifts.

"And that ties in with the prophecy how?" she asked.

Uther strolled to the window and peeked behind one panel. "Something ancient. Handed down through my family from the first generations." He dropped the curtain and faced her. "I don't know its details, but I know the legend promises power. Loads of it."

A slow, steady roar of adrenaline built in her bloodstream. She'd never had a means to out-power Eryx before. No one had. But this, this could be huge. "With strength and rank comes the need for politics. Are you prepared to navigate those waters?"

A flicker of doubt flashed in his eyes. Not much, but enough to let her know she'd hit a nerve.

"I am," she said before he could answer. She ambled closer, this time not with a gait of seduction, but defiance. "I'm damned good at it. Enough I got a jury to look past my crimes."

"Did you use the same trick you threw on me a few minutes ago to make it happen?"

His blocking skill. She'd assumed it might be a factor. At least now she knew it applied to her influence as well. "One and the same." She smiled, strength and certainty fueling a confidence she hadn't felt in days. "Now, are we going to partner up and get us both what we want? Or are you going to keep wasting time?"

CHAPTER 26

*T*hree days. Three idyllic, magical days, and Trinity still couldn't shake the bubble-bursting paranoia that dogged her every waking moment.

Ramsay's hand tightened around hers, his usual long strides shortened so she could keep up as they wound through the thick forest. "You okay? You seem distant."

"Yep." Perfect. Couldn't find a thing to complain about and hadn't since he'd emotion-bombed her after her awakening, which was precisely the problem. Nothing this good lasted. "Just thinking. Where are we headed anyway? I thought we were having a picnic."

"We are."

That devilish grin of his hadn't dimmed once. Not when he'd all but ordered her to shower after telling her he intended to marry her. Or whatever it was Myrens called it. Not when he'd shown her how to levitate pebbles and rocks the size of her fist at the beach later that day, or when he'd taught her to fly the day after. Certainly not when he set about physically pleasuring her, which seemed to be any spare second they were alone.

"I'm taking you to one of my favorite spots," he said. "There's a clearing in the middle of all this that's quiet and private. I go there a lot for natxu or when I want to clear my head."

"Natxu?"

He held a branch back so she could pass a tight spot. "I guess you might compare it to something like Tai Chi, but on a much more demanding scale. Our warriors use it as a part of daily training."

Warrior training. Another perk of her recent stay in Eden. He'd taken her with him the last two days to watch him work with his men, just as Eryx had taken Lexi.

Man, talk about visual gratification. Ramsay in motion, chest bare, sun beating off his sweat-covered skin, and black leather molding the rest of his delicious assets. Oh, yeah. Perfect. Lexi had laughed herself silly and teased Trinity for the way she gapped through most of day one.

A fallen tree lay directly in her path, but before she could jump over it, Ramsay levitated her up and over the barely decayed wood. Her half-gasp, half-giggle bounced between the tall, chocolate-colored tree trunks and the thick canopy of huge pearlescent leaves. "You should warn me before you do stuff like that."

"All right." He tugged her so she faced him and wrapped her up tight. The picnic basket Orla had made them dangled from one of his hands and grazed the back of her legs. "I plan to see to your needs for an indefinite period of time, including, but not limited to navigating you through difficult terrain either mentally or physically." He kissed her. Not chaste, and not wild, but a perfect mesh of his full lips against hers. "Consider that a blanket warning."

She laughed and playfully shoved his shoulders, though the last thing she wanted was escape. For the life of her, she couldn't figure out what to do about their situation. Ramsay had been dangerous when all he'd seemed to want was decadent sex. Ramsay on a mission for the whole enchilada, which was what he kept insisting he was after, was downright lethal.

"Come on. We're not far now." He released her and reclaimed her hand, striding toward the edge of the forest.

"Why not fly in? Wouldn't that be faster?" More fun for sure. She'd never imagined what it would be like to be Superman, but now that she'd done it for herself, she'd pick it over a car any day.

Ramsay shrugged. "Peaceful, I guess. Kind of a way to center my mind and prep for natxu."

A very Zen-ish attitude. Yet another surprising aspect to the man who'd swept into her world and turned it upside down.

They stepped from the last line of trees and her breath left on a rush.

Green grass with scattered tiny white flowers stretched out in a misshaped oval nearly three football fields long. Unlike the sod back home, Eden's glinted in the sun, the silver-tinted blades making everything seem magical.

Trinity pointed to the odd rectangular stones arranged like doors, or monuments, at the end closest to them. Kind of like the pictures she'd seen of Stonehenge but in an arch instead of a circle. "What's that?"

Ramsay shrugged and pulled her forward. "Not a clue. My dad said they date back to our first generation and the first malran, but that's all anyone knows. Rumor has it the castle was purposefully built to be close to this spot, but for all we know, it's just that. Rumor." He smiled back at her. "Wanna eat there?"

And give her librarian/fantasy girl a little chance to indulge her curiosity and imagination in one swoop? "Heck, yes."

Ramsay laid out the thick blanket Orla had packed while Trinity rifled through the basket.

"Good grief," she said, setting aside a fourth sandwich made of the buttery, crusty bread she'd helped Orla make the day before. "How many of us did she think she was feeding?"

Ramsay peeked over her shoulder. "Looks like enough for us. Three for me, one for you." He kissed her cheek, then lay on his back and stared up at the holographic rainbow sky. "Soon as we eat, we can spend some time figuring out what your best element is."

Oh, that. She'd been avoiding the whole fire-throwing, water-conjuring, and whatever else Myrens could do. What if she burned something down? Or worse, couldn't do anything? "No rush. I'm not in any hurry."

"That's a different spin than Lexi gave it. She wouldn't give playing with her new gifts a rest. 'Course she also thought she was gonna have to go head-to-head with Maxis and Serena solo, so she had a bit more incentive."

Trinity handed him a sandwich and settled in to devour her own. "So, Serena's contained now?" She knew Maxis was dead, but the idea Serena could still cause problems for her new friends, or worse, somehow pair with the Spiritu who'd forced Serena into killing Maxis, didn't sit well.

"She's under guard. Whether or not she's the one who took people to Eden we can't prove yet, but Eryx has men on the house."

Which meant the humans being brought to Eden might not have anything to do with Serena at all and everything to do with the prophecy. Lexi had given her updates on that score everyday too. The journal she'd seen in her box was apparently written in an old language. One no one used anymore, which made deciphering tricky.

"I tried to help Lexi translate some pages from the journal while you were huddled up with Eryx yesterday," she said.

Ramsay popped the last bite of his sandwich in his mouth.

Trinity snagged a drishen and ate it, waiting for him to say something.

He stared back at her.

"She said Eryx told her written communications from that time period were less literal than ours. That because of the pictorial slant to the words, it was easy to misinterpret things. Have you tried working on it?"

He wiped his hands on his napkin. "A little."

Well, gee, Trinity. Why not tiptoe around the subject a little more?

"Why don't you talk about it anymore?" she said. "The prophecy, I mean."

"Because you're more than a means to an end, and I want it to be clear my intent with you is completely separate."

Her belly did a barrel roll and her heart missed at least two beats. The message alone was enough to bowl a girl over, but added with his rumbly voice, her mind clocked out. "And when we..." She motioned between them. "You know."

He cocked one eyebrow and grinned. "When we what?"

Ugh. Stubborn Ass. "You know. When we've been together. Every time since my awakening, I seem to be the only one getting to fully enjoy things. Does that have anything to do with your intent?"

He grabbed her hand and stretched back out on the blanket, pulling her so she lay half on and half off him. "You mean the fact that I've only gotten you off with my mouth and my fingers? That you're the only one who's come? Yeah, it's got something to do with my intent." He caressed her neck and his thumb skated back and forth along her hairline. "Telling you I love you and proving it are two very different things." His eyes locked onto her lips. "I'm more interested in the latter."

What if I said I love you too? Was it really possible to feel such a thing so quickly? And what if everything changed after she said it? For all she knew, she was just a challenge to Ramsay. A shiny new toy that would lose its luster the minute she uttered the words.

She pushed the thought aside. Ramsay might be a lot of things, but shallow wasn't one of them. He might have been deceptive at first, but it wasn't without cause. Now that everything was out in the open, there was no point in him jumping through hoops for something he'd been willing to flat-out say he wanted a few days ago.

Ramsay shifted beneath her, tilting his head to one side. "If I wanted to talk with your father, how would I do that?"

Why would he want to? "Honestly, I don't know. I've never needed to call him. He just shows when I need him. When I think of him."

"So you talk to him at will? Like telepathy?"

Another good question. Not that she knew yet how telepathy worked since she had no Myren family to connect with. She'd tried to communicate with Lexi, but came up with a big nothing. Which sucked because it confirmed they weren't related.

"No," she said. "I wouldn't call it telepathy. I mean, except for during the awakening. I heard his voice in my head then, but most of the time I just think of him and he poofs in."

Ramsay grinned. "He poofs in?"

She smiled back, his boyish charm infecting her the way it always did. "Yeah."

"Tell me about him."

She traced the metal torc at his neck, mostly platinum, but with yellow gold bars at either side of a black Pegasus etched at its center. Except for the first day after her awakening, he'd always worn it, along with the drast and black leather pants the rest of the warriors wore. "His name is

Kazan. His build is similar to yours, about the same height as you too. My mom must've been the blond because his hair is as black as it gets."

"He's with the Black contingent?"

She nodded and reality dimmed for a minute, warm memories flooding up from the countless easy conversations she'd had with her father. "The good side, he'd say. Passion. Lust for life." She met Ramsay's gaze. "Personally, I've never seen that side of him. He's always calm with me. Reserved, like a part of him is missing."

Ramsay tucked a strand of hair behind her ear. "Sounds like a good man. Though I don't think he'd appreciate the term poof. Pop, maybe. Or appear. Not poof. Men do not poof."

A happy giggle bubbled up. When was the last time she'd felt this light? This unencumbered by responsibility and have-nots? "Why all the questions?"

His gaze slid to the skies for a second, then returned to her. "I'd like to talk to him. Do you think you could tell him that?"

Ramsay and her father? In the same room?

Oh, wait. It was probably prophecy talk. "He can't help you with the prophecy. If he does, he'll forfeit his existence. He barely survived the penalty for his indiscretion with Mom."

Ramsay cupped the back of her head. If she weren't sprawled across him already, the intensity of his expression would've knocked her over. "It's something more important than the prophecy, Sunshine."

"Then what is it?"

His ornery grin flipped back into place, and he rolled them until he had her pinned against the blanket. "Things a man who wants another man's daughter needs to say one-on-one." He studied her a minute. "Now, are you going to help me out and give Dad a jingle, or do I need to persuade you?"

A towering form solidified behind them. Black T-shirt, black jeans, black boots. Her father, who, from the scowl on his face, appeared to be in a black mood.

His powerful voice sounded above them before Trinity could say a word to warn Ramsay. "I can hear you fine."

RAMSAY FROZE ABOVE TRINITY, biceps flexed and ready for action.

It had to be her dad. And didn't that figure. His first introduction to the guy, and he was nearly on top of his daughter, forearms braced on either side of her head. Logic said to roll away and spring to his feet. Something far more primitive kept him rooted in place, the need to protect, even mark her as his, knocking reason out of the way.

Trinity pushed on his chest, urging him to move, her eyes wide and locked on the man behind her.

"Look at me," Ramsay said, quiet enough to keep the communication between the two of them.

Her gaze slid to his. With every second the pretty pink flush on her cheeks strengthened.

He kissed her, a soft, innocent touch, and murmured against her lips. "Breathe."

Kazan's shadow fell across them. "A little hard for her to do that considering the circumstances, don't you think?"

Fuck. He'd forgotten their powers. The Great One only knew how vast they were.

"Far more than yours," Kazan said, answering Ramsay's thought. "And I think I've been more than patient holding them back where my daughter's concerned."

So, he could read minds on top of exceptional hearing. Good to know.

He eased back to his knees and helped Trinity up, keeping his back to Kazan despite his instincts to do otherwise until she was steady. Weird how centered he felt. No need for posturing or anger, just a single-minded focus to handle what needed handling.

He turned and squared his shoulders, wrapping one arm around Trinity's waist and offering his hand to her father. "Ramsay Shantos."

Man, she wasn't kidding about Kazan being big. The guy would be a good contender in a sparring match with Ludan. Right now said contender had his arms crossed and glared at the hand Ramsay offered like it was the gravest insult he'd ever been given.

"Dad," Trinity whispered beside him.

Kazan took the hand, giving it the extra squeeze Ramsay anticipated.

Once the non-verbal male tango finished, Ramsay focused on Trinity. "Do you remember the way back to the castle?"

She nodded, shuttling her attention between her dad and Ramsay.

He squeezed her shoulder. "Do you feel safe flying back on your own?"

"I think it's smarter if I stay here."

Ramsay tried to hold back his smile, but the quick pinch of her eyebrows said he'd pretty much blown it. "Do you think I need protection?"

Trinity leaned in, her voice an irritated grumble. "You don't know how powerful my father is."

He edged even closer. "Is he a fair man? Reasonable?"

She glanced at Kazan. "So far."

Ramsay chuckled at that, her protective kitten routine

pouring a fresh layer of concrete on his already rock solid resolve. He kissed her forehead. "Then whatever happens will be as it needs to be. Now go."

Trinity worried her lip for a second and aimed a warning scowl at her father. "Please don't—"

"Trinity," Ramsay said.

Kazan's eyebrow lifted.

Why? Because Ramsay had cut her off, or to get her to finish the statement? Had to be the first option because he had to be able to hear her thoughts.

"I'll be in the library with Lexi," she said.

Of course she would. Every second she hadn't been with him, she'd spent with Lexi, either learning new skills, or trying to help with the prophecy.

She shot to the skies without the slightest hesitation, the same confidence Lexi had shown when she'd learned to fly.

Ramsay turned in time to catch an unguarded splash of pride on Kazan's face. "She caught on fast."

The hard mask slid back into place. "Of course, she did. She's my daughter."

Ramsay had already caught a glimmer of the same determined attitude a time or two with Trinity. He hoped to histus it grew even stronger the more she learned to trust him. Going toe to toe with her for the rest of his life would be one heck of a ride.

Now wasn't about wishes though. It was about asking for what he wanted. "You already know my thoughts, but I'd dishonor her if I didn't ask formally."

Kazan's head tilted to an angle that screamed, *"I dare you,"* and his biceps flexed above his still crossed arms.

Not a complete shut down, so that was promising. "I would give her my vow and have her for my mate if she accepts me."

"You don't deserve her."

Something prickled at Ramsay's thoughts. Something foreign. No, not foreign, more like forgotten. He homed in on it. "Is that a statement from a father sharing his honest opinion? Or a Spiritu nudging us away from a dangerous future by trying to piss me off?"

"If I told you it was the latter, would it make a difference?"

His mouth opened to toss out some smart-ass remark, but he shut it just as fast and let the question simmer. "That depends," he said working through it out loud. "If it's me doing the suffering, I'd take it to be her mate. If it's her…"

Inside, his emotions raged and burned, flaying him from the inside out. Is that what her dad was trying to tell him? That he'd finally found a woman worth risking his heart for, only to be told he can't have her without hurting her?

"No," Ramsay ground out. "If it put her in danger, I wouldn't claim her."

"But you'd stay with her."

Ramsay clenched his jaw so hard a sharp pain shot up the back of his head. "No. Not if it meant hurting her. I'd hang on to what she's already given me and keep my distance."

Kazan glowered at him, not moving a muscle.

Ramsay itched to move, his bloodstream flooded with so damned much adrenaline he thought he might combust at any moment. Praise The Great One, couldn't the guy throw a punch or something? Maybe let loose some of those wicked powers?

Kazan let out a resigned breath and unfolded his arms. "I want to mislead you. Want to do whatever it takes to keep you as far away from her as possible."

"For her safety?"

"Yes."

Fuck. The guy hadn't lifted a finger, but blasted his whole damned life to histus with a single word.

"But you mating with her won't change anything," he added. "Her path is her own. Decisions will be placed in front of her whether you're together or apart."

Air rushed into Ramsay's lungs, and he rewound the last few sentences in his head to make sure he hadn't misheard.

"She wants you," Kazan said. "If it means happiness for her as she faces the choices destiny gives her, then she should have it."

The world righted itself and the nearly drunken fury that had swamped him in less than two heartbeats eked, leaving him vibrating with relief. A cool wind whipped behind him, brushing against the fine sheen of sweat at his neck and chilling his skin. "Then you give your blessing?"

Kazan's lips tightened, then he nodded. "Though I should warn you, hurting her would be an act I would happily give up my existence to avenge."

Ramsay stepped forward, the certainty and power he'd felt days before with Trinity mushrooming up into something impenetrable. He offered his hand to the father of his would-be mate, assuming she'd have him. "Anything that is within my power to give is hers. Even if it isn't, I'll still try. She'll have my vow and my protection."

Kazan studied his outstretched hand for the second time in less than ten minutes, this time with an entirely different expression. Maybe resignation, but could be worry too. Lifting his gaze to Ramsay, Kazan clasped Ramsay's hand.

A heady buzz rattled him head to toe.

A second later Kazan released him and stepped back. His form started to fade.

Ramsay lurched forward. "Wait."

Kazan's image stabilized, partially gone, but still visible.

"These decisions," Ramsay said. "If she's in danger, tell me. Help me protect her."

Kazan's body wavered and the man hung his head in

something Ramsay could only categorize as defeat. "That's something you'll have to figure out how to do on your own."

TRINITY PROPPED her chin on one palm, elbow grounded on the library's trestle table, and glared down at the open journal. The edges of the aged leather covers framed the ivory parchment, and bold masculine writing in smudged black ink scrolled down both sides.

What was taking Ramsay so long? She'd been back more than an hour. Plenty of time for her dad and Ramsay to say whatever needed saying. Maybe she should go find Eryx and have him check things out. She'd never seen her dad that mad before. Heck, if Orla had thought to pack marshmallows, she could've roasted a few in the line of her dad's death glare.

A hand swiped between Trinity's face and the book. "Hello?"

Trinity jerked back and locked eyes with Lexi across the table. "Sorry. I was thinking."

"I can see that." Lexi leaned over the table, craning her neck to see which journal entry she was on, then sat back down. "We already have that one deciphered, so I'm guessing you're not thinking about translating."

Hardly. God, what if her dad thought she didn't love Ramsay? He could read her mind as easily as anyone else's. If she couldn't admit it to herself, then why would her dad think anything different? She should've said something. At least stuck around to do what she could to protect Ramsay.

"Wow." Lexi snapped her fingers in front of Trinity's face. "That's twice in under a minute. Do you really think your dad's gonna hurt him?"

Trinity traced one of the symbols near the corner of the

page. "I don't know. I never had a boyfriend before. I couldn't tolerate so much as holding hands growing up, and Mom wasn't big on me dating anyway, so it's not like I've got experience in the dad versus date thing."

Lexi rounded the table and slid onto the long bench next to her. She covered Trinity's hand. "Do you believe in them?"

"Individually, sure. Butting heads against each other, I have no idea."

"Pfft. Neither one of them is going to do anything that upsets you in the long run. You'll see. Things always turn out like they need to." Lexi grinned and patted Trinity's hand. "Gotta admit, I kind of like imagining Ramsay tap dancing around someone more bad-ass than him, though. Monster Playboy versus Super Daddy."

"You're incorrigible."

"Ooo. Big words from the librarian." Lexi waggled her eyebrows and pulled the journal out from under her hand. "Admit it. You're not as tense as before, right?"

Trinity half-chuckled and shook her head. "No, I guess not."

"All right then. Scoot up here close and we'll kill time going over what we learned while you were out playing kissey-kissey." Lexi pulled a tablet from the corner of the table beside the journal. "Remember how the earlier entries eluded to Myrens and humans being here at the same time?"

Trinity nodded and shuttled her attention between the symbol Lexi pointed out and the translation she referenced on her right.

"Well, the next few passages seemed to be about some kind of fight. Or a battle. That part's fuzzy. But what's cool, or scary as hell, depending on how you look at it, is this page seems to indicate that the wall between our world and Evad is fueled by someone's powers."

Trinity leaned in closer, comparing the symbols to the

translation tablets Eryx had gathered from the sacred libraries. "So, someone's fueling them now?"

Lexi shook her head and laid the tablet on top of the journal. "Nope. Someone gave their powers up to fuel it. Had something to do with the battle, but we haven't tied together what it was yet."

Huh. "Then the wall is what, like the super power lottery win of a lifetime?"

"Yep. Something like that."

Trinity stared at the journal, seeing it without really connecting. "And the prophecy's about a new era for the race."

"Exactly." Lexi scooted sideways on the bench with one leg crossed on the top of the honey-stained surface. "If someone were to find a way to retract the wall and claim the powers fueling it for themselves, it would definitely be a new era. And not necessarily a good one."

"Unless we find a way to prevent that from happening."

Lexi's smile hopped to full bright. "I like the way you say 'we.' It's got a nice ring to it."

The clunk of heavy metal on metal sounded a second before the double doors swung open.

Trinity shot to her feet, her heart about two paces ahead of her as she rounded the long table.

Ramsay strode through the opening, his gait purposeful but not at all frantic, eyes locked on her.

She met him before he'd made it halfway to the table and wrapped him up tight, the odd slick-rough combination of his drast firm against her cheek. "You're okay."

"Of course I'm okay." Ramsay kissed the top of her head. "I'm sure I could find a way to make your dad decrease my lifespan, but today's topic didn't put that task on the short list."

Heavy footsteps sounded through the doorway.

"Lexi, I need you to help me with something."

Eryx. Funny, they were twins and their voices were almost as identical as their appearance, but she could still tell them apart without the visual.

"Sure, babe. Just give us a second. I was going over what we'd found with Trinity and—"

The harsh halt to Lexi's voice ripped Trinity's head upright.

Lexi frowned, her gaze lasered on Eryx. "Um...sure. Yeah." She sidestepped from between the bench and table, closed the journal, and packed it with the tablet in the dark wood box. She took a few steps forward, glanced at Trinity, and stopped. "You know, maybe Trinity and I should have a quick word first."

"Lexi," Eryx warned.

"Well, she's new," Lexi said. "I mean, you can't just throw her in there without—"

"I've got this," Ramsay said.

Trinity twisted to see Lexi, but Ramsay's arms tightened so she couldn't make it all the way around. "He's got what?" She looked back to Ramsay. "What's going on?"

Ramsay's focus was locked on Lexi. "I love her. Trust me. I've got this."

Whoa. Ramsay and those three dangerous words uttered solo were one thing. Amplifying the message with a public declaration unplugged Trinity's processor and turned everything from the neck down soft and squishy.

"Let it go, Lexi." Eryx hadn't budged from his place at the door, but he spoke with an intimacy palpable from across the room. "You'll have time with her before, I promise."

The three kept staring at each other. The tension between them was weird. Not imminent danger weird, but the same as that sketchy feeling you had when you thought you left the iron on and were five miles across town where you couldn't do anything about it.

Lexi clutched the box tighter against her chest. The second she shifted her gaze to Trinity the expression softened, all except her eyes which seemed pinched with worry. "Listen to your heart. Trust it and everything will work out like it needs to."

With one last threatening glare at Ramsay, she marched toward Eryx.

Ramsay chuckled under his breath and pulled Trinity flush against him, inhaling deep in a cozy Saturday morning kind of way.

Behind them the door snicked shut.

"How can you laugh? Lexi looked like she was about to take garden shears to your neck."

His laughter grew to the point it rattled through Trinity pinned against him. "If you knew how many times I've had my general existence threatened where you're concerned in the last few days you'd chuckle too."

She snapped her head back for eye contact. "Dad threatened you?"

"And Lexi. Though for some reason her threats always entail the loss of my genitals. I'm more inclined to be worried about hers over your dad's. At least if he took me out, it'd be short and quick."

Trinity fisted her hand in his drast as all the thoughts and worries of the last hour rushed to the front row of her mind. "I should have told you. Should have stayed and told him too."

"Told me what?"

Damn but the room felt hot. Ramsay's body practically burned against hers, and her heart seemed saturated with adrenaline. If Ramsay could say it, surely she could.

The words battled up her throat. "That I love you."

Ramsay froze and his smile faltered.

Oh, boy. Not exactly the reaction she'd hoped for. "If I'd said it out loud, admitted it instead of holding it in, he wouldn't have threatened you."

His smile faded entirely, a heavy lidded smolder taking its place and tapping into every erotic point without so much as a touch. He cupped the back of her head. "Say it again."

She tried to swallow. Tried to breathe. Not an easy task with his intensity bearing down on her. "I love you, too."

Ramsay's gaze roamed her face, lingering on her lips before lifting to her eyes. "Sunshine."

"What?"

"Everything about you is bright. The kind of light that makes a solitary man step out of the shadows."

Her belly rippled in one of those mark-that-one-down-for-history flutters. For a guy who claimed not to know how to do relationships, he seemed to be a quick study.

He traced her cheekbone with his thumb. "Your dad would have threatened me whether you told him how you felt or not. It's what a father does when a man states his intentions toward his daughter. A last chance to ensure her happiness before he lets her go."

"You asked him?"

Ramsay nodded, his eyes never wavering from hers.

"And he said?"

"He said he'll bless and support whatever choice you make." His fingers flexed against her nape and he pulled her closer. "Choose me, Trinity. Take me as your fireann. Bear my mark and be my mate."

Oh, God. Oh-God-oh-God-oh-God. She gripped his drast so tight her nails snagged in the fine weave. "Don't we need more time? I mean, get to know each other better first?"

"Why? I already know you're the brightest, purest thing to ever touch my life. I know you've got an innocent passion that stirs something in me I'd never thought to connect with. I know I'd work until I couldn't stand to give you what you want or need, and that I'd happily give up my life to protect you." His lips hovered close. "What else do I need to know?"

Her heartbeat was the only sound that registered. A warbled and frantic *ka-thump-a, ka-thump-a, ka-thump-a* that left a sharp pain in its wake. Not one dog-gone thing from her mind to add to the conversation.

Listen to your heart. Trust it and everything will work out like it needs to.

Could she really leap like this?

When passion hits you, don't run from it. Embrace it. Revel in it. Then you'll know what it means to truly live.

One of the last things her dad had said before she met Ramsay that fateful night.

She was Spiritu. A Dark Spiritu. Why couldn't she follow her heart? Her passion? Her love?

She curled her fingers around his nape, knuckles brushing against the delicious weight of his thick hair as she let loose and tumbled into the risky abyss. "I choose you."

CHAPTER 27

$\mathcal{R}$amsay paced the castle foyer and paused beside the mammoth arched window overlooking the terrace and gardens. Five minutes. That's all he'd give Trinity's posse to deliver her before he headed up to collect her himself.

He turned for a fresh lap. Over a hundred and fifty years old and the last twenty-four hours had been the longest, most uncomfortable of them all. A heck of a statement considering some of the battles he'd been in. Since the time she'd agreed to be his mate, he'd barely seen Trinity save holding her while they slept the night before. Or, more accurately, while she slept. He'd tossed and turned, rehashing his plans for the mating and worrying through details he might have left uncovered.

Laughter trilled from the royal suite on the top floor.

Damned women. Lexi had corralled Trinity the minute she heard the news and hoarded her away with the rest of the girls to plan. According to Eryx, they'd re-assembled *en masse* hours ago. Lexi, Orla, Galena, Jillian and Brenna, all laughing and huddled around Trinity in a way that promised unacceptable delays.

He mentally checked the sun's position. Maybe he should tell Eryx to bring her down now. Any longer and they'd risk missing sunset.

Heavy, muted footsteps sounded at the top of the stairs.

Ramsay spun, a battle's worth of excitement peaking all at once.

Eryx started down the staircase and cast a bemused grin at Ramsay.

"Where's Trinity?" Ramsay said.

"Coming." The bastard didn't seem the least bit worried.

Damn it, he knew how important tonight was. How he'd hustled to get everything just right. "You're supposed to bring her down."

"Not anymore I'm not." He glanced up at the landing. "You should brace."

A man dressed all in black and a woman in white strolled onto the staircase landing above. The man guided his partner with her hand in his in an old-fashioned, courtly gesture.

Something breeze-like swept down the staircase and billowed out into the foyer, though instead of cooling his skin, it snipped and tingled the same as an oncoming electrical storm.

"Who in histus is that?" he said to Eryx.

"The Black King and the White Queen. Quite the sendoff for your woman."

No shit. Size-wise they weren't anything special, but their presence was larger than life. Awe inspiring and terrifying all at once. *"They say why?"*

"Something about the monumental joining of two races making their attendance necessary."

Ramsay stalked to the foot of the stairs, Eryx in lockstep beside him.

The couple floated down the stairway, their legs seemingly motionless.

A flash of red caught his eye from above, Trinity with Kazan and Lexi on either side.

Screw the king and queen. They might be powerful enough to flatten the damned castle, or maybe even their whole race, but in that moment they were inconsequential.

Instead of the white gown he'd found and delivered to her, Trinity was decked out in a fire-engine-red dress, its train so full and long it still hadn't made its way out of the hallway behind her. Whatever the fabric was, it suited her, like what a ballet dancer would wear, but lighter. The body of it had a Grecian style, accenting her curves and fastened with a sparkling silver clasp at the shoulder.

Trinity smiled, a heart-stopping, ear-to-ear one capable of obliterating any shadows in its trajectory.

"Always gratifying to see a suitor tongue-tied," the White Queen said. Her attire was too sensual to be called anything but erotic, her breasts covered in a nearly translucent fabric that hinted at dark areolas beneath, and a long skirt hanging low and provocative on her hips. Sparkling crystals marked her midriff to match the circlet atop her head.

"I think he likes our gift," the queen said to her mate before sliding her gaze back to Ramsay. "Red's a fine color on her, don't you think?"

Nothing about Trinity in that dress fell under the definition of fine. Gorgeous. Devastating. Fucking dangerous.

The queen hooked her arm around the king's and snuggled close. Her low chuckle filtered through the room, the same resonance and beauty of distant sanctuary bells on a spring morning. "Oh, yes. I think he likes our gift." She lifted her face to her mate. "Mayhap now that our Trinity has opened his heart he'll be more receptive to the voice of his Spiritu."

Ramsay's mind lurched out of its stupor. "What's that supposed to mean?"

The Black King laughed, a full-bodied sound meant for feasts and post-battle celebrations. "Your Spiritu. Vyree. She's a persistent thing for all the good it's done her. Of all her charges, she complains of your stubborn resistance the most."

His Spiritu was a woman? He didn't remember hearing a woman in his head. Did that mean—

"You haven't heard her because you've blocked her voice," the Black King answered. "Your thoughts have been your own. No spark save those generated by your own mind or The Great One himself. Only the most lost soul can ignore His influence."

Trinity neared the bottom of the stairs. A pretty flush marked her cheeks, nowhere near as deep as the color of her dress, but a perfect accent all the same. She started to duck her head, but checked it at the last second and kept her eyes locked to his.

Mine.

No outside sway to push them against their will. No dictate save fate and their own hearts.

With his gaze still on Trinity, he spoke to Eryx. "You talked to her?"

"All she needs to know," Eryx said.

Lexi covered her mouth with one hand and looked away, clearing her throat.

"And someone else may have added a hair more than they should have," Eryx tacked on dryly.

Figured. Lexi wasn't exactly on board with the rigid Myren custom of keeping mating details from unmated women, even if she'd been through it herself and understood its purpose.

Ramsay stepped forward, ready to collect his would-be mate and get his plans in motion.

"A moment." The Black King lifted his hand with a flourish, and a thick black lacquer box about twelve inches wide appeared in his palm. He drifted toward Trinity in the odd manner of movement all Spiritu seemed to employ. Well, all except Kazan. For some reason, he seemed more human than the rest. Did that mean they all had individual nuances? Or just certain ones?

The Black King opened the lid and showed the contents to Trinity.

From Ramsay's vantage point, all he could make out was a black velvet surface and something large nestled in the center. A rock, or a gemstone of some kind.

Low words rumbled from the Black King for Trinity alone, the string of information too hushed for Ramsay to catch even with his Myren hearing.

Beside Trinity, Lexi hunched closer to the box, scrutinizing its contents.

The Black King closed the lid and handed the box to Trinity.

Trinity bobbed a tiny bow and passed it to Lexi, who tucked it close.

Floating back to his place beside the White Queen, the king grinned at Ramsay. "I believe we've kept your patience at bay long enough. Make your request and do so with the blessing of those who share her heritage."

Ramsay strode forward. With every step, the people around him seemed to fade.

Everyone save Trinity.

He wanted to sweep her up and out the door. To cart her away and peel the red confection off her. To fit his body against hers and take what the most primal part of him recognized as his. He offered his hand instead. "Will you go with me, Trinity? Will you hear my vow and consider our future?"

Her smile nearly knocked him over, the power of it blinding. She glanced up at her father.

Warmth shone in his response, but pain was there too. Or worry.

Would he feel that someday? Have a daughter of his own and fight back his own worries and demons as he watched her leave under the care of another man?

Kazan released Trinity's hand and she placed it in Ramsay's.

He tucked her in the circle of his arm and guided her to the entrance, pushing the double doors wide with his mind.

Sunshine spilled through the entry, deep shades of gold and orange coloring the beams as the sun began its final decent.

Almost alone. Almost time to claim the one thing he'd never thought he'd have.

"A reminder, warrior," the Black King said.

Ramsay hesitated.

The Black King continued, "This mating is the first of its kind. One that may not be easily formed. I suggest you use the resources at your disposal."

Trinity tried to pull away and opened her mouth.

Before she could speak, Ramsay said, "I've noticed the Spiritu prefer hints over explicit directions. I take it this is one of those intricately laid clues?"

The king smirked and wrapped his arm around his queen. "Consider it my mating gift."

TRINITY MASHED and wriggled the red tulle train bundled in her arms beneath her chin for the fourth time in under ten minutes. No way was she missing one minute of the fantastic colors stretched along the western horizon as she and Ramsay flew through the air.

Ramsay tightened his arm around her waist and tucked the escaped portion of her train back with the rest. "Not the most practical gown they could've picked out, but I have to admit it makes a killer impact."

She twisted enough to meet his eyes. "You're not mad I didn't wear the one you got me?"

He shook his head and kissed her temple. His lips lingered and he pressed his hips suggestively against her bottom. "As long as you're happy and I'm the one unwrapping you, I don't care how you dress the package."

She smacked his shoulder, a playful swat that let the tail end of her train slip free again, whipping in the wind behind them. Another gust caught it and yanked the bundle from her arms.

Trinity shrieked and tried to pull the fluttering tulle back in.

"Leave it." Ramsay turned her so her chest pressed to his. He rolled to his back so the ground skimmed by below them, her train waving in the wind like an elegant kite on a perfect windy day. "We're almost there, and I don't plan on letting you keep it on long anyway."

Her belly fluttered to match the fabric waving behind them. Ramsay on the prowl was one thing, but the man holding her tonight was something more. His whole demeanor was different. Raw. Vulnerable. A fearless man who'd tossed his emotional armor aside.

"Kiss me, Trinity." He swept a hand up the length of her spine and cupped her nape. "Close your eyes and kiss me, and I'll show you my surprise."

He seemed so blasé, utterly confident in seducing her a good hundred or so feet above the ground without so much as a glance to check the direction they were headed. Then again, he'd been doing this a heck of a lot longer than she had.

He grinned, a little lopsided and a whole lot devious. The same daring look he'd used on her the night they'd met.

She lowered her head.

God, but she loved the feel of his mouth against hers. So, full and warm. A perfect fit that scattered her thoughts and worries with a single press.

She anchored her fingers in his hair and levered herself up to deepen the kiss. He tasted of his favorite Scotch, spicy and bold with a hint of vanilla. A nearly addicting warmth, like everything else she'd grown to crave about him. The brazen sweep of his tongue against hers, the way he lured her surrender, the absolute command and control he exercised against her senses—yeah, she was definitely a goner. And darn it if letting go didn't feel divine.

He fisted her hair, limiting the depth of their kiss. He nipped her lower lip. "Easy." He licked the same spot and teased his mouth against hers. "Too much of that and you'll make me flub all my carefully laid plans."

The world around them shifted as Ramsay rotated their bodies so their feet aimed toward the earth.

She smiled against his lips, reveling in the way his warm breath mingled with hers and the hard beat of his heart beneath her palm. "You're not supposed to be able to resist me. I might need to call in my tutor for additional instruction."

He froze, pulled away, and studied her face. The salt-tinged ocean breeze batted them on all sides. "Resisting you isn't an option. I tried and it didn't work. My heart might have been gun shy at the start, but my soul recognized yours from the first instant." His mouth twitched in a sheepish smile. Kind of like his internal man-meter had kicked in and cried foul for treading into sappy territory. "Ready for the surprise?"

Nope, not really.

My soul recognized yours from the first instant.

Yeah, that was way too high on the raw confession scale to rush into more surprises. "Okay," she said instead.

His smile jumped to killer proportions, a flash of the vibrant youth he'd likely once been mingled with the powerful man he'd become. No walls between them. No pretense or playboy moves.

All her emotions resonated into one unrepentant blast. Joy, wonder, gratitude and love. Each of them nestled deep in her heart, something profoundly protective and compelling mushrooming up with determination to protect what he'd laid bare.

He turned her around and pulled her back against his chest. "What do you think?"

The ocean rolled in firm, steady waves on her right, the late afternoon sun spilling across the turquoise water in deep red and mango. Three birds with long cobalt wings and lavender tips dipped and chirped in singsong voices against the wind. To her left was a private, peaceful cove, black rock walls surrounding it on all sides with varied gemstone colors glinting off the setting sun.

Sunlight winked off a glass surface in her periphery.

Oh. My. God. Was that a house?

As if sensing her thoughts, Ramsay guided them closer to the tall rock bluff jutting out in a long point between the ocean and the cove. The towering bluff was shaped in an L, a man-made cave with wall-to-wall windows and modern architecture lining the top.

Centered at the lower part of the L was a circular outdoor living space with casual loungers and futons, all topped with plush smoky black cushions piped with dove gray fabric at the edges. A skinny, but long rectangular fire pit stretched wide at the center.

"Where are we?" Everything else she'd seen in Eden had a more renaissance-meets-new-age feel to it. This was somewhere closer to Batman-meets-old-world-Greece.

Ramsay navigated them to the circular outdoor area, lifting her up as he landed and easing her to her feet. "Where I go when I need time to myself."

She spun to face him. "You live here?"

"When I'm not at the castle, which isn't often." He shrugged, eyes on the well-hidden residence above. "Took me forever to build it. Eryx helped when he had time or when I needed an extra set of hands."

"You built it yourself?"

He grinned, the devilish orneriness he wore like a second skin rising to the occasion. "I'm a resourceful guy."

Indeed. Resourceful enough to gain her father's blessing, and sweep her into a sacred ritual that would change the rest of her life in just over twenty-four hours. Too bad she didn't have a clue how to hold up her end of whatever the night held in store.

"I'm scared." She could almost feel the little minions in her mind scampering about, shouting all manner of clipped commands, and flipping levers to handle her unplanned outburst. Kind of a Willy Wonka environment in a Titanic situation.

Ramsay tucked a windswept lock of her hair behind her ear and caressed the side of her face. "Eryx said he told you what tonight was about?"

She nodded. The warmth from his hand slithered down to unwind the tension in her neck. "He said Myren women never knew what would happen on their mating night. That it's supposed to be about the man demonstrating his sincerity. To show how he means to care for the woman he wants to claim, and that he's responsible for guiding her through the process."

"And Lexi?"

Lexi. Trinity couldn't decide if she loved the woman for trying to help her out, or wanted to choke her for her less than helpful cryptic comments. "Well, for starters, she said she wasn't sure she agreed with the whole concept of keeping women in the dark about the ritual, but that she could see how it came about."

"That's a big shift for Lexi. The first time I saw her after she and Eryx were mated, I was a little afraid she'd publish a step-by-step guide. At least now she gets there's a purpose." He slid his hand down her arm and clasped her hand. "What else did she say?"

Her heart slowed and steadied under the slow back and forth of his thumb above her knuckles. "She asked me if I believed you'd be there for me going forward. If I thought you were done with running and would catch me no matter the circumstance."

The casual stroke of his thumb stopped. His calm attention shifted to that of a predator keen to prey gallivanting in his lair. "And you said?"

She swallowed, and her fingers tightened against his. Her blood surged with adrenaline, the kind of disorienting, heady rush every student got when the teacher singled them out in front of the whole class. "I told her trust was a two-way street. A man can't catch a woman who never allows herself to fall."

For the longest time he didn't move, just studied her with what she could only classify as bewilderment. Either that, or he desperately wanted to hightail it for home and couldn't figure out a good exit line.

"I don't deserve you." He traced her cheekbone, then palmed the back of her head and pulled her against his chest in a fierce, almost needy hug. "I haven't earned a tenth of what you give me, but I swear I'll spend the rest of my life catching up."

He held her there for long, peaceful minutes. The beat of his heart beneath her cheek lulled and comforted, and his heat counterbalanced the cool ocean breeze at her back.

Pulling back only enough to meet her gaze, he cupped his hands on either side of her head. His mouth parted as if to speak, then closed. He peered over her shoulder at the horizon and his eyes sharpened. He motioned behind her with his chin and turned her to match his line of sight. "This is why I brought you here."

Trinity gasped and staggered backward into Ramsay's solid chest. His strong hands steadied her at each shoulder, but the bulk of her attention was riveted on the sunset. Midnight blue covered the skies high above her and a fire red swath stretched along the ocean line, but it was the span of colors between the two that stole her breath. The odd, red-rimmed Myren sun cast sharp beams up into the skies to make its own powerful rendition of the aurora borealis, mingling with the holographic sky for a mesmerizing display.

"It's beautiful." Really, the word didn't do the visual justice, but her mind was too dumbfounded by the view to bother digging up the right description.

Ramsay's voice was quiet behind her, peaceful, and yet a little sad. "My dad brought me here when I was little. The only time I remember ever having him to myself. Eryx and I had fought about something, a worse blow up than normal. Dad thought me having a place to go and gather my thoughts might be in the best interest of the whole castle."

Trinity paced her breathing and kept her eyes locked on the majestic sun as it tipped into the teal water. She could see this sight tomorrow, or the day after, but the story bubbling up from Ramsay's memory was huge. The intensity of it crackled and snapped around her.

"Aside from Eryx, I've never brought anyone here, and even he has only been a time or two." He pulled in a slow breath. "It was the only thing I had of my dad I didn't have to share with anyone else." His fingers tightened on her shoulders. "I wanted to share it with you."

Honest to God, a battering ram couldn't have impacted her senses more than his simple, heart-felt gift. She was dumbfounded. Too stunned and humbled to formulate even the basest response.

"Look at it, Trinity. That sunset is the same impression you made on me the first time I saw you. Powerful. Colorful. Bright and warm." He slid his hands around her waist and wrapped her up tight, his mouth at her ear. "Every time I see or think of you, this is what fills me."

She tried to turn, her body and senses clamoring for eye contact. To anchor herself in his steel-gray eyes.

He stopped her with a flex of his arms. "Not yet. I need you to watch it until it's gone. To know that it's the last sunset you'll see without a mate. And know that the sunrise we watch tomorrow will be ours."

CHAPTER 28

*A*rms wrapped snug around Trinity's middle with her back pressed tight against his chest, Ramsay skimmed the shell of her ear with his lips and dragged in a deep, indulgent breath. She smelled even better than she looked, like her red dress had sparked a chemical reaction and added a touch of warm spice to her skin.

Her arms lay over his at her waist and her fingers pushed and pulled in an absentminded, almost anxious rhythm.

He'd have to work on that. Her saying trust was a two-way street eased the bulk of his worries about tonight, but that didn't mean he could afford to get complacent. The Black King's warnings of their mating being the first of its kind, one that might not easily be formed, kept circling in his head. A tiny, niggling itch he couldn't quite reach.

Only a sliver of orange and the sun's red rim hovered above the horizon. Another minute or two and the night would be theirs.

"Watch this," he said low in her ear.

Ten seconds passed. Fifteen. Twenty.

The orange disappeared, leaving only a blood red arc atop

the stretch of dark ocean. Shards of crimson shot up into the skies, a last gasp of daylight streaming into the heavens like lasers against midnight blue. Swirls of silver energy danced between them.

Trinity laughed into the quiet night, her eyes open in innocent wonder while the breeze brushed her platinum hair off her face. So beautiful. And she would be his baineann. His mate.

So long as he didn't screw things up.

I suggest you use the resources at your disposal.

Helluva mating gift. One would think the guy could've thrown him a bone and offered something a little less vague.

The last of the sun dipped below the sea, and Trinity laid her head back on his chest with a sigh. She craned her neck and studied him. Her eyes sparkled bright in the moonshine, tiny pools of unshed tears rimming the lower edge. "Thank you for sharing that with me."

She understood. Actually comprehended the importance of him bringing her here, and it rattled every square inch of him. Though why he was surprised, he didn't know. This was Trinity. He'd never met a more self-aware, giving person in his life.

"I wanted you to know," he said. "To have some demonstration that, until I die, my life is yours. I couldn't think of a better way to show you than to share the one place I've held safe from everyone else."

She turned in his arms and laid her palm over his heart. "You don't have to prove anything to me. If I didn't believe in you, I wouldn't be here."

He hoped that was true. One way or another, they were about to find out.

"Come on." He tucked her beside him and cast a narrow flame at the waiting fire pit.

The kindling he'd laid earlier in the day flared bright and

the massive logs crackled against the breeze. Sparks drifted upward.

Trinity watched the glowing particles as they sailed higher with the same open, wide-eyed fascination she'd given the sunset. "Okay, maybe I should get around to learning those tricks."

"Most people jump on learning the elements the minute they feel good enough to get out of bed. Well, either that or flying." He sat in the center of a wide fireside cushion with a mountain of pillows behind him, and pulled her between his legs so she reclined against his chest. "What gives?"

Trinity shrugged. "I don't know. I might be a little afraid of burning something I shouldn't. Or shocking something too much." She glanced back at him, a wry twist to her lips. "Mostly I'm just hesitant."

"Hesitant of what?"

She rested her head on his shoulder and studied the stars and wild swirls of Eden's extra energy. "The power, I think. I'm not sure if I have a healthy respect for it, or if I'm afraid it'll go to my head." She rolled her head to meet his gaze. "Or maybe I just like my humanity."

Ramsay stroked her jaw. "You think you've got some human mixed up with the Spiritu and the Myren, huh? Kind of a genetic trifecta?"

She huffed out a laugh and resumed her skyward perusal. "I think I've given up trying to figure out what I am. Better to focus on just being."

He traced the neckline of her gown, the bold red fabric slashing from one shoulder across her chest before dipping around the back. "Where's your pendant?"

Her hand shot to the hollow of her throat where the pendant usually lay. Her eyebrows dipped low in the center before snapping back into a relaxed line. "For a minute I forgot." She rubbed the bare skin. "I thought it looked clunky with the dress, so I took it off. Lexi said she'd put it in our room."

Our room.

And he wouldn't just be sharing his room. He'd be sharing his life. His thoughts. His emotions.

You won't be alone anymore.

Or wouldn't be if he'd stop stalling and get busy binding the two of them. "There's another reason I chose this spot. Why we're outside."

Curiosity glittered in her dark eyes.

"The elements. Fire, energy, air, water, earth, they're all here." He laid his head back and savored his heart's resounding rhythm. The heady buzz of anticipation in his veins. He skimmed his hands along her upper arms and her tiny goose bumps tickled his palms. "It's important the gifts The Great One gave us be present on a night when two people become one."

"I like that." She said it on an almost sing-songy exhale, the kind of sound usually reserved for love-struck teens and the sappy parts in romance novels. Maybe the sentiment would work to his advantage. The Great One knew what was coming would be a shock to her system.

From beneath the pillows, he tugged free the long, mahogany box he'd stashed while preparing for their night. He sat upright, taking Trinity with him. "Cross your legs."

She situated herself Indian style and settled the bulk of her train so it lay to one side of them.

With his legs bent at either side of her, he placed the box in her lap. "Open it."

She regarded him for a good three or four seconds, then ran her fingers along the polished surface. Gently, she pried the lid open.

The Shantos dagger lay nestled in onyx velvet, its nearly

nine-inch silver blade glinting orange, red, and yellow from the firelight.

Trinity fingered the rubies and sapphires embedded in the ebony hilt. "It's beautiful."

"It's been in my family for a long time. At least four generations that we're sure of." He kissed her temple and centered himself in her scent, in her presence, then stood and held out his hand. "Hand me the dagger, Trinity."

Her gaze shot back and forth between his hand and the weapon. She lifted the entire box.

He shook his head. "Just the dagger, Sunshine. Put the hilt in my palm."

With careful fingers, she lifted the blade free.

Fisting the cool metal in his palm, he offered his free hand. "Will you stand with me?"

She frowned, confusion painting her features.

Hard to blame her. Frankly, he was taking things off-script by asking her to stand beside him for his vow, but having her there felt right. Another way to let her know he wouldn't keep her at a distance. Not tonight. Not any time in their hopefully long future.

Her fingers settled in his outstretched hand and he pulled her to her feet.

He snatched the towel he'd left on a nearby table, guided her upwind of the fire pit, and shoved his drast above his elbow.

Trinity moved in close, her body tight. "What are you doing?"

Keeping the dagger at his side, he lifted his free hand parallel to the ground and fisted his hand over and over. "What's more important to our existence than the elements?"

She met his stare then eyeballed the dagger at his side. "I don't think I like this."

"For a Myren man willing to take a baineann, offering a

blood vow is the most sacred act there is. Would you ask me to forgo honoring you with it?"

"But it's not necessary." Her focus didn't budge from the knife, but she rested gentle fingers at his wrist as though prepared to shove it away. "I told you I believe in you. I don't need blood to prove it."

"I need it."

Her mouth snapped shut.

"I need for you and my Creator to know what I'm committing to isn't done lightly," he said. "Not something I'll run from when you need me most." He flexed his hand again. The veins along the inside of his arm rose and his heart pounded in a furious beat. "You don't have to watch if it's too much, but this is important. A testament that I need you as much as the blood in my veins."

She swallowed, grimacing a little before lowering her hand from his wrist. She nodded.

Before she could change her mind or overthink what would come next, he slit a long gash along the tender inside of his forearm. Nerve endings shrieked in protest and he nearly lost his grip on the hilt. Fire-intense pain radiated out in all directions, and for a second or two his sight glazed over.

He set his blade on the fire pit's rim and angled his arm so the blood flowed thick and easy. It dripped to the steel grate with an angry hiss. His forearm throbbed. His biceps and triceps cramped beneath his fist's brutal clench.

Trinity stared at the blood pulsing from the gash, her face slack and white as the moon above.

His voice rumbled against the ocean gusts, pained and grated. "Look at me, Trinity."

Her eyes were rounded with fear. For him. The concept knocked him silly. This sweet woman worried over a simple flesh wound, one easily healed with a moment or two of concentration.

He cupped her nape with his free hand and pulled her close. "I vow to The Great One to love and provide for this woman until I leave this life. To see to her needs and the needs of those she holds dear. To protect her at all costs, even to the point of death." He kissed her forehead. All the emotion wrapped around his heart surged to the surface, leaving what felt like a boulder lodged in his throat. "No other will be placed before her, and she will be cherished until I breathe no more."

A log snapped in two and the fire crackled against the ocean breeze.

Trinity's fingers dug into his waist. "Ramsay?"

"Mmm?"

She stayed pressed beside him, one arm curled around his back and the other now fisted in the bottom of his drast. "That was really beautiful, and I don't want to seem insincere, but can we take care of your arm now? I don't think we'll have much of a wedding night if you're passed out from blood loss."

A laugh ripped free before he could stop it, the sharp, loud sound echoing off the cove's high walls. He kissed the top of her head. "Can't leave my baineann-to-be unsatisfied, now can I?"

He snatched the towel and handed it to her, then angled his arm so she could better see. "It's not deep enough for serious damage. Easy enough to heal." Running the flat of his hand along the wound, he worked from his elbow to his wrist, mending the flesh and muscle underneath.

Trinity gently swiped the pink, barely-healed trail. "You fixed it." She wiped again, this time a little more boldly, and inspected his work. Turning his arm over, she shoved the sleeve of his drast up as far as it would go. "There's no mark though. Isn't that how it works?"

Damn. So much for subtle transitions. "I think that's better explained up in the lodge, preferably with you naked on my bed where I can find all kinds of ways to distract you."

"Are we done with knives?"

"Absolutely."

"Will the rest of it hurt?"

Ah, histus. How to get around this one without a complete lie or blowing the whole point of the ritual? "I only know what other mated women have told me. You'll definitely feel, but they say it's not painful."

Okay, so he left out how he'd be in enough pain for both of them. Technically, that made it more textbook male avoidance than a lie.

Trinity's gaze slid over his shoulder to the lodge nestled in the black rock wall, then shifted to the cushions where they'd started their night. "What's wrong with staying out here?"

Her husky question spun up an instantaneous visual. Trinity stretched out on the cushions, moonlight and the fire's glow on her creamy skin, knees up and wide as he tunneled deep. His cock shot from semi to concrete in less time than his Porsche could hit sixty.

"I thought you might be more comfortable someplace private." Charcoal and dove gray silk pillows waited, almost daring him to take her up on her suggestion. "I need you relaxed, Trinity. Not worried about your surroundings. If this is what you want, I'll give it to you and enjoy the hell out of every minute, but I want you comfortable. No inhibitions."

She bit her lower lip. "Would anyone see us?" she near-whispered, shy and curious all at once.

"My senses are highly accurate, capable of sensing other Myrens at a high distance when I'm focused, but something tells me I'll be distracted." He turned her to fully face the cushions and wrapped his arms around her waist. Nuzzling the sweet spot behind her ear, he pressed his aching erection against her perfect ass. "Isn't that the thrill of it? Knowing nothing is for certain?"

Her breaths deepened and her eyelids grew heavy. "I want this." So much passion in her voice, raspy and rumbling with desire. With such innocent sensuality, he'd drive a bargain with the diabhal himself to get her anything she wanted.

He spanned her waist with his hands, teasing slowly up her torso until his thumbs skimmed below her breasts. "Tell me why. Tell me how you imagine it. What you want."

A tiny tremor rattled through her. "It's the wildness of it. The wind. The water. The fire. Becoming yours in the middle of everything you hold sacred."

Becoming yours.

He wouldn't rush this. Couldn't rush this, but his hands fairly shook with the need to rip her dress free and sheath himself in her heat. "My little hedonist." He gave into a fraction of his need and cupped her breasts through the fabric, worrying her tight nipples with his thumbs. "Then I'll claim you under the stars and make you scream your release loud enough to reach the castle."

Eyes closed and lips parted, Trinity moaned and arched into his touch, her head falling back onto his shoulder.

He kissed the side of her neck, slow teasing sweeps of his lips along her skin. "Tell me you're ready." He nipped her earlobe and followed it with a soothing lick. "Tell me you'll give me everything I ask."

"Everything." Her eyes opened to meet his. "I'm not afraid. Whatever it is, whatever you have to do, I know you'll keep me safe."

Heavy words, laden with responsibility.

I suggest you use the resources at your disposal.

Damn right he would. And even those that weren't his to use if it kept her happy. Even if it meant prying his eager hands off her body to heighten her pleasure. He stepped away and checked the fire. Plenty to keep them warm for at least another hour, and more wood stacked neatly beside it.

Circling away, he strolled toward the cushion with the high mound of pillows and pulled off his drast.

Trinity followed.

Ramsay stopped and shook his head, toeing off one boot. "Oh, no you don't. You stay right there. I want to make sure I'm ready to watch my little exhibitionist in action." He tossed the second boot to join its mate, freed the fastenings on his leather pants, and shrugged them past his hips. His cock practically sang at the freedom, one barrier eradicated with only one more between it and the slick heat between Trinity's legs. He stretched out on the cushion and reclined into the pillows, legs bent and wide.

Her gaze slid to his blatant erection.

He fisted himself at the root and one of her hands fluttered to the sweet roundness above her mound. "Now it's your turn." He stroked his length. Once. Twice. Teased her while he pacified the throbbing need in his dick. "Lose the dress."

She clenched the hand at her waist.

Ramsay guided a gentle breeze against her shoulders and face.

Trinity closed her eyes and let her head fall back, savoring the salt-tinged caress.

"Feels good, doesn't it?" He swirled the air around her, tousling her hair and brushing against every inch of exposed skin. "Imagine how it would feel without the dress. Just you. The wind. The fire at your back. My eyes on you." He released the stream to its normal pattern and she lifted her head. "You wanted this. Lose the dress and come claim my mark."

Exposing herself might have come with second thoughts, but the mention of his mark shook her into action. She pulled off her sandals. Straightening, she fumbled with the sparkling broach at her shoulder, first with one hand, then with both. The latch sprang free and tumbled from her fingers.

Ramsay caught it with a thought before it made contact with the rock floor and guided it to join his dagger.

Trinity clutched the gown at her breast, held his stare for three eager heartbeats, and let go. The fabric slithered to the ground, coiling around her sumptuous curves along the way.

The Great One be praised, she was perfect. A damned sexual nymph. Rounded in all the right places, breasts firm and peaked by rock hard nipples he couldn't wait to get in his mouth.

A fresh gust of wind swept in, this one guided only by nature's hand.

Trinity gasped against the sensation, her hair wild in the breeze and eyes wide with wonder and desire. "Ramsay."

"I'm right here, Sunshine." He added a few extra streams along the back of her thighs, teasing between her legs and up around her torso. "Waiting on you."

She crept toward him, each step tentative. As though her footfalls on the stone reverberated through her body. "Where do you want me?"

Here. In his lodge. At the castle, and every surface or location in between. God, the things he wanted to do to her. To do with her. At this rate, he wasn't sure he'd ever want to resurface in reality.

"Right here." He held out his hand. "Straddle me."

Hesitant, she scanned his body like she couldn't quite figure out how to navigate the situation or where to land.

A chuckle slipped free before he could check it. He snatched her hand and tugged her forward. "Feet on either side of my hips."

She did as he asked and kneeled, knees spread wide so her slick sex sat low on his belly.

His cock nestled against her ass and he nearly came on contact. "Fuck, you feel good." He gripped her hips and flexed his own on reflex.

The movement knocked her off balance, and she caught herself with hands at his shoulders, those perfect tits of hers jiggling deliciously close to his mouth.

Damn, but he needed to be inside her. Now. To feel her heat fisting him. To thrust his energy into her heart and claim her as his mate.

"Wait."

The voice tingled more than spoke in the back of his head. Not his own, but feminine and vaguely familiar. Clipped and focused.

Trinity stared down at him, her mouth parted and close enough her jagged breaths fanned his face. She undulated against him. "Touch me. Please."

No. No waiting. He'd done that his whole damned life. Trinity was here. Eager for his touch. His cock. His mark.

He cupped her breasts, lifting the heavy globes and flicking his thumbs across her nipples. "Give me your lips."

She fit her mouth to his with a broken groan and arched into his palms. Her tongue tangled with his, her taste better than any sweet treat from Orla's kitchen and tinged with cinnamon.

Instinctively, he pressed his hand above her heart. Energy built inside his chest, something wild and primal bursting from a part of him he hadn't known existed. It tunneled down his arm. Close. So close.

"Wait."

The voice rang louder. More stern. Not Trinity, but a voice he was sure he'd heard before.

The energy pooled in his palm, eager for release. Ready to claim.

Trinity moaned against his mouth and wiggled her soft ass against his aching erection. Her lips and tongue dueled with his and her hands fisted in his hair. "Please."

His shaft throbbed against her wind-cooled skin. It was torture. Sweet, mind-bending torture. A push and pull between physical need and instinct. He wanted—needed—the link, but the voice kept echoing in his head.

I suggest you use the resources at your disposal.

He snapped his head back.

Trinity gasped, her kiss-swollen lips parted in surprise. "What?"

Mayhap now that our Trinity has opened his heart, he'll be more receptive to the voice of his Spiritu.

Vyree. The Black King had called her Vyree.

This mating is the first of its kind. One that may not be easily formed.

"Ramsay, what's wrong?"

He stroked the smooth flesh between her breasts. Beneath his skin, his energy swirled and fought for release. Was this it? What the king was warning him about?

Partially levitating them both, he spun them so fast Trinity let out a startled cry. He splayed her flat against the cushion, kneeling between her spread thighs. "It's different." The wind whipped around them in what felt like silent agreement, chilling his sweat-slick skin and slashing his hair across his face.

She gripped his wrists, stilling his hands as he stroked the tops of her legs. "What's different?"

"You. Us." He leaned over her, propping himself up with one arm and lowering himself to one breast. He licked the tip and locked his eyes with hers. "Close your eyes. Feel and let go." Another lick, circling the dusty pink areola. "I've got you."

He latched onto the hard bud and suckled deep.

Trinity bowed beneath him, her hands threading in his hair for a brutal, demanding grip.

"Tell me." Two simple words he thought into the nothingness, praying for the Black King's promised guidance.

Years of stubborn isolation shattered. Light swept in and surrounded him, peace and certainty rushing in behind it. The voice came again. More of a relieved sigh at first, then words. Faint. Barely discernible. *"Look with your spirit."*

Energy snapped above him, indignant blue arcs clashing against the dark and the fire's orange glow as his anger surged. What the hell good was a Spiritu if they talked in riddles?

"Look with your spirit." More tangible this time. Almost stubborn in its tone. *"Find what protects her heart and merge your energy with hers."*

Trailing slow, indulgent kisses along the way, he shifted to her other breast and teased the top of her mound with his knuckles. He could do this. If it meant having Trinity, he could do anything. Face anything.

"Find what protects her heart," the almost spunky woman repeated.

Cautiously, he sent his spirit forward, circling her heart.

Blinding gold flashed against his mind's eye, so radiant it rippled through him in a shock wave. Like the night he'd tried to read her memories, only more bearable. But then, he hadn't made contact this time either.

"Merge your energy with hers."

Shit. Just looking at the awesome barrier nearly knocked him silly. How in histus was he supposed to merge his own with hers?

"You suck it up and grab on tight. Better brace though. It's gonna hurt. Bad. But she's worth it, right?"

"Ramsay?"

Still focused on the golden shield and the edgy voice in his head, he barely registered Trinity's question. Distant. Concerned.

His hand was at her heart, the steady rhythm beneath his palm luring him in. Comforting despite the pain that waited. He hoped he didn't screw this up. For all he knew, he was about to grab onto a Spiritu equivalent of a live wire.

He sent his energy into her chest, surrounding the pulsating gold light with his silver essence. Only a thin, neutral layer ran between them. "Put your hand on my heart." He eked the words past his strained throat. The arm he used to hold himself above her shook with fatigue and his pulse reverberated along his arms and legs.

Trinity's fingers splayed above his heart. Firm. Not the least bit hesitant. "It's okay." Her throaty voice barely carried over the wind. "I'm ready. I trust you."

Man, this woman undid him. How could she? He didn't even know what the hell he was doing. He lowered himself against her, needing the skin-to-skin contact and the press of her mouth. "I love you," he whispered against her lips. "Never doubt it."

Before she could answer, he breached the thin layer between the barrier and his energy.

∽

QUIET. Eerie, golden quiet.

Quick as a blink, reality had flashed to nothing, leaving her alone with nothing but an odd sparkling void. Not unlike her sometimes bizarre dreams, though without the sound. No ocean waves or wind. No crackling fire. Just the same muted sensation that came from a good set of earplugs.

No, wait...

A long agonized wail registered, muffled as though it came from a great distance.

She strained her mental vision against the shimmering wall. There was something on the other side of the veil. Something important.

Think, Trinity. Focus.

This couldn't be a dream. She'd been awake. With Ramsay and ready to become his mate.

The cry sounded again. Ragged and closer.

Ramsay.

Grated shouts billowed up like something from the bowels of a torturer's dungeon. But where was he? Why couldn't she see him?

Heat radiated along her front and a steady weight pressed against her heart.

The image of him above her, his long, dark hair spilling over his shoulders as he whispered against her lips. *I love you. Never doubt it.*

It wasn't a dream. He was still here. Hurting.

And she was failing him.

She pushed against the golden fog, a mental equivalent of swimming toward the water's surface from the deepest ocean. Over and over again she reached with her mind, wading through the seemingly impenetrable gate.

This couldn't happen. She'd told him she trusted him. Told him she believed in him. How could she let this happen?

"Let me in." Faint. Barely there, but unmistakably Ramsay. A simple thought echoing through her head.

She needed to calm down. To center herself and think.

Destiny is what you make it. The last words her father had spoken the night she'd met Ramsay. Maybe that was the key.

Her will was hers. Who she trusted. Who she took as her mate. Who she let behind the walls of her Spiritu self.

A picture formulated in her head. The barrier thinned from gold to the color of wheat, then to a buttery yellow. Streams of sparkling silver glinted in the distance, swirling at the furthest edge of what remained of the gold veil.

She reached for him with her thoughts and a shimmering gold stream shot forward. It spiraled through the tunnel she'd created in an almost playful dance. Like a water nymph set free from a land-bound prison.

The silver threads at the far side slithered closer, cautious, but purposeful. Such a beautiful color. Vibrant and powerful like his dagger. One of the strands wound around hers, the movement so beautifully sensual her heart quaked.

Tighter and tighter the strands blended.

A warm, peaceful burn sparked deep in her chest, a place so intimate she wasn't even sure it was of her physical body. Something far more important. Spiritual.

The strands snapped together. A flash of perfectly woven gold and silver blasted through every corner of her mind, blinding her to everything. The strands, the barrier.

"Trinity."

Big, warm hands cradled her face. Ramsay hovered above her, his eyes wide and tanned skin flushed from exertion. His hair clung to the sides of his face and neck, damp with sweat. Over his heart, angry welts sprawled in a huge starburst pattern. "You said it wouldn't hurt."

He smiled. A beautiful, genuine smile that ricocheted through every fiber of her being. God, she could swear she actually felt his happiness. A carefree rush of emotion. "I said *you* wouldn't hurt."

He guided her hand from his chest, laid a reverent kiss to her knuckles, and lifted her arm so she could better see it. "You're mine." He traced the proud horse reared back and ready for flight. "My baineann." He fingered the detailed wings. "My Spiritu."

Oh. My. God.

She sat up so quickly she nearly knocked heads with her new husband. "There's color." She glanced at Ramsay, now kneeling in front of her. "Lexi's doesn't look like this."

"No one's looks like that." He leaned in to appreciate the silver and gold glinting in the feathers. "But then no other Myren has a Spiritu for a mate, now do they?"

It was beautiful. An amazing artistic feat that shouldn't be possible on a living body.

Her gaze drifted to the welts deepening to bloody crimson on his chest. "I can't believe you did that. For me."

He lifted her face with a gentle touch beneath her chin. "I'd do it all again. I'd do it every day, if it meant having you."

A thousand flutters winged inside her chest. The world around them dimmed and the sweetest instinct tugged her forward. Nothing mattered right now save his touch. The perfect press of his lips against hers.

She smoothed his hair off his face. "You said you'd give me what I want?"

His trademark bad boy grin kicked into place. A little weary and more lopsided than normal, but there all the same. "Anything."

She rolled to her knees. "All this uncertainty and guesswork has left me a little out of balance." She nudged his shoulders, urging him to lie back on the cushions.

A wicked glint fired in his silver eyes. He shifted to his back, centering her between his bent legs and giving her the most delicious view of his impeccable body. "Can't have that. I suppose you have an idea what would get you centered again?"

She stood tall on her knees and ran her hands along his upper thighs toward his hips. The sparse hair tickled her palms, a stark contrast to the powerful muscles beneath. "I think I'd like to drive."

His eyes darkened and his smile slipped.

The wind snapped around her like the tail of an angry cat. She scraped her nails down the prominent V at his hips, stopping just short of his rapidly hardening erection. "Does that bother you?"

His cock jerked in answer before he could. "Does it look like I'm bothered?" He thrust his pelvis up suggestively and threaded his hands behind his head. "Take what you want. Just get your hands on me before I take over."

His shaft lay long and thick against his belly, the flared head slightly darker than the tanned skin beneath it. Shadows from the firelight accented every dip and groove of muscles along his abdomen, chest, and arms. So much to enjoy. The question was where to start.

"Hands, Trinity." The heat behind his stare nearly engulfed her. A giant inferno so violent it wouldn't leave so much as ash behind. "Unless you've changed your mind."

She crawled over him, purposefully avoiding his cock. "Just thinking about how my instructor would have suggested I tackle my assignment." She anchored her hands at either side of his head. "He seems to be a fan of long, drawn-out torment. I'm thinking I should give that approach a try."

His eyes were locked on her breasts, his mouth slightly ajar and ready for action.

She dipped her torso just enough to tease him, then shifted downward and pressed a kiss to the starburst welts above his heart.

"I've created a damned monster." Playful, but strained. Talk about a boost for her feminine morale. He didn't just sound like a man who wanted sex. He sounded like he'd die in the next few minutes if he didn't find release.

She licked along the center of his chest, tracing each indentation with slow, lingering kisses. His skin tasted of salt and warmth, one hundred percent male and potent. With every inch and every kiss, his anticipation became her own, his need, her want.

She flicked her tongue against his navel, careful to avoid the waiting erection just beneath.

His abdominals rippled and his breath hissed between clenched teeth. "Need your hands on my dick, Trinity." He flexed his hips. "Now."

Angling sideways, she nipped the tight flesh at his hip. "Hands?" She kissed the same spot and inhaled deep. His earthy, exotic scent blended with the wood smoke and the ocean's salty breeze.

She lifted her head, mouth poised over his cock, and clashed into his silver gaze. "I was thinking of something a little more..." She licked her lower lip and cast a coy glance at his staff. "Wet."

He uncurled one arm from behind his head and fisted his hand in her hair. To his credit, he didn't force her so much as an inch, but the tension was there. Demanding need. Fierce determination. "You enjoying yourself?"

A smile spread wide before she could stop it, one she was sure her Black brethren would be pretty darned proud of. "Infinitely."

"Good." He undulated again, bringing the tip of his sex to her lips. "Remember that when I've got you begging for my cock."

Her core clenched and the image of him behind her, fingers digging into her hips as he plunged deep flashed vivid in her mind.

Okay. Maybe she'd toyed with him enough. Especially if it meant making that picture a reality. She licked the slick head and his tangy pre-cum settled at the back of her tongue, a carnal taste that drew her back for more. Sucking him in, she flattened her tongue against his hot length and swallowed.

"Daaamn." His guttural exclamation vibrated like a living presence all around them, and his other hand joined its mate, clenching in her hair. No force, but tightly leashed power. An unspoken testament to the strength he held in check. For her.

She cupped his tight sack and gloried in the mix of soft skin and formidable strength. The stark veins along his cock rasped against her tongue with each push and pull of her mouth. So thick. Stretching her lips. Promising the same glorious sensation as he tunneled deep.

A slow, tingling warmth pooled in her belly. Faint at first, then growing. Ribbons of pure ecstasy slithered towards her breasts and between her thighs.

She moaned around his shaft and widened her knees. Her hips lifted in wanton invitation, but met only a sharp stroke of cool air. God, whatever he was doing beat any vibrator known to man. She wanted more of it. Now.

"Like that?" The rumble in his voice matched the ever-increasing vibration at each pleasure point.

She took all of him that she could in answer, his cockhead meeting the back of her throat as she swallowed. This was supposed to be about him, giving back the selfless sensual indulgence he'd shown her. She'd never last. Not with his unfathomable assault running wild at her core.

"Crawl up here, Sunshine." He urged her upward with firm hands at the back of her head. "Fucking love your mouth, but need your pussy."

His claim plucked her already taut strings of pleasure, nearly pushing her to climax without so much as a physical touch.

His cock slipped free of her mouth and bobbed against

her lips. She tongued the ridge and met his heavy-lidded gaze. "Is it terrible I like how dirty that sounds?"

He gripped her under each arm and half dragged, half lifted her on top of him. His cock lay flat against his skin, her slick labia splayed deliciously around his length. He clasped her hips and prodded her into a decadent motion, rubbing her wet center up and down his shaft. Teasing her with yet an additional sensation. A promise without fulfillment.

"There's nothing wrong with dirty." He flexed upward, grazing her clit with his cockhead, then pulled back. Back and forth, he guided her. Again and again. Always ending with his head in perfect alignment, but never thrusting where she needed him. The tingling sensation grew at every pleasure point. "Tell me what you want, Sunshine."

"Stop teasing me." She tried to overpower his rhythm, but his hands held her steady.

"Uh-uh. Told you I'd make you beg for it." He nudged her sex and grinned. The swirling vibration behind her clit jumped so high she flinched. He teased the fine hairs on her mound in a soft touch. "Tell me. Make it dirty. I dare you."

Dirty. She couldn't think, let alone conjure up dirty. She tumbled forward and gripped his shoulders, angling her hips for the extra pressure at her clit.

He took full advantage of the adjustment, cupping one breast and flicking her hard nipple with his tongue. "Tell me to fuck you. Beg me to fill your pussy with my cock." He sucked the point into his mouth. He prodded her entrance. Ready. Waiting.

Her body shook. Sweat misted her back and the space between her breasts. Air whipped around them and the fire radiated against her skin, heightening already overpowered sensations.

The words sat eager on her tongue. Her insides coiled so

tense she thought she might explode. She could do this. Wanted it. "Fuck me."

Ramsay's gaze bore into hers, hotter than the fire. A scorching stare that obliterated what was left of her hesitancy.

"Fill my pussy with your cock. Make me yours."

A blast of pure lust washed across his face. Animal surging beyond the man for just a glimpse before he filled her in one unyielding thrust.

So full. Hard and thick. Pistoning into her sensitive channel and holding her firm against each advance. Flesh slapped against flesh. Moans and grated pleas tangled with the wind. This was connection. A primal, perfect joining. No shame. No rules. Just desire, need, and the flawless melding of two souls.

He flicked the neglected nipple with his tongue then murmured against it, his hot breath nothing short of glorious. "My naughty little Spiritu." He nipped the peak with his teeth. "Time for you to fly."

He sucked her nipple deep and shifted the angle of his thrusts, rasping the sweet spot inside her. Once. Twice.

Her walls clamped tight, fisting his shaft with a desperation she felt all the way to her soul. Her pulse roared to match the ragged shout rattling up her throat, at her neck, her wrists, the arches of her feet, between her legs.

His cock tunneled in and out, matching the beat of her heart perfectly, drawing out the sweet uproar rolling through her and pushing it to an even higher apex.

He gripped her hair, dragging her head back. "Look at me."

She pried her eyelids open. Was it her imagination or did the fire beside them burn higher? Brighter? Above them sharp, blue arcs of electricity snapped and crackled.

He held her hips stationary and slammed deep, the whites

of his eyes glowing neon. Wild. Completely untamed. "Mine."
He speared to the hilt and threw back his head, unleashing a
roar that shook everything around them. His cock jerked
inside her.

Her pussy contracted, a whole new level of pleasure
mingled with his, body shaking as she writhed against him.
There was no world, no reality, save the press of his hot body
against hers.

Slowly her muscles loosened. Relaxed into the soothing
stroke of his hand along her spine and the brush of the
ocean's breeze.

Amazing. Utterly, mind-alteringly amazing. Too good to
ever recreate. Which was just as well. She wasn't sure she
could live through such a profound moment twice.

He kissed her forehead, lips warm, fingers massaging the
back of her neck. *"Not too good. Perfect."* The words formed in
her mind as clearly as her own thoughts.

Telepathy. How odd that it worked like a thought. And
how exciting that she finally had a link with someone. Had a
family connection of her own.

"Not just family," he answered. *"A mate. And what you just
felt? It's what you deserve. What I'll give you every single time."*

CHAPTER 29

*S*erena strode down the long open breezeway towards Thyrus' office, two of Eryx's guards flanking her. She gripped her fur-trimmed jacket tight beneath her breasts and ducked her head against the unseasonably cold wind. As weather went, she couldn't have picked a worse time to leave her home. Cush and Havilah favored comfortable climates most of the time, warm days and brisk nights, but every now and then Great Mother threw a tantrum.

Fine with her. She needed time away from home, bad weather or not. More importantly, she needed out from under Uther's watchful eyes. His visits the last three days had kept to the overnight hours, but she got the distinct impression he kept close tabs on the activities at her home during the day. If her instincts steered her right, today's outing was a pursuit best kept to herself.

She flicked her fingers toward Thyrus' office at the furthest end of the corridor and the ebony door with its etched detail opened wide. "I'll be a while," she said to the men behind her, barely sparing them a withered glance. She gripped her satchel a bit tighter. "I suggest you find some-place warm to occupy yourself. I'll send a runner to fetch you when I'm ready to return."

"We'll wait," the dark-headed one on her left said, pausing just outside the threshold.

Warmth wafted through the opening. She stepped inside just as Thyrus lumbered around his wide mahogany desk. Overcast skies lit the otherwise comfortably furnished room through a wide picture window that spanned the far wall. In the corner, his assistant scribbled diligently in a thick jour-nal. "My counsel's office is protected space." She waved her hand at their warrior garb. "You'll be miserable out here dressed like that."

The other warrior turned his back and crossed his arms, feet braced defiantly. His long wavy hair whipped madly in the wind. No mark graced his forearm.

Unmated and free of current entanglement. Eryx might be a pain in her ass, but his warriors were exceptional speci-mens. This one in particular would be a pleasant distraction if she had more time to kill.

"We'll be fine." The dark-haired man's voice dripped with disgust.

She shrugged and gripped the door. "Suit yourself," she said with a smile and shoved the panel shut.

"You'd do better to develop good relations with them." Thyrus hustled closer and held out his hand. "How was the trip over?"

"Miserable." Keeping her jacket on, she settled beside the roaring hearth in a crimson wingback. "And I'd be more than willing to foster a very intimate relationship with the blond, though I do believe his fellow warrior thinks I'm the diabhal incarnate."

Thyrus sprawled on the ivory couch beside her. "Can I get you something to drink? It might not yet be noon, but a finger or two of strasse might be just the thing to fight your chill."

As if pulled to attention with the snap of a finger, his assistant stood and waited beside his desk, ready for action.

The harsh scent of the berries used to ferment the brew upended her stomach on a good day, let alone one where she needed her mind sharp. "A minute or two by the fire and I'll be fine."

Thyrus waved dismissively at his assistant. "Go. Take some extra time for lunch. Maybe spend some time at the market."

As if anyone would willingly spend time in this blustering morning. Still, the prepubescent-looking man scurried off, snatching a poor excuse for an over robe off a hall tree on the way.

"Now." Thyrus threaded his meaty paws on top of his wide girth and wiggled deeper into the already strained cushions. "What brings you out in such foul weather?"

"The second book I asked you to keep for me, you said you'd keep it safely stored here?"

Thyrus rolled his lower lip out in a thoughtful pout and nodded. "Have it in the safe as you asked."

"Good. Would it be possible for you to give me some time to study it? Maybe take an hour or two alone in your conference room?"

"Yes, of course." He pried himself from the couch and motioned toward the back room. "Don't know why you got out for the occasion, though. Would've happily sent the tome via carrier."

She picked her satchel up off the floor and followed him. "I've assured Angus the copies would be kept safe. I'm uncomfortable enough with the more recent copy unprotected in my home. Housing one a thousand years older would worry me to no end." And would give Uther an excuse to have a copy of his own. Not something she was amenable to.

Compared to the main office, Thyrus' conference room was a sterile gray offset only by the Blackwood table stretched from end to end and a wall of legal texts in all manner of leather bindings. Maybe it was the overcast gloom, but the room felt twenty degrees colder than the one behind them.

"I thought you said the journals were the same." He set the candles spaced down the table's center alight with a wave of his hand and pulled out a chair for her.

"According to Angus, they are," she lied quickly. "Some of the markings in the newer copy are too worn to decipher. I was hoping the same translations would be more apparent in the older text." In actuality, Angus had warned of subtle differences between the two texts. Most might be identical, but rumor had it some of the symbols had alternate meanings in the older texts. A factor she hoped would shed light on a few nonsensical, yet apparently key translations.

Thyrus spun the old-fashioned combination safe, a human contraption that looked like it had been hand-delivered from the wild, Wild West. "Perhaps I could be of assistance? I have something of a knack for languages."

Praise The Great One, no. She'd given Uther only enough to whet his whistle, but the full breadth of what she'd already uncovered was enough to spur the most conscientious of men to a greedy pursuit of power.

"I have no doubt you'd be a great help, but I find the solitary time soothes me." She nudged an air of woe and helplessness toward her colleague. "I have a feeling the next year will be filled with many such projects to pass the time."

He grunted in agreement and pulled the worn brown book from a shelf. Tiny dust motes stirred the muted gray light from the windows. "Here you go then." He slid the book across the table and dusted his hands. "Take your time. I've got a few errands to run and an ellan to meet for midday meal. Just pack up the journal if I'm not here when you're done and give the dial a spin." He waddled across the room, breath heaving from his barely accelerated endeavors. "Help yourself to snacks and drinks at the bar while you're here."

The door shut behind him with a quiet *thunk*.

She traced the journal's spine. Cracked, aged leather scraped the pad of her finger.

Muted shuffles and footsteps sounded from the outer room, followed by the clunk of the main door.

She fingered the satchel flaps, waiting.

No sounds save the intermittent wind gusts on the windows.

She flipped the fasteners and pulled her tablet free, smoothing the crinkled pages. Front and center, the scribbled notes she'd toiled over nearly non-stop for the last three days stared back at her. Not the shambled bits and pieces she'd placated Uther with, but the ones that stirred her visions. Made her re-think all her plans in the most dramatic of ways. The words of The Great One. The long foretold prophecy, save the most important words she needed to complete the puzzle.

A safe haven will be created for your human brethren and a barrier formed between the two realms, fueled by your most formidable powers and grief. A reckoning will come, marked by the joining of one who leads and one who bears the mark of a sword twined in ivy. A human will stand as judge, one versed in both races and injured in similar kind to the one wronged this day. The mark ???? will be the key, the tool that will ???? ???? ???? the powers you give freely this day, or that will keep the wall in place forever more.

So close. She'd wasted nearly a whole day wading through the sketchy drama outlined in the early passages of Uther's tattered family journal. Some nonsense about the transgressions of Myren men against a human woman that had triggered the whole bloody affair, but this...

She re-read the last passage. This had to be it. The key to it all. A few, frustratingly vague symbols worn by too many years and second-rate care all that stood between her and all she ever wanted. If the rest of Uther's family wasn't already dead, she'd recommend he torture and kill every last one of them for their foolish disregard of the legacy they'd held all these years.

She gently pulled Uther's felt-wrapped journal from her satchel. Peeling away the black fabric, she opened the book to the last passage and laid it side by side with the ancient translation from Thyrus' safe. Tension held her spine rigid, and the ache of days pouring over the texts tugged at the base of her neck. Her arms shook with each cautiously turned page, a dangerous mix of the room's chill and the hunt.

One symbol after another, she worked through the older translation. Some easily distinguished from others, some varying only by a small mark or nuance. Time passed too quickly. The sun's overcast beams shifted through the high window and everything from her waist down tingled with near numbness.

An open palm with wavy lines above it sat near the bottom of the page, the second of the two images she'd failed to translate. All she'd garnered from the more recent translation was that the symbol represented food, which made no sense.

She pulled a candle closer and leaned in.

To strengthen. To provide for. To feed.

Shifting to her tablet, she set the options to paper.

Feed. It had to be feed. But feed who?

Four pages later another word clicked into place. Family.

The mark of your family will be the key, the tool that will feed ????
the powers you give freely this day, or that will keep the wall in
place forever more.

Damn it. Feed who? She'd reached the end of the translation and hadn't seen one reference to the last symbol.

She flipped to the start of the translation again. One image was all she had left, two circles with a box on top.

Carefully, she turned the page. Then another. She started to turn the third and froze. It was the last on the page. No wonder she'd missed it.

To convey. To porter. To bear.

To bear. That had to be it.

The mark of your family will be the key, the tool that will feed its
bearer the powers you give freely this day, or that will keep the
wall in place forever more.

Her heart surged in an eager sprint. If she wielded the key, she could have the powers. No man between her and her desires. No reliance on others to keep their vows. Just because a man had always been the one to command the sum of all Myren powers didn't mean it had to remain that way.

A muted thud sounded from the outer room.

Serena ripped the full translation from her tablet and stuffed it in her satchel. With her mind she navigated the older book to the safe and pushed the door closed with a heavy swoosh as the door latch behind her clunked. She gave the safe's dial a quick mental twist and perched over her tablet.

"Hard at work," Uther said from behind her.

What in histus was he doing here?

"I wondered what had you out and about." He hovered over her shoulder. "Any more luck?"

A damned treasure trove. Not that he needed to know. She showed him the same heavily parsed section she'd shown him the day before and waved to the wall of books behind her. "I can't seem to get past this section. I'd hoped Thyrus' library might offer up some clues, but I haven't had much luck." She tucked the tablet in her satchel, careful to keep the full translation hidden. "I think it's best I move on to the next section and see if it brings any more success."

Uther studied her, the shrewd narrowing of his eyes amplifying her pulse to the point it pounded in her ears. "Why aren't there any books on the table?"

She flipped the latches on her satchel into place and lifted an arrogant eyebrow. "You're going to tell me how to do my research now? I don't see you making any progress on your own. I hardly think you're in a place to question my methods." She stood and lifted her satchel. "For the record though, I'd already finished my research and cleaned up before you got here. Speaking of, how did you get past the guards?"

Uther's gaze slid along the wall of books, considering, before he met hers and smirked. "Masking is one of my stronger skills. Particularly when there are sufficient distractions that help me hide my presence."

"How?"

"Now you're questioning my methods?"

She waved him off and headed to the main room. "Not the same thing at all. You were calling mine into question. I was learning."

She was halfway to the door, her heart almost back to a bearable rhythm.

Uther grasped her arm and spun her to face him. "I won't tolerate lies."

Of course, he wouldn't. The man had as much sympathy in him as her father. It didn't matter. The gamble would be worth it in the end if she could find that key.

She smiled with more confidence than she felt. "Neither will I. Now, if you won't tell me how you got past the guards, then at least tell me if your tricks would work in a more secure environment."

"How secure?"

She gave him her back and continued her trek to the door and the guards waiting beyond. "I want you to get us in the castle. They've got the official translations, and we'll never get past where I'm at without them."

"You want to steal right out from under the malran's nose?"

Well, not the translation tables. Something far more important than that. But Uther didn't need to know that detail. Not yet anyway. She twisted the latch and tossed a mocking smirk his direction. "If you want the power, you'll have to take the risk."

CHAPTER 30

Trinity flew toward the Shantos castle, Ramsay within touching distance at her back. A little more than forty-eight hours they'd had all to themselves, and it had been utter bliss. Two sunrises she'd been able to watch with him, vivid corals and pinks lifting over the distant mountains and his black rock cove.

Their cove, Ramsay had called it. Their home. Compared to the castle, the lodge was tiny. Cozy, but with clean lines. One large open room, a minimal kitchen along one wall, small sitting area in one corner with a moderate hearth, and a monstrous bed along the back wall. Kind of like the loft she'd almost rented in Dallas, but more manly and with a much better view.

The landscape *and* the man.

That mysterious, but oh-so pleasant flutter she'd wrestled with since the day she met Ramsay scampered beneath her sternum. What a fairy tale. In two weeks her life had turned on its head. From lonely librarian with a secret heritage, to a multi-cultural woman with a devastatingly handsome husband.

No, not husband. Fireann. If she was going to live a Myren life, she needed to get those terms right.

And family. She had family.

She twisted and laid eyes on the mark spanning Ramsay's entire arm. An exact replica of Lexi's mark and the pendant she'd worn nearly every day since she was ten. Well, exactly the same except Ramsay's mark had silver and gold just like her Pegasus, though his was accented in the blade and hilt.

God, but she was happy. Connected. Her soul beaming brighter than the red-rimmed sun creeping up the rainbow sky.

"Crazy," Ramsay half muttered, half chuckled.

"What's crazy?"

He shook his head and gazed down at her. It was weird seeing him with his hair bound, but the first thing he'd done upon waking was to pull his thick hair into a tight ponytail. With a satisfied smirk, he'd proceeded to braid a lock of hers. A custom, he'd explained. One that signified their relationship.

An almost misty wonderment filled his eyes. "I swear I can feel your emotions. I don't know if it's the Spiritu factor in our link, or if I just can't turn off my Myren emotional radar, but right now I'd say you're somewhere between a kid with a new toy and Cinderella."

She gave in to temptation and touched the sword hilt on his forearm. He wasn't wrong. Not on either count. "I'm pretty sure I'm feeling yours too, like an echo." She navigated closer, nearly snuggled with him midair. "You didn't want to leave this morning, but you did it anyway. For me."

"You wanted to officially meet your family and show off your pretty new mark. I get that." He stroked one tip of the horse's wing near her shoulder. The gold and silver accents shimmered in the brilliant morning light. "Kind of looking forward to one-upping Eryx myself."

She shook her head, a little of her early confusion clouding her happy mood. "I don't get it though. If Lexi and I are related, why wouldn't the telepathy work after my awakening?"

Ramsay laughed and laid a comforting hand at the small of her back. "Stop analyzing it. Could just be we needed to blast a hole in your Spiritu firewall."

"So you think it'll work now?"

"You could try calling ahead and find out."

The castle sat nestled on an ocean-side point, growing closer by the second. Tall mountains looked down on it from one side and lush gardens with flowers in bold, exotic colors surrounded the perimeter. They were nearly there already. Not much point in testing things out now. "Nope, I'd rather keep it a surprise."

"Works for me." He shifted to land and swept her into his arms. "I'd rather Eryx not know we're coming anyway. He might put me back to work early, and I'm not done playing with my baineann."

Her happy laughter trailed behind them, her stomach lagging along with it. Someday she'd be as adept in the air as he was, but right now every aerial shift registered on par with a corkscrew roller coaster.

The guards positioned outside the main castle entrance pulled the mammoth double doors wide and dipped their heads in acknowledgement. She could have sworn Ramsay puffed his chest out a tad further as they strode past. She'd wondered why he'd chosen the more informal drast this morning, especially with how cold it had been. But with her mark plastered big and bold down his entire arm the pieces clicked.

"And you think I'm a show off." She laced her fingers with his and traipsed beside him as he wound through the main hallway. "At least I wore a jacket."

Granted it was Ramsay's jacket, heavy leather with the sleeves clumsily rolled back to free her hands, but it was all he'd had at the lodge to combat the unexpected cold front.

"Hey, I should get points for having a change of clothes for you. The Great Mother, her moods I can't predict. If I hadn't worn that to Evad a few weeks ago, we'd have had to roll you up in a blanket like a burrito to get you home."

They hurried through the kitchen. A castle worker stood perched on a step stool in the open pantry, stowing a nearly bursting burlap sack on a high shelf. A small fire burned in the wide, skinny brick oven, and the scent of fresh bread filled the room.

"Where are we going?" she asked.

Ramsay lifted his chin toward the back of the castle. "Eryx is up front in his study with Ludan. Lexi's in the private garden out back."

She stopped, pulling Ramsay to a standstill in the process. "How do you know that?"

His head jerked back as if she'd shocked him, then a slow smile spread across his face. "Their links. You can use 'em to locate where they're at. It's kind of second nature once you learn how to do it. Guess we forgot to cover that point." He pulled her in front of him and aimed her toward the garden beyond. "Close your eyes and give it a shot."

"Will she know I'm doing it?"

"Nope. Not a clue unless you say something." He cupped her shoulders. "Just open your mind and search her out. You'll feel it like a tug. Or maybe a compass. Kind of hard to explain."

She closed her eyes and tried to relax. Muted sounds pinged in and around the house. Two women chatting somewhere near the foyer. A steady clang from outside, like a hammer on metal. Maybe they had a blacksmith. Did they even need things like that in Eden?

"Start with me," he whispered in her mind. *"Follow the thread you feel when we talk this way. Feel the presence that goes with it?"*

Instinct urged her to face his voice. *"Like your brain is trying to line up with the person."*

"Exactly like that." He pressed a kiss to the top of her head. *"Now look for Lexi. Find your family."*

She focused on Ramsay's link and stilled her mind. His had a certain resonation. A sparkling silver thread floating easy in her mind's eye.

A blue stream wiggled nearby, soft in tone and so close to gray she nearly missed it beside Ramsay's.

Wait a minute. In her mind's eye, there was another strand near Ramsay's. This one deeper gray and more restrained in its movement. Peaceful. Calm.

Eryx.

"I see it." She clamped onto Ramsay's hand at her shoulder and held her breath for fear she'd lose the vision. "Hers and Eryx's. Because he's family now too, right?"

"That's right. You should see Lena and Reese too, though Reese's might be a little dimmer."

A green strand. Vibrant as Myren grass and set further away, a pale green strand close beside it. The two undulated as though floating in a soft breeze, in perfect alignment. "They're all different colors. And they all act a little different too."

"Because every person is different." He wrapped his arms around her waist and hugged her tight. "Now follow Lexi's. See where it leads you."

She singled out the blue thread and her thoughts shifted. A kind of mental pointer her body responded to almost instantly. "That way." She opened her eyes and found herself aimed straight toward the rear castle exit.

"Nailed it." He grabbed her hand and pulled her forward. "Now come on. Let's go meet your sister."

She stumbled in his wake. Her emotions rattled in all directions. Sister? She'd let her thoughts fiddle with the idea of family, but sister?

Ramsay opened the door. The guards at either side snapped to attention, drawing the focus of a cluster of women, all animatedly chatting near the fire pit.

Lexi and Galena. Orla. Ian's daughter, Jillian. At the center of their group was Brenna, the sweet little human she'd caught watching her as Lexi had taught her to levitate things shortly after her awakening. Her dark eyes seemed way too ancient for her young body.

All eyes were trained on her.

"Time to strut your stuff, Sunshine." He peeled the jacket off her shoulders and playfully swatted her butt. "Let's go show the girls what we made together."

She swallowed and kept her focus on Lexi as she navigated the twisting sand path. A sister. Wow. She'd barely made it halfway to them when their expressions shifted, welcome smiles morphing to stunned looks. Every one of them had eyes locked on Ramsay's arm.

Lexi's head snapped up as Trinity reached the flagstone circle. Her smile reached ear-to-ear, joy shining from her face to match what danced around in Trinity's heart.

Trinity focused on the blue strand and aimed her thoughts. *"Surprise."*

Lexi's eyes rounded and her mouth dropped open. "I can hear you!"

Ramsay chuckled beside Trinity and cupped the back of her neck. "I guess my firewall theory was right."

Lexi shot forward and wrapped Trinity up in a tight hug, the impact nearly knocking her off center. For long seconds, it seemed as if both of them held their breath, uncertain what to say. Lexi shook against Trinity and a sniffle sounded at Trinity's ear.

"It wasn't a fluke," Lexi whispered. "We are family."

Oh, God. Not tears. If Lexi cried, there was no way Trinity would be able to contain her own. Her throat was already clogged with more emotion than she knew what to do with. Any more and she'd be a blubbering mess. "Ramsay thinks we're sisters."

Lexi's arms tightened, and then she pulled away still grasping Trinity's shoulders. Tears trailed down her cheeks and her eyes were shiny with more yet to fall, but her smile was huge. Pure joy. Bold and as vibrant as the woman herself. "We'll figure it out."

Her vision swam, Lexi and the women behind her going fuzzy as reality surfaced.

Ramsay stroked her nape.

Lexi laughed and dashed away a fresh tear. "Now look what I did." She motioned at Ramsay beside her. "You're crying and your big bad fireann's all prickly and ready to cart you off somewhere safe."

"She's right where she needs to be." He moved closer to Trinity and wrapped an arm around her waist.

Did he realize the way he grounded her? How much she needed his strength right now?

"Besides," he said, "she's probably ready for some girl talk, and I'm kind of looking forward to showing off with Eryx."

"Showing off what?" Eryx strode toward them, a few of his many braids hanging long over one shoulder, metals beads at the end glinting in the sun

Next to Eryx, Ludan scowled and scanned the women behind Lexi. Whatever it was that had brought them to the garden didn't look to be warm and fuzzy.

Eryx didn't stop until he had Lexi plastered next to him, a nearly mirror grip at her neck to the one Ramsay so often used with her. He glared at his twin. "You want to tell me why my baineann's crying?"

"Unwind your panties," Ramsay drawled from behind Trinity. He uncoiled his marked arm from around her and held it out where Eryx could see. "Just confirming family ties and sharing all 'round good cheer."

Eryx gaped.

Ludan leaned in, studied the sword on Ramsay's arm then ran his gaze up and down Trinity's. His mouth quirked into an almost awkward grin he seemed determined to keep in check. "Sparkly."

"Fuck you, Forte," Ramsay said.

"Ignore him," Eryx said. "He's just scared the mating biz is contagious." He offered Ramsay his hand. "Pretty damned impressive, brother. Guess that's one way to make sure people tell us apart."

Ramsay clapped hands with his brother, or more like forearms. The weird grip looked like something she'd expect in a gladiator movie. "Yeah, well, the fancy upgrades came with a few extra up-charges." He winked at Trinity as he released Eryx's forearm. "Made for a wild night."

"Ugh." Lexi swatted Eryx on the shoulder. "Male posturing. You guys go beat on your chests somewhere else and let me and the rest of the girls plot out how to unravel our mysterious family tree."

All the humor in Eryx's face fled. "Yeah, about that." He locked stares with Ramsay and jerked his head toward the castle. "Just had a meeting with one of the senior ellan, Maron Deesus. He showed up unannounced about an hour ago and dropped some intel we can't ignore."

"Serena?" Lexi said.

"Angus." Eryx aimed an apologetic smile at Trinity. "I was coming to tell Lexi we were headed out to get Ramsay. Need him to run down a lead."

Ramsay tensed. "What kind of lead?"

"Angus visited the ellan a few days ago. Unexpected. Didn't really have a good reason for being there either. Next day, the ellan realized an ancient text was missing from his library."

Pinpricks sizzled along Trinity's nape and a low, aggravating hum tickled her ears. A warning. Bolder than usual. Nearly as potent as the day her adopted father had died.

"Translation tables?" Lexi glanced between Eryx and Ludan. "I thought we got the only ones that were left."

"Seems there are a few more circulating than we thought, two of them in this ellan's family library." Eryx pegged Ramsay with a stern look. "Need you to pay a visit to Angus. Everything's circumstantial at this point. If you can get him to slip, we can bring him in formally."

"Why me?" Ramsay said. "You're the one he's got a beef with."

"Exactly. He'll be on guard with me. With you, I'm hoping he'll take the questions less serious. Besides, Ian's tracked down the last two humans we haven't checked out from the mystery sightseeing trips. Ludan and I are gonna split up and see if we can get any evidence Serena's the one behind them."

The space behind Trinity's solar plexus cramped up tight, almost like someone had reached in and fisted the muscles.

Beside her, Ramsay shifted. His hands were clenched tight enough the veins along the back of his hand popped up in angry ridges.

Guess that answered whether or not they were imagining feeling each other's emotions. She covered his hand with both of hers. "You go and see what you can find. I'll stay here with Lexi."

He uncurled his fist and laced his fingers with hers. Bright white shards flickered in his darkened gray gaze and his mouth was pinched in a nearly flat line.

"Go." She stroked his arm and feigned a carefree attitude her insides railed against. "It'll take what? An hour?"

"We need two or three hours, tops," Eryx said. "We can all meet back here and figure out next steps."

Ramsay pulled her close and glared at his brother. "I do this, then my next step is time alone at the lodge with Trinity."

Eryx shook his head, laid a quick kiss to Lexi's temple, and headed toward the castle. "Best not to plan that far ahead in this household."

CHAPTER 31

hree hours. Three fucking hours Ramsay had tracked that crotchety old shit, Angus, all over Cush from one ellan's office to another. He might be old, but he sure as histus got around quick.

Ramsay prowled the far wall of Angus' dreary study. For a guy who'd spent his whole life in public office and made a damned fine living off the opportunities it created, his home didn't show it. From the minute Ramsay had stepped across the threshold, his lungs had struggled against the moldy stench, and the maroon rugs looked like they'd been around since before Angus was born. The guy was what? Nearing six hundred now?

Muted voices sounded in the hallway beyond.

About time. He'd finally caught a break running into Angus' page at the main council hall and learned Angus would be headed home after a quick appointment across town. He'd thought about waiting for the old fart outside, especially after he'd got a whiff of the living tomb, but figured a little unsupervised tour couldn't hurt.

The dark walnut door opened and Angus shuffled in.

His stark white council robe was painfully bright after thirty minutes in the windowless office. "A visit from the spare Shantos. Can't say I ever expected to find you in my study."

He shut the door behind him with a flick of his hand and scanned the tiny room as he shuffled to his desk. "I've got plans this evening with a colleague. Whatever you need, get on with it."

"You're a busy man."

Angus sat gingerly on the stiff wooden chair, the type one might expect to find in an old legal drama. "Yes well, not all of us were born with a castle and full coffers."

Yeah, but he had plenty now. Too bad he didn't put a little of it into his box of a home. Maybe it was Angus' crude upbringing that made him hesitant to spend what he'd earned.

Didn't matter. How the guy lived wasn't Ramsay's problem and Trinity was waiting. "I understand you paid a visit to Maron Deesus a few days ago."

Angus paused in riffling through his desk drawer, but kept his head down. Not much, just a little hesitancy. Could have been a tell. Could have just been he'd startled the guy with his voice. "I did. What of it?"

"He seemed surprised by the visit. Said he hadn't been expecting you."

Angus slowly shut the drawer and lifted his head. "I wasn't aware the ellan were required to report each and every visitor to you or your brother. Am I unaware of some new protocol?"

"No requirement." Ramsay eased into a spindly chair across from Angus' desk. The damned thing creaked like it might fall apart at any minute. "It's just your visit was timed with an unfortunate loss in his household."

"Loss?"

Damn. If the guy was guilty of anything, he did a good job of covering it. "A book. Something from a family library."

"And he accused me of taking it?"

"He didn't accuse you of anything," Ramsay said. "Just reported a missing valuable. We're tracking all the people who happened to be in the house around the same time."

Angus harrumphed and pulled a well-worn planner from the side of his desk. He wrote something in the far corner. "I'm afraid you've wasted your time coming to me. I was with Maron the entire time. Never left his sight."

"You take anyone with you?"

His grip tightened on the pencil, and his smooth writing motion turned jerky for a few strokes. "My page. He's usually with me on my visits. Helps keep me organized."

Interesting. He'd have to see if Maron had mentioned the page to Eryx. He leaned in and motioned to Angus' planner. "That list out all your appointments over the last few weeks?"

Angus' gaze snapped to Ramsay. "Something in particular you want to know?"

"Just running down leads. Being thorough." He shrugged like he didn't consider the request any big deal. More of a nuisance. "Figured since you had it handy you wouldn't mind."

His thumb moved up and down along the pencil's shaft. Once. Twice. "I don't see any reason why not." He turned the book around and shoved it across the desk.

Ramsay sat back with the beat-up planner in his lap. The guy's scrawl matched Angus' attitude, all jagged edges and angry angles. Busy day today for sure. Yesterday, not so much. Council session the day before that in the morning and an afternoon visit to Maron.

Serena. Four days ago. The day before the texts went missing.

He kept his head down and turned the page to the week

prior, pretending a bored perusal. "You visited Serena Steysis?"

"Of course I paid her a visit. The woman did our race an enormous favor ridding the world of Maxis Steysis, far more than you or your brother have done. I made no secret in voting in favor of leniency with her sentence. I felt the least I could do was visit and give my personal thanks."

Bullshit. A damned good excuse and one he'd obviously prepped before he'd turned over the planner to Ramsay, but bullshit all the same. "You mind sharing your memories from that visit?"

Angus chuckled low and reclined against his seat, fingers laced across his lap. "Ellan conversations with their constituents are protected. I'd no more share my conversation with her than I would yours with her. It defeats the purpose of providing our race a safe harbor for conveying their concerns."

Nice. Extremely well played. "True. Just thought you might be willing to help your malran keep a close eye on someone we're not yet convinced has our race's best interests at heart."

"I'm always interested in protecting our race. Even those held in disfavor by the malran." He steepled his fingers under his chin. "If you want me to share the memories of my conversations with Serena, you'll have to petition the council for the right. That, of course, would require a charge against me. Is there one?"

Lousy fucker.

"Nope." Ramsay stood, tossed the planner on the desk like he couldn't care less what happened, and headed to the door. As he exited, he said, "Not yet anyway."

≈

TRINITY ROLLED the cinnamon-scented dough Orla had given her in a long line on the flour-covered counter. Lexi and Brenna already had theirs coiled up in a close representation of the roll Orla had demonstrated, but Trinity was having a hard time multi-tasking worry alongside baking.

"You okay, Trin?" Lexi said.

Trin. The same nickname her girlfriends back home used. At some point she was going to have to talk to Ramsay about getting word to them she was safe. She might not be in a hurry to get back to the human realm just yet, but that didn't mean she was willing to give up her friends. "Yeah, sorry. Just thinking."

Lexi swirled the rest of her dough with a whole lot more flair than Trinity thought she could ever manage for any kitchen activity. "Wanna talk about it?"

Orla and Brenna stopped their side chatter, but kept working, heads down.

Probably not the best topic for a group, but a little color commentary might take her worry down a notch. "The stolen texts. Do you think they've got anything to do with the prophecy?"

Lexi cocked her head and pursed her mouth. "Hard to say for sure." She scooped up the finished roll and laid it on a baking sheet waiting by the oven. "Kind of fishy timing. Probably smart Ramsay's running it down."

Brenna peeked up from her dough, met Trinity's eyes, then snapped her head back down to business.

"Somehow I doubt that's all that's on your mind." Lexi pinched a new section of dough and started another roll. That was two to Trinity's not yet one.

Trinity started the wide circle like Orla had shown them, patting the top with her flour-covered fingers to hold the dough in place. "What would happen if someone brought the wall down? With the powers, I mean?"

"Ah, prophecy worries." Lexi shrugged. "Well, for one, humans would have a free back and forth path from here to Evad. Not saying that's bad. I'd just be worried about people like Maxis and Serena taking advantage of them."

Brenna dropped the dough she'd been coiling in a nearly perfect replication of Orla's steady work.

Orla patted Brenna's hand. "Maxis is gone, dear. He can't hurt you anymore. And my boys won't let Serena anywhere near you."

"Personally, I'm hoping I get a chance to gut the bitch. Maxis died waaay too fast and easy. Seems to me a little karmic justice in the form of Serena's long, drawn out demise would be fitting after all he put Brenna through the last fifteen years." Lexi flicked the last bit of dough into place, and then jerked her head up. "Sorry. Too morbid for kitchen convo?"

Not in Trinity's book. She couldn't even fathom how Brenna had survived the horror Maxis had heaped on her. Kidnapped at only eight years old and forced to serve as a slave. And according to Ramsay, the serving part didn't stop at just menial labor.

Brenna grinned and ducked back to her work.

Orla smiled, but it sure looked like she was trying to hold back the bulk of it. Probably thought it was better not to encourage Lexi.

Trinity straightened and let out a heavy breath. Not too bad of a roll. Kind of an oval more than a circle, but overall it looked pretty even. "What do you call these again?"

"Lastas," they all said at once.

"I should have known better than to feed them to Lexi as a first meal," Orla said. "She's had them nearly every day since."

"And we're not stoppin' anytime soon," Lexi added.

Silence settled in the cozy kitchen.

Orla popped a pinch of the dough into her mouth and shuffled to the sink to wash her hands.

"What about the powers?" Trinity asked.

Lexi dusted her hands and joined Orla at the sink. "What about 'em?"

"You said Eryx was the malran because he had the most powers. That no one was strong enough to challenge him. If someone else had the same, what would happen?"

Lexi clutched the kitchen towel in a death grip. Clearly, she'd considered the question before, because her mood shot straight from balanced to murderous. "Eryx said he'd likely be challenged for the throne, and odds are good it would come down to skill and experience. If someone else won, it would be up to Ramsay to win it back." She tossed the towel aside. "If he could."

Trinity stared down at the untouched lump of dough in the bowl in front of her. Stupid. So damned stupid. She was playing housewife, while her husband—fireann—was out trying to protect his family's legacy and the overall human race.

Stupid, stupid, stupid.

And selfish.

She could fix it if she wanted to. Give them all the information they needed if she'd just suck it up and accept what was rightfully hers.

But then you'll lose Ramsay. No way would they let such a huge violation go without serious reprimand, most likely her life.

Something splattered onto the flour-covered surface. A tear.

She dashed the next one slipping down her cheek aside with the back of her hand before Lexi could see or comment on it.

Brenna came up beside her. "Lexi can you grab another

cookie sheet?" She waited until Lexi bustled to the large side closet filled with all manner of pans, and then quickly dusted a trace of flour from Trinity's check. She leaned in quick and quiet. "You're not selfish. If I could have what you have, I'd never let it go." She squeezed Trinity's fisted hand on the counter then got back to work like she'd never said a thing.

Trinity held stock still, shocked and more than a little worried Brenna had managed to home in on her thoughts. She might be human, but there was definitely more to her than met the eye.

And there was more to Trinity than just being Myren. She was Spiritu too. Maybe it was time she started acting like one.

CHAPTER 32

*R*amsay took the castle stairs two at a time and followed his brother's link toward the third floor. Things in Evad had either gone tremendously well or fallen to shit fast if Eryx was in the rec room. He, Eryx, and Ludan had spent the better part of twenty years building out the Myren equivalent of a man cave after their awakenings, making it their own. Histus, during their training days, Ludan and Reese crashed there more often than they did at home.

And then Eryx and Ramsay's dad had died.

Ready or not, Eryx had stepped into his place as malran. Ludan replaced his father, Graylin, as somo, and Ramsay had assumed the role of strategos. Exploring life one minute, disciplined vigilance and loaded responsibility the next. What he'd lost in companionship with his brother he'd made up for in his time off in Evad. Parties, music, women. Years of it. All out from under the watchful eyes of his race.

And utterly empty.

Two weeks he'd been with Trinity. Two roller coaster

emotional weeks, but he'd wrung more out of life in that span than he had in over a century prior.

He rounded the last flight of stairs and strode down the dark corridor. The thick burgundy rugs muted his booted footsteps. An unfamiliar, itchy aggravation scraped at his insides. Probably just antsy to get back to Trinity. If he was lucky, Eryx would trust Wes and Troy to tie up whatever loose ends were needed with Angus and Serena. Dodging his duties forever wasn't an option, but he didn't think another day with his new baineann was an over the top request.

He opened the mahogany door at the end of the hall with a thought, and the late afternoon sun pierced the opening. The rounded turret wall came into focus, varied shades of gray stone and picture windows spanning a heart-stopping view.

Graylin's low, cultured voice rumbled from somewhere deep in the room. "You don't have enough evidence to bring charges against her. You'd be better served to wait it out. She'll trip up again. She's too impatient not to."

What the hell was Ludan's father doing at the castle? He'd barely left his cottage for more than supplies and formal ceremonies in the last sixty or so years. In the last month, he'd been here two or three times a week. Come to think of it, almost every time he'd seen Graylin, he'd been in the kitchen.

Scratch that. He'd been wherever Orla was, which was usually in the kitchen. Surely the two of them weren't…

He shook his head to clear the odd image and strode in the room.

Graylin perched on the edge of a barstool, one of three they'd acquired from White's gentlemen's club just after a renovation in the late 1800's. Always a supporter of the old-school Myren ways, he sported loose silk pants and tank with a long over robe, and his hair was pulled back in a queue in deference to his late wife.

Eryx bent over the red felt billiard table and lined up a shot. "Wondered when you were gonna finally show, brother. Tell me you got something I can use. I'm not sure waiting for Serena or Angus to trip up again is smart for any of us." He took the shot. The cue ball snapped against the red-stripped eleven and sent it sailing into the far right corner pocket. "Well?"

Ramsay looked up from the table to find all eyes on him. "Shit. Thought you were talking to Ludan." He ambled to the antique bar loaded with pretty much every enviable liquor over a two-hundred dollar price point and went straight for the Scotch. Maybe that would take the edge off. "Nothing worth jumping on right away, but a lead. I take it your trip turned a goose egg?"

"Nothin'." Ludan's gaze was locked on the pool table, cue stick planted butt end in the black rug between his braced feet and both hands fisted on the shaft.

Eryx chalked his cue and circled the table, sizing up his next shot. For all his focus on the table, his thoughts seemed directed somewhere else. "What's the lead?"

The Balvenie laid a warm satisfying path down his throat, but clashed a little too heavy in his stomach. "Two, really. First, Angus has got some mighty detailed records showing every appointment he's had since The Great One knows when. One of 'em was a visit to Serena the day before he visited Maron."

Eryx stopped in his tracks and turned to Ramsay. "You scan his memories?"

"Claimed protected constituent conversation. Said he'd have to be instructed by the council to divulge his memories, and that would take formal charges."

Graylin reclined in his barstool and set his drink on the bar beside him. "A shrewd move on his part."

"He tell you why he was there?" Eryx said.

"Said it was a visit to show his support and to thank her for doing what we failed to do." Ramsay circled the Scotch in the tumbler. "Was thinking we might be wise to see if Serena will offer up her memories instead. You got her to do it once. Might be able to charm her a second time."

Eryx grunted and leaned over the table for another shot. "Doubtful. I let Ludan do it last time."

"I wasn't nice about it," Ludan added.

The cue ball cracked against its target.

"What's the other lead?" Eryx said.

"Angus says he was never out of Maron's sight the whole time he was there," Ramsay said. "Did Maron share his memories with you?"

Eryx stood, eyes distant. "He did. And now that I think on it, he's right. He was with Maron in every image."

"What about his page?" Ramsay said.

Gaze aimed at the floor, Eryx loosely gripped the cue stick. "They left Maron's study," he said, almost to himself. "The page stayed behind."

His head snapped up and he locked eyes with Ramsay. "Round up the page. See if you can get a read from Serena. Neither of them are protected by ellan laws. They'll either clear Angus or give us the proof we need."

Fuck. Orders didn't get more direct than that. He could try to play the new mate card and send Wes or Troy in his place, but that didn't feel right. Not with such an important issue. Surely Trinity would understand given the situation.

He reached for her through their link and a crackling, almost painful, reverberation echoed back at him. His stomach lurched, and the Scotch swished in a way that promised it was almost headed topside. The sensation he'd been stifling for the last few hours billowed up, blockading his throat. Shit. Her emotions. Something was wrong. Very wrong. And he hadn't been paying attention. "Have you seen Trinity?"

Eryx put up the pool cue. "When we got back from Evad, she was huddled up with Lexi, Brenna, and Orla in the kitchen."

Ramsay took off toward the hallway. "Check in with Lexi. See if she's there."

"Check in...Ramsay!" Eryx shouted. "What the fuck is wrong?"

Ramsay stopped at the door. "I can't reach Trinity. Where's Lexi?"

Eryx's face blanked. "Kitchen."

Ramsay bolted toward the stairs, heavy steps pounding behind him. He skipped the spiral staircase and leapt over the balcony railing, levitating down the open center in a swoosh. He landed on the thick rugs.

A castle maid cleaning the long foyer side table shrieked.

He stormed down the main hallway, past the receiving room. Past the library and the dining room. How long had it been since the unease had started? An hour? Two?

Closer to two. Just after he'd arrived at Angus' house and settled in to wait.

He stalked into the kitchen. Lexi and Brenna sat with Orla at the kitchen counter, each cradling a cup of coffee with the sun streaming over them through the bay window. "Where's Trinity?"

All three women faced him at once.

Lexi smiled and opened her mouth as if to greet him, but stopped and scowled. "She went to take a nap. Something wrong?"

Brenna ducked her head and looked away.

He tried the link again. Still broken. There, but hard to

hold onto without getting a nauseous punch to the gut. And distant. Too damned far away.

"Ramsay, what's wrong?" Lexi said.

Eryx, Ludan, and Graylin came up behind him.

Ramsay headed up the back staircase and glanced at the three men. "Check the grounds. Lock everything down."

Voices and the scrape of chair legs on stone sounded behind him. Sharp commands. Eryx at the back of the house, Ludan and Graylin further away.

Ramsay pounded down the hallway toward his suite and pushed open the door. Black bedspread stretched taut across the perfectly made wide bed. Windows open to the breeze and the nearing sunset. Not one thing out of place and no sign of Trinity.

Lexi came in behind him and shot to the bathroom. "Trinity!"

Ramsay couldn't move. His legs seemed locked in place, and the queasy mess in his gut solidified to lead. She wouldn't be there. Wouldn't be at the castle or anywhere outside. He didn't know how he knew it, but he knew it.

He stared at the bed. Their bed.

Lexi paced from the bathroom and made a circuit through the suite. "I swear to God, Ramsay. She said she was going up to take a nap. She was fine."

No, she wasn't fine. His senses had been telling him otherwise, but he hadn't listened.

"Shit." Lexi strode to the dresser behind him and picked up the Black King's black lacquer box. "The jewel is gone." Lexi stared at the empty black velvet interior, a gaping hole where the gem had nestled. Her pendant sat beside it, neatly arranged and untouched.

He'd never asked Trinity about the gift. Figured she'd tell him when she was ready, or when he wasn't buried so deep in her he could manage normal conversation. "What's that mean?"

Eryx marched into the room, Brenna and Ludan tight behind him. "Everyone's combing the estate," Eryx said. "No one in and no one out."

Lexi turned the box and showed Eryx. "I don't think you'll find her. I think she went to Winrun."

Eryx darted looks between Lexi and Ramsay. "Winrun?"

"The Spiritu realm," Lexi said. "The Black King said she could use the stone to take her there if she chose to accept her gifts."

Ramsay shook his head and tried to piece together the information with the sticky unease he'd been fighting all day. "Why would she do that? I mean, if she wants her gifts, fine, but right now?"

"She wants to help you." Brenna's sweet, soft voice slashed through the room's intensity.

Every head whipped her way.

She ducked her head, but only for a second. She met Ramsay's stare. "I felt her concern. Her worry."

"You felt it?" Lexi said. "Like me?"

"Yes and no. Yes, the same way you feel emotions, but not on my own." She focused on Eryx. "I didn't want to say anything. Not until I was sure, but I think you healing Ian and I made it so we could echo other people's gifts. At least when we're close to them. It's why Ian can hear things when you talk to each other."

"Can you do the same?" Lexi asked.

Brenna nodded and clenched her hands at her waist. "I didn't mean to."

"Anything else?" Eryx asked sharply.

Brenna flinched. Her gaze slid down and to the side. "I made a flower bloom in the garden yesterday when I was working with Orla, and I fixed a torn cuticle the other day when Galena was here."

"But nothing when you're alone?" Lexi said.

Brenna shook her head. "Just the normal me."

It didn't make sense. Why in histus would Trinity need her gifts to help him? The emotions he felt weren't anywhere near what a woman gaining more power should feel. They were thick. Filled with dread. He looked to Lexi. "Did you pick up anything?"

Lexi glanced at Eryx and Ludan. "I keep it turned off unless I need it. Too hard on my insides."

He stepped closer to Brenna, careful not to scare her. "Did you pick up anything else?"

Ludan edged in behind her, though if Ramsay read it right, he was ready to step in and kick Ramsay's ass more than keep Brenna from bolting.

Brenna swallowed and lifted her head. "She's really scared," she whispered. "She may be going to accept her gifts like Lexi said, but I'm not so sure it's a good thing."

Scared. Scared of what? The king and queen appeared to love her. And her dad wouldn't let anything happen to her. He'd die first.

"Shit," Lexi said. "She went for answers." She scanned everyone in the room. In her hand she gripped Trinity's pendant. "They see the future right?"

"Until we change it," Erxy said. "Remember, it's only valid at any given point in time. One shift of free will and the whole thing alters."

Lexi pegged Brenna with a knowing look. "All those questions she was asking us. The prophecy," she clarified, looking at Eryx. "She knows this is a big deal and she went for answers."

Her path is her own. Decisions will be placed before her whether you're together or apart, Kazan had said. *If it means happiness for her as she faces the choices destiny gives her, then she should have it.*

"They're not supposed to divulge destiny," Lexi said. "We were talking about how we might be related. How her dad ended up with her mother after she was abandoned by another man. We're guessing my father. She told me her dad nearly forfeit his existence for being with her. Can you imagine the penalty for up-ending a whole prophecy?"

Answers. Everything he'd wanted in the beginning, but not if it cost him his mate. He stormed toward the door.

Eryx caught him with a merciless grip at his bicep. "Where the hell are you headed?"

Ramsay jerked his arm free and stormed out the door. "The lodge. Winrun. Wherever the fuck I need to go to find and stop my mate."

CHAPTER 33

*S*erena peeked around one of the tall twin pillars marking the front castle garden entrance, her mask fortified by Uther behind her.

"Popular place," he whispered in her ear.

"Too popular." Something was up. She'd anticipated increased guards after Lexi's capture months before, but warriors prowling the perimeter with shrewd, calculating eyes screamed red alert. Far more security than what was needed to keep those inside protected. "I'm not sure even Eryx or Ramsay could navigate masked through that many men."

"Hunger and desperation make pretty effective teachers. I don't give a shit how powerful they are. I doubt any Shantos ever had that kind of motivation."

A petty thief. She'd heard of such stories, young Myrens in need of food honing their skills on simple street vendors. Something she'd need to think on. Maybe try to hone her own gifts. Assuming she got past today. "You really think you can get us inside?"

"On my own, easy. Carting you along for the ride? It's a

crapshoot. Better if you just tell me where you think the translations are and let me go in."

"I don't know exactly." Not a complete lie. "I might have had full run of the castle once, but I rarely went beyond the public rooms or Eryx's suite."

"Then tell me what you know and I'll explore the rest."

No way. The key was in there. It had to be. "I'm going with you. Just tell me what you need me to do."

Keeping one hand at her shoulder, he covered her hand where it rested against the gray stone pillar. "Give me your link."

She started to turn.

Uther clamped her shoulder and held her in place. "Don't move." He waited long enough to ensure she'd comply then relaxed his fingers. "I don't like the idea of being tied to you any more than you like it, but whispering's not going to cut it once we're in the thick of it."

Histus, no, she didn't like it. Links meant vulnerability. The Great One only knew what other special gifts Uther had yet to reveal.

The castle doors burst open and one of the Shantos brothers stormed onto the wide veranda. No braids, so it had to be Ramsay. Eryx never went anywhere without those barbaric commitment braids. Odd, though. Ramsay's hair was bound as well.

Two warriors rushed from the gardens to meet him, both elites, given the white gold torques and wrist cuffs.

"Can you get us closer?" Serena whispered to Uther.

Uther hesitated. "Halfway. No further. And if you deviate from any direction I give, I'll leave you to fend for yourself. Understand?"

"Agreed."

He wrapped his arms around her waist and levitated

them both. "Regulate your breathing. Stay calm and do not move."

They floated forward on an odd pattern. Slow. Swift. Then nothing at all. A kind of ebb and flow, like the lap of small waves at the shore's edge. Wind. He was working with the breeze. Blending into it.

Damn, but she should have formed the link. How was she going to convey direction to Uther without it?

"...the gardens twice and the perimeter nonstop," the dark-headed warrior said to Ramsay as Serena and Uther drifted into hearing range. "If she's outside, she's well beyond the castle by now."

"The castle's clean," the blond said. "Any place else you want us to cover?"

Ramsay spun, looked back at the castle, and fisted his hair at the top of his head, pulling a good chunk of what he'd bound free. Something glittered on his forearm.

Serena shifted for a better angle.

Uther's hands tightened in warning.

A mark. The son of a bitch was mated. And not to just anyone apparently, but someone related to Lexi, the same damned ivy-twined sword stretching the length of his arm. Slightly different though. Black like most marks, but with gold and silver highlights in it.

He faced his men. "No. I think I know where she is." He focused on the dark-headed one. "Take half the men. Round up Angus Rallion's page and Serena Steysis. Bring them to the training center."

Serena flinched inside Uther's nearly crushing grip.

"Any charges?" the warrior asked.

"Voluntary." Ramsay stared toward the ocean. "Hold them there until Eryx arrives. He'll know what to do." He pinned the blond warrior with a cold glare. "Keep the rest of the men here on high alert. No one gets in or out you don't know."

The men dipped their heads once and took off in separate directions. Ramsay scanned the perimeter, hands fisted at his side, then shot to the skies.

"You wanna make it back before they do, we have to go now," Uther said quietly.

As the blond warrior marched down the veranda barking orders, the men combing the grounds paired off. Fewer warriors meant more access. If she could find that key, she'd never answer to another man. Ever.

Who knew what Eryx wanted her for. If she played it safe and went home, she might never get this chance again. "I'm staying."

"There's no going back from this. Fugitives rarely know where their next meal is coming from, let alone live with a staff that sees to their needs. You sure you're ready for that?"

Fugitive. No safety net. Her neck burned with tension, and her heart pulsed so heavily it hurt. She covered his hand at her waist with her own and pushed her energy through and up his forearm. "Give me your link. We're going in."

CHAPTER 34

*T*rinity stood beside the ceremonial slab and ran her fingers along the cold, black and white swirled marble. Everything in Winrun was one or the other, stark black or purest white. Everything, that was, save the varied hair colors and skin tones of the people who lived there. Even the sky was white, every surface beneath her feet a never ending ebony that left her feeling like she'd fall at any given moment.

"You don't have to do this." Kazan's voice was thick with emotion. Garbled almost. "Think before you act."

She let her hand fall to her side and glanced at the Black King and White Queen at either end of the waist-high slab. "Ramsay needs me. My new family needs me."

"Not like this, they don't. You know the penalty for interfering."

Trinity whirled and faced him. "Was being with my mother worth the cost?"

Kazan jerked back. "That's different."

"How? You loved her. I love Ramsay. This will help him."

"It's different because the destiny I messed with dealt

with two people, not two races. This is a big deal, kiddo. Not the kind of thing that comes with a tiny ten-year, but painful slap on the wrist."

The slab stood like a gravestone behind her. Cold and so very final.

"Think about it," Kazan said. "My interference cost me ten years of pain, but it cost your mother her sanity and her life. She never knew why I'd been taken from her. Imagine how alone she felt. How devastated. If you can't think of the price you'll pay, think of the pain you'll deal Ramsay."

"Ramsay would pay it to save his race."

"Are you sure? Do you really think he'd give you up? Even to save his race? Because I don't." He held his silence until she met his eyes. "Please, sweetheart. Don't do this. Trust them to find a way. Encourage him, but don't—"

"You're crossing the line, Kazan." The Black King's voice rumbled like thunder. "Her will is her own."

"I'm her father, not her Spiritu."

The Black King's eyes met hers, warm and chilling all at once. "It's her choice."

"Then give her the facts." Kazan lurched forward, invading the Black King's space. "You know what she means to do. Tell her what the consequences are if she goes through with it."

"She knows enough to weigh her conscience," the king said. "No decisions can be made with absolute certainty. Hers are no exception."

"Does it hurt?" Trinity asked.

The Black King smiled, slow and sensual. Her body heated instantly, the pleasure so intense she could barely pull in a full breath. "Far from it. Your body was made to cradle your gifts. It will welcome your powers the way a mother welcomes her babe. Nestle into your soul the way you curl around your mate late at night."

Something tugged at her heart. To accept her gifts? Or to return to Ramsay? Surely this was the right thing. A purpose that served the greater good.

"Can you face the punishment, Trinity?" her father said quietly. "Is it worth never seeing Ramsay again?"

Her pleasure or Ramsay's entire life? That's what it really came down to. If someone else led the Myren race, someone not as fair as the Shantos line, what would happen to his race? Or humans?

She faced the black and white marble and pressed both hands against its chilly surface. The colors seemed to move and swirl on their own, imitating the riotous emotions pushing and pulling her heart. She could do this. Ramsay would do it for her. "I want this."

RAMSAY PACED the black rock ledge outside his lodge, impatience and fear crippling what speck of logic he had left. Trinity wasn't in the lodge, not that he'd really expected her to be. In his gut, he knew where she was.

Winrun.

There had to be a way to get there. To stop her. But damned if his head would get its shit together and form some kind of strategy.

The ocean wind whipped a few loose chunks of hair against his forehead and cheeks in an almost painful lash. Not nearly the punishment he deserved. He should've stayed with her. Should've made sure she knew she came before the prophecy.

He glared at the red-rimmed setting sun. He needed help. Bad. Maybe he should bounce some ideas off Eryx. Or Lexi. Lexi had a way of thinking things through. And she was a woman. The Great One knew he could use a little guidance in with navigating the feminine mindset right now.

"What am I? Chopped liver?"

Ramsay spun toward the lodge. No one behind him. No presence pinging against his Myren senses. Just the sun's red reflected in the lodge's window above and rocks, plants, and the fire pit on the terrace below.

"My presence won't ever register unless I want it to."

That voice. He knew it.

"Of course, you know it. Not that you listened to it very well up until now."

His Spiritu. Vyree.

A circular space near the terrace wall wavered and a woman dressed all in black shimmered into view. She lay on her back atop the hip-high stone wall, one leg crossed over the other, casual as could be. Her maroon hair with its cobalt blue streaks hung loose, nearly to the ground.

"The waitress," he said mostly to himself. He shook himself out of his stupor. "You were the waitress at Louis, the night Trinity and I went out."

"Yep." She rolled her head toward him, then propped herself on one elbow. "Couldn't get you to listen to me the normal way. Figured I'd drop in and meddle face to face." Her mouth screwed up in a dramatic pucker. "You're a tough nut to crack, Ramsay Shantos. Good thing I'm not a quitter."

"I thought you weren't supposed to show yourself."

She swung upright, cocked her head, and grinned. "You want me to go? I could have sworn you were asking for help, but if you'd rather stick to folks you know—"

"No!" He stepped forward and then checked his impulse. The last thing he needed right now was to scare off someone with a roadmap to Winrun. "I didn't know you were an option. I mean..." Damn, he was really fucking this up. "I mean I was too stupid to remember you were there."

Vyree smiled so bright it seemed the setting sun moved in reverse and brightened the whole hillside. "Oh, that's smooth. I'll give you points for a quick save." She swung her legs and hunched forward, gripping the side of the wall. "Do you have any clue what you're about to go up against?"

"I know my baineann's about to make a decision based on what she thinks I want instead of what she wants. If it means keeping her safe and making sure she's making decisions for the right reasons, then it doesn't really matter what I'm up against."

Vyree's legs kept swinging.

"Please," he said. "Help me find her."

Her legs stopped. "You'll do anything?"

"Anything."

"Whatever it takes?"

"Anything."

She narrowed her eyes and an unnatural gust of wind tossed her wine-colored hair in a wild mess. With a sharp nod, she hopped off the wall and crossed her arms. "Good, 'cause penance for this is going to suck. Glad to know it's going to be worth it."

Thank The Great One. For a minute there, he'd thought she was Splitsville.

"You ever watch *The Wizard of Oz*?" she asked.

"The what?"

"*The Wizard of Oz*. You know, Dorothy, Toto, and the rest of the crew."

Oh, for fuck's sake, she wanted to talk pop culture now? "Yeah, I know it."

"It's kind of like that," she said. "'There's no place like home.' That kind of thing."

"You're kidding me," he bit back. "Seriously?"

"Seriously." She waved her hand at him in an up and

down motion. "Close your eyes. Focus on your link and follow it."

Hands down, this had to be the trippiest conversation of his lifetime. Not like he had a shit-ton-full of options right now, and she'd damn sure come through with the mating. He closed his eyes.

"Now focus," she said. "Center on the link. Lose your physical self and follow it."

He opened himself to the link and his body seemed to pitch to one side, like a boat caught off guard by a big wave.

"Yep, like that," Vyree said. "Stay focused. Don't let go."

His stomach heaved. He'd done some crazy aerial antics, but this was brutal. Tilt-a-Hurl times twenty. "Praise The Great One…"

"Hang in there," she said from not too far away. Her voice had dropped. Far more serious. "Don't let go. Will it. Want it."

A buzz started in his ears. Loud. Louder. Growing until he thought his eardrums would surely pop.

Silence.

Kazan growled from somewhere beside him, "What are you doing here?"

Ramsay opened his eyes. Pitch black stretched out beneath Ramsay and white fog surrounded everything else. At the end of the formless room was a tall marble slab with Trinity laid out on top, a white gauzy fabric covering her.

Kazan stood two steps down from Trinity, a murderous scowl on his face. At the foot of the slab stood the White Queen, hands clasped peacefully at her waist. The Black King hovered near Trinity's head. He lifted his hands and held them over Trinity's face.

"No!" Ramsay shot forward.

An unseen power circled his waist and jerked him to a stop just out of Trinity's reach.

"You cannot stop what she has requested." Though his lips hadn't moved, the Black King's voice rumbled all around.

"I'm not here to stop her." The words shot out on instinct.

The Black King dropped his hands, twisted, and met Ramsay's gaze. "What other purpose would bring you here?"

Ramsay scrambled for answers. The answer was important. He didn't know how he knew it, but every part of him screamed to state his purpose carefully.

Vyree could help him. Maybe.

"Wow," Vyree said with a chuckle. *"Twice in one day. This will take some getting used to."*

He stifled a groan. *"Please. Help me."*

"It's easy. Tell him what you told me."

Fuck. He could barely remember what he had for breakfast, let alone all the serious conversations from today. He shook his head and replayed the time since Vyree had appeared.

A spunky faery. Realizing she was the waitress. Tough nut to crack. Making decisions for the right reasons...

"I just need to talk to her first," he blurted. "If she wants her gifts because that's what she wants, then I will fully support her. But if she wants them to give me answers, that's the wrong reason. I need her to know before she accepts them that she comes first. Not the prophecy. Not my race. Not my family. Nothing comes before her."

The White Queen dipped her head and covered her mouth, but smiled behind her fingers.

The force around his waist relented.

The Black King stepped to Trinity's side and peeled the gauzy fabric back. He waved a hand over her face. "Your fireann is most anxious to speak with you."

Trinity's eyes fluttered open. She stared at the misty white cloud above them for one or two heartbeats and rolled her head toward him. "Ramsay."

Ramsay closed the distance between them and gripped her hand. Cold. Too damned cold. "You don't have to do this. I mean, if you want your gifts, I'm great with that. But I don't need answers. Not like this."

"What makes you think that's why I'm here?"

"Lexi. She told me about your questions. And Brenna. She said you were worried. Scared."

Her gaze drifted to Kazan, who'd moved in close. "A lot of people would be saved, Ramsay. Your people. My people." She squeezed his hand. "Tell me the truth. You'd do it for me, wouldn't you?"

He leaned in and brushed her hair off her forehead. "It's not the same, Sunshine. I'd give anything for you. My family. My life. Anything."

She smiled and a tear slid down her temple. "Exactly." She stared at him for long seconds. Heartbeats that stabbed brutally within his chest. She lifted her gaze to the Black King. "Go ahead."

A second, maybe less, and the same unforgiving force ripped him from Trinity's side.

"This is wrong," Kazan rumbled beside him. Even with his formidable size and strength, Trinity's father fought against the same unbending force. "She's doing this for the wrong reason. You know that. How can you let her do this?"

The Black King pulled the fabric back over Trinity's head and her eyelids slid shut.

Ramsay struggled against the power coiled around him. "Trinity!"

"Damn it all!" Kazan banged against the invisible wall and the air between them rippled like a pebble cast against a smooth lake. He focused on the White Queen. "Stop this! She shouldn't be forced to choose this way. It's wrong."

Ramsay dug his feet into the onyx ground and strained against the transparent wall. Every muscle stretched. Every ligament and bone creaked to the point of breaking. *Please, God. Not this. Not Trinity.*

"If the circumstances change, she should be granted re-evaluation," Kazan said to the White Queen. "Do you agree?"

The White Queen lifted her head, her expression tense.

"Do you agree?" Kazan asked again.

The White Queen nodded.

Kazan gripped Ramsay's shoulder in an iron grip. "Then I forfeit. What I give him is freely given and my life forfeit."

Trinity's eyes opened.

The Black King lowered his hand and the White Queen nodded.

Pain jolted through Ramsay, unforgiving, torturous pain, woven with a fire's burn. A tormented scream echoed all around him.

No, not one. Two screams. His and Trinity's.

And then, nothing but black.

CHAPTER 35

Serena steadied her breath and focused on keeping her mind calm as Uther levitated them through the castle front door in the path of a hurried warrior. *"So that's how you do it."*

Uther grunted a mental agreement and tightened his arm around her waist in warning. *"Now where?"*

Histus if she knew. Off to one side of the foyer, the formal receiving room doors stood open. Easy enough to navigate in the quieter portion of the castle. *"Try the receiving room. Up and on the left."*

Uther hesitated, then drifted forward.

Damn but this was going to be a pain in the ass situation. With Uther glued to her back, she'd never be able to swipe the key even if she did manage to find it. There had to be some way to get him to let her go on her own.

He combed the room in slow, cautious movements. *"Anything?"*

"No. Nothing here. We need books. A library maybe."

As they floated toward the doors, a feminine voice sounded on the staircase. "You did the right thing, Brenna,"

Lexi said. "Ramsay needed to know. There's not a thing for you to worry about."

Uther and Serena crested the threshold just as Lexi and a petite, young brunette with light skin reached the first floor.

Lexi clasped the girl's hand. "Remember. We're in this together." She smiled, wrapped the girl in a side hug, and dangled a black pendant in front of them. "Come on. We'll get Trinity's stuff locked up and then track down Galena and Orla. Something tells me we'll need all the female backup we can stand when the guys get back."

Trinity. Not a name Serena recognized. Brenna though, she looked familiar. *"Follow them."*

Uther dropped in behind the women, far enough back their murmured words were indistinguishable, but close enough to hide their presence in the women's energy wake.

Two arched panels Serena had always thought to be ornate walls opened beneath the staircase. Beyond them stretched a long room with books lining either side, casual sitting areas clustered in homey sections throughout, and a two-story window at the end.

Brenna paced to the window and hugged herself as though chilled.

Lexi hustled to an elegant antique desk angled in one corner. The malress' desk. The same one Eryx's mother had sat behind and countless malresses before her.

Heat blasted Serena from the inside out. Lexi's voice registered in some dim corner of her mind, but the content didn't stick. That should be her desk. Would be hers.

Her gaze slid to the matching, albeit larger desk in the opposite corner. Eryx's.

Scratch that. She'd take the malran's desk and use Lexi's to fuel the hearth.

With the soft scrape of wood on wood, Lexi pulled a dark box from her desk drawer and carefully placed the pendant inside. She studied whatever lay inside a moment, thoughtful, then closed up the box and tucked it back in the drawer.

"Does it bother you?" Lexi looked up at Brenna, still staring out the window and the ocean beyond. "The powers and knowing how different your life can be now?"

"This is the only life I've known. What I'd really like is a chance to know the life I didn't get to live." Brenna turned at Lexi's approach. "Do you think he'll ever let me visit? Maybe spend a little time in Evad and get to know my mom?"

The human. Maxis' little slave. Though she sure looked a lot better now than she had under Maxis' control. More color to her skin and a mass of wavy dark hair well past her shoulders. Her figure wasn't too shabby either. No wonder Maxis had kept her in those sack-like slave robes. Better to keep his little toy hidden from envious male guests.

Lexi steered Brenna away from the window and through the library doors. "Maybe once all the hubbub dies down and we get a better handle on the prophecy. We're already close, with or without whatever answers Trinity brings home."

Uther's arm tightened at her waist.

"Relax," she told him. *"If we get the translation tables, we'll slow them down. Check Eryx's desk. I'll check Lexi's."*

"Hold your mask in place," he said as he drifted away.

Serena hurried to the drawer Lexi had opened. The Shantos mark was etched in black atop the box, deep and carefully detailed by someone with substantial skill. She opened it where it sat. A smallish journal in worn chocolate leather, the pendant, and the picture of a woman with long, nearly platinum hair. It was a profile shot, the woman laughing up at some unseen presence.

"What am I looking for?" Uther's irritation bristled down her spine to match his words.

She fingered the black filigree pendant. A sword twined in ivy. An exact match to Lexi's mark. Funny. It didn't look like a pendant. Not really. It was too clunky for anyone to consider it pretty. She certainly wouldn't wear it.

"Serena, what am I looking for?" Uther barked.

"Something big. Similar to the one I got from Angus. Maybe older," she said.

The mark of your family will be the key.

Of whose family? Lexi's?

She glanced at Eryx's desk. Nothing there save a drawer sliding outward seemingly on its own. Thank The Great One Uther couldn't see her any more than she could see him. She tucked the journal and the pendant into her pocket and moved to the next drawer.

"Something like this?"

Serena checked the foyer beyond for any signs of movement and levitated toward Uther. Nestled in the lowest compartment of Eryx's desk was a wide tome wrapped in black felt, an edition almost identical to the one locked up in Angus' safe.

She fingered the pendant in her pocket. A mark. Drab and sturdy. Was the pendant what she needed? Or should she keep looking?

"Grab it," she said. *"If they're getting close, then losing it will slow them down."* And if she was lucky, by the time they figured out what they needed, she'd be long gone with the key.

~

VOICES. Lots of them rattling around in Ramsay's head. So many none of what they said made sense.

He tried to shift, looking for a visual. Something to ground him and help him pick apart the conversations, but his body wouldn't move. Black surrounded him on all sides, snippets of color flashing in random bursts in all directions.

Backward. The voices were running backward.

Cool air streamed around his bare neck, pushing hair around his face.

The horizon lightened. Deepest gray at first, then lighter. The color of storm clouds one minute then a murky fog the next, color swishing around him in a kind of time tunnel as the voices rewound.

A flash of white blasted and everything stopped. No sound. No wind. No color. Just white. Everywhere.

A ragged cry echoed and a vision came into focus. A woman in a loose black shift, torn on one side and bunched nearly to her hips. Her body lay at an awkward angle. Bruises marked her fair skin.

And she looked just like Brenna.

He blinked and tried to shift for a better look.

A man dropped to his knees beside her, blocking Ramsay's view. He had blond hair. Nearly white, like Trinity's. He tossed a blood-streaked blade to the grass and pulled the woman carefully onto his lap, stroking her cheek. A crimson smudge marked its path, blood from his hands.

Raped. How Ramsay knew the woman had been so vilely abused he wasn't sure, but he felt the man's pain and knowledge as though it was his own. The man had avenged her. Slain the six responsible. Myrens who'd used their powers against his helpless human mate.

Another man came up beside him and gripped his shoulder, a cuff bearing the Shantos mark on the man's wrist. "It wasn't your fault, Hagan."

Hagan. Hagan Xenese. And the man beside him was Kentar Shantos. The first malran. Hagan's dearest friend.

This was their history. The first generation of Myrens playing out like a dream, though Ramsay's emotions and thoughts were connected with theirs. Their knowledge, their experiences, implanting themselves on top of his own.

"She was defenseless. Innocent." Hagan gripped his mate tight to his chest and rocked back and forth. "All my powers and I still failed her."

"But you had your vengeance." The booming voice came from all corners. Peaceful and powerful in one breath. All encompassing.

Hagan and Kentar looked into the heavens, silver and gold sparkling against the rainbow Eden skies.

Kentar dropped to one knee.

The Great One, their creator, was talking to them. Communicating with them one-on-one. "In grief, you've wrought the same damage as those who injured the one you loved. They have atoned for their actions with their lives. Are you prepared for your own reparation?"

Hagan bowed his head. His soul was dead. Cold as the ceremonial stones in the standing circle. Nothing that happened to him now mattered.

Kentar held the same powers as Hagan. He could lead their people on his own and protect his own family. But he could not protect the humans. They'd be as vulnerable as Mitia had been. Unless someone looked out for them.

Hagan stared into the sky. "It will happen again. Those who believe their powers superior to humans will cause her family and those like her to suffer. I accept whatever fate, but ask you watch over them. Protect her family. Her people."

The silver and gold sparks wavered in the sky, and nature stilled around them. "They will not always be so powerless," The Great One said. "Are you willing to act as their protector? To sacrifice the gifts I have given you to do so? Even if, in doing so, your sentence proves a greater torture?"

There could be no greater torture. His heart beat as only an afterthought, an instinct he would quash on his own if he could find the strength. "I would sacrifice whatever you ask. Anything to right the failure I wrought this day."

Wind whistled through the green valley where the men stood, and loose blades of grass and leaves whipped in a mini tempest. "Then you have my decree. My vow. I will return your woman to you, whole and unharmed without memory of the pain visited upon her. She and her race will be given a new land to call their own, a safe haven with a barrier formed between the two realms."

Kentar tightened his hand on Hagan's shoulder and bowed his head.

Hagan cupped Mitia's head and kissed her forehead.

"The Spiritu will watch over both races," The Great One said. "The space of time where all three walked together will be stricken from human and Myren memories. Only when one who bears the blood of all three races returns to Eden will the knowledge of your history be returned. A reckoning will come, marked by the joining of one who leads and one who bears the mark of a sword twined in ivy. A human will stand as judge, one versed in both races and injured in similar kind to the one wronged this day. The mark of your family will be the key, the tool that will feed its bearer the powers you give freely this day, or that will keep the wall in place forever more."

Hagan looked up. "And my sentence?"

"Your powers and six millennium among those you protect, one for each life you've taken this day. Your powers and grief will fuel the wall that separates the realms. You will journey through the years, loving and losing those dearest to you while propagating your Myren line among those you protect."

Stillness settled in the valley.

"Kentar Shantos," The Great One said. "Mark these words and use your powers to ensure your race abides. Your people will be held by two tenets. Never shall your existence be revealed to those your brother protects, and never shall they interfere in human destiny as they have today." The gold and silver sparks dimmed, still glimmering, but calmer. "Such is my command and so shall be your destinies."

"Ramsay." Trinity's voice, distant and thick with weariness, pierced through Ramsay's altered consciousness and shattered the image.

His spirit catapulted forward, hurtling back through the tunnel in a twisted, spiraling mess.

"Ramsay, please wake up." So desperate, but getting closer. "I can't lose you too. Please. I need you."

CHAPTER 36

*T*rinity clutched Ramsay's slack hand at his side and hung her head. *"Please, God. Let him be okay. Whatever it takes...anything..."*

"Trinity?" Brenna said from her chair on the opposite side of Ramsay's bed.

No more. Dear God, no more platitudes on how everything would be okay. How nothing happened without a purpose. It was all she'd heard from Eryx, Lexi, and Galena for the last twelve hours, each of them taking turns watching over Ramsay with her and trying to get her to take a break.

"Trinity, look," Brenna said as the bed dipped. "His eyes. I think he's waking up."

His eyelids were still closed, but behind them, his eyes darted back and forth and he shifted slightly as though he dodged an attacker in his sleep.

"Ramsay." She leaned in and smoothed a damp strand of hair off his brow. "Ramsay, it's okay. Relax. I'm here. Just wake up."

His head jerked once, twice. His eyes snapped open and he sucked in a sharp breath, shooting nearly upright in bed.

He propped himself up and blinked over and over, glazed eyes locked on the far wall of his room.

She stroked his shoulder, his chest. His skin was cool but slick with sweat. "Ramsay?"

He shook his head and scanned the room. His chest rose and fell in a labored rhythm. His arms shook as he pushed himself backward on the bed and reclined against the cushioned black headboard. "We're home."

Thank God. He was okay. Alert, despite whatever her father had put him through. "Yeah. We're home. The Black King..." Words lodged in her throat, mangled with emotions she couldn't bear to process. Not yet. "He sent us back. He..." The tears she'd tried to hold back slipped free and her chest burned.

"Hey." He pulled her across him and cradled her in his lap. His arm at the small of her back shook with obvious exhaustion, but he held her anyway, tucking her cheek to his chest as everything she'd bottled up broke free. He caressed her face. "I'm fine. Feel like I've been to histus and back, but I'm fine."

"You should tell her." Brenna's raspy voice barely penetrated Trinity's sobs. Probably wouldn't have if Ramsay's hand had not frozen in place as he tucked a strand of hair behind her ear.

"Tell her what?" he said.

"What you saw. Where you've been," she said.

Trinity twisted in Ramsay's lap.

A look passed between Ramsay and Brenna. The age-old stare of disbelief, two people trying to gauge without words if the unbelievable could be believed.

"You saw it too, didn't you?" Ramsay said. "With the echo."

Brenna's lips tightened and her chin quivered. "She was me. The woman. That was me, wasn't it?"

343

Ramsay's hand tightened on Trinity's forearm. He opened his mouth to speak.

"What the voice said…" Brenna swallowed and fisted her hands in her lap. "I don't want…I can't do that." She started to stand.

Ramsay shot forward, shifting Trinity beside him and halting Brenna with a grip on her arm. "It's all right." He urged Brenna to sit, voice modulated in an easy cadence. "Don't get ahead of yourself. We'll figure it out. Better two of us saw it than just one, right?"

"Saw what?" Trinity said.

Ramsay kept eye contact with Brenna for two long agonizing breaths, then slowly let go of Brenna's hand and covered Trinity's fisted hand on the bed. "The prophecy. How it all came about. How it's all supposed to end."

The prophecy. What she'd gone to learn about. "Dad," she whispered.

"That's my guess," Ramsay said. "He gripped my shoulder and about a nanosecond later I was somewhere else. Or more like some*when* else. With our first generation."

His thumb shuttled in a comforting back and forth atop the back of her hand. So warm. Strong. In that moment it was all she could bear to look at. All she could face or hold on to. "He gave himself up. For me."

"He gave information, Trin. Nothing else."

Trinity shook her head, replaying those last seconds in her mind. "Not just the information. His existence. That's the penance."

His thumb stopped and his fingers tightened.

She lifted her gaze to his. "After you passed out, he kneeled in front of the White Queen. She laid her hand on his head and a snowy kind of fog built around him. Before I could see any more, the Black King stepped between us and then we were here." Words queued up on her tongue, bitter. Ugly. "My dad's gone."

Brenna stood so abruptly her chair nearly toppled. "You should be alone. I'll let Eryx and Galena know you're awake."

Ramsay's eyes narrowed as he watched Brenna go. Whatever he was worried about, he quickly shut it off and refocused on Trinity. "You don't know he's gone. Could've been—"

"What did he say?" Trinity said. "What were the words he used before he touched you?"

Ramsay scrunched his brow for a second, thoughtful. A second later the furrow disappeared and his gaze lifted to hers, heavy with remorse.

A fresh tear slipped free. "Tell me," she said. "What did he say?"

He gripped the back of her head, like the contact might brace her for impact. "He said, 'What I give is freely given and my life forfeit.'"

Forfeit. The word wrecking-balled into her sternum and yanked a ragged sob past her burning throat. Weight pressed her shoulders and rounded her spine until she all but fell into Ramsay beside her. "It's my fault. I pushed him into this."

Ramsay pulled her close and rocked her back and forth. "I'm so sorry." Over and over he said it, pressing tender kisses to her temple and soothing her in calming, patient strokes.

"I was stupid." She lifted her head, eyes burning and cheeks as hot as embers. "I was trying to do what was right. To help you. I killed my own father."

"You didn't. You did what you thought was right and he did the same. He chose, Trinity. He wanted life for you. Joy. It's his gift. Don't darken it by blaming yourself."

"But if I'd waited...he told me to wait. Said to let you

figure things out on your own. If I'd listened, he'd still be here. I forced him."

"You don't know that."

"I do."

"Your mate is wise, child." The White Queen's soft airy voice sounded behind her.

Trinity shot to her feet.

Ramsay stood as well and stepped cautiously between them.

The White Queen noted his protective stance with a pointed look and a wry grin. "You have nothing to fear for your mate, warrior. I come only to support the guidance you share and to offer comfort of my own."

Ramsay held his place.

Trinity squeezed his arm and stepped from behind him. "Tell me he's still alive."

"A soul never dies, child." She floated forward, the fabric of her white gown flowing in a nonexistent breeze. "You are right. He no longer lives on our own plane, but exists with The Great One. What you should know is that his sacrifice comes with great peace."

She held out her hand and a huge Opal shaped like an Easter egg filled her palm. She handed the gem to Trinity.

The surface was so cold it sent a sharp pain up Trinity's arm to the base of her neck.

The queen swept her hand above the gem. "Open your heart and ease your fears."

Warmth, slow at first, then growing to the comfortable glow of a well-tended fire. The gem's surface wavered, the veins of green, blue, and pink flattened to a murky white.

Her father's image formed, another coming into focus beside it. A woman. The same one shown in the picture from her box, long platinum hair that matched her own nearly to her waist and beautiful blue gray eyes like Lexi's. They were talking. A tree stood behind them with dark chocolate limbs and perfect bell shaped white blossoms.

"He looks different." Gone was the strain and tension he always seemed to carry, and his smile was easy. Light. Even his eyes were brighter, bits of amber brightening eyes that had always been close to black.

"He's with your mother. He never told you the details behind her death, mostly because he didn't want to burden you with it. She took her life only months after your birth. He blamed himself for her actions. For not being there when she needed him most. He mourned her loss deeply."

Trinity felt more than saw the White Queen drift away. "You are no longer alone. Your father knew that and sought to give you a life free of pain. What he gave, he did so willingly. What you see is his reward. A life in true paradise with The Great One and the woman he loved."

No sound issued from the image, but her father threw his head back in what looked like a rumbling laugh. He was happy. Genuinely happy.

Her heart warmed to match the stone in her hand and the guilt and tension she'd held knotted in her core slowly unwound.

"He's at peace," The White Queen said. "He knows you're safe. That you have many years with the man you love, and that your race has what they need to fight. Heed your fire-ann's advice and accept your father's gift for what it is, the love of a father for his wonderful child."

Trinity shifted and lifted the gem up for Ramsay. The motion knocked a tear free from her cheek. "Can you see him?"

"No. Tell me."

"His cheeks have color. Not just his normal skin tone, but like he's been running in the sun. His shoulders are back and proud, but they look relaxed too. And his smile. God,

Ramsay. He used to look dead before. Emotionless. But now his arm is curled around my mom's shoulders and he looks like he has everything. Like he's whole." She looked up, a thank you on her lips.

The White Queen was gone.

She looked to Ramsay instead. "He's alive."

"That happens to a man when he's able to be with the woman he loves." Ramsay turned her, carefully took the gem, and set it on the nightstand. He cupped her nape and walked her backward until the bed hit the back of her knees. "Your dad and I, we have something in common."

"You? And my dad? He's all grumpy and serious." She glanced at the gem. Its soft pastels glimmered in the midday sun. Happy. Just like her father's smile. "You're a fun and games playboy who likes to get into trouble."

"I *was* a playboy." He tugged her tunic over her head in one quick swoosh and tossed it in a yellow heap on the floor. His gaze locked on her bare chest and he licked his lips. "And those fun and games...all bullshit." He pulled her leggings past her hips and nudged her just enough to knock her off center and onto his big bed.

"Ramsay, now's not a good time for this." She checked the door. "Your brother was really worked up about something. He wouldn't tell me what it was, but he's been in and out ever since we got back and seemed really worried."

Iron clinked on iron.

"There. Now it's locked," he said, dragging the soft cotton past her feet. "So long as the castle's not on fire and no one's bleeding out, I don't care what my brother wants." He unfastened his leather pants and shoved them to the floor. "My baineann is safe. Her father's happy. You're naked in my bed and no one's banging on the door, so right now all I want is to be next to you and see if I can't teach you something new."

"Now? You've got all the answers to the prophecy, your brother's in a tizzy, and you want to pause for Sex Ed?"

He crawled over her, his sheer size and power radiating over every inch of her. A sizzling match to her own growing burn. "That's what you need to get, Sunshine. The prophecy brought me to you, but you're what I want first. What I need. Not answers. Not power. I can live without the rest of my race. Histus, I could even live without the rest of my family."

He pressed himself against her, elbows planted at either side of her head, hips cradled deliciously between her thighs. "What I can't live without is you. I was as dead and emotionless as your father was when you met me. I was living, but I wasn't alive. Asleep at the wheel."

His thumb skimmed her cheekbone and his breath fluttered against her face, his lips close enough that hers tingled in anticipation. "You woke me up, Trinity. Brought me to life. You're my sunshine. The reason I'm awake and alive in a way I never thought possible." His mouth touched hers. Reverent and full of so much emotion. "And you're mine."

~

BOOKS BY RHENNA MORGAN

The Eden Series

Unexpected Eden

Healing Eden

Waking Eden

Eden's Deliverance

Men of Haven Series

Rough & Tumble

Wild & Sweet

Claim & Protect

Tempted & Taken

Stand & Deliver

Down & Dirty

Ancient Ink

Guardian's Bond

Healer's Need

NOLA Knights

His To Defend

Hers To Tame

Mine To Have

Standalone

What Janie Wants

MEET THE AUTHOR

Rhenna Morgan is a happily-ever-after addict—hot men, smart women, and scorching chemistry required. A triple-A personality with a thing for lists, Rhenna's a mom to two beautiful daughters who constantly keep her dancing, laughing and simply happy to be alive.

When she's not neck deep in writing, she's probably driving with the windows down and the music up loud, plotting her next hero and heroine's adventure. (Though trolling online for man-candy inspiration on Pinterest comes in a close second.)

She'd love to share her antics and bizarre since of humor with you and get to know you a little better in the process. You can sign up for her newsletter and gain access to exclusive snippets, upcoming releases, fun giveaways, and social media outlets at www.rhennamorgan.com.

Ready to see what happens in the final installment of The Eden Series? Here's a sneak peek from

EDEN'S DELIVERANCE

Fate is the life we're given. Destiny is what we do with it.

Captured as a child and forced into slavery by the Rebellion's leader, Brenna Haven was raised in near isolation with the utmost cruelty. She knew nothing of kindness, or compassion, until Fate orchestrated her rescue. Finally free, she wants nothing more than to return to her home. To reconnect with her human family and live a simple, quiet life. But her newfound powers demand an entirely different future. One fraught with danger, and a terrifying role in an ancient Myren prophecy.

A battle-hardened warrior and sworn bodyguard to the king, Ludan Forte wields a powerful, memory stealing gift. But his skill comes with a price. A torturous burden he's hidden since his awakening over a hundred years ago. He never dreamed he'd find relief, let alone be tempted to forgo his vows to the king. Yet in Brenna's sweet, beguiling presence, the weight he bears is lifted. And when her role in the prophecy threatens her life, he'll stop at nothing to keep her safe.

CHAPTER 1 - EDEN'S DELIVERANCE

A human will stand as judge, one versed in both races and injured in similar kind to the one wronged this day.

Brenna staggered down the castle's darkened hallway toward the servant's staircase, echoes of The Great One's booming proclamation dogging every unsteady step. Streaming tears and the vision she'd unintentionally shared with Ramsay blinded her to the thick, maroon rugs in front of her. Even now, awake and alert, the flashback burned as bold as real life in her mind's eye. The gold and silver flecks amid a rainbow-laden sky. The standing stones. The ancient Myren warrior who'd brought the prophecy to pass—and his dead human mate splayed across his lap.

She couldn't be the judge The Creator had referred to. Surely God wouldn't put the weight of all races on her shoulders. Not after all she'd been through. Not now that she finally had a chance at peace.

The vicious knot at the base of her throat blossomed thicker and larger, the specters of her past clawing their way free and unleashing her buried terror until she could barely breathe. She shook her head and hurried forward. The dead woman she'd seen wasn't her. The vision was of the past, and she was alive. Safe. Free from the bruises and shameful way she'd been used. Maxis was dead and couldn't hurt her anymore.

Her footsteps quickened and her blood raced. The room spun around her, hazy and out of focus, but the cool stone walls were steady beneath her palms, guiding her to the soft glow ahead. Air. She needed air. And space.

Freedom.

Grasping the wrought iron stair rail, she padded down the gray stone steps, careful to silence her sandaled steps. Fresh baked bread and cinnamon weighted the air, and muted feminine chatter drifted from the kitchen. Orla and the other morning castle workers, maybe even Lexi and Galena, preparing for another day full of hungry warriors and family members. Compassionate people who'd saved and sheltered her, but came with keen eyes and probing questions.

Skirting the voices, she cut through the formal dining room and angled to the main foyer and the massive gardens beyond. Mid-morning sunshine slanted through the open two-story arched windows, and the salt-tinged ocean breeze swept her tear-streaked cheeks. Her heart kicked at the scent, luring her as it had since she'd first awakened here. Calling as it had all those years ago with her parents. The day before Maxis kidnapped her and destroyed everything.

She shoved one of the two thick mahogany doors wide, gasped, and staggered backward.

A warrior, backlit by the rising sun, towered in her path. A big one, dressed in full warrior garb of black leather pants, boots, and silver drast. He caught the door before it could shut in a quick, easy grip, and stepped out of the sun's glare.

Her lungs seized. Not just any warrior. This was Ludan Forte, right hand and somo to the malran. Six foot, six of pure intimidation with twice the muscle mass of his peers. Framed by the brilliant light behind him, he loomed like an avenging legend come to life.

He cocked his head and assessed her head to toe, a wayward strand of wavy, blue-black hair falling across his forehead. His mouth tightened. Framed by his closely cropped beard, his frown reeked of menace.

"You're crying." An accusation and a demand for information all rolled up into one, as crisp and gruff as everything else he did.

"I..." Her thoughts fizzled, any hope for words dried up on her tongue. She ducked her head and swiped her cheek with the back of her hand. Her feet refused to move, frozen beneath his searing ice-blue gaze. "I'm fine I just—"

"Ludan, you going to let the poor girl by, or glare at her until she keels over?" Ian Smith's raspy voice drifted from behind her, his heavy tread sounding on the main foyer staircase. A perfect distraction.

"Excuse me." Her breathy words barely registered as she ducked beneath Ludan's arm and stumble-scurried across the castle's veranda. Her sandals slapped against the stone. Her lungs burned with the need for a full, unimpeded breath, and her heart slammed against her sternum in time with each footfall. Just a little further. Around the castle's edge to the cove and the ocean's peaceful rhythm. Then she could stop. Re-evaluate. Smother the past so it couldn't touch her. Couldn't blemish the tiny scrap of good she'd finally found.

Rounding the final corner, the wind whipped her loose, dark hair and tangled her simple sapphire gown around her ankles. The bluff's waist-high wall stretched along the cove's crescent edge, gray and taupe stone blending with the perfect azure and rainbow-laced Myren sky. Chocolate wood gates marked each quarter mile interval, the closest one unlatched and open, welcoming her escape.

She trudged across the vibrant green grass, the color similar to what she remembered from her home in Evad, but tinged with silver that glinted off the red-rimmed Myren sun. Memories from before her capture barely registered anymore, only foggy snippets remaining where there were once finite details. So much lost. Her family. Her future and any hope for tenderness or love. No man could ever want her, not with her tainted past. And now this? Thrust into the middle of a prophecy hinged on the very cruelness that shaped her life? It wasn't fair. At the very least she deserved a fresh start. Peace and contentment, if not solace.

Below, the turquoise waves crashed against the powder-white sand and black stone walls. As deep as the soaring three-story castle was tall, the turbulent waters seemed forever away. She inched closer to the edge, the toes of her sandals lining the bluff's rocky edge.

The dead human from the vision wavered in the forefront of her mind, her twin not just in appearance, but in the fate they'd suffered. Except that Brenna had lived.

That's not the only difference.

The snide, biting thought razored across her heart and left a frozen wake in its path. That woman had been loved. Her mate mourned her death. Avenged the damage brought upon her and offered his gifts to protect those like her. She had no one.

A pebble slipped from beneath her feet and bounced off the black stone walls once, twice, then free-falled to the water below. All this time she'd believed. Clung to the hope of going home and finding her family. Kept the faith and believed she'd someday set her misfortune behind and build

CHAPTER 1 - EDEN'S DELIVERANCE

something new and fresh. For what? To have the weight of all races thrust on her unwilling shoulders?

The wind whipped faster, and reality blurred, only the back and forth of the waves below in focus. In the distance, a larken trilled a string of sing-song notes. Fifteen years she'd suffered, no choices left to her but life and death.

No more.

She was done with accepting what others thrust on her. If she didn't want this role in the prophecy, she didn't have to take it. Didn't have to play the parts deigned appropriate by others. This was her life. To build however she saw fit. Myren laws and prophecies be damned. No one else could force her how to live.

Lifting her head, she focused on the horizon and sucked in a deep breath. She could do this. For once, she'd stand up for what she wanted and make this life her own. Voice her demands. Her needs.

She shifted to look back at the castle.

The rocks beneath her crumbled, and her body pitched to one side. Her feet slipped past the bluff's edge and she flailed her arms, barely catching the ledge. Wind whipped her gown and tugged her dangling legs. Straining to pull herself up and over the ledge, she dug her work roughened fingers into the damp earth and pushed with everything she had.

The clay fragmented, slipped between her fingers, and surrendered her to the water below.

She's not your concern.

Ludan tightened his grip on the castle's thick mahogany door until he thought the wood would snap. He'd fed himself the same damned mantra since the first time he'd seen Brenna, over and over in an endless loop.

Along with all the other voices.

Ian ambled up beside him and stared down the veranda in time to see Brenna disappear around the far side of the castle. "What the hell did you say to her?"

"I didn't say anything." Forcing his fingers free, Ludan let the door slip shut. The land on the far end of the castle was quiet. No other energy patterns registered near the ocean where Brenna had headed, nor in the forest beyond. Only blinding mid-morning sun and the bold blue Myren sky filled the quiet landscape in-between.

He still didn't like it. Too much weirdness had gone down in the last few months. Serena and Angus' page, Sully, disappearing. The Spiritu. The prophecy. He glanced at Ian beside him. "Go find Lexi. Have her take you to Evad today. I'll find Brenna and bring her back."

"You sure that's a good idea?"

The bite in Ian's tone cut through Ludan's focus. "Why wouldn't it be?"

"Because you looked like you were an inch away from ripping her head off."

Hardly. A hopeless junkie would surrender his fix before he'd hurt Brenna. Not that Ian would know that. None of them would. Ever. "I had things on my mind." Like how anytime she got within fifteen feet of him the non-stop racket in his head downgraded to a more tolerable decibel.

Ian cocked his head and anchored his hands in the pockets of his jacket, studying Ludan with a level of scrutiny that probably came in slow-mo precision. The son of a bitch was too damned perceptive. Cops, or former-cops turned PI in Ian's case, usually were.

"Track down Lexi," Ludan grumbled before Ian could latch onto any ideas. "The sooner I find Brenna and you're in Evad running reconnaissance, the sooner I can get back to work."

He strode away and shook the weight of Ian's stare off his back. This whole damned place was one giant microscope lately. Suspicious stares. People digging into his personal life and asking questions they had no right to ask. Ian could think whatever the fuck he wanted. Tracking Brenna and making sure no other shit storms were on the horizon was just common sense, nothing more.

Justify it however you want, but you'd follow her with or without a prophecy.

His conscience's uppercut nailed him square in the gut and yanked him to a halt at the castle's edge.

Beyond the stone safety wall, Brenna stood staring down at the cove. Her dark hair whipped in the heavy ocean winds while the rest of her stood still as a statue. In the past few months, he'd watched from the sidelines as she'd fought her way back from near death. Seen her creep from the timid shell she'd survived behind after fifteen long years with Maxis. Studied how every day her posture got a little taller, her shoulders squared and her chin had raised a fraction higher.

Today was different. Something in her near-black eyes seemed fractured. Broken. Off in a way that tripped all kinds of warning bells.

Pushing his Myren senses out along the cove, he gauged for any disturbance he might have missed. A larken swooped and sang high overhead, his deep blue body a near perfect match to Brenna's gown. Except for the bird and Brenna, no other forms of energy stirred. No visible threats, which meant whatever plagued her had already happened, or originated in her head.

He should leave her be and get Lexi. Combat and stealth were all he had to offer. If either were worth a damn when it came to emotions, he'd have slain his own demons years ago. Histus, even Ian would be better at this than him. At least Ian shared something in common with her. Two humans whose lives had been turned upside down by Maxis Steysis.

A memory surged to the forefront of his mind and his knees nearly buckled. His mother, bloody and battered. Defiled and broken in a way no woman should ever know. Her screams roared above all the other memories battling for space in his head, sending painful shards between his temples.

He shook his head and focused on the grass beneath his boots. How the silver on the bold green blades sparked on the morning sun. How the rich, dark soil beneath it was still damp from storms the night before. It was just a memory. The worst of all the ones he had to relive, for sure, but in the past. This was now.

Brenna still hadn't moved. She probably just needed time alone, a concept he of all people understood, but he could check on her without making her uncomfortable. Pulling his mask into place, he blended with the elements, hiding his form as he took to the sky, and circled up and over the cove. A desperate, almost palpable propulsion urged him faster, directing him no more than twenty feet in front of her.

She stared out at the sea, her gaze empty and unfocused. He knew that look. Resignation and defeat. Had staggered beneath the weight of both for too damned many years. Her hands were fisted tight at her sides and her toes touched the bluff's edge. Surely she wouldn't try to take her life. Not now. Not after all she'd survived.

As if in answer to his thoughts, Brenna's head snapped up and her focus sharpened on the horizon.

The muscles along his shoulders uncoiled and he huffed out a relieved exhale. Whatever had gripped her was gone now. Even her energy sparked brighter than moments before, as if the ocean's breeze had slipped beyond the confines of her skin and swept the sleeping monsters from her soul. Still, he'd be smart to keep an eye on her.

The dark, untamed presence inside him lifted its head, ears perked. The clawing hunger and compulsion he kept hidden and buried from everyone else rippled to the surface. Too close. An animal scenting the most succulent prey.

He forced himself an extra twenty feet away. Being closer to Brenna was a bad idea. Blissful in the way she dampened the backlash of his gift, but far too risky with the beast. That ugly, unpredictable part of him was only fit for battle. He'd mention his concerns for Brenna to Lexi, or Galena. Brenna would be more comfortable with them anyway.

He turned for the castle, the memory of her soulful, near black eyes and the way they'd focused on his lips this morning superimposing the brilliant sunrise in front of him. For the sweetest, most torturous moment, he could have sworn she wanted him. Craved him the way he wanted her. But that couldn't be right. She was afraid of men. All of them.

Beneath him, the tossing seas transitioned to the plush green grass surrounding the castle. He had a job to do. The job he was born to do. The sooner he got back to it, the sooner that taut, insistent tug that stretched between he and Brenna would go away. At least he hoped it would. Either that, or he'd have to spar and drink himself into a stupor like he had the last few weeks.

A shriek rang out behind him, the sheer terror of it searing white hot shrapnel inside his chest.

Before his mind had fully registered Brenna as its source, his body acted on instinct. The distance he'd created between them swept by in a blur. The only object in perfect focus was Brenna, her fingers digging in the loose clay and her slender arms pushing with all she had.

The slick, moss covered edges crumbled.

Brenna's fingers slipped through the clay and she dropped out of sight.

The beast roared and lashed him from the inside out. Fear supercharged his powers and shot him through the air so fast the wind burned his face. The powdered sand and black boulders rushed closer, Brenna only two arm spans away.

Three feet from the ground, he swooped beneath her and angled up at a sharp pitch. His heart slammed an angry protest, and his lungs burned for air, but Brenna was flush against him. Shaking violently in his arms with a brutal grip on his shoulders, but safe.

He held them there, high above the ocean, and cradled her closer.

Her breath chuffed against his skin and something wet trailed down the side of his neck. Tears. A river of them mixed with gentle sobs.

And he could hear them. Each raspy inhalation as clear as a whisper in the dead of night. The ocean and the larken, too. No voices clouding the sounds around him. No memories trampling each other for headspace. They weren't just dimmed the way they normally were around her, they were gone. Absolute silence. The first reprieve in over a hundred years.

His arms tightened on instinct, as though she might somehow fly away, or dissipate into nothingness. Rubbing his cheek against the top of her head, he savored the silk texture against his skin and lowered his voice to a near whisper. "You're safe."

She huddled closer, drawing her knees to her chest as her whimpers continued. The ocean tossed bold and loud beneath them. Probably not the most reassuring view from a non-flying human's point of view.

Fuck, like she'd have any other response. She'd nearly

died. He couldn't exactly expect her to lift her head and beam sunshine and roses.

He drifted to a flat-topped boulder at the cove's base and settled with the bluff wall behind him. Leaning back, he gave the wall his weight and pulled his knees in to angle Brenna closer.

Damn, but she felt good. So tiny and soft. Her hand opened and closed against his chest, dragging the slick-rough fabric of his drast against his adrenaline soaked skin in a way he probably shouldn't enjoy, but abso-fucking-lutely did. Considering Brenna couldn't get a solid breath in, it was also entirely the wrong thing to think about. There had to be something he could do. Something to help her find her balance.

For once, a decent memory came to mind. The day he'd tried to imitate his father by jumping off their cottage roof in an attempt to fly. He'd been too little to comprehend that flight required an awakening, something that didn't happen to eight year old boys. His mother had healed his wounds and held him in her lap while he cried, rocking slowly side to side.

He'd liked that. A lot. So much so, he'd pretended to cry longer so he could stay.

Gently, he imitated the movement, albeit more clunky than his mother. He stroked a hand from the top of her head to the small of her back, her glossy hair slick against his calloused palm. Since the first time he'd seen her, he'd been fascinated by it. The darkest chocolate to match her eyes.

Wind whispered through the cove, wrapping a faint vanilla scent around them. He dipped his head, his nose only inches from her temple, and inhaled deep. It was Brenna, either her hair, or her skin, but whatever it was, was perfect. Comforting and soft.

The darkness inside him settled. Stilled in a way he hadn't

felt since before his awakening. Countless battles he'd fought, and bone chilling memories he'd absorbed in the name of protecting his malran and his race, but no act felt as important as this moment. This was what armies fought to provide. What men died to protect.

Brenna let lose a long, body-shuddering sigh. Uncoiling her arms from around his neck, she smoothed her hands across his shoulders and down to his biceps.

His muscles tightened, every inch of him poised for her touch. Her presence.

Her fingers tightened, a tentative combination of exploration and reflex, before she pushed upright. Her nearly black eyes were glassy with the last of her tears, and her cheeks were a mottled red. It shouldn't have impacted him the way it did, but damned if he didn't want to pull her back against him and demand she stay put.

She didn't meet his gaze, but neither did she avert her face. Definitely a step up from the first day he'd met her.

"Thank you," she muttered.

Her voice. Praise The Great One, it was beautiful. He'd heard it plenty of times before, always shy with a breathiness born of well-earned caution, but now it was clear. Unhindered by the noise in his head.

He dipped his chin in acknowledgement. There wasn't much he could say she'd appreciate at this point, and all he really wanted was to hear her say something else. Anything. Histus, she could recite the damned alphabet and he'd be happy.

Instead, her focus drifted to where her hands rested on his biceps. A curious light flickered for a second, maybe two, before she blinked, shook her head, and tried to wiggle off his lap.

Ludan tightened his hold. "I'm not gentle." The words came out rougher than he'd intended, driven solely on compulsion and a need he couldn't quite define. "My words aren't as pretty as Eryx's, but I can listen."

For the longest time she stayed locked in place, studying him with a deep scrutiny he felt clear to his soul. As though she gauged the meaning of his entire existence from her gaze alone. A fresh tear slipped down her cheek.

He traced its path, captivated by the contrasts between them. Her smooth, creamy skin, to his dark, roughened fingers. His brutish-sized paw against her pixy face.

"I don't want to talk about where I've been." Her voice ripped him from his thoughts, the angst behind it prodding the beast out from his all too brief respite. "I don't want him to have any more of me than he already got."

And by *him* she meant Maxis. That bastard.

Ludan exhaled slow, but held Brenna's gaze. In that moment, he'd give a lot to resurrect the son of a bitch and kill him all over again with nothing more than his fists. "Then tell me what made you run."

"Only my memories." She looked away, scanning the cove with the pretense of gaining her bearings, but he recognized it for what it was. Diversion. The same tactic he'd used for years to throw people off track.

She smoothed her gown along her thigh, all business but for the sniffles that came between her still uneven breaths. Whatever it was that had chased her from the castle this morning was tucked neatly back in its place. For now. "I need to get back. Ramsay's awake, but Trinity's in a bad place. I told them I'd tell Eryx and Galena he was okay, and give them some time alone."

The casually dropped information punched through Ludan's languid state as little else could in that moment. Ever since Ramsay and Trinity had come back from Winrun, Ramsay out cold and Trinity a mess of nerves, Eryx's temper had run sharper than any blade Ludan had fought against. He nodded and set her on her feet, clinging to her hips until she was steady.

The second he lost contact, the voices rose. Nowhere near their normal levels, but the quiet vanished, the chatter of memories he'd consumed the last hundred plus years kicking back into full gear.

So, it wasn't a fluke. Brenna really was the key. The calming presence he'd sensed from the beginning.

He stood and shook the thoughts off. Eryx needed him. Ramsay needed him. The tiny break was more than he deserved anyway. He'd already learned in the worst possible way what happened when responsibilities went ignored. "I asked Ian to find Lexi before I came after you. Eryx is at the training center, but I'll contact him and have him meet us at the castle."

He stepped forward to pick her up, but she staggered back a step and raised her hands to hold him away. "What are you doing?"

"Getting you back to the castle." Ludan glanced up and over his shoulder at the towering bluff behind them. "Unless you'd rather climb."

This time she ducked her chin, but it was sweet and paired with a pretty flush on her cheeks. "All right."

He scooped her up and the voices disappeared. Amazing. A damned miracle in sweet innocent form. He stepped forward, ready to launch to the skies.

"Ludan."

He stopped and nearly choked at the depth in her dark eyes. Large and full of emotion, full of knowledge no woman her age should know. "You're wrong."

Like before, the pleasant brush of her voice sent him sideways, enough so it took at least a seven-second delay before the meaning of her words registered. He lifted an eyebrow, wanting more of her beautiful voice no matter what she had to say.

Her gaze slid sideways and her arms tightened around his neck. "You might not use pretty words, but you were gentle with me."

GLOSSARY

Aron - Mainstay livestock in Eden used for food and clothing. The hide is tanned to provide a soft, supple leather and is the predominant source of protective outerwear in the colder regions. The animal's fur is a cross between that found on a buffalo and a beaver in the human realm. The thickness and warmth of buffalo, but shiny and soft as beaver.

Asshur - A region in Eden. Sun isn't unheard of, but Asshur tends to be cloudier and rainier than other regions. The population has dropped off in the last few centuries with inhabitants moving to more hospitable areas.

Awakening - A Myren ceremony where people between the ages of eighteen and twenty-one are brought into their powers. The father (or paternal representative) is typically the trigger for the process, where the mother (or maternal influence) acts as an anchor for the awakened individual.

Baineann - The female within a bonded union.

Briash - The Myren equivalent of oatmeal. Its color is deep brown and the flavor has a hint of chocolate and cinnamon.

Brasia - A region in Eden. The terrain is mountainous. Heavy snow and difficult conditions prevail in the higher elevations.

Briyo - Brother-in-law.

Cootya - A type of cafe that sells common Myren beverages and snacks. Myren fruits and vegetables are the most common menu items, but some pastries can be found. Most feature an open air area where customers can relax, while kitchen and serving areas remain indoor.

Cush - The capital region of Eden, densely populated with elaborate buildings.

Diabhal - Devil.

Drast - Field-issue protective garment worn by warriors to protect their most vital organs in battle. Made of fine, metal threads, the garments fit their bodies closely. Day-to-day drasts are sleeveless, but the more formal version covers 3/4 of their arms. The necks are boat shaped to allow for greater comfort when fighting. Metal threads block most fire and electrical attacks.

Drishen - A fruit found in Eden. Looks like a grape and tastes like lemonade.

Eden - Another dimension, unknown to humans, within the fabric surrounding Earth.

Ellan - Elected officials who govern the Myren race alongside the Malran or Malress. Like most governing bodies, there are a mix of honest servants who seek prosperity and growth for the Myrens and corrupt lifers who stand on antiquated ideas and ceremonies.

Evad - The realm in which humans reside.

Fireann - The male within a bonded union.

Havilah - A more affluent and less populated region in Eden. Rain occurs, but mostly in the evenings with pleasant days full of sun and comfortable temperatures.

Histus - The human equivalent of hell.

Kilo - A fish that swims in many lakes in Eden, but is most prevalent in Brasia. A popular mainstay of protein in the Myren race, most often prepared by smoking in apple wood and basting with an apple and cinnamon glaze.

Larken - A long-winged bird known for its sing-song chirp. Primarily cobalt blue, while their wingtips are lavender.

Lastas - A favorite Myren breakfast pastry.

Leabrash - Library

Lomos Rebellion - A faction of Myrens that has long pursued the enslavement of humans and sought to overthrow the tenets of the Great One.

Lyrita Tree - An exotic tree exclusive to the Havilah region. Trunks are dark brown. Leaves are long, slender, and sage-green. The blooms are exceptionally large and run from pearl to pale pink in color. Average height for a mature lyrita is thirty to forty feet.

Malran - The male leader of the Myren people and the equivalent of a king in the human realm. Leadership has descended down through the Shantos family line since the birth of the Myren race, with the mantle of Malran (or Malress) falling to the first born.

Malress - The female leader of the Myren people and the equivalent of a queen in the human realm.

Myrens - A gifted race in existence for over six thousand years that lives in another dimension called Eden. They are deeply in tune with the Earth and the elements that surround her. Their powerful minds and connection to the elements allow them to communicate silently with those they are linked to, levitate, and command certain elements. Women typically have more healing or nurturing gifts, where men trend toward protective and aggressive abilities.

Natxu - A regular and expected practice of physical discipline for all Myren warriors. The moves and postures are grueling yet meditative, resulting in peak physical performance and enhanced ties to the elements.

Nirana - The human equivalent of heaven.

Oanan - Daughter-in-law.

Quaran - The Myren equivalent of a General within the warrior ranks.

Runa - Region in Eden, predominantly used for farming. The black soil is rich and sparkles with minerals. It's surrounded by a crescent-shaped formation of mountains that appear blue from ground level.

Shalla - Sister-in-law.

Somo - Sworn personal guard to the Malran or Malress.

Strasse - A highly intoxicating Myren beverage made from berries found only in Eden.

Strategos - Leader of the Myren warriors.

Torna - An annoying Myren rodent. Larger than an armadillo, but similar in color to an eel. While not typically aggressive, their teeth function similar to a shark. Torna almost always come out fighting.

Underlands - Not considered a region by most, but

more of an uninhabited wasteland. Lack of rain makes agriculture nearly impossible.

Vicus - A vegetable known for its extremely tart flavor, popular among the older generation.

Zurun - A thick flaky pastry with a thin layer of icing in the middle, twisted in the shape of a bow.